SWING, BROTHER, SWING

Dame Ngaio Marsh, a tall, vigorous New Zealander, published her twenty-seventh novel in 1972—at the age of seventy-two. Her best-selling whodunnits are in the classic tradition of Dorothy Sayers and Agatha Christie.

Dame Ngaio, in common with many white New Zealand children, was given a Maori name. (The 'g' is silent.) It is a 'portmanteau' word which can mean 'light-on-the-tree', or a type of tree with a white flower which she describes as 'undistinguished'. It can also mean 'clever'.

Despite her enormous output, the writing of crime fiction is only her second love. The first is the theatre, and she developed the New Zealand public's interest in live theatrical performances almost single-handed. Now the University of Canterbury has a theatre named after her. Almost as splendid an honour as what she likes to call 'me damery'.

NGAIO MARSH

Swing, Brother, Swing

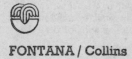

FONTANA / Collins

First published 1949
First issued in Fontana Books 1956
Second Impression 1958
Third Impression April 1964
Fourth Impression October 1966
Fifth Impression February 1974

Printed in Great Britain
Collins Clear-Type Press London and Glasgow

For Bet
who asked for it and
now gets it
with my love

Contents

Cast of Characters

LORD PASTERN AND BAGOTT

LADY PASTERN AND BAGOTT

FÉLICITÉ DE SUZE, her daughter

THE HON. EDWARD MANX, Lord Pastern's second cousin

CARLISLE WAYNE, Lord Pastern's niece

MISS HENDERSON, Companion-Secretary to Lady Pastern

SPENCE ⎫

MISS PARKER ⎪

WILLIAM ⎪

MARY ⎬ Domestic staff at Duke's Gate

MYRTLE ⎪

HORTENSE ⎭

BREEZY BELLAIRS ⎫

HAPPY HART, pianist ⎪ of Breezy

SYDNEY SKELTON, tympanist ⎬ Bellair's Boys

CARLOS RIVERA, piano accordionist ⎭

CAESAR BONN, Maitre de café at The Metronome

DAVID HAHN, his secretary

NIGEL BATHGATE, of *The Evening Chronicle*

DR. ALLINGTON

MRS. RODERICK ALLEYN

CAST OF CHARACTERS

CHIEF DETECTIVE-INSPECTOR ALLEYN

DETECTIVE-INSPECTOR FOX

DR. CURTIS

DETECTIVE-SERGEANT BAILEY,
  fingerprint expert

DETECTIVE-SERGEANT THOMPSON,
  photographer

DETECTIVE-SERGEANTS GIBSON,
  MARKS, SCOTT AND SALLIS

of the
Criminal
Investigation,
Department
New
Scotland Yard

Sundry policemen, waiters, bandsmen, etc.

CHAPTER ONE

LETTERS

FROM Lady Pastern and Bagott to her niece by marriage, Miss Carlisle Wayne:

3 DUKE'S GATE,
EATON PLACE,
LONDON, S.W.1.

MY DEAREST CARLISLE,—I am informed with that air of inconsequence which characterises all your uncle's utterances, of your arrival in England. Welcome Home. You may be interested to learn that I have rejoined your uncle. My motive is that of expediency. Your uncle proposes to give Clochemere to the nation and has returned to Duke's Gate, where, as you may have heard, I have been living for the last five years. During the immediate post-war period I shared its dubious amenities with members of an esoteric Central European sect. Your uncle granted them what I believe colonials would call squatters' rights, hoping no doubt to force me back upon the Cromwell Road or the society of my sister Desirée with whom I have quarrelled since we were first able to comprehend each other's motives.

Other aliens were repatriated, but the sect remained. It will be a sufficient indication of their activities if I tell you that they caused a number of boulders to be set up in the principal reception room, that their ceremonies began at midnight and were conducted in antiphonal screams, that their dogma appeared to prohibit the use of soap and water and that they were forbidden to cut their hair. Six months ago they returned to Central Europe (I have never inquired the precise habitat) and I was left mistress of this house. I had it cleaned and prepared myself for tranquillity. Judge of my dismay! I found tranquillity intolerable. I had, it seems, acclimatised myself to nightly pandemonium. I had become accustomed to frequent encounters with persons who resembled the minor and dirtier

prophets. I was unable to endure silence, and the unremarkable presence of servants. In fine. I was lonely. When one is
lonely, one thinks of one's mistakes. I thought of your uncle.
Is one ever entirely bored by the incomprehensible? I doubt
it. When I married your uncle (you will recollect that he was
an attaché at your Embassy in Paris and a frequent caller at my
parents' house), I was already a widow. I was not, therefore,
jeune fille. I did not demand Elysium. Equally I did not anti-
cipate the ridiculous. It is understood that after a certain time
one should not expect the impossible of one's husband. If he
is tactful, one remains ignorant. So much the better. One is
reconciled. But your uncle is not tactful. On the contrary, had
there been liaisons of the sort which I trust I have indicated,
I should have immediately become aware of them. Instead of
second or possibly third establishments I found myself confronted in turn by Salvation Army Citadels, by retreats for
Indian yogis, by apartments devoted to the study of Voodoo;
by a hundred and one ephemeral and ludicrous obsessions.
Your uncle has turned with appalling virtuosity from the tenets
of Christadelphians, to the practice of nudism. He has perpetrated antics which, with his increasing years, have become
the more intolerable. Had he been content to play the panta-
loon by himself and leave me to deplore, I should have perhaps
been reconciled. On the contrary, he demanded my collabora-
tion.

For example, in the matter of nudism. Imagine me, a de
Fouteaux, suffering a proposal that I should promenade without costume, behind laurel hedges in the Weald of Kent. It
was at this juncture and upon this provocation that I first left
your uncle. I have returned at intervals only to be driven away
again by further imbecilities. I have said nothing of his temper,
of his passion for scenes, of his minor but distressing idiosyn-
crasies. These failings have, alas, become public property.

Yet, my dearest Carlisle, as I have indicated, we are together
again at Duke's Gate. I decided that silence had become intolerable and that I should be forced to seek a flat. Upon this
decision came a letter from your uncle. He is now interested
in music and has associated himself with a band in which he
performs upon the percussion instruments. He wished to use
the largest of the reception rooms for practice; in short he pro-

posed to rejoin me at Duke's Gate. I am attached to this house. Where your uncle is, there also is noise and noise has become a necessity for me. I consented.

Félicité, also, has rejoined me. I regret to say I am deeply perturbed on account of Félicité. If your uncle realised, in the smallest degree, his duty as a stepfather, he might exert some influence. On the contrary he ignores, or regards with complacency, an attachment so undesirable that I, her mother, cannot bring myself to write more explicitly of it. I can only beg, my dearest Carlisle, that you make time to visit us. Félicité has always respected your judgment. I hope most earnestly that you will come to us for the first week-end in next month. Your uncle, I believe, intends to write to you himself. I join my request to his. It will be delightful to see you again, my dearest Carlisle, and I long to talk to you.

Your affectionate aunt,
CECILE DE FÔUTEAUX PASTERN AND BAGOTT

From Lord Pastern and Bagott to his niece, Miss Carlisle Wayne:

3 DUKE'S GATE,
EATON PLACE,
LONDON, S.W.1.

DEAR 'LISLE,—I hear you've come back. Your aunt tells me she's asked you to visit us. Come on the third and we'll give you some music.

Your aunt's living with me again.

Your affectionate uncle,
GEORGE

From "The Helping Hand," G.P.F.'s page in *Harmony*:

DEAR G.P.F.,—I am eighteen and unofficially engaged to be married. My fiancé is madly jealous and behaves in a manner that I consider more than queer and terribly alarming. I enclose details under separate cover because after all he might read this and then we *should* be in the soup. Also five shillings for a special Personal Chat letter. Please help me.

"TOOTS"

Poor Child in Distress, let me help you if I can. Remember I shall speak as a man and that is perhaps well, for the masculine mind is able to understand this strange self-torture that is clouding your fiancé's love for you and making you so unhappy. Believe me, there is only *one* way. You must be patient. You must prove your love by your candour. Do not tire of reassuring him that his suspicions are groundless. Remain tranquil. *Go on loving him.* Try a little gentle laughter but if it is unsuccessful *do not continue. Never* let him think you impatient. A thought. *There are some natures so delicate and sensitive that they must be handled like flowers. They need sun. They must be tended. Otherwise their spiritual growth is checked.* Your Personal Chat letter will reach you to-morrow.

Footnote to G.P.F.'s Page. —G.P.F. will write you a very special Personal Chat if you send postal order to " Personal Chat, *Harmony*, 5 Materfamilias Lane, E.C.2."

From Miss Carlisle Wayne to Miss Félicité de Suze.

> FRIAR'S PARDON,
> BENHAM,
> BUCKS.

DEAR FEE,—I've had rather a queer letter from Aunt 'Cile who wants me to come up on the third. What have you been up to?

> Love,
> LISLE

From The Hon. Edward Manx to Miss Carlisle Wayne:

> HARROW FLATS,
> SLOANE SQUARE,
> LONDON, S.W.1.

DEAREST LISLE,—Cousin Cecile says you are invited to Duke's Gate for the week-end on Saturday the third. I shall come down to Benham in order to drive you back. Did you know she wants to marry me to Félicité? I'm not at all keen and neither, luckily is Fée. She's fallen in a big way for an extremely dubious number who plays a piano accordion in Cousin George's band. I imagine there's a full-dress row in the offing *à cause*, as Cousin Cecile would say, *de* the band and particularly *de* the dubious number whose name is Carlos something. They aren't 'alf cups-of-tea are they? Why do you go away to foreign parts? I shall arrive at about 5 p.m. on the Saturday.

Love,

NED

From the *Monogram* gossip column:

Rumour hath it that Lord Pastern and Bagott, who is a keen exponent of boogie-woogie, will soon be heard at a certain restaurant "not a hundred miles from Piccadilly." Lord Pastern and Bagott who, of course, married Madame de Suze (*née* de Fouteaux), plays the tympani with enormous zest. His band includes such well-known exponents as Carlos Rivera and is conducted by none other than the inimitable Breezy Bellairs, both of the Metronome. By the way, I saw lovely Miss Félicité (Fée) de Suze, Lady Pastern and Bagott's daughter by her first marriage, lunching the other day at the Tarmak *à deux* with the Hon. Edward Manx who is, of course, her second cousin on the distaff side.

From Mr. Carlos Rivera to Miss Félicité de Suze:

102 BEDFORD MANSIONS,
AUSTERLY SQUARE,
LONDON, S.W.1.

LISTEN GLAMOROUS,—You cannot do this thing to me. I am not an English Honourable This or Lord That to sit complacent while my woman makes a fool of me. No. With me it is all or nothing. I am a scion of an ancient house. I do not permit trespassers and I am tired. I am very tired indeed, of waiting. I wait no longer. You announce immediately our engagement or—finish! It is understood? Adios.

CARLOS DA RIVERA

Telegram from Miss Félicité de Suze to Miss Carlisle Wayne:

Darling for pity's sake come everything too tricky and peculiar honestly do come genuine cri de coeur tons of love darling Fée.

Telegram from Miss Carlisle Wayne to Lady Pastern and Bagott:

Thank you so much love to come arriving about six Saturday 3rd Carlisle.

CHAPTER TWO

THE PERSONS ASSEMBLE

I

At precisely 11 o'clock in the morning G.P.F. walked in at a side door of the *Harmony* offices in 5 Materfamilias Lane, E.C.2. He went at once to his own room. Private G.P.F. was written in white letters on the door. He unwound the scarf with which he was careful to protect his nose and mouth from the fog, and hung it, together with his felt hat and overcoat, on a peg behind his desk. He then assumed a green eyeshade and shot a bolt in his door. By so doing he caused a notice, Engaged, to appear on the outside.

His gas fire was burning brightly and the tin saucer of water set before it to humidify the air, sent up a little drift of steam. The window was blanketed outside by fog. It was as if a yellow curtain had been hung on the wrong side of the glass. The footsteps of passers-by sounded close and dead and one could hear the muffled coughs and shut-in voices of people in a narrow street on a foggy morning. G.P.F. rubbed his hands together, hummed a lively air, seated himself at his desk and switched on his green-shaded lamp. " Cosy," he thought. The light glinted on his dark glasses, which he took off and replaced with reading spectacles.

"One, two. Button your boot," sang G.P.F. in a shrill falsetto and pulled a wire basket of unopened letters towards him. "Three four, knock on the gate," he sang facetiously and slit open the top letter. A postal order for five shillings fell out on the desk.

"DEAR G.P.F. [he read],—I feel I simply must write and thank you for your *lush* Private Chat letter—which I may as well confess has rocked me to my foundations. You couldn't be more right to call yourself Guide, Philosopher and Friend, honestly you couldn't. I've thought so much about what you've told me and I can't help wondering what you're *like*. To look at and listen to, I mean. I think your voice must be rather deep ('Oh, Crumbs!' G.P.F. murmured), and I'm sure you are tall. I wish——"

He skipped restlessly through the next two pages and arrived at the peroration: "I've tried madly to follow your advice but my young man really is! I can't help thinking that it would be immensely energising to talk to you. I mean really *talk*. But I suppose that's hopelessly out of bounds, so I'm having another five bob's worth of Private Chat." G.P.F. followed the large flamboyant script and dropped the pages, one by one, into a second wire basket. Here at last, was the end. "I suppose he would be madly jealous if he knew I had written to you like this but I just felt I had to.

"Yours grateful,
'TOOTS'"

G.P.F. reached for his pad of copy paper, gazed for a moment in a benign, absent manner at the fog-blinded window and then fell to. He wrote with great fluency, sighing and muttering under his breath.

"Of course I am happy," he began, "to think that I have helped" The phrases ran out from his pencil "——you must think of G.P.F. as a friendly ghost—write again if you will—more than usually interested—best of luck and my blessing——" When it was finished he pinned the postal note to the top sheet and dropped the whole in a further basket which bore the legend "Personal Chat."

The next letter was written in a firm hand on good note-paper. G.P.F. contemplated it with his head on one side, whistling between his teeth.

" The writer," it said, " is fifty years old and has recently consented to rejoin her husband who is fifty-one. He is eccentric to the verge of lunacy but, it is understood, not actually certifiable. A domestic crisis has arisen in which he refuses to take the one course compatible with his responsibilities as a stepfather. In a word, my daughter contemplates a marriage that from every point of view, but that of unbridled infatuation, is disastrous. If further details are required I am prepared to supply them, but the enclosed cuttings from newspapers covering a period of sixteen years will, I believe, speak for themselves. I do not wish this communication to be published, but enclose a five shilling postal order which I understand will cover a letter of personal advice.

" I am, etc.,
" CECILE DE FOUTEAUX PASTERN AND BAGOTT "

G.P.F. dropped the letter deliberately and turned over the sheaf of paper clippings. " PEER SUED FOR KIDNAPPING STEP-DAUGHTER," he read, " PEER PRACTISES NUDISM," " SCENE IN MAYFAIR COURTROOM." " LORD PASTERN AGAIN." " LADY PASTERN AND BAGOTT SEEKS DIVORCE." " PEER PREACHES FREE LOVE." " REBUKE FROM JUDGE." " LORD PASTERN NOW GOES YOGI." " ' BOOGIE-WOOGIE PEER.' " " INFINITE VARIETY."

G.P.F. glanced through the letterpress beneath these head-lines, made a small impatient sound and began to write very rapidly indeed. He was still at this employment when, glancing up at the blinded window, he saw, as if on a half-developed negative, a shoulder emerge through the fog. A face peered, a hand was pressed against the glass and then closed to tap twice. G.P.F. unlocked his door and returned to his desk. A moment later the visitor came coughing down the passage. " Entrez!" called G.P.F. modishly and his visitor walked into the room.

" Sorry to harry you," he said. " I thought you'd be in this morning. It's the monthly subscription to that relief fund. Your signature to the cheque."

G.P.F. swivelled round in his chair and held out Lady Pastern's letter. His visitor took it, whistled, read it through and burst out laughing. "Well!" he said. "Well, *honestly*."

"Press cuttings," said G.P.F. and handed them to him.

"She *must* be in a fizz! That it should come to this!"

"Damned if I know why you say that."

"I'm sorry. Of course there's no reason, but . . . How have you replied?"

"A stinger."

"May I see it?"

"By all means. There it is. Give me the cheque."

The visitor leant over the desk, at the same time reading the copy-sheets and groping in his breast pocket for his wallet. He found a cheque and still reading, laid it on the desk. Once he looked up quickly as if to speak but G.P.F. was bent over the cheque so he finished the letter.

"Strong," he said.

"Here's the cheque," said G.P.F.

"Thank you." He glanced at it. The signature was written in a small, fat and incredibly neat calligraphy: "G. P. Friend."

"Don't you ever sicken of all this?" the visitor asked abruptly with a gesture towards the wire basket.

"Plenty of interest. Plenty of variety."

"You might land yourself in a hell of a complication one of these days. This letter, for instance——"

"Oh, fiddle," said G.P.F., crisply.

2

"Listen," said Mr. Breezy Bellairs, surveying his band. "Listen, boys, I know he's dire but he's improving. And listen, it doesn't matter if he's dire. What matters is this, like I've told you: he's George Settinjer, Marquis of Pastern and Bagott, and he's Noise Number One for publicity. From the angle of news-value, not to mention snob-value, he's got all the rest of the big shots fighting to buy him a drink."

"So what?" asked the tympanist morosely.

" ' So what!' Ask yourself, what. Look, Syd, I'm keeping you on with the boys, first, last and all the while. I'm paying you full-time same as if you played full-time."

" That's not the point," said the tympanist. " The point is I look silly, stepping down half-way through the bill on a gala night. Me! I tell you straight, I don't like it."

" Now, listen Syd. Listen boy. You're featured, aren't you? What am I going to do for you? I'm going to give you a special feature appearance. I'm going to fetch you out on the floor by me to take a star-call, aren't I? That's more than I've ever done, boy. It's good, isn't it? With that coming to you, you should worry if the old bee likes to tear himself to shreds in your corner for half an hour, on Saturday night."

" I remind you," said Mr. Carlos Rivera, " that you speak of a gentleman who shall be my father-in-law."

" O.K., O.K., O.K. Take it easy, Carlos, take it easy, boy! That's fine," Mr. Bellairs gabbled, flashing his celebrated smile. " That's all hunky-dory by us. This is in committee, Carlos. And didn't I say he was improving? He'll be good, pretty soon. Not as good as Syd. That'd be a laughable notion. But good."

" As you say," said the pianist. " But what's all this about his own number?"

Mr. Bellairs spread his hands. " Well, now, it's this way, boys. Lord Pastern's got a little idea. It's a little idea that came to him about this new number he's written."

" Hot Guy, Hot Gunner?" said the pianist, and plugged out a phrase in the treble. " What a number!" he said without expression.

" Take it easy now, Happy. This little number his lordship's written will be quite a little hit when we've hotted it up."

" As you say."

" That's right. I've orchestrated it and it's snappy. Now, listen. This little idea he's got about putting it across is quite a notion, boys. In its way. It seems Lord Pastern's got round to thinking he might go places as a soloist with this number. You know. A spot of hot drumming and loosing off a six-shooter."

" For chrisake!" the tympanist said idly.

" The idea is that Carlos steps out in a spotlight and gives. Hot and crazy, Carlos. Burning the air. Sky the limit."

Mr. Rivera passed the palm of his hand over his hair. "Very well. And then?"

" Lord Pastern's idea is that you get right on your scooter and take it away. And when you've got to your craziest, another spot picks him out and he's sitting in tin-can corner wearing a cowboy hat and he gets up and yells ' yippi-yi-dee' and shoots off a gun at you and you do a trick fall——"

" I am not an acrobat——"

" Well, anyway, you fall and his lordship goes to market and then we switch to a cod funeral march and swing it to the limit. And some of the boys carry Carlos off and I lay a funny wreath on his breast. Well," said Mr. Bellairs after a silence, " I'm not saying it's dynamic, but it might get by. It's crazy and it might be kind of good, at that."

" Did you say," asked the tympanist, " that we finish up with a funeral march? Was that what you said?"

" Played in the Breezy Bellairs Manner, Syd."

" It was what he said, boys," said the pianist. " We sign ourselves off with a corpse and muffled drums. Come to the Metronome for a gay evening."

" I disagree entirely," Mr. Rivera interposed. He rose gracefully. His suit was dove-grey with a widish pink stripe. Its shoulders seemed actually to curve upwards. He was bronzed. His hair swept back from his forehead and ears in thick brilliant waves. He had flawless teeth, a slight moustache and large eyes and he was tall. " I like the idea," he said. " It appeals to me. A little macabre, a little odd, perhaps, but it has something. I suggest, however, a slight alteration. It will be an improvement if, on the conclusion of Lord Pastern's solo, I draw the rod and shoot *him*. He is then carried out and I go into my hot number. It will be a great improvement."

" Listen, Carlos——"

" I repeat, a great improvement."

The pianist laughed pointedly and the others grinned.

" You make the suggestion to Lord Pastern," said the tympanist. " He's going to be your ruddy father-in-law. Make it and see how it goes."

"I think we better do it like he says, Carl," said Mr. Bellairs. "I think we better."

The two men faced each other. Mr. Bellairs' expression of geniality had become habitual. He might have been a cleverly made ventriloquist's doll with a pale rubber face that was constantly and arbitrarily creased in a roguish grimace. His expressionless eyes with their large pale irises and enormous pupils might have been painted. Wherever he went, whenever he spoke, his lips parted and disclosed his teeth. Two dimples grooved his full cheeks, the flesh creased at the corners of his eyes. Thus, hour after hour, he smiled at the couples who danced slowly past his stand; smiled and bowed and beat the air and undulated and smiled. He sweated profusely from these exertions and at times would mop his face with a snowy handkerchief. And behind him every night his Boys, dressed in soft shirts and sculptured dinner-jackets with steel pointed buttons and silver revers, flexed their muscles and inflated their lungs in obedience to the pulse of his celebrated miniature baton of chromium-tipped ebony, presented to him by a lady of title. Great use was made of chromium at the Metronome by Breezy's Boys. Their instruments glittered with it, they wore wristwatches on chromium bracelets, the band-title appeared in chromium letters on the piano which was painted in aluminium to resemble chromium. Above the Boys, a giant metronome, outlined in coloured lights, swung its chromium-tipped pendulum in the same measure. "Hi-dee-ho-dee-oh," Mr. Bellairs would moan. "Gloomp-gloomp, giddy-iddy, hody-oh-do." For this and for the way he smiled and conducted his band he was paid three hundred pounds a week by the management of the Metronome, and out of that he paid his Boys. He was engaged with an augmented band for charity balls, and sometimes for private dances. "It was a grand party," people would say, "they had Breezy Bellairs and everything." In his world he was a big noise.

His boys were big noises. They were all specialists. He had selected them with infinite pains. They were chosen for their ability to make the hideous and extremely difficult rumpus known as The Breezy Bellairs Manner and for the way they looked while they made it. They were chosen because of their sex appeal and their endurance. Breezy said : " The better they like you the more you got to give." Some of his players he could replace fairly easily ; the second and third saxophonists and the double-bass, for instance, but Happy Hart, the pianist and Syd Skelton the tympanist and Carlos Rivera the piano accordionist, were, he said and believed, the Tops. It was a constant nagging anxiety to Breezy that some day, before his public had *had* Happy or Syd or Carlos, one or all of them might get hostile or fed up or something, and leave him for The Royal Flush Swingsters or Bones Flannagan and His Merry Mixers or The Percy Personalities. So he was always careful how he handled these three.

He was being careful now, with Carlos Rivera. Carlos was good. His piano accordion talked in The Big Way. When his engagement to Félicité de Suze was announced it'd be A Big Build-up for Breezy and the Boys. Carlos was as good as they come.

" Listen, Carlos," Breezy urged feverishly. " I got an idea. Listen, how about we work it this way? How about letting his lordship fire at you like what he wants and miss you. See? He looks surprised and goes right ahead pulling the triggers and firing and you go right ahead in your hot number and every time he fires, one of the other boys acts like *he's* been hit and plays a queer note and how about these boys playing a note each down the scale? And you just smile and sign off and bow kind of sardonically and leave him flat? How about that, boys?"

" We-ell," said the boys judicially.

" It is a possibility," Mr. Rivera conceded.

" He might even wind up by shooting himself and getting carried off with the wreath on his breast."

" If somebody else doesn't get in first," grunted the tympanist.

" Or he might hand the gun to me and I might fire it at him and it might be empty, and he might go into his act and end up with a funny faint and get carried out."

" I repeat," Rivera said, " it is a possibility. We shall not quarrel in this matter. Perhaps I may speak to Lord Pastern myself."

"Fine!" Breezy cried, and raised his tiny baton. "That's fine. Come on, boys. What are we waiting for? Is this a practice or is it a practice? Where's this new number? Fine! On your marks. Everybody happy? Swell. Let's go."

3

"' Carlisle Wayne,' " said Edward Manx, "' was thirty years old, but she retained something of the air of adolescence, not in her speech, for that was tranquil and assured, but in her looks and manner. Her movements were fluid; boyish perhaps. She had long legs, slim hands and a thin beautiful face. Her clothes were wisely chosen and gallantly worn but she took no great trouble with them and seemed to be well-dressed rather by accident than design. She liked travel but dreaded sight-seeing and would retain memories as sharp as pencil drawings of unimportant details; a waiter, a group of sailors, a woman in a bookstall. The names of the streets or even the towns where these persons had been encountered would often be lost to her; it was people in whom she was really interested. For people she had an eye as sharp as a needle and she was extremely tolerant.' "

"' Her remote cousin, The Honourable Edward Manx,' " Carlisle interrupted, "' was a dramatic critic. He was thirty-seven years old and of romantic appearance but not oppressively so. His professional reputation for rudeness was cultivated with some pains for, although cursed with a violent temper, he was by instinct of a courteous disposition!' "

"Gatcha!" said Edward Manx, turning the car into the Uxbridge Road.

"' He was something of a snob but sufficiently adroit to disguise this circumstance under a show of social indiscrimination. He was unmarried——' "

"' ——having a profound mistrust of those women who obviously admired him——' "

"' ——and a dread of being rebuffed by those of whom he was not quite sure.' "

"You *are* as sharp as a needle you know," said Manx, uncomfortably.

" Which is probably why I, too, have remained unmarried."

" I wouldn't be surprised. All the same I've often wondered——"

" I invariably click with such frightful men."

" Lisle, how old were we when we invented this game?"

" 'Novelettes?' Wasn't it in the train when we came back from our first school holidays with Uncle George? He wasn't married then so it must have been over sixteen years ago. Félicité was only two when Aunt Cecile married him and she's eighteen now."

" It was then. I remember you began by saying : ' There was once a very conceited, bad-tempered boy called Edward Manx. His elderly cousin, a peculiar peer——' "

" Even in those days, Uncle George was prime material, wasn't he?"

" Lord, yes ! Do you remember——"

They told each other anecdotes, familiar to both, of Lord Pastern and Bagott. They recalled his first formidable row with his wife, a distinguished Frenchwoman of great composure who came to him as a widow with a baby daughter. Lord Pastern, three years after their marriage, became an adherent of a sect that practised baptism by total immersion. He wished his stepdaughter to be rechristened by this method in a sluggish and eel-infested stream that ran through his country estate. Upon his wife's refusal he sulked for a month and then, without warning, took ship to India where he immediately succumbed to the more painful austerities of the yogi. He returned to England, loudly proclaiming that almost everything was an illusion and, going by stealth to his stepdaughter's nursery, attempted to fold her infant limbs into esoteric postures, exhorting her, at the same time, to bend her gaze upon her navel and say " Om." Her nurse objected, was given notice by Lord Pastern and reinstated by his wife. A formidable scene ensued.

" My Mama was there, you know," said Carlisle. " She was supposed to be Uncle George's favourite sister but she made no headway at all. She and Aunt Cecile held an indignation meeting with the nanny in the boudoir, and Uncle George sneaked down the servants' stairs with Félicité and drove her thirty miles in his car to some sort of yogi boarding-house.

They had to get the police to find them. Aunt 'Cile laid a charge of kidnapping."

"That was the first time Cousin George became banner headlines in the press," Edward observed.

"The second time was the nudist colony."

"True. And the third was the near-divorce."

"I was away for that," Carlisle observed.

"You're always going away. Here I am, a hard-working pressman who ought to be in constant transit to foreign parts, and you're the one to go away. He was taken with the doctrine of free love, you remember, and asked a number of rather odd women down to Clochemere. Cousin Cecile at once removed with Félicité, who was by now twelve years old, to Duke's Gate, and began divorce proceedings. But it turned out that Cousin George's love was only free in the sense that he de-livered innumerable lectures without charge to his guests and then told them to go away and get on with it. So the divorce fell through, but not before counsel and bench had enjoyed an orgy of wisecracks and the press had exhausted itself."

"Ned," Carlisle asked, "do you imagine that it's at all hereditary?"

"His dottiness? No, all the other Settinjers seem to be toler-ably sane. No, I fancy Cousin George is a sport. A sort of monster, in the nicest sense of the word."

"That's a comfort. After all I'm his blood-niece, if that's the way to put it. You're only a collateral on the distaff side."

"Is that a cheap sneer, darling?"

"I wish you'd put me wise to the current set-up. I've had some very queer letters and telegrams. What's Félicité up to? Are you going to marry her?"

"I'll be damned if I do," said Edward with some heat. "It's Cousin Cecile who thought that one up. She offered to house me at Duke's Gate when my flat was wrested from me. I was there for three weeks before I found a new one and naturally I took Fée out a bit and so on. It now appears that the invita-tion was all part of a deep-laid plot of Cousin Cecile's. She really is excessively French, you know. It seems that she went into a sort of state-huddle with my mama and talked about Félicité's *dot* and the desirability of the old families standing firm. It was all terrifically Proustian. My mama, who was born in the colonies and doesn't like Félicité, anyway, kept her head and preserved an air of impenetrable grandeur until the last second when she suddenly remarked that she never interfered in my affairs and wouldn't mind betting I'd marry an organising secretary in the Society for Closer Relations with Soviet Russia."

" Was Aunt 'Cile at all rocked?"

" She let it pass as a joke in poor taste."

" What about Fée, herself?"

" She's in a great to-do about her young man. He, I don't mind telling you, is easily the nastiest job of work in an unreal sort of way that you are ever likely to encounter. He glistens from head to foot and is called Carlos Rivera."

" One mustn't be insular."

" No doubt, but wait till you see him. He goes in for jealousy in a big way and says he's the scion of a noble Spanish-American family. I don't believe a word of it and I think Félicité has her doubts."

" Didn't you say in your letter that he played the piano accordion?"

" At the Metronome, in Breezy Bellairs' Band. He walks out in a spotlight, and undulates. Cousin George is going to pay Breezy some fabulous sum to let him, Cousin George, play the tympani. That's how Félicité met Carlos."

" Is she really in love with him?"

" Madly, she says, but she's beginning to take a poor view of his jealousy. He can't go dancing with her himself, because of his work. If she goes to the Metronome with anyone else he looks daggers over his piano accordion and comes across and sneers at them during the solo number. If she goes to other places he finds out from other bandsmen. They appear to be a very close corporation. Of course, being Cousin George's stepdaughter, she's used to scenes, but she's getting a bit rattled nevertheless. It seems that Cousin Cecile, after her interview with my mama, asked Félicité if she thought she could love me. Fée telephoned at once to know if I was up to any nonsense and asked me to lunch with her. So we did and some fool put it in the paper. Carlos read it and went into his act with unparalleled vigour. He talked about knives and what his family do with their women when they are flighty."

" Fée *is* a donkey," said Carlisle after a pause.

" You, my dearest Lisle, are telling me."

4

Three, Duke's Gate, Eaton Place, was a pleasant Georgian house of elegant though discreet proportions. Its front had an air of reticence which was modified by a fan-light, a couple of depressed arches and beautifully designed doors. One might have hazarded a guess that this was the town house of some tranquil, wealthy family who in pre-war days had occupied it at appropriate times and punctually left it in the charge of caretakers during the late summer and the shooting seasons. A house for orderly, leisured and unremarkable people, one might have ventured.

Edward Manx dropped his cousin there, handing her luggage over to a mild elderly manservant and reminding her that they would meet again at dinner. She entered the hall and noticed with pleasure that it was unchanged.

" Her ladyship is in the drawing-room, miss," said the butler. " Would you prefer——?"

" I'll go straight in, Spence."

" Thank you miss. You are in the yellow room, miss. I'll have your luggage taken up."

Carlisle followed him to the drawing-room on the first floor. As they reached the landing a terrific rumpus broke out beyond a doorway on their left.

A saxophone climbed through a series of lewd dissonances into a prolonged shriek; a whistle was blown and cymbals clashed. " A wireless, at last, Spence?" Carlisle ejaculated. " I thought they were forbidden."

" That is his lordship's band, miss. They practise in the ballroom."

" The band," Carlisle muttered. " I'd forgotten. Good heavens!"

" Miss Wayne, my lady," said Spence, in the doorway.

Lady Pastern and Bagott advanced from the far end of a long room. She was fifty and tall for a Frenchwoman. Her figure was impressive, her hair rigidly groomed, her dress admirable. She had the air of being encased in a transparent, closely-fitting film that covered her head as well as her clothes and permitted no disturbance of her surface. Her voice had edge. She used the faultless diction and balanced phraseology of the foreigner who has perfect command but no love of the English language.

"My dearest Carlisle," she said crisply, and kissed her niece with precision, on both cheeks.

"Dear Aunt 'Cile, how nice to see you."

"It is charming of you to come."

Carlisle thought that they had uttered these greetings like characters in a somewhat dated comedy, but their pleasure, nevertheless, was real. They had an affection for each other, an unexacting enjoyment of each other's company. "What I like about Aunt Cecile," she had said to Edward, "is her refusal to be rattled about anything." He had reminded her of Lady Pastern's occasional rages and Carlisle retorted that these outbursts acted like safety-valves and had probably saved her aunt many times from committing some act of physical violence upon Lord Pastern.

They sat together by the large window. Carlisle, responding punctually to the interchange of inquiries and observations which Lady Pastern introduced, allowed her gaze to dwell with pleasure on the modest cornices and well-proportioned panels; on chairs, tables and cabinets which, while they had no rigid correspondence of period, achieved an agreeable harmony born of long association. "I've always liked this room," she said presently. "I'm glad you don't change it."

"I have defended it," Lady Pastern said, "in the teeth of your uncle's most determined assaults."

"Ah," thought Carlisle, "the preliminaries are concluded. Now, we're off."

"Your uncle," Lady Pastern continued, "has, during the last sixteen years, made periodic attempts to introduce prayer-wheels, brass Buddhas, a totem-pole, and the worst excesses of the surrealists. I have withstood them all. On one occasion I reduced to molten silver an image of some Aztec deity. Your uncle purchased it in Mexico City. Apart from its repellent appearance I had every reason to believe it spurious."

" He doesn't change," Carlisle murmured.

" It would be more correct, my dear child, to say that he is contant in inconstancy." Lady Pastern made a sudden and vigorous gesture with both her hands. " He is ridiculous to contemplate," she said strongly, " and entirely impossible to live with. A madman, except in a few unimportant technicalities. He is not, alas, certifiable. If he were, I should know what to do."

" Oh, come ! "

" I repeat, Carlisle, I should know what to do. Do not misunderstand me. For myself, I am resigned. I have acquired armour. I can suffer perpetual humiliation. I can shrug my shoulders at unparalleled buffooneries. But when my daughter is involved," said Lady Pastern with uplifted bust, " complaisance is out of the question. I assert myself. I give battle."

" What's Uncle George up to, exactly?"

" He is conniving where Félicité is concerned, at disaster. I cannot hope that you are unaware of her attachment."

" Well——"

" Evidently you are aware of it. A professional bandsman who, as no doubt you heard on your arrival, is here, now, at your uncle's invitation, in the ballroom. It is almost certain that Félicité is listening to him. An utterly impossible young man of a vulgarity——" Lady Pastern paused and her lips trembled. " I have seen them together at the theatre," she said. " He is beyond everything. One cannot begin to describe. I am desperate."

" I'm so sorry, Aunt 'Cile," Carlisle said uneasily.

" I knew I should have your sympathy, dearest child. I hope I shall enlist your help. Félicité admires and loves you. She will naturally make you her confidante."

" Yes, but Aunt 'Cile——"

A clamour of voices broke out in some distant part of the house. " They are going," said Lady Pastern, hurriedly. " It is the end of the *repetition*. In a moment, your uncle and Félicité will appear. Carlisle, may I implore you——"

" I don't suppose——" Carlisle began dubiously, and at that

juncture, hearing her uncle's voice on the landing, rose nervously to her feet. Lady Pastern, with a grimace of profound significance, laid her hand on her niece's arm. Carlisle felt a hysterical giggle rise in her throat. The door opened and Lord Pastern and Bagott came trippingly into the room.

CHAPTER THREE

PRE-PRANDIAL

I

HE WAS short, not more than five foot seven, but so compactly built that he did not give the impression of low stature. Everything about him was dapper, though not obtrusively so; his clothes, the flower in his coat, his well-brushed hair and moustache. His eyes light grey with pinkish rims, had a hot impertinent look, his underlip jutting out and there were clearly defined spots of local colour over his cheek-bones. He came briskly into the room, bestowed a restless kiss upon his niece and confronted his wife.

" Who's dinin'? " he said.

" Ourselves, Félicité, Carlisle, of course, and Edward Manx. And I have asked Miss Henderson to join us, to-night."

" Two more," said Lord Pastern. " I've asked Bellairs and Rivera."

" That is quite impossible, George," said Lady Pastern, calmly.

" Why? "

" Apart from other unanswerable considerations, there is not enough food for two extra guests."

" Tell 'em to open a tin."

" I cannot receive these persons for dinner."

Lord Pastern grinned savagely. " All right. Rivera can take Félicité to a restaurant and Bellairs can come here. Same number as before. How are you, Lisle? "

" I'm very well, Uncle George."

"Félicité will not dine out with this individual, George. I shall not permit it."

"You can't stop 'em."

"Félicité will respect my wishes."

"Don't be an ass," said Lord Pastern. "You're thirty years behind the times, m'dear. Give a gel her head and she'll find her feet." He paused, evidently delighted with the aphorism. "Way you're goin', you'll have an elopement on your hands. Comes to that, I don't see the objection."

"Are you demented, George?"

"Half the women in London'd give anything to be in Fée's boots."

"A Mexican bandsman."

"Fine well set-up young feller. Inoculate your old stock. That's Shakespeare, ain't it, Lisle? I understand he comes of a perfectly good Spanish family. Hidalgo, or whatever it is," he added vaguely. "A feller of good family happens to be an artist and you go and condemn him. Sort of thing that makes you sick." He turned to his niece: "I've been thinkin' seriously of givin' up the title, Lisle."

"George!"

"About dinner, 'Cile. Can you find something for them to eat or can't you? Speak up."

Lady Pastern's shoulders rose with a shudder. She glanced at Carlisle who thought she detected a glint of cunning in her aunt's eye. "Very well, George," Lady Pastern said. "I shall speak to the servants. I shall speak to Dupont. Very well."

Lord Pastern darted an extremely suspicious glance at his wife and sat down. "Nice to see you, Lisle," he said. "What have you been doin' with yourself?"

"I've been in Greece. Famine relief."

"If people understood dietetics there wouldn't be all this starvation," said Lord Pastern, darkly. "Are you keen on music?"

Carlisle returned a guarded answer. Her aunt, she realised, was attempting to convey by means of a fixed stare and raised eyebrows, some message of significance.

"I've taken it up, seriously," Lord Pastern continued. "Swing. Boogie-woogie. Jive. Find it keeps me up to the mark." He thumped with his heel on the carpet, beat his hands together and in a strange nasal voice, intoned: "'Shoo-shoo-shoo, Baby. Bye-bye, Bye, Baby.'"

The door opened and Félicité de Suze came in. She was a striking young woman with large black eyes, a wide mouth, and an air of being equal to anything. She cried: "Darling—you're Heaven its very self," and kissed Carlisle with enthusiasm. Lord Pastern was still clapping and chanting. His step-daughter took up the burden of his song, raised a finger and jerked rhythmically before him. They grinned at each other. "You're coming along very prettily indeed, George," she said.

Carlisle wondered what her impression would have been if she were a complete stranger. Would she, like Lady Pastern, have decided that her uncle was eccentric to the point of de-rangement? "No," she thought, "probably not. There's really a kind of terrifying sanity about him. He's overloaded with energy, he says exactly what he thinks and he does exactly what he wants to do. But he's an over-simplification of type, and he's got no perspective. He's never mildly interested in anything. But which of us," Carlisle reflected, "has not, at some time, longed to play the big drum?"

Félicité, with an abandon that Carlisle found unconvincing, flung herself into the sofa beside her mother. "Angel!" she said richly, "don't be so *grande dame*. George and I are having fun!"

Lady Pastern disengaged herself and rose: "I must see Dupont."

"Ring for Spence," said her husband. "Why d'you want to go burrowin' about in the servants' quarters?"

Lady Pastern pointed out, with great coldness, that in the present food shortage one did not, if one wished to retain the services of one's cook, send a message at seven in the evening to the effect that there would be two extra for dinner. In any case, she added, however great her tact, Dupont would almost certainly give notice.

"He'll give us the same dinner as usual," her husband rejoined. "'The Three Courses of Monsieur Dupont!'"

"Extremely witty," said Lady Pastern coldly. She then withdrew.

"George!" said Félicité. "Have you won?"

"I should damn' well think so. Never heard anything so preposterous in me life. Ask a couple of people to dine and your mother behaves like Lady Macbeth. I'm going to have a bath."

When he had gone, Félicité turned to Carlisle, and made a wide helpless gesture. "Darling, *what* a life! Honestly! One prances about from moment to moment on the edge of a volcano, *never* knowing when there'll be a major eruption. I suppose you've heard all about ME."

"A certain amount."

"He's madly attractive."

"In what sort of way?"

Félicité smiled and shook her head. "My dear Lisle, he just does things for me."

"He's not by any chance a bounder?"

"He can bound like a ping-pong ball and I won't bat an eyelid. To me he's Heaven; *but* just plain Heaven."

"Come off it, Fée," said Carlisle. "I've heard all this before. What's the catch in it?"

Félicité looked sideways at her. "How do you mean, the catch?"

"There's always a catch in your young men, darling, when you rave like this about them."

Félicité began to walk showily about the room. She had lit a cigarette and wafted it to-and-fro between two fingers, nursing her right elbow in the palm of the left hand. Her manner became remote. "When English people talk about a bounder," she said, "they invariably refer to someone who has more charm and less *gaucherie* than the average Englishman."

"I couldn't disagree more; but go on."

Félicité said loftly : "Of course I knew from the first, Mama would kick like the devil. *C'la va sans dire.* And I don't deny Carlos is a bit tricky. In fact, 'It's Hell but it's worth it' is a fairly accurate summing-up of the situation at the moment. I'm adoring it, really. I think."

"I don't think."

"Yes, I am," said Félicité violently. "I adore a situation. I've been brought up on situations. Think of George. You know, I honestly believe I've got more in common with George than I would have had with my own father. From all accounts, Papa was excessively *rangé*."

"You'd do with a bit more orderliness yourself, old girl. In what way is Carlos tricky?"

"Well, he's just *so* jealous he's like a Spanish novel."

"I've never read a Spanish novel unless you count *Don Quixote* and I'm certain you haven't. What's he do?"

"My dear, everything. Rages and despairs and sends frightful letters by special messenger. I got a stinker this morning, *à cause de*—— Well, *à cause de* something that really is a bit diffy."

She halted and inhaled deeply. Carlisle remembered the confidences that Félicité had poured out in her convent days, concerning what she called her "raves." There had been the music master who had fortunately snubbed Félicité and the medical student who hadn't. There had been the brothers of the other girls and an actor whom she attempted to waylay at a charity matinée. There had been a male medium, engaged by Lord Pastern during his spiritualistic period, and a dietician. Carlisle pulled herself together and listened to the present recital. It appeared that there was a crisis : a "*crise*" as Félicité called it. She used far more occasional French than her mother and was fond of laying her major calamities at the door of Gallic temperament.

"——And as a matter of fact," Félicité was saying, "I hadn't so much as smirked at another *soul*, and there he was seizing me by the wrists and giving me that shattering sort of look that begins at your boots and travels up to your face and then makes the return trip. And, breathing loudly, don't you know, through the nose. I don't deny that the first time was rather fun. But after he got wind of old Edward it really was, and I may say still is, beyond a joke. And now to crown everything, there's the *crise*."

"But what crisis. You haven't said——"

For the first time Félicité looked faintly embarrassed.

"He found a letter," she said. "In my bag. Yesterday."

"You aren't going to tell me he goes fossicking in your bag? And what letter, for pity's sake? Honestly, Fée !"

"I don't expect you to understand," Félicité said grandly.

S.B.S.   B

" We were lunching and he hadn't got a cigarette. I was doing my face at the time and I told him to help himself to my case. The letter came out of the bag with the case."

" And he—well, never mind, *what* letter?"

" I know you're going to say I'm mad. It was a sort of rough draft of a letter I sent to somebody. It had a bit in it about Carlos. When I saw it in his hand I was pretty violently rocked. I said something like ' Hi-hi you can't read that,' and of course Carlos with that tore everything wide open. He said ' So.' "

" ' So what?' "

" ' So,' all by itself. He does that. He's Latin-American."

" I thought that sort of ' so ' was German."

" Whatever it is I find it terrifying. I began to fluff and puff and tried to pass it off with a jolly laugh but he said that either he could trust me or he couldn't and if he could, how come I wouldn't let him read a letter? I completely lost my head and grabbed it and he began to hiss. We were in a restaurant."

" Good lord! "

" Well, I know. Obviously he was going to react in a really big way. So in the end the only thing seemed to be to let him have the letter. So I gave it to him on condition he wouldn't read it till we got back to the car. The drive home was hideous. But hideous."

" But what was in the letter, if one may ask, and who was it written to? You are confusing, Fée."

There followed a long uneasy silence. Félicité lit another cigarette. " Come on," said Carlisle at last.

" It happened," said Félicité haughtily, " to be written to a man whom I don't actually know, asking for advice about Carlos and me. Professional advice."

" What can you mean! A clergyman? Or a lawyer?"

" I don't think so. He'd written me rather a marvellous letter and this was thanking him. Carlos, of course, thought it was for Edward. The worst bit, from Carlos point of view was where I said : ' I suppose he'd be madly jealous if he knew I'd written to you like this.' Carlos really got weaving after he read that. He——"

Félicité's lips trembled. She turned away and began to speak rapidly, in a high voice. " He roared and stormed and wouldn't listen to anything. It was devastating. You can't conceive what it was like. He said I was to announce our engagement at once. He said if I didn't he'd—he said he'd go off and just simply end it all. He's given me a week. I've got till next Tuesday. That's all. I've got to announce it before next Tuesday."

"And you don't want to?" Carlisle asked gently. She saw Félicité's shoulders quiver and went to her. "Is that it, Fée?"

The voice quavered and broke. Félicité drove her hands through her hair. "I don't know *what* I want," she sobbed. "Lisle, I'm in such a muddle. I'm terrified, Lisle. It's so damned awful, Lisle. I'm terrified."

2

Lady Pastern had preserved throughout the war and its exhausted aftermath, an unbroken formality. Her rare dinner parties had, for this reason, acquired the air of period pieces. The more so since, by feat of superb domestic strategy she had contrived to retain at Duke's Gate a staff of trained servants, though a depleted one. As she climbed into a long dress, six years old, Carlisle reflected that if the food shortage persisted, her aunt would soon qualify for the same class as that legendary Russian nobleman who presided with perfect equanimity at in interminable banquet of dry bread and water.

She had parted with Félicité, who was still shaking and incoherent, on the landing. "You'll see him at dinner," Félicité had said. "You'll see what I mean." And with a spurt of defiance: "And anyway, I don't care what anyone thinks. If I'm in a mess, it's a thrilling mess. And if I want to get out of it, it's not for other people's reasons. It's only because—— Oh, God, what's it *matter*!"

Félicité had then gone into her own room and slammed the door. It was perfectly obvious, Carlisle reflected, as she finished her face and lit a cigarette, that the wretched girl was terrified and that she herself would, during the week-end, be a sort of buffer-state between Félicité, her mother and her stepfather. "And the worst of it is," Carlisle thought crossly, "I'm fond of them and will probably end by involving myself in a major row with all three at once."

She went down to the drawing-room. Finding nobody there, she wandered disconsolately across the landing and opening a pair of magnificent double-doors, looked into the ballroom. Gilt chairs and music stands stood in a semi-circle like an island in the vast bare floor. A grand piano stood in their midst. On its closed lid, with surrealistic inconsequence, was scattered a number of umbrellas and parasols. She looked more closely at them and recognised a black and white, exceedingly Parisian, affair, which ten years ago or more her aunt had flourished at Ascot. It had been an outstanding phenomenon, she remembered, in the Royal Enclosure and had been photographed. Lady Pastern had been presented with it by some Indian plenipotentiary on the occasion of her first marriage and had clung to it ever since. Its handle represented a bird and had ruby eyes. Its shaft was preposterously thin and was jointed and bound with platinum. The spring catch and the dark bronze section that held it were uncomfortably encrusted with jewels and had ruined many a pair of gloves. As a child, Félicité had occasionally been permitted to unscrew the head and the end section of the shaft and this, for some reason, had always afforded her extreme pleasure. Carlisle picked it up, opened it, and, jeering at herself for being superstitious, hurriedly shut it again. There was a pile of band-parts on the piano seat and on the top of this a scribled programme.

" Floor Show," she read. " (1) A New Way with Old Tunes. (2) Skelton. (3) Sandra. (4) Hot Guy."

At the extreme end of the group of chairs and a little isolated, was the paraphernalia of a dance-band tympanist— drums, rattles, a tambourine, cymbals, a wire whisk and coco-nut shells. Carlisle gingerly touched a pedal with her foot and jumped nervously when a pair of cymbals clashed. " It would be fun," she thought, " to sit down and have a whack at everything. What can Uncle George be like in action!"

She looked round. Her coming-out ball had been here; her parents had borrowed the house for it. Utterly remote, those years before the war! Carlisle repeopled the hollow room and felt again the curious fresh gaiety of that night. She felt the cord of her programme grow flossy under the nervous pressure of her gloved fingers. She saw the names written there and read them again in the choked print of casualty lists. The cross against the supper dances had been for Edward. "I don't approve," he had said, guiding her with precision, and speaking so lightly that, as usual, she doubted his intention. "We've no business to do ourselves as well as all this." "Well, if you're not having fun——" "But I am. I am." And he had started one of their "novelettes": "In the magnificent ballroom at Duke's Gate, the London House of Lord Pastern and Bagott, amid the strains of music and the scent of hot-house blooms——" And she had cut in: "Young Edward Manx swept his cousin into the vortex of the dance." "Lovely," she thought. Lovely it had been. They had had the last dance together and she had been tired yet buoyant, moving without conscious volition; *really* floating, she thought. "Good-night, good-night, it's been perfect." Later, as the clocks struck four, up the stairs to bed, light-headed with fatigue, drugged with gratitude to all the world for her complete happiness.

"How young," thought Carlisle, looking at the walls and floor of the ballroom, "and how remote. The Spectre of the Rose," she thought, and a phrase of music ended her recollections on a sigh.

There had been no real sequel. More balls, with the dances planned beforehand, an affair or two and letters from Edward who was doing special articles in Russia. And then the war.

She turned away and recrossed the landing to the drawing-room.

It was still unoccupied. "If I don't talk to somebody soon," Carlisle thought, "I shall get a black dog on my back." She found a collection of illustrated papers and turned them over, thinking how strange it was that photographs of people eating, dancing, or looking at something that did not appear in the picture, should command attention.

"Lady Dartmoor and Mr. Jeremy Thringle enjoyed a joke at the opening night of *Fewer and Dearer*." "Miss Penelope Santon-Clarke takes a serious view of the situation at Sandown. With her, intent on his racing-card, is Captain Anthony Barr-Barr." "At the Tarmac: Miss Félicité de Suze in earnest conversation with Mr. Edward Manx." "I don't wonder," thought Carlisle, "that Aunt Cecile thinks it would be a good match," and put the paper away from her. Another magazine lay in her lap: a glossy publication with a cover-illustration depicting a hill-top liberally endowed with flowers and a young man and woman of remarkable physique gazing with every expression of delight and well-being at something indistinguishable in an extremely blue sky. The title *Harmony* was streamlined across the top of the cover.

Carlisle turned the pages. Here was Edward's monthly review of the shows. Much too good, it was, mordant and penetrating, for a freak publication like this. He had told her they paid very well. Here, an article on genetics by " The Harmony Consultant," here something a bit over-emotional about famine relief, which Carlisle, an expert in her way, skimmed through with disapproval. Next an article : " Radiant Living," which she passed by with a shudder. Then a two-page article headed : " Crime Pays," which proved to be a highly flavoured but extremely outspoken and well-informed article on the drug-racket. Two Latin American business firms with extensive connections in Great Britain were boldly named. An editorial note truculently courted information backed by full protection. It also invited a libel action and promised a further article. Next came a serial by a Big Name and then, on the centre double-page with a banner headline :

" The Helping Hand."
Ask G.P.F. about it.
(Guide, Philosopher, Friend.)

Carlisle glanced through it. Here were letters from young women asking for advice on the conduct of their engagements and from young men seeking guidance in their choice of wives and jobs. Here was a married woman prepared, it seemed, to follow the instructions of an unknown pundit in matters of the strictest personal concern, and here a widower who requested an expert report on remarriage with someone twenty years his junior. Carlisle was about to turn the page when a sentence caught her eye :

" I am nineteen and unofficially engaged to be married. My fiancé is madly jealous and behaves——"

She read it through to the end. The style was vividly familiar. The magazine had the look of having been frequently opened here. There was cigarette ash in the groove between the pages. Was it possible that Félicité——? But the signature: "Toots!" Could Félicité adopt a nom-de-plume like Toots? Could her unknown correspondent——? Carlisle lost herself in a maze of speculation from which she was aroused by some faint noise; a metallic click. She looked up. Nobody had entered the room. The sound was repeated and she realised it had come from her uncle's study, a small room that opened off the far end of the drawing-room. She saw that the door was ajar and that the lights were on in the study. She remembered that it was Lord Pastern's unaltered habit to sit in this room for half an hour before dinner, meditating upon whatever obsession at the moment enthralled him, and that he had always liked her to join him there.

She walked down the long deep carpet to the door and looked in.

Lord Pastern sat before the fire. He had a revolver in his hands and appeared to be loading it.

3

For a few moments Carlisle hesitated. Then, in a voice that struck her as being pitched too high, she said: "What *are* you up to, Uncle George?"

He started and the revolver slipped in his hands and almost fell.

"Hallo," he said. "Thought you'd forgotten me."

She crossed the room and sat opposite him. "Are you preparing for burglars?" she asked.

"No." He gave her what Edward had once called one of his leery looks and added: "Although you might put it that way. I'm gettin' ready for my big moment." He jerked his hand towards a small table that stood at his elbow. Carlisle saw that a number of cartridges lay there. "Just goin' to draw the bullets," said Lord Pastern, "to make 'em into blanks, you know. I like to attend to things myself."

"But what is your big moment?"

"You'll see to-night. You and Fée are to come. It ought to be a party. Who's your best young man?"

"I haven't got one."

"Why not?"

"Arst yourself."

"You're too damn' standoffish, me gel. Wouldn't be surprised if you had one of those things—Oedipus and all that. I looked into psychology when I was interested in companionate marriage."

Lord Pastern inserted his eyeglass, went to his desk, and rummaged in one of the drawers.

"What's happening to-night?"

"Special extension night at the Metronome. I'm playin'. Floor show at 11 o'clock. My first appearance in public. Breezy engaged me. Nice of him, wasn't it? You'll enjoy yourself, Lisle."

He returned with a drawer filled with a strange collection of objects; pieces of wire, a fret-saw, razor blades, candle-ends, wood-carving knives, old photographs, electrical gear, plastic wood, a number of tools and quantities of putty in greasy paper. How well Carlisle remembered that drawer. It had been a wet-day solace of her childhood visits. From its contents, Lord Pastern, who was dexterous in such matters, had concocted mannikins, fly-traps and tiny ships.

"I believe," she said, "I recognise almost everything in the collection."

"Y' father gave me that revolver," Lord Pastern remarked. "It's one of a pair. He had 'em made by his gunsmith to take special target ammunition. Couldn't be bored having to re-load with every shot like you do with target pistols, y'know. Cost him a packet these did. We were always at it, he and I. He scratched his initials one day on the butt of this one. We'd had a bit of a row about differences in performance in the two guns, and shot it out. Have a look."

She picked up the revolver gingerly. "I can't see anything."

"There's a magnifying glass somewhere. Look underneath near the trigger-guard."

Carlisle rummaged in the drawer and found a lens. "Yes," she said. "I can make them out now. C.D.W."

"We were crack shots. He left me the pair. The other's in the case, somewhere in that drawer."

Lord Pastern took out a pair of pliers and picked up one of the cartridges. "Well, if you haven't got a young man," he said, "we'll have Ned Manx. That'll please your aunt. No good asking anyone else for Fée. Carlos cuts up rough."

"Uncle George," Carlisle ventured as he busied himself over his task, "do you approve of Carlos? Really?"

He muttered and grunted. She caught disjointed phrases : "——take their course—own destiny—goin' the wrong way to work. He's a damn' fine piano accordionist," he said loudly and added, more obscurely : "They'd much better leave things to me."

"What's he like?"

"You'll see him in a minute. I know what I'm about," said Lord Pastern crimping the end of a cartridge from which he had extracted the bullet.

"Nobody else seems to. Is he jealous?"

"She's had things too much her own way. Make her sit up a bit and a good job, too."

"Aren't you making a great number of blank cartridges?" Carlisle asked idly.

"I rather like making them. You never know. I shall probably be asked to repeat my number lots of times. I like to be prepared."

He glanced up and saw the journal which Carlisle still held in her lap. "Thought you had a mind above that sort of stuff," said Lord Pastern, grinning.

"Are you a subscriber, darling?"

"Y' aunt is. It's got a lot of sound stuff in it. They're not afraid to speak their minds, b'God. See that thing on drug-runnin'? Names and everything and if they don't like it they can damn' well lump it. The police," Lord Pastern said obscurely, "are no good. Pompous incompetent lot. Hidebound. Ned," he added, "does the reviews."

"Perhaps," Carlisle said lightly, "he's G.P.F. too."

"Chap's got brains," Lord Pastern grunted bewilderingly. "Hog-sense in that feller."

"Uncle George," Carlisle demanded suddenly, " you don't know by any chance, if Fée's ever consulted G.P.F.?"

" Wouldn't let on if I did, m'dear. Naturally."

Carlisle reddened. " No, of course you wouldn't if she'd told you in confidence. Only usually Fée can't keep anything to herself."

" Well, ask her. She might do a damn' sight worse."

Lord Pastern dropped the two bullets he had extracted into the waste-paper basket and returned to his desk. " I've been doin' a bit of writin' myself," he said. " Look at this, Lisle."

He handed his niece a sheet of music manuscript. An air had been set down, with many rubbings out, it seemed, and words had been written under the appropriate notes. " This Hot Guy," Carlisle read, " does he get mean? This Hot Gunner with his accord-een. Shoots like he plays an' he tops the bill. Plays like he shoots an' he shoots to kill. Hide oh hi. Yip. Ho de oh do. Yip. Shoot buddy, shoot and we'll sure come clean. Hot Guy, Hot Gunner and your accord-een. Bo. Bo. Bo."

" Neat," said Lord Pastern complacently. " Ain't it?"

" It's astonishing," Carlisle murmured and was spared the necessity of further comment by the sound of voices in the drawing-room.

" That's the Boys," said Lord Pastern briskly. " Come on."

The Boys were dressed in their professional dinner suits. These were distinctive garments, the jackets being double-breasted with steel buttons and silver revers. The sleeves were extremely narrow and displayed a great deal of cuff. The taller of the two, a man whose rotundity was emphasised by his pallor, advanced, beaming upon his host.

" Well, well, well," he said. " Look who's here."

It was upon his companion that Carlisle fixed her attention. Memories of tango experts, of cinema near-stars with cigarette holders and parti-coloured shoes, of armoured women moving doggedly round dance floors in the grasp of younger men; all these memories jostled together in her brain.

"——and Mr. Rivera——" her uncle was saying. Carlisle withdrew her hand from Mr. Bellairs' encompassing grasp and it was at once bowed over by Mr. Rivera.

" Miss Wayne," said Félicité's Carlos.

He rose from his bow with grace and gave her a look of

automatic homage. "So we meet, at last," he said. "I have heard so much." He had, she noticed, a very slight lisp.

Lord Pastern gave them all sherry. The two visitors made loud conversation : "That's very fine," Mr. Breezy Bellairs pronounced and pointed to a small Fragonard above the fireplace. "My God, that's beautiful, you know, Carlos. Exquisite."

"In my father's hacienda," said Mr. Rivera, "there is a picture of which I am vividly reminded. This picture to which I refer, is a portrait of one of my paternal ancestors. It is an original Goya." And while she was still wondering how a Fragonard could remind Mr. Rivera of a Goya, he turned to Carlisle. "You have visited the Argentine, Miss Wayne, of course?"

"No," said Carlisle.

"But you must. It would appeal to you enormously. It is a little difficult, by the way, for a visitor to see us, as it were from the inside. The Spanish families are very exclusive."

"Oh."

"Oh, yes. An aunt of mine, Donna Isabella da Manuelos-Rivera used to say ours was the only remaining aristocracy." He inclined towards Lord Pastern and laughed musically. "But, of course, she had not visited a certain charming house in Duke's Gate, London."

"What? I wasn't listening," said Lord Pastern. "Look here, Bellairs, about to-night——"

"To-night," Mr. Bellairs interrupted, smiling from ear to ear, "is in the bag. We'll rock them, Lord Pastern. Now, don't you worry about to-night. It's going to be wonderful. You'll be there, of course, Miss Wayne?"

"I wouldn't miss it," Carlisle murmured, wishing they were not so zealous in their attentions.

"I've got the gun fixed up," her uncle said eagerly. "Five rounds of blanks, you know. What about those umbrellas, now——"

"You are fond of music, Miss Wayne? But of course you are. You would be enchanted by the music of my own country."

"Tangos and rhumbas?" Carlisle ventured. Mr. Rivera inclined towards her. "At midnight," he said, "with the scent of magnolias in the air—those wonderful nights of music. You will think it strange, of course, that I should be "—he shrugged up his shoulders and lowered his voice—" performing in a dance band. Wearing these appalling clothes! Here, in London! It is terrible, isn't it?"

" I don't see why."

" I suppose," Mr. Rivera sighed, " I am what you call a snob. There are times when I find it almost unendurable. But I must not say so." He glanced at Mr. Bellairs who was deep in conversation with his host. " A heart of gold," he whispered. " One of nature's gentlemen. I should not complain. How serious we have become," he added gaily. " We meet and in two minutes I confide in you. You are *simpatica*, Miss Wayne. But of course, you have been told that before."

" Never," said Carlisle firmly, and was glad to see Edward Manx come in.

" Evenin', Ned," said Lord Pastern, blinking at him. " Glad to see you. Have you met——"

Carlisle heard Mr. Rivera draw in his breath with a formidable hiss. Manx, having saluted Mr. Bellairs, advanced with a pleasant smile and extended hand. " We haven't met, Rivera," he said, " but at least I'm one of your devotés at the Metronome. If anything could teach me how to dance I'm persuaded it would be your piano accordion."

" How do you do," said Mr. Rivera, and turned his back. " As I was saying, Miss Wayne," he continued. " I believe entirely in first impressions. As soon as we were introduced——"

Carlisle looked past him at Manx who had remained perfectly still. At the first opportunity, she walked round Mr. Rivera and joined him. Mr. Rivera moved to the fireplace before which he stood with an air of detachment, humming under his breath. Lord Pastern instantly buttonholed him. Mr. Bellairs joined them with every manifestation of uneasy geniality. " About my number, Carlos," said Lord Pastern, " I've been tellin' Breezy——"

" Of all the filthy rude——" Manx began to mutter.

Carlisle linked her arm in his and walked him away. " He's just plain frightful, Ned. Félicité must be out of her mind," she whispered hastily.

"If Cousin George thinks I'm going to stand round letting a bloody fancy-dress dago insult me——"

"For *pity's* sake don't fly into one of your rages. Laugh it off."

"Heh-heh-heh——"

"That's better."

"He'll probably throw his sherry in my face. Why the devil was I asked if he was coming. What's Cousin Cecile thinking of?"

"It's Uncle George—shut up. Here come the girls."

Lady Pastern, encased in black, entered with Félicité at her heels. She suffered the introductions with terrifying courtesy. Mr. Bellairs redoubled his geniality. Mr. Rivera had the air of a man who never blossoms but in the presence of the great.

"I am so pleased to have the honour, at last, of being presented," he said. "From Félicité I have heard so much of her mother. I feel, too, that we may have friends in common. Perhaps, Lady Pastern you will remember an uncle of mine who had, I think, some post at our Embassy in Paris many years ago. Señor Alonza da Manuelos-Rivera."

Lady Pastern contemplated him without any change of expression. "I do not remember," she said.

"After all it was much too long ago," he rejoined gallantly. Lady Pastern glanced at him with cold astonishment, and advanced upon Manx. "Dearest Edward," she said, offering her cheek, "we see you far too seldom. This is delightful."

"Thank you, Cousin Cecile. For me, too."

"I want to consult you. You will forgive us, George. I am determined to have Edward's opinion on my *petit-point*."

"Let me alone," Manx boasted, "with *petit-point*."

Lady Pastern put her arm through his and led him apart. Carlisle saw Félicité go to Rivera. Evidently she had herself well in hand : her greeting was prettily formal. She turned with an air of comradeship from Rivera to Bellairs and her stepfather. "Will anyone bet me," she said, "that I can't guess what you chaps have been talking about?"

Mr. Bellairs was immediately very gay. "Now, Miss de Suze, that's making it just a little tough. I'm afraid you know much too much about us. Isn't that the case, Lord Pastern?"

"I'm worried about those umbrellas," said Lord Pastern moodily and Bellairs and Félicité began to talk at once.

Carlisle was trying to make up her mind about Rivera and failing to do so. Was he in love with Félicité? If so, was his jealousy of Ned Manx a genuine and therefore an alarming passion? Was he, on the other hand, a complete adventurer? Could he conceivably be that to which he pretended? Could any human being be as patently bogus as Mr. Rivera or was it within the bounds of possibility that the scions of noble Spanish-American families behaved in a manner altogether too faithful to their Hollywood opposites? Was it her fancy or had his olive-coloured cheeks turned paler as he stood and watched Félicité? Was the slight tic under his left eye, that smallest possible muscular twitch really involuntary or, as everything else about him seemed to be, part of an impersonation along stereotyped lines? And as these speculations chased each other through her mind, Rivera himself came up to her.

"But you are so serious," he said. "I wonder why. In my country we have a proverb: a woman is serious for one of two reasons; she is about to fall in love or already she loves without success. The alternative being unthinkable, I ask myself: to whom is this lovely lady about to lose her heart?"

Carlisle thought: "I wonder if this is the line of chat that Félicité has fallen for." She said: "I'm afraid your proverb doesn't apply out of South America."

He laughed as if she had uttered some brilliant equivocation and began to protest that he knew better, indeed he did. Carlisle saw Félicité stare blankly at them and, turning quickly, surprised just such another expression on Edward Manx's face. She began to feel acutely uncomfortable. There was no getting away from Mr. Rivera. His raillery and archness mounted with indecent emphasis. He admired Carlisle's dress, her modest jewel, her hair. His lightest remark was pronounced with such a killing air that it immediately assumed the character of an impropriety. Her embarrassment at these excesses quickly gave way to irritation when she saw that while Mr Rivera bent upon her any number of melting glances he also kept a sharp watch upon Félicité. "And I'll be damned," thought Carlisle, "if I let him get away with that little game." She chose her moment and joined her aunt who had withdrawn Edward Manx to the other end of the room and, while she exhibited her embroidery, muttered anathemas upon her other guests. As Carlisle came up, Edward was in the middle of some kind of uneasy protestation. "——but, Cousin Cecile, I don't honestly think I can do much about it. I mean—— Oh, hallo, Lisle, enjoying your Latin-American petting party?"

"Not enormously," said Carlisle, and bent over her aunt's embroidery. "It's lovely, darling," she said. "How do you do it?"

"You shall have it for an evening bag. I have been telling Edward that I fling myself on his charity, and" Lady Pastern added in a stormy undertone, "and on yours, my dearest child." She raised her needlework as if to examine it and they saw her fingers fumble aimlessly across its surface. "You see, both of you, this atrocious person. I implore you——" Her voice faltered. "Look," she whispered, "look now. Look at him."

Carlisle and Edward glanced furtively at Mr. Rivera who was in the act of introducing a cigarette into a jade holder. He caught Carlisle's eye. He did not smile but glossed himself over with appraisement. His eyes widened. "Somewhere or another," she thought, "he has read about gentlemen who undress ladies with a glance." She heard Manx swear under his breath and noted with surprise her own gratification at this circumstance. Mr. Rivera advanced upon her.

"Oh, lord!" Edward muttered.

"Here," said Lady Pastern loudly, "is Hendy. She is dining with us. I had forgotten."

The door at the far end of the drawing-room had opened and a woman plainly dressed came quietly in.

"Hendy!" Carlisle echoed. "I had forgotten Hendy," and went swiftly towards her.

CHAPTER FOUR

THEY DINE

I

MISS HENDERSON had been Félicité's governess and had remained with the family after she grew up, occupying a post that was half-way between that of companion and secretary to both Félicité and her mother. Carlisle called her controller-of-the-household and knew that many a time she had literally performed the impossible task this title implied. She was a greyish-haired woman of forty-five; her appearance was tranquil but unremarkable, her voice pleasant. Carlisle, who liked her, had often wondered at her faithfulness to this turbulent household. To Lady Pastern, who regarded all persons as neatly graded types, Miss Henderson was no doubt an employee of good address and perfect manners whose presence at Duke's Gate was essential to her own peace of mind. Miss Henderson had her private room where usually she ate in solitude. Sometimes, however, she was asked to lunch or dine with the family; either because a woman guest had slipped them up, or because her employer felt it was suitable that her position should be defined by such occasional invitations. She seldom left the house and if she had any outside ties, Carlisle had never heard of them. She was perfectly adjusted to her isolation and if she was ever lonely, gave no evidence of being so. Carlisle believed Miss Henderson to have more influence than anyone else with Félicité, and it struck her now as odd that Lady Pastern should not have mentioned Hendy as a possible check to Mr. Rivera. But then the family did not often remember Hendy until they actually wanted her for something. "And I myself," Carlisle thought guiltily, "although I like her so much, had forgotten to ask after her." And she made her greeting the warmer because of this omission.

"Hendy," she said, "how lovely to see you. How long is it? Four years?"

" A little over three, I think." That was like her. She was always quietly accurate.

" You look just the same," said Carlisle, nervously aware of Mr. Rivera close behind her.

Lady Pastern icily performed the introductions. Mr. Bellairs bowed and smiled expansively from the hearth-rug. Mr. Rivera, standing beside Carlisle, said : " Ah, yes, of course. Miss Henderson." And might as well have added : " The governess, I believe." Miss Henderson bowed composedly and Spence announced dinner.

They sat at a round table; a pool of candlelight in the shadowed dining-room. Carlisle found herself between her uncle and Rivera. Opposite her, between Edward and Bellairs, sat Félicité. Lady Pastern, on Rivera's right, at first suffered his conversation with awful courtesy, presumably, thought Carlisle, in order to give Edward Manx, her other neighbour, a clear run with Félicité. But as Mr. Bellairs completely ignored Miss Henderson, who was on his right and lavished all his attention on Félicité herself, this manœuvre was unproductive. After a few minutes Lady Pastern engaged Edward in what Carlisle felt to be an extremely ominous conversation. She caught only fragments of it as Rivera had resumed his crash tactics with herself. His was a simple technique. He merely turned his shoulders on Lady Pastern, leant so close to Carlisle that she could see the pores of his skin, looked into her eyes, and, with rich insinuation, contradicted everything she said. Lord Pastern was no refuge, as he had sunk into a reverie from which he roused himself from time to time only to throw disjointed remarks at no one in particular, and to attack his food with a primitive gusto which dated from his Back-to-Nature period. His table-manners were defiantly and deliberately atrocious. He chewed with parted lips, glaring about him like a threatened carnivore, and as he chewed he talked. To Spence and the man who assisted him and to Miss Henderson who accepted her isolation with her usual composure, the conversation must have come through like the dialogue in a boldly surrealistic broadcast.

". . . such a good photograph, we thought, Edward, of you and Félicité at the Tarmac. She so much enjoyed her party with you . . ."

" . . . but I'm not at all musical . . ."

" . . . you must not say so. You are musical. There is music in your eyes—your voice . . ."

" . . . now that's quite a nifty little idea, Miss de Suze. We'll have to pull you in with the boys . . ."

" . . . so it is arranged, my dear Edward."

" . . . thank you, Cousin Cecile, but . . ."

" . . . you and Félicité have always done things together, haven't you? We were laughing yesterday over some old photographs. Do you remember at Clochemere . . .?"

" . . . C, where's my sombrero?"

" . . . with this dress you should wear flowers. A cascade of orchids. Just here. Let me show you . . ."

" . . . I beg your pardon, Cousin Cecile, I'm afraid I didn't hear what you said . . ."

" Uncle George, it's time you talked to me . . ."

" Eh? Sorry, Lisle, I'm wondering where my sombrero . . ."

" Lord Pastern is very kind in letting me keep you to myself. Don't turn away. Look. Your handkerchief is falling."

" *Damn!*"

" Edward!"

" I beg your pardon, Cousin Cecile, I don't know what I'm thinking of."

" Carlos."

" . . . in my country, Miss Wayne . . . no, I cannot call you Miss Wayne. Car-r-r-lisle! What a strange name. Strange and captivating."

" Carlos!"

" Forgive me. You spoke?"

" About those umbrellas, Breezy."

" Yes, I did speak."

" A thousand pardons, I was talking to Carrlisle."

" I've engaged a table for three, Fée. You and Carlisle and Ned. Don't be late."

" My music to-night shall be for you."

" I am coming, also, George."

" *What!*"

" Kindly see that it is a table for four."

" Maman! But I thought . . ."

" You won't like it, C."

" I propose to come."

" Damn it, you'll sit and glare at me and make me nervous."

" Nonsense, George," Lady Pastern said crisply. " Be good enough to order the table."

Her husband glowered at her, seemed to contemplate giving further battle, appeared suddenly to change his mind and launched an unexpected attack at Rivera.

" About your being carried out, Carlos," he said importantly, " it seems a pity I can't be carried out, too. Why can't the stretcher party come back for me."

" Now, now, now," Mr. Bellairs interrupted in a great hurry. " We've got everything fixed, Lord Pastern, now, haven't we? The first routine. You shoot Carlos. Carlos falls. Carlos is carried out. You take the show away. Big climax. Finish. Now don't you get me bustled," he added playfully. " It's good and it's fixed. Fine. That's right, isn't it?"

" It is what has been decided," Mr. Rivera conceded grandly. " For myself, I am perhaps a little dubious. Under other circumstances I would undoubtedly insist upon the second routine. I am shot at but I do not fall. Lord Pastern misses me. The others fall. Breezy fires at Lord Pastern and nothing happens. Lord Pastern plays, faints, is removed. I finish the number. Upon this routine under other circumstances, I should insist." He executed a sort of comprehensive bow, taking in Lord Pastern, Félicité, Carlisle and Lady Pastern. " But under these exclusive and most charming circumstances, I yield. I am shot. I fall. Possibly I hurt myself. No matter."

Bellairs eyed him. " Good old Carlos," he said uneasily.

" I still don't see why I can't be carried out, too," said Lord Pastern fretfully.

Carlisle heard Mr. Bellairs whisper under his breath : " For the love of Pete!" Rivera said loudly : " No, no, no, no. Unless we adopt completely the second routine, we perform the first as we rehearsed. It is settled."

" Carlisle," said Lady Pastern, rising, " shall we . . .?"

She swept her ladies into the drawing-room.

2

Félicité was puzzled, resentful and uneasy. She moved restlessly about the room, eyeing her mother and Carlisle. Lady Pastern paid no attention to her daughter. She questioned Carlisle about her experiences in Greece and received her somewhat distracted answers with perfect equanimity. Miss Henderson, who had taken up Lady Pastern's box of embroidery threads, sorted them with quiet movements of her hands and seemed to listen with interest.

Suddenly Félicité said : " I don't see much future in us all behaving as if we'd had the Archbishop of Canterbury to dinner. If you've got anything to say about Carlos, all of you, I'd be very much obliged if you'd say it."

Miss Henderson, her hands still for a moment, glanced up at Félicité and then bent again over her task. Lady Pastern having crossed her ankles and wrists, slightly moved her shoulders and said : " I do not consider this a suitable occasion, my dear child, for any such discussion."

" Why?" Félicité demanded.

" It would make a scene, and under the circumstances," said Lady Pastern with an air of reasonableness, " there's no time for a scene."

" If you think the men are coming in, Maman, they are not. George has arranged to go over the programme again in the ballroom."

A servant came in and collected the coffee cups. Lady Pastern made conversation with Carlisle until the door had closed behind him.

" So I repeat," Félicité said loudly, " I want to hear, Maman, what you've got to say against Carlos."

Lady Pastern slightly raised her eyes and lifted her shoulders. Her daughter stamped. " Blast and hell !" she said.

" Félicité !" said Miss Henderson. It was neither a remonstrance nor a warning. The name fell like an unstressed comment. Miss Henderson held an embroidery stiletto firmly between her finger and thumb and examined it placidly.

Félicité made an impatient movement. " If you think," she

said violently, "anybody's going to be at their best in a
strange house with a hostess who looks at them as if they
smelt!"

"If it comes to that, dearest child, he does smell. Of a
particularly heavy kind of scent, I fancy," Lady Pastern added
thoughtfully.

From the ballroom came a distant syncopated roll of drums
ending in a crash of cymbals and a loud report. Carlisle
jumped nervously. The stiletto fell from Miss Henderson's
fingers to the carpet. Félicité bearing witness in her agitation,
to the efficacy of her governess's long training, stooped and
picked it up.

"It is your uncle, merely," said Lady Pastern.

"I ought to go straight out and apologise to Carlos for the
hideous way he's been treated," Félicité stormed, but her voice
held an overtone of uncertainty and she looked resentfully at
Carlisle.

"If there are to be apologies," her mother rejoined, "it is
Carlisle who should receive them. I am so sorry, Carlisle, that
you should have been subjected to these"—she made a fastidious gesture—"to these really insufferable attentions."

"Good lord, Aunt 'Cile," Carlisle began in acute embarrassment, and was rescued by Félicité who burst into tears and
rushed out of the room.

"I think, perhaps . . .?" said Miss Henderson, rising.

"Yes, please go to her."

But before Miss Henderson reached the door, which Félicité had left open, Rivera's voice sounded in the hall. "What
is the matter?" it said distinctly and Félicité, breathless,
answered. "I've got to talk to you." "But certainly, if you
wish it." "In here, then." The voices faded, were heard again,
indistinctly, in the study. The connecting door between the
study and the drawing-room was slammed-to from the far side.
"You had better leave them, I think," said Lady Pastern.

"If I go to my sitting-room, she may come to me when this
is over."

"Then go," said Lady Pastern, drearily. "Thank you, Miss
Henderson."

"Aunt," said Carlisle when Miss Henderson had left them,
"what are you up to?"

Lady Pastern, shielding her face from the fire, said: "I have made a decision. I believe that my policy in this affair has been a mistaken one. Anticipating my inevitable opposition, Félicité has met this person in his own setting and has, as I think you would say, lost her eye. I cannot believe that when she has seen him here, and has observed his atrocious antics, his immense vulgarity, she will not come to her senses. Already one can see, she is shaken. After all, I remind myself, she is a de Fouteaux and a de Suze. Am I not right?"

"It's an old trick, darling, you know. It doesn't always work."

"It is working, however," said Lady Pastern, setting her mouth. "She sees him, for example, beside dear Edward to whom she has always been devoted. Of your uncle as a desirable contrast, I say nothing, but at least his clothes are unexceptionable. And though I deeply resent, dearest child, that you should have been forced, in my house, to suffer the attentions of this animal, they have assuredly impressed themselves disagreeably upon Félicité."

"Disagreeably—yes," said Carlisle turning pink. "But look here, Aunt Cecile, he's shooting this nauseating little line with me to—well, to make Fée sit up and take notice." Lady Pastern momentarily closed her eyes. This, Carlisle remembered, was her habitual reaction to slang. "And, I'm not sure," Carlisle added, "that she hasn't fallen for it."

"She cannot be anything but disgusted."

"I wouldn't be astonished if she refuses to come to the Metronome to-night."

"That is what I hope. But I am afraid she will come. She will not give way so readily, I think." Lady Pastern rose. "Whatever happens," she said, "I shall break this affair. Do you hear me Carlisle? I shall break it."

Beyond the door at the far end of the room, Félicité's voice rose, in a sharp crescendo, but the words were indistinguishable.

"They are quarrelling," said Lady Pastern with satisfaction.

3

As Edward Manx sat silent in his chair, a glass of port and a cup of coffee before him, his thoughts moved out in widening circles from the candle-lit table. Removed from him, Bellairs and Rivera had drawn close to Lord Pastern. Bellairs' voice, loud but edgeless, uttered phrase after phrase. "Sure, that's right. Don't worry, it's in the bag. It's going to be a world-breaker. O.K., we'll run it through. Fine." Lord Pastern fidgeted, stuttered, chuckled, complained. Rivera, leaning back in his chair, smiled, said nothing and turned his glass. Manx, who had noticed how frequently it had been refilled, wondered if he was tight.

There they sat, wreathed in cigar-smoke, candle-lit, an unreal group. He saw them as three dissonant figures at the centre of an intolerable design. "Bellairs," he told himself, "is a gaiety merchant. Gaiety!" How fashionable, he reflected, the word had been before the war. Let's be gay, they had all said, and glumly embracing each other had tramped and shuffled, while men like Breezy Bellairs made their noises and did their smiling for them. They christened their children "Gay," they used the word in their drawing-room comedies and in their dismal, dismal songs. "Gaiety!" muttered the disgruntled and angry Edward. "A lovely word, but the thing itself, when enjoyed is unnamed. There's Cousin George, who is undoubtedly a little mad, sitting, like a mouthpiece for his kind, between a jive-merchant and a cad. And here's Fée antic-ing inside the unholy circle while Cousin Cecile solemnly gyrates against the beat. In an outer ring, I hope unwillingly, is Lisle, and here I sit, as sore as hell, on the perimeter." He glanced up and found that Rivera was looking at him, not directly, but out of the corners of his eyes. "Sneering," thought Edward, "like an infernal caricature of himself."

"Buck up, Ned," Lord Pastern said, grinning at him. "We haven't had a word from you. You want takin' out of yourself. Bit of gaiety, what?"

"By all means, sir," said Edward. A white carnation had

fallen out of the vase in the middle of the table. He took it up and put it in his coat. " The blameless life," he said.

Lord Pastern cackled and turned to Bellairs. " Well, Breezy, if you think it's all right, we'll order the taxis for a quarter past ten. Think you can amuse yourselves till then?" He pushed the decanter towards Bellairs.

" Sure, sure," Bellairs said. " No, thanks a lot, no more. A lovely wine, mind you, but I've got to be a good boy."

Edward slid the port on to Rivera, who, smiling a little more broadly, refilled his glass.

" I'll show you the blanks and the revolver, when we move," said Lord Pastern. " They're in the study." He glanced fretfully at Rivera who slowly pulled his glass towards him. Lord Pastern hated to be kept waiting. " Ned, you look after Carlos, will you? D'you mind, Carlos? I want to show Breezy the blanks. Come on, Breezy."

Manx opened the door for his uncle and returned to the table. He sat down and waited for Rivera to make the first move. Spence came in, lingered for a moment, and withdrew. There followed a long silence.

At last Rivera stretched out his legs and held his port to the light. " I am a man," he said, " who likes to come to the point. You are Félicité's cousin, yes?"

" No."

" No?"

" I'm related to her stepfather."

" She has spoken of you as her cousin."

" A courtesy title," said Edward.

" You are attached to her, I believe?"

Edward paused for three seconds and then said, " Why not?"

" It is not at all surprising," Rivera said, and drank half his port. " Carlisle also speaks of you as her cousin. Is that too a courtesy title?"

Edward pushed back his chair. " I'm afraid I don't see the point of all this," he said.

" The point? Certainly. I am a man," Rivera repeated, " who likes to come to the point. I am also a man who does not care to be cold-shouldered or to be—what is the expression—taken down a garden path. I find my reception in this house unsympathetic. This is displeasing to me. I meet, at the same time, a lady who is not displeasing to me. Quite on the contrary. I am interested. I make a tactful inquiry. I ask, for example, what is the relationship of this lady to my host. Why not?"

"Because it's a singularly offensive question," Edward said and thought : "My God, I'm going to lose my temper."

Rivera made a convulsive movement of his hand and knocked his glass to the floor. They rose simultaneously.

"In my country," Rivera said thickly, "one does not use such expressions without a sequel."

"Be damned to your country."

Rivera gripped the back of his chair and moistened his lips. He emitted a shrill belch. Edward laughed. Rivera walked towards him, paused, and raised his hand with the tips of the thumb and middle finger daintily pressed together. He advanced his hand until it was close to Edward's nose and, without marked success, attempted to snap his finger. "Bastard," he said cautiously. From the distant ballroom came a syncopated roll of drums ending in a crash of cymbals and a deafening report.

Edward said : "Don't be a fool, Rivera."

"I laugh at you till I make myself vomit."

"Laugh yourself into a coma if you like."

Rivera laid the palm of his hand against his waist. "In my country this affair would answer itself with a knife," he said.

"Make yourself scarce or it'll answer itself with a kick in the pants," said Edward. "And if you worry Miss Wayne again I'll give you a damn' sound hiding."

"Aha!" cried Rivera, "so it is not Félicité but the cousin. It is the enchanting little Carlisle. And I am to be warned off, ha? No, no, my friend." He backed away to the door. "No, no, no, no."

"Get out."

Rivera laughed with great virtuosity and made an effective exit into the hall. He left the door open. Edward heard his voice on the next landing. "What is the matter?" and after a pause, "But certainly if you wish it."

A door slammed.

Edward walked once round the table in an irresolute

manner. He then wandered to the sideboard and drove his
hands through his hair. "This is incredible," he muttered.
"It's extraordinary. I never dreamt of it." He noticed that
his hand was shaking and poured himself a stiff jorum of
whisky. "I suppose," he thought, "it's been there all the
time and I simply didn't recognise it."

Spence and his assistant came in. "I beg your pardon, sir,"
said Spence. "I thought the gentlemen had left."

"It's all right, Spence. Clear, if you want to. Pay no attention to me."

"Are you not feeling well, Mr. Edward?"

"I'm all right, I think. I've had a great surprise."

"Indeed, sir? Pleasant, I trust."

"In its way, wonderful, Spence. Wonderful."

4

"There y'are," said Lord Pastern complacently. "Five
rounds and five extras. Neat, aren't they?"

"Look good to me," said Bellairs, returning him the blank
cartridges. "But I wouldn't know." Lord Pastern broke open
his revolver and began to fill the chamber. "We'll try 'em,"
he said.

"Not in here, for Pete's sake, Lord Pastern."

"In the ballroom."

"It'll rock the ladies a bit, won't it?"

"What of it?" said Lord Pastern simply. He snapped the
revolver shut and gave the drawer a shove back on the desk.
"I can't be bothered puttin' that thing away," he said. "You
go to the ballroom. I've a job to do. I'll join you in a minute."

Obediently, Breezy left him and went into the ballroom
where he wandered about restlessly, sighing and yawning and
glancing towards the door.

Presently his host came in looking preoccupied.

"Where's Carlos?" Lord Pastern demanded.

"Still in the dining-room, I think," said Bellairs with his
loud laugh. "Wonderful port you've turned on for us, you
know, Lord Pastern."

" Hope he can hold it. We don't want him playin' the fool with the show."

" He can hold it."

Lord Pastern clapped his revolver down on the floor near the tympani. Bellairs eyed it uneasily.

" I wanted to ask you," said Lord Pastern sitting behind the drums. " Have you spoken to Sydney Skelton?"

Bellairs smiled extensively: " Well, I just haven't got round . . ." he began.

Lord Pastern cut him short. " If you don't want to tell him," he said, " I will."

" No, no!" cried Bellairs in a hurry. " No. I don't think that'd be quite desirable, Lord Pastern, if you can understand." He looked anxiously at his host who had turned away to the piano and with an air of restless preoccupation, examined the black-and-white parasol. Breezy continued: '" I mean to say, Syd's funny. He's very temperamental, if you know what I mean. He's quite a tough guy to handle, Syd. You have to pick your moment with Syd, if you can understand."

" Don't keep on asking if I can understand things that are as simple as falling off a log," Lord Pastern rejoined irritably. " You think I'm good on the drums, you've said so."

" Sure, sure."

" You said if I'd made it my profession I'd have been as good as they come. You said any band'd be proud to have me. Right. I am going to make it my profession and I'm prepared to be your full-time tympanist. Good. Tell Skelton and let him go. Perfectly simple."

" Yes, but——"

" He'll get a job elsewhere fast enough, won't he?"

" Yes. Sure. Easy. But . . ."

" Very well, then," said Lord Pastern conclusively. He had unscrewed the handle from the parasol and was now busy with the top end of the shaft. " This comes to bits," he said. " Rather clever, what? French."

" Look!" said Bellairs winningly. He laid his soft white hand on Lord Pastern's coat. " I'm going to speak very frankly, Lord Pastern. *You* know. It's a hard old world in our game,

if you under—— I mean, I have to think all round a proposi-
tion like this, don't I?"

"You've said you wished you had me permanently," Lord
Pastern reminded him. He spoke with a certain amount of
truculence but rather absent-mindedly. He had unscrewed a
small section from the top end of the parasol shaft. Breezy
watched him mesmerised, as he took up his revolver and, with
the restless concentration of a small boy in mischief, poked
this section a short way up the muzzle, at the same time holding down with his thumb the spring catch that served to keep
the parasol closed. "This," he said," would fit."

"Hi!" Breezy said, "is that gun loaded?"

"Of course," Lord Pastern muttered. He put down the piece
of shaft and glanced up. "You said it to me and Rivera," he
added. He had Hotspur's trick of reverting to the last remark
but four.

"I know, I know," Bellairs gabbled, smiling to the full
extent of his mouth, "but listen. I'm going to put this very
crudely . . ."

"Why the hell shouldn't you!"

"Well, then. You're very keen and you're good. Sure,
you're good! But, excuse my frankness, will you stay keen?
That's my point, Lord Pastern. Suppose, to put it crudely, you
died on it."

"I'm fifty-five and as fit as a flea."

"I mean, suppose you kind of lost interest. Where,"
asked Mr. Bellairs passionately, "would I be then?"

"I've told you perfectly plainly . . ."

"Yes, but . . ."

"Do you call me a liar, you bloody fellow?" shouted Lord
Pastern, two brilliant patches of scarlet flaming over his
cheekbones. He clapped the dismembered parts of the parasol
on the piano and turned on his conductor who began to
stammer.

"Now, listen, Lord Pastern. I—I'm nervy to-night. I'm
all upset. Don't get me flustered, now."

Lord Pastern bared his teeth at him. "You're a fool," he
said. "I've been watchin' you." He appeared to cogitate and
come to a decision. "Ever read a magazine called *Harmony*?"
he demanded.

Breezy shied violently. "Why, yes. Why—I don't know what your idea is, Lord Pastern, bringing that up."

"I've half a mind," Lord Pastern said darkly, "to write to that paper. I know a chap on the staff." He brooded for a moment, whistling between his teeth and then barked abruptly : "If you don't speak to Skelton to-night, I'll talk to him myself."

"O.K., O.K. I'll have a wee chat with Syd. O.K."

Lord Pastern looked fixedly at him. "You'd better pull y'self together," he said. He took up his drumsticks and without more ado beat out a deafening crescendo, crashed his cymbals and snatching up his revolver pointed it at Bellairs and fired. The report echoed madly in the empty ballroom. The piano, the cymbals and the double-bass zoomed in protest and Bellairs, white to the lips, danced sideways.

"For chrissake!" he said violently and broke into a profuse sweat.

Lord Pastern laughed delightedly and laid his revolver on the piano. "Good, isn't it?" he said. "Let's just run through the programme. First, there's 'A New Way With Old Tunes.' 'Any Ice To-day?' 'I Got Everythin',' 'The Peanut Vendor,' and 'The Umbrella Man.' That's a damn' good idea of mine about the umbrellas."

Bellairs eyed the collection on the piano and nodded.

"The Black and White parasol's m'wife's. She doesn't know I've taken it. You might put it together and hide it under the others will you? We'll smuggle 'em out when she's not lookin'."

Bellairs fumbled with the umbrellas and Lord Pastern continued : "Then Skelton does his thing. I find it a bit dull, that number. And then the Sandra woman does her songs. And then," he said with an affectation of carelessness, "then you say somethin' to introduce me, don't you?"

"That's right."

"Yes. Somethin' to the effect that I happened to show you a thing I'd written, you know, and you were taken with it and that I've decided that my métier lies in this direction and all that. What?"

"Quite."

"I come out and we play it once through and then we swing

it, and then there's shootin', and then, by God, I go into my solo. Yes."

Lord Pastern took up his drumsticks, held them poised for a moment and appeared to go into a brief trance. "I'm still not so sure the other routine wasn't the best after all," he said.

"Listen! Listen!" Breezy began in a panic.

Lord Pastern said absently: "Now, you keep your hair on. I'm thinkin'." He appeared to think for some moments and then, ejaculating: "Sombrero!" darted out of the room.

Breezy Bellairs wiped his face with his handkerchief, sank on to the piano stool and held his head in his hands.

After a considerable interval the ballroom doors were opened and Rivera came in. Bellairs eyed him. "How's tricks, Carlos?" he asked dolefully.

"Not good." Rivera stroking his moustache with his forefinger, walked stiffly to the piano. "I have quarrelled with Félicité."

"You asked for it, didn't you? Your little line with Miss Wayne . . ."

"It is well to show women that they are not irreplaceable. They become anxious and, in a little while, they are docile."

"Has it worked out that way?"

"Not yet, perhaps. I am angry with her." He made a florid and violent gesture. "With them all! I have been treated like a dog. I Carlos de . . ."

"Listen," said Breezy, "I can't face a temperament from you, old boy. I'm nearly crazy with worry myself. I just can't face it. God, I wish I'd never taken the old fool on! God, I'm in a mess! Give me a cigarette, Carlos."

"I am sorry. I have none."

"I asked you to get me cigarettes," said Breezy and his voice rose shrilly.

"It was not convenient. You smoke too much."

"Go to hell."

"Everywhere," Rivera shouted, "I am treated with impertinence. Everywhere I am insulted." He advanced upon Bellairs, his head thrust forward. "I am sick of it all," he said. "I have humbled myself too much. I am a man of quick decisions. No longer shall I cheapen myself by playing in a common dance band . . ."

" Here, here, here!"

" I give you, now, my notice."

" You're under contract. Listen, old man . . ."

" I spit on your contract. No longer shall I be your little errand boy. ' Get me some cigarettes.' Bah!"

" Carlos!"

" I shall return to my own country."

" Listen, old boy . . . I—I'll raise your screw . . ." His voice faltered.

Rivera looked at him and smiled. " Indeed? By how much? It would be by perhaps five pounds?"

" Have a heart, Carlos."

" Or if, for instance, you would care to advance me five hundred . . ."

" You're crazy! Carlos, for Pete's sake . . . Honestly, I haven't got it."

" Then," said Rivera magnificently, " you may look for another to bring you your cigarettes. For me it is . . . finish."

Breezy wailed loudly : " And where will I be? What about me?"

Rivera smiled and moved away. With an elaborate display of nonchalance, he surveyed himself in a wall-glass, fingering his tie. " You will be in a position of great discomfort, my friend," he said. " You will be unable to replace me. I am quite irreplaceable." He examined his moustache closely in the glass and caught sight of Breezy's reflection. " Don't look like that," he said, " you are extremely ugly when you look like that. Quite revolting."

" It's a breach of contract. I can . . ." Breezy wetted his lips. " There's the law," he mumbled. " Suppose . . ."

Rivera turned and faced him.

" The law?" he said. " I am obliged to you. Of course, one can call upon the law, can one not? That is a wise step for a band leader to take, no doubt. I find the suggestion amusing. I shall enjoy repeating it to the ladies who smile at you so kindly, and ask you so anxiously for their favourite numbers. When I no longer play in your band their smiles will become infrequent and they will go elsewhere for their favourite numbers."

" You wouldn't do that, Carlos."

"Let me tell you, my good Breezy, that if the law is to be invoked, it is I who invoke it."

"Damn and blast you," Breezy shouted in a frenzy.

"What the devil's all the row about?" asked Lord Pastern. He had entered unobserved. A wide-brimmed sombrero decorated his head, its strap supporting his double-chin. "I thought I'd wear this," he said. It goes with the shootin' don't you think? Yipee!"

5

When Rivera left her, Félicité had sat on in the study, her hands clenched between her knees, trying to bury quickly and forever the memory of the scene they had just ended. She looked aimlessly about her, at the litter of tools in the open drawer at her elbow, at the typewriter, at familiar prints, ornaments and books. Her throat was dry. She was filled with nausea and an arid hatred. She wished ardently to rid herself of all memory of Rivera and in doing so to humiliate and injure him. She was still for so long that when at last she moved, her right leg was numb and her foot pricked and tingled. As she rose stiffly and cautiously, she heard someone cross the landing, pass the study and go into the drawing-room next door.

"I'll go up to Hendy," she thought. "I'll ask Hendy to tell them I'm not coming to the Metronome."

She went out on the landing. Somewhere on the second floor her stepfather's voice shouted: "My sombrero, you silly chap—somebody's taken it. That's all. Somebody's collared it." Spence came through the drawing-room door, carrying an envelope on a salver.

"It's for you, Miss," he said. "It was left on the hall table. I'm sure I'm very sorry it was not noticed before."

She took it. It was addressed in typescript. Across the top was printed a large "Urgent" with "by District Messenger" underneath. Félicité returned to the study and tore it open.

Three minutes later Miss Henderson's door was flung open and she, lifting her gaze from her book, saw Félicité, glowing before her.

"Hendy—Hendy, come and help me dress. Hendy, come and make me lovely. Something marvellous has happeend. Hendy, darling, it's going to be a wonderful party."

CHAPTER FIVE

A WREATH FOR RIVERA

I

AGAINST a deep blue background the arm of a giant Metronome kept up its inane and constant gesture. It was outlined in miniature lights, and to those patrons who had drunk enough, it left in its wake a formal ghost-pattern of itself in colour. It was mounted on part of the wall overhanging the band alcove. The ingenious young man responsible for the décor had so designed this alcove that the band platform itself appeared as a projection from the skeleton tower of the metronome. The tip of the arm swept to and fro above the bandsmen's heads in a maddening reiterative arc, pointing them out, insisting on their noise. This idea had been considered "great fun" by the ingenious young man but it had been found advisable to switch off the mechanism from time to time and when this was done the indicator pointed downwards. Either Breezy Bellairs or a favoured soloist was careful to place himself directly beneath the light-studded pointer at its tip.

On their semi-circular rostrum the seven performers of the dance band crouched; blowing, scraping and hitting at their instruments. This was the band that worked on extension nights, from dinner-time to eleven o'clock, at the Metronome: it was known as The Jivesters, and was not as highly paid or as securely established as Breezy Bellairs and His Boys. But of course it was a good band, carefully selected by Caesar Bonn, the manager and *maître de café*, who was also a big shareholder in the Metronome.

Caesar himself, glossy, immeasurably smart, in full control of his accurately graded cordiality, moved, with a light waggle

of his hips, from the vestibule into the restaurant and surveyed his guests. He bowed roguishly as his head-waiter, with
raised hand, preceded a party of five to their table. " Hallo,
Caesar. ' Evenin'," said Lord Pastern. " Brought my family,
you see."

Caesar flourished his hands. " It is a great evening for the
Metronome, my lady. A gala of galas."

" No doubt," said her ladyship.

She seated her guests. Herself, with erect bust, faced the
dance floor, her back to the wall. She raised her lorgnette.
Caesar and the head-waiter hovered. Lord Pastern ordered
hock.

" We are much too close, George," Lady Pastern shouted
above The Jivesters who had just broken out in a frenzy. And
indeed their table had been crammed in alongside the band
dais and hard by the tympanist. Félicité could have touched
his foot. " I had it put here specially," Lord Pastern yelled.
" I knew you'd want to watch me."

Carlisle, sitting between her uncle and Edward Manx, nervously clutched her evening bag and wondered if they were all
perhaps a little mad. What, for instance, had come over
Félicité? Why, whenever she looked at Edward, did she blush?
Why did she look so often and so queerly at him, like a
bewildered and—yes—a besotted schoolgirl? And why, on
the landing at Duke's Gate, after a certain atrocious scene
with Rivera (Carlisle closed her memory on the scene) had
Ned behaved with such ferocity? And why, after all, was she,
in the middle of a complicated and disagreeable crisis, so
happy?

Edward Manx, seated between Félicité and Carlisle, was also
bewildered. A great many things had happened to him that
evening. He had had a row with Rivera in the dining-room.
He had made an astonishing discovery. Later (and, unlike
Carlisle, he found this recollection entirely agreeable) he
had come on to the landing at the precise moment when
Rivera was making a determined effort to embrace Carlisle
and had hit Rivera very hard on the left ear. While they were
still, all three of them, staring at each other, Félicité had
appeared with a letter in her hands. She had taken one look
at Edward and going first white under her make-up and then

scarlet, had fled upstairs. From that moment she had behaved in the most singular manner imaginable. She kept catching his eye and as often as this happened she smiled and blushed. Once she gave a mad little laugh. Edward shook his head and asked Lady Pastern to dance. She consented. He rose, and placing his right hand behind her iron waist, walked her cautiously down the dance floor. It was formidable, dancing with Cousin Cecile.

"If anything," she said when they had reached the spot farthest away from the band, "could compensate for my humiliation in appearing at this lamentable affair, my dearest boy, it is the change your presence has wrought in Félicité."

"Really?" said Edward nervously.

"Indeed, yes. From her childhood, you have exerted a profound influence."

"Look here, Cousin Cecile——" Edward began in extreme discomfort, but at that moment the dance band which had for some time contented itself with the emission of syncopated grunts and pants, suddenly flared into an elaborate rumpus. Edward was silenced.

Lord Pastern put his head on one side and contemplated the band with an air of critical patronage. "They're not bad, you know," he said, "but they haven't got enough guts. Wait till you hear us, Lisle. What?"

"I know," Carlisle said encouragingly. At the moment his naïveté touched her. She was inclined to praise him as one would a child. Her eyes followed Edward who now guided Lady Pastern gingerly past the band-dais. Carlisle watched them go by and in so doing caught the eye of a man who sat at the next table. He was a monkish-looking person with a fastidious mouth and well-shaped head. A woman with short dark hair was with him. They had an air of comradeship. "They look nice," Carlisle thought. She felt suddenly uplifted and kindly disposed to all the world, and, on this impulse, turned to Félicité. She found that Félicité, also, was watching Edward and still with that doting and inexplicable attention.

"Fée," she said softly, "what's up? What's happened?" Félicité without changing the direction of her gaze, said: "Something too shattering, darling. I'm all *bouleversée* but I'm in Heaven."

Edward and Lady Pastern, after two gyrations, came to a halt by their table. She disengaged herself and resumed her seat. Edward slipped in between Carlisle and Félicité. Félicité leant towards him and drew the white carnation from his coat. "There's nobody else here with a white flower," she said softly.

"I'm very *vieux jeu* in my ways," Edward rejoined.

"Let's dance, shall we?"

"Yes, of course."

"Want to dance, C.?" asked Lord Pastern.

"No, thank you, George."

"Mind if Lisle and I trip a measure? It's a quarter to eleven, I'll have to go round and join the Boys in five minutes. Come on, Lisle."

You had, thought Carlisle, to keep your wits about you when you danced with Uncle George. He had a fine sense of rhythm and tremendous vigour. No stickler for the conventions, he improvised steps as the spirit moved him, merely tightening his grip upon her as an indication of further variations and eccentricities. She noticed other couples glancing at them with more animation than usually appears on the faces of British revellers.

"D'you jitter-bug?" he asked.

"No, darling."

"Pity. They think 'emselves too grand for it in this place. Sickenin' lot of snobs people are, by and large, Lisle. Did I tell you I'm seriously considerin' givin' up the title?"

He swung her round with some violence. At the far end of the room she caught a glimpse of her cousin and his partner. Ned's back was towards her. Félicité gazed into his eyes. Her hand moved farther across his shoulders. He stooped his head.

"Let's rejoin Aunt 'Cile, shall we?" said Carlisle in a flat voice.

2

Breezy Bellairs hung up his overcoat on the wall and sat down, without much show of enthusiasm, at a small table in the inner room behind the office. The tympanist, Syd Skelton, threw a pack of cards on the table and glanced at his watch. "Quarter-to," he said. "Time for a brief gamble."

He dealt two poker hands. Breezy and Skelton played show poker on most nights at about this time. They would leave the Boys in their room behind the band dais and wander across to the office. They would exchange a word with Caesar or David Hahn, the secretary, in the main office, and then repair to the inner room for their gamble. It was an agreeable prelude to the long night's business.

"Hear you've been dining in exalted places," said Skelton acidly.

Breezy smiled automatically and with trembling hands picked up his cards. They played in a scarcely broken silence. Once or twice Skelton invited conversation, but without success.

At last he said irritably: "What's the trouble? Why the great big silence?"

Breezy fiddled with his cards and said: "I'm licked all to hell, Syd."

"For the love of Mike! What's the tragedy this time?"

"Everything. I'll crack if it goes on. Honest, I'm shot to pieces."

"It's your own show. I've warned you. You look terrible."

"And how do I feel! Listen, Syd, it's this stunt, to-night. It's his lordship. It's been a big mistake."

"I could have told you that, too. I did tell you."

"I know. I know. But we're booked to capacity, Syd."

"It's cheap publicity. Nothing more nor less and you know it. Pandering to a silly dope, just because he's got a title."

"He's not all that bad. As an artist."

"He's terrible," said Skelton briefly.

"I know the number's crazy and full of corn but it'll get by. It's not that, old boy, it's him. Honest, Syd, I think he's crackers." Breezy threw his cards face down on the table. "He's got me that *nervy*," he said. "Listen, Syd, he's—he hasn't said anything to you, has he?"

"What about?"

"So he hasn't. All right. Fine. Don't take any notice if he does, old man."

Skelton leant back in his chair. "What the hell are you trying to tell me?" he demanded.

"Now, don't make me nervous," Breezy implored him. "You know how nervy I get. It's just a crazy notion he's got. I'll stall him off, you bet." He paused. Skelton said ominously, "It wouldn't be anything about wanting to repeat this fiasco, would it?"

"In a way it would, Syd. Mind, it's laughable."

"Now, you get this," Skelton said, and leant across the table. "I've stood down once, to-night, to oblige you, and I don't like it and I won't do it again. What's more it's given me a kind of unpleasant feeling that I'm doing myself no good, working with an outfit that goes in for cheap sensationalism. You know me. I'm quick tempered and I make quick decision. There's other bands."

"Now, Syd, Syd, Syd! Take it easy," Breezy gabbled. "Forget it, old boy. I wouldn't have mentioned anything only he talked about chatting to you, himself."

"By God," Skelton said, staring at him, "are you trying to tell me, by any chance, that this old so-and-so thinks he'd like my job? Have you got the flaming nerve to . . ."

"For chrisake, Syd! Listen, Syd, I said it was crazy. Listen, it's going to be all right. It's not my fault, Syd. Be fair, now, it's not my fault."

"Whose fault is it then?"

"Carlos," said Breezy, lowering his voice to a whisper. "Take it easy, now. He's next door, having a drink with Caesar. It's Carlos. He's put the idea into the old bee's head. He wants to keep in with him on account of the girl can't make up her mind and him wanting the old bee to encourage her. It's all Carlos, Syd. He told him he was wonderful."

Skelton said briefly what he thought of Rivera. Breezy looked nervously towards the door. "This settles it," Skelton said, and rose. "I'll talk to Carlos, by God." Breezy clawed at him. "No, Syd, not now. Not before the show. Keep your voice down, Syd, there's a pal. He's in there. You know how he is. He's thrown a temperament once to-night. Geeze," cried Breezy, springing to his feet, "I nearly forgot! He wants us to use the other routine in the new number, after all. Can you beat it? First it's this way and then it's what-have-you. He's got me so's I'm liable to give an imitation of a maestro doing two numbers at once. Gawd knows how his lordship'll take it. I got to tell the boys. I as near as damn it forgot, I'm that nervy. Listen, you haven't heard what's really got me so worried. You know what I am. It's that gun. It's such a hell of a thing, Syd, and his lordship's made those blanks himself and, by God, I'm nervous. He's dopey enough to mix the real things up with the phoney ones. They were all mucked up together in a bloody drawer, Syd, and there you are. And he really points the thing at Carlos, old boy, and fires it. Doesn't he now?"

" I wouldn't lose any sleep if he plugged him," said Skelton with violence.

"Don't talk that way, Syd," Breezy whispered irritably. " It's a hell of a situation. I hoped you'd help me, Syd."

" Why don't you have a look at the gun?"

" Me? I wouldn't know. He wouldn't let me near it. I tell you straight, I'm scared to go near him for fear I start him up bawling me out."

After a long pause, Skelton said : " Are you serious about this gun?"

" Do I look as if I was kidding?"

" It's eight minutes to eleven. We'd better go across. If I get a chance I'll ask him to show me the ammunition."

" Fine, Syd. That'd be swell," said Breezy, mopping his forehead. " It'd be marvellous. You're a pal, Syd. Come on. Let's go."

" Mind," Skelton said, " I'm not passing up the other business. I've just about had Mr. Carlos Rivera. He's going to find something out before he's much older. Come on."

They passed through the office. Rivera, who was sitting there with Caesar Bonn, disregarded them. Breezy looked timidly at him. " I'm just going to fix it up with the Boys, old man," he said. " You'll enter by the end door, won't you?"

" Why not?" Rivera said acidly. " It is my usual entrance. I perform as I rehearse. Naturally."

" That's right. Naturally. Excuse my fussiness. Let's go, Syd."

Caesar rose. " It is time? Then I must felicitate our new artist."

He preceded them across the vestibule where crowds of late arrivals still streamed in. Here they encountered Félicité, Carlisle and Edward. "We're going in to wish George luck," said Félicité. "Hallo, Syd. Nice of you to let him have his fling. Come on, chaps."

They all entered the bandroom which was immediately behind the dais end of the restaurant and led into the band alcove. Here they found the Boys assembled with their instruments. Breezy held up his hand and, sweating copiously, beamed at them. "Listen, Boys. Get this. We'll use the other routine, if it's all the same with the composer. Carlos doesn't feel happy about the fall. He's afraid he may hurt himself on account he's holding his instrument."

"Here!" said Lord Pastern.

"It's the way you wanted it, Lord Pastern, isn't it!" Breezy gabbled. "That's fine, isn't it? Better egzzit altogether."

"I faint and get carried out?"

"That's right. The other routine. I persuaded Carlos. Everybody happy? Swell."

The Boys began to warm up their instruments. The room was filled with slight anticipatory noises. The double-bass muttered and zoomed.

Skelton strolled over to Lord Pastern. "I had to come in and wish the new sensation all the best," he said, looking hard at him.

"Thank yer."

"A great night," Caesar Bonn murmured. "It will be long remembered."

"Would this be a loaded gun?" Skelton asked, and laughed unpleasantly.

The revolver lay, together with the sombrero, near the drums. Lord Pastern took it up. Skelton raised his hands above his head. "I confess everything," he said. "*Is* it loaded?"

"With blanks."

"By cripes," said Skelton with a loud laugh, "I hope they *are* blanks."

"George made them himself," said Félicité.

Skelton lowered his right hand and held it out towards Lord Pastern who put the revolver into it.

Breezy, at a distance, sighed heavily. Skelton broke the revolver, slipped a finger nail behind the rim of a cartridge and drew it out.

"Very nice work, Lord Pastern," he said. He spun the cylinder, drawing out and replacing one blank after the other. "Very nice work, indeed," he said.

Lord Pastern, obviously gratified, embarked on a history of the revolver, of his own prowess as a marksman, and of the circumstances under which his brother-in-law had presented it to him. He pointed out the initials scratched under the butt. Skelton made a show of squinting down the barrel, snapped the revolver shut, and returned the weapon to Lord Pastern. He turned away and glanced at Breezy. "O.K.," he said. "What are we waiting for?" He began to heighten the tension of his drums. "Good luck to the new act," he said, and the drums throbbed.

"Thanks, Syd," said Breezy.

His fingers were in his waistcoat pocket. He looked anxiously at Skelton. He felt in one pocket after another. Sweat hung in fine beads over his eyebrows.

"What's up, boy?" said Happy Hart.

"I can't find my tablet."

He began pulling his pocket linings out. "I'm all to pieces without it," he said. "God, I know I've got one somewhere!"

The door leading to the restaurant opened and The Jivesters came through with their instruments. They grinned at Breezy's Boys and looked sideways at Lord Pastern. The room was full of oiled heads, black figures and the strange shapes of saxophones, double-basses, piano accordions and drums.

"We'd better make ourselves scarce, Fée," Edward said. "Come on, Lisle. Good luck, Cousin George."

"Good luck."

"Good luck."

They went out. Breezy still searched his pockets. The others watched him nervously.

"You shouldn't let yourself get this way," said Skelton.

Lord Pastern pointed an accusing finger at Breezy: "Now perhaps you'll see the value of what I was tellin' you," he admonished. Breezy shot a venomous glance at him.

"For Heaven's sake, boy," said Happy Hart. "We're *on*."

"I've got to have it. I'm all shaky. I can't look. One of you . . ."

"What *is* all this!" Lord Pastern cried with extreme irritation. He darted at Breezy.

"It's only a tablet," Breezy said. "I always take one. For my nerves."

Lord Pastern said accusingly, "Tablet be damned!"

"For chrisake, I *got* to have it, blast you."

"Put your hands up."

Lord Pastern began with ruthless efficiency to search Breezy. He hit him all over and turned out his pockets, allowing various objects to fall about his feet. He opened his cigarette case and wallet and explored their contents. He patted and prodded. Breezy giggled. "I'm ticklish," he said foolishly. Finally Lord Pastern jerked a handkerchief out of Breezy's breast pocket. A small white object fell from it. Breezy swooped on it, clapped his hand to his mouth and swallowed. "Thanks a lot. All set, boys? Let's go."

They went out ahead of him. The lights on the walls had been switched off. Only the pink table-lamps glowed. A floodlight, hidden in the alcove ceiling, drove down its pool of amber on the gleaming dais; the restaurant was a swimming cave filled with dim faces, occasional jewels, many colours. The waiters flickered about inside it. Little drifts of cigarette smoke hung above the tables. From the restaurant the band dais glowed romantically in its alcove. The players and their instruments looked hard and glossy. Above them the arm of the giant Metronome pointed motionless at the floor. The Boys, smiling as if in great delight, seated themselves. The umbrellas, the sombrero and the tympani were carried in by waiters.

In the band room Lord Pastern, standing beside Breezy, fiddled with his revolver, whistled under his breath, and peered sideways through the door. Beyond the tympani, he could see the dimly glowing faces of his wife, his stepdaughter, his niece and his cousin. Félicité's face was inclined up to Ned Manx's. Lord Pastern suddenly gave a shrill cackle of laughter.

Breezy Bellairs glanced at him in dismay, passed his hand over his head, pulled down his waistcoat, assumed his ventriloquist's doll smile and made his entrance. The Boys played

him on with their signature tune. A patter of clapping filled
the restaurant like a mild shower. Breezy smiled, bowed,
turned and, using finicking sharp gestures that were expressly
his own, conducted.

Syd Skelton bounced slightly in his seat. His foot moved
against the floor, not tapping but flexing and relaxing in a
constant beat and against the syncopated, precise, illogic of the
noises he made. The four saxophonists swayed together, their
faces all looking alike, expressionless because of their com-
pressed lips and puffed cheeks. When they had passages of
rest they at once smiled. The band was playing tunes that
Carlisle knew; very old tunes. They were recognisable at
first and then a bedevilment known as the Breezy Bellairs
Manner sent them screeching and thudding into a jungle of
obscurity. " All swing bandsmen," Carlisle thought, " ought to
be negroes. There's something wrong about their not being
negroes."

Now three of them were singing. They had walked forward with long easy steps and stood with their heads close
together, rocking in unison. They made ineffable grimaces.
" Peea-nuts," they wailed. But they didn't let the song about
peanuts, which Carlisle rather liked, speak for itself. They
bedevilled and twisted and screwed it and then went beaming
back to their instruments. There was another old song : " The
Umbrella Man." She had a simple taste and its quiet mono-
tony pleased her. They did it once, quietly and monotonously.
The flood-light dimmed and a brilliant spotlight found the
pianist. He was playing by himself and singing. That was all
right, thought Carlisle. She could mildly enjoy it. But a
piercing shriek cut across the naïve tune. The spotlight
switched to a doorway at the far end of the restaurant. Carlos
Rivera stood there, his hands crawling over the keys of his
piano accordion. He advanced between the tables and
mounted the dais. Breezy turned to Rivera. He hardly moved
his baton. His flesh seemed to jump about on his submerged
skeleton. This was his Manner. Rivera, without accompaniment, squeezed trickles, blasts and moans from his piano accordion. He was a master of his medium. He looked straight
at Carlisle, widening his eyes and bowing himself towards
her. The sounds he made were frankly lewd, thought Edward

Manx. It was monstrous and ridiculous that people in evening clothes should sit idly in a restaurant, mildly diverted, while Rivera directed his lascivious virtuosity at Carlisle.

Now the spotlight was in the centre of the dais and only the tympanist played, while the double-bass slapped his instrument. The others moved one by one through the spotlight, holding opened umbrellas and turning them like wheels.

It was an old trick and they did it, Carlisle thought, sillily. They underdid it. Lady Pastern during a quieter passage said clearly : " Félicité, that is my Ascot parasol."

" Well, Maman, I believe it is."

" Your stepfather had no right whatsoever. It was a wedding present of great value. The handle is jewelled."

" Never mind."

" I object categorically and emphatically."

" He's having difficulty with it. Look, they've stopped turning their parasols."

The players were all back in their seats. The noise broadened and then faded out in an unanticipated wail and they were silent.

Breezy bowed and smiled and bowed. Rivera looked at Carlisle.

A young woman in a beautiful dress and with hair like blonde seaweed came out of a side door and stood in the spotlight, twisting a length of scarlet chiffon in her hands. She contemplated her audience as if she was a sort of willing sacrifice and began to moo very earnestly : " Yeoo knee-oo it was onlee summer lightning." Carlisle and Edward both detested her.

Next Syd Skelton and a saxophonist played a duet which was a *tour de force* of acrobatics, and earned a solid round of applause.

When it was over Skelton bowed and with an expression of huffy condescension walked into the band room.

In the ensuing pause, Breezy advanced to the edge of the dais. His smile was broad and winning. He said in a weak voice that he wanted to thank them all very very much for the wonderful reception his Boys had been given and that he had a little announcement to make. He felt sure that when he

told them what was in store for them, they would agree with
him that this was a very, very special occasion. (Lady Pastern
hissed under her breath.) Some weeks ago, Breezy said, he
had been privileged to hear a wonderful little performance
on the tympani by a distinguished—well, he wouldn't say
amateur. He had prevailed upon this remarkable performer
to join the Boys to-night and as an additional attraction
the number given would be this performer's own composition.
Breezy stepped back, pronounced Lord Pastern's names and
title with emphasis and looked expectantly towards the door
at the rear of the alcove.

Carlisle, like all other relations, distant or close, of Lord
Pastern, had often suffered acute embarrassment at his hands.
To-night she had fully expected to endure again that all too
familiar wave of discomfort. When, however, he came through
the door and stood before them with pink cheeks and
a nervous smile, she was suddenly filled with compassion. It
was silly, futile and immensely touching that he should make a
fool of himself in this particular way. Her heart went out to
him.

He walked to the tympani, made a polite little bow, and
with an anxious expression, took his seat. They saw him, with
a furtive air, lay his revolver on the dais close to Félicité's
chair and place his sombrero over it. Breezy pointed his baton
at him and said, " Ladies and Gentlemen : ' Hot Guy. Hot
Gunner.' " He gave the initial down-beat and they were off.

It sounded, really, much like all the other numbers they
had heard that night, Carlisle thought. Lord Pastern banged,
and rattled, and zinged much in the same way as Syd Skelton.
The words, when the three singers came out, were no sillier
than those of the other songs. The tune was rather catchy.
But, " Oh," she thought, " how vulnerable he is among his
tympani ! "

Edward thought : " There he sits, catsmeat to any satirist
who feels as I do about the social set-up. You might make
a cartoon of this or a parable. A cartoon, certainly. Cousin
George, thumping and banging away under Breezy's baton
and in the background a stream of displaced persons. The
metronome is Time . . . finger of scorn . . . making its inane

gesture to society. A bit too obvious, of course," he thought, dismissing it, " false, because of its partial truth." And he turned his head to watch Carlisle.

Félicité thought : " There goes George. He has fun, anyway." Her glance strayed to Lord Pastern's sombrero. She touched Edward's knee. He bent towards her and she said in his ear : " Shall I pinch George's gun? I could. Look ! " She reached out towards the edge of the dais and slipped her hand under the sombrero.

" Fée, don't ! " he ejaculated.

" Do you dare me? "

He shook his head violently.

" Poor George," said Félicité, " what *would* he do? " She withdrew her hand and leant back in her chair turning the white carnation in her fingers. " Shall I put it in my hair? " she wondered. " It would probably look silly and fall out but it might be a good idea. I wish he'd say something—just one thing—to show we understand each other. After this we can't just go on for ever, pretending."

Lady Pastern thought : " There is no end to one's capacity for humiliation. He discredits me and he discredits his class. It's the same story. There will be the same gossip, the same impertinences in the paper, the same mortification. Nevertheless," she thought, " I did well to come. I did well to suffer this torment to-night. My instinct was correct." She looked steadily at Rivera who was advancing into the centre of the stage. " I have disposed of you," she thought triumphantly.

Lord Pastern thought : " No mistakes so far. And one, bang and two bang and one crash bang zing. One two and three with his accord-een and wait for it. This is perfectly splendid. I *am* this noise. Look out. Here he comes. Hi-de oh hi. Yip. Here he comes. It's going to work. Hot gunner with his accord-een."

He crashed his cymbal, silenced it and leant back in his seat.

Rivera had advanced in the spotlight. The rest of the band was tacit. The great motionless arm of the Metronome stabbed its pointer down at his head. He seemed rapt : at once tormented and exalted. He swayed and jerked and ogled. Although he was not by any means ridiculous, he was the puppet of his own music. The performance was a protracted crescendo, and as it rocketed up to its climax he swayed backwards at a preposterous angle, his instrument raised, the pointer menacing it as it undulated across his chest. A screaming dissonance abruptly tore loose from the general din, the spotlight switched abruptly to the tympani. Lord Pastern, wearing his sombrero, had risen. Advancing to within five feet of Rivera he pointed his revolver at him and fired.

The accordion blared grotesquely down a scale. Rivera sagged at the knees and fell. The accordion crashed a final chord and was silent. At the same moment as the shot was fired the tenor saxophonist played a single shrill note and sat down. Lord Pastern, apparently bewildered, looked from the recumbent Rivera to the saxophonist, paused for a second and then fired three more blanks. The pianist, the trombone, and finally the double-bass each played a note in a descending scale and each imitated a collapse.

There was a further second's pause. Lord Pastern, looking very much taken aback, suddenly handed the revolver to Bellairs, who pointed it at him and pulled the trigger. The hammer clicked but there was no discharge. Bellairs aped disgust, shrugged his shoulders, looked at the revolver and broke it open. It discharged its shells in a little spurt. Breezy scratched his head, dropped the revolver in his pocket and made a crisp gesture with his baton-hand.

"Yipee," Lord Pastern shouted. The band launched itself into a welter of noise. He darted back and flung himself at his tympani. The spotlight concentrated upon him. The metronome, which had been motionless until now, suddenly swung its long arm. Tick-tack, tick-tack, it clacked. A kaleidoscopic welter of coloured lights winked and flickered along its surface and frame. Lord Pastern went madly to work on the drums.

"Hell!" Edward ejaculated, "at this pace he'll kill himself."

Breezy Bellairs had got a large artificial wreath. Dabbing his eyes with his handkerchief he knelt by Rivera, placed the wreath on his chest and felt his heart. He bent his head, groped frantically inside the wreath and then looked up with a startled expression in the direction of the tympani, where the spotlight revealed Lord Pastern in an ecstatic fury, wading into his drums. His solo lasted about eighty seconds. During this time four waiters had come in with a stretcher. Bellairs spoke to them excitedly. Rivera was carried off while the saxophones made a grotesque lugubrious sobbing and Lord Pastern, by hitting the big drum and immediately releasing the tension, produced a series of muffled groans.

The metronome clacked to a standstill, the restaurant lights went up and the audience applauded generously. Breezy, white to the lips and trembling, indicated Lord Pastern who joined him, glistening with sweat, and bowed. Breezy said something inaudible to him and to the pianist and went out followed by Lord Pastern. The pianist, the double-bass and the three saxophonists began to play a dance tune.

" Good old George ! " cried Félicité, " I think he was superb, Maman darling, don't you? Ned, wasn't he Heaven?"

Edward smiled at her : " He's astonishing," he said, and added : " Cousin C., do you mind if Lisle and I dance? You will, won't you, Lisle?"

Carlisle put her hand on his shoulder and they moved away. The head-waiter slid past them and stooped for a moment over a man at a table further down the room. The man rose, let his eyeglass fall and with a preoccupied look passed Carlisle and Edward on his way to the vestibule.

They danced in silence, companionably. At last Edward said : " What will he do next, do you suppose? Is there anything left?"

" I thought it dreadfully pathetic."

" Quintessence of foolery. Lisle, I haven't had a chance to talk to you about that business before we left. I suppose I oughtn't to have hit the fellow, considering the set-up with Fée, but really it was a bit too much. I'm sorry if I made an unnecessary scene, but I must say I enjoyed it." When she didn't answer, he said uncertainly : " Are you seriously annoyed? Lisle, you didn't by any chance . . ."

" No," she said. " No, I didn't. I may as well confess I was extremely gratified." His hand tightened on hers. " I stood," she added, " in the door of my cave and preened myself."

" Did you notice his ear? Not a cauliflower, but distinctly puffy, and a little trickle of blood. And then the unspeakable creature had the infernal nerve to goggle at you over his hurdy-gurdy."

"It's all just meant to be one in the eye for Fée."

"I'm not so sure."

"If it is, he's not having much success."

"How do you mean?" Edward asked sharply.

"Arst yourself, dearie."

"You mean Fée . . ." He stopped short and turned very red. "Lisle," he said "about Fée . . . Something very odd has occurred. It's astonishing and well, it's damned awkward. I can't explain but I'd like to think you understood."

Carlisle looked up at him. "You're not very lucid," she said.

"Lisle, my dear . . . Lisle, see here . . ."

They had danced round to the band dais. Carlisle said: "Our waiter's standing over there, watching us. I think he's trying to catch your eye."

"Be blowed to him."

"Yes, he is. Here he comes."

"It'll be some blasted paper on my tracks. Yes, do you want me?"

The waiter had touched Edward's arm. "Excuse me, sir. An urgent call."

"Thank you. Come with me, Lisle. Where's the telephone?"

The waiter hesitated, glanced at Carlisle, and said: "If Madame will excuse me, sir . . ." His voice sank to a murmur.

"Good lord!" Edward said and took Carlisle by the elbow. "There's been some sort of trouble. Cousin George wants me to go in. I'll drop you at the table, Lisle."

"What's he up to now, for pity's sake?"

"I'll come as soon as I can. Make my excuses."

As he went out Carlisle saw, with astonishment, that he was very pale.

In the vestibule, which was almost deserted, Edward stopped the waiter. "How bad is it?" he asked. "Is he badly hurt?"

The man raised his clasped hands in front of his mouth. "They say he's dead," said the waiter.

3

Breezy Bellairs sat at the little table in the inner office where he had played poker. When Edward came through the outer office he had heard scuffling and expostulations and he had opened the door upon a violent struggle. Breezy was being lugged to his feet from a squatting position on the floor and hustled across the room. He was slack now, and unresisting. His soft hands scratched at the surface of the table. He was dishevelled and breathless; tears ran out of his eyes, and his mouth was open. David Hahn, the secretary, stood behind him and patted his shoulder. "You shouldn't have done it, old boy," he said. "Honest. You shouldn't have done a thing like that."

"Keep off me," Breezy whispered. Caesar Bonn, wringing his hands in the conventional gesture of distress, looked past Edward into the main office. The man with the eyeglass sat at the desk there, speaking inaudibly into the telephone.

"How did it happen?" Edward asked.

"Look," Lord Pastern said.

Edward crossed the room. "You must not touch him," Caesar Bonn gabbled. "Excuse me, sir, forgive me. Doctor Allington has said at once, he must not be touched."

"I'm not going to touch him."

He bent down. Rivera lay on the floor. His long figure was stretched out tidily against the far wall. Near the feet lay the comic wreath of flowers and a little farther off his piano accordion. Rivera's eyes were open. His upper lip was retracted and the teeth showed. His coat was thrown open and the surface of his soft shirt was blotted with red. Near the top of the blot a short dark object stuck out ridiculously from his chest.

"What is it? It looks like a dart."

"Shut that door," Bonn whispered angrily. Hahn darted to the communicating door and shut it. Just before he did so, Edward heard the man at the telephone say: "In the office. I'll wait for you, of course."

"This will ruin us. We are ruined," said Bonn.

" They will think it an after-hours investigation, that is all,"
said Hahn. " If we keep our heads."

" It will all come out. I insist we are ruined."

In a voice that rose to a weak falsetto, Breezy said : " Listen,
boys. Listen, Caesar, I didn't know it was that bad. I couldn't
see. I wasn't sure. I can't be blamed for that, can I? I passed
the word something was wrong to the boys. It wouldn't have
made any difference if I'd acted different, would it, Dave?
They can't say anything to me, can they?"

" Take it easy, old man."

" You did right," Bonn said, vigorously. " If you had done
otherwise—what a scene! What a debacle! And to no purpose. No, no, it was correct."

" Yes, but look, Caesar, it's terrible, the way we carried on.
A cod funeral march and everything. I knew it was unlucky.
I said so when he told me he wanted the other routine. All
the boys said so!" He pointed a quivering finger at Lord
Pastern. " It was your big idea. You wished it on us. Look
where it's landed us. What a notion, a cod funeral march!"

His mouth sagged and he began to laugh, fetching his
breath in gasps and beating on the table.

" Shut up," said Lord Pastern, irritably. " You're a fool."
The door opened and the man with the eyeglass came in.
" What's all this noise?" he asked. He stood over Breezy. " If
you can't pull yourself together, Mr. Bellairs," he said, " we
shall have to take drastic steps to make you." He glanced at
Bonn. " He'd better have brandy. Can you beat up some
aspirin?"

Hahn went out. Breezy sobbed and whispered.

" The police," said the man, " will be here in a moment. I
shall, of course, be required to make a statement." He looked
hard at Edward. " Who is this?"

" I sent for him," said Lord Pastern. " He's with my party.
My cousin, Ned Manx—Dr. Allington."

" I see."

" I thought I'd like to have Ned," Lord Pastern added wist-
fully.

Dr. Allington turned back to Breezy and picked up his
wrist. He looked sharply at him. " You're in a bit of a mess,
my friend," he remarked.

" It's not my fault. Don't look at me like that. I can't be held responsible, my God."

" I don't suggest anything of the sort. Is brandy any good to you? Ah, here it is."

Hahn brought it in. " Here's the aspirin," he said. " How many?" He shook out two tablets. Breezy snatched the bottle and spilt half a dozen on the table. Dr. Allington intervened and gave him three. He gulped them down with the brandy, wiped his face over with his handkerchief, yawned broadly and shivered.

Voices sounded in the outer office. Bonn and Hahn moved towards Breezy. Lord Pastern planted his feet apart and lightly flexed his arms. This posture was familiar to Edward. It usually meant trouble. Dr. Allington put his glass in his eye. Breezy made a faint whimpering.

Somebody tapped on the door. It opened and a thickset man with grizzled hair came in. He wore a dark overcoat, neat, hard and unsmart, and carried a bowler hat. His eyes were bright and he looked longer and more fixedly than is the common habit at those he newly encountered. His sharp impersonal glance dwelt in turn upon the men in the room and upon the body of Rivera, from which they had stepped aside. Dr. Allington moved out from the group.

" Trouble here?" said the newcomer. " Are you Dr. Allington, sir? My chaps are outside. Inspector Fox."

He walked over to the body. The doctor followed him and they stood together, looking down at it. Fox gave a slight grunt and turned back to the others. " And these gentlemen?" he said. Caesar Bonn made a dart at him and began to talk very rapidly.

" If I could just have the names," said Fox and took out his note-book. He wrote down their names, his glance resting longer on Breezy than upon the others. Breezy lay back in his chair and gaped at Fox. His dinner jacket with its steel buttons sagged on one side. The pocket was dragged down.

" Excuse me, sir," Fox said, " are you feeling unwell?" He stooped over Breezy.

" I'm shot all to hell," Breezy whimpered.

" Well, now, if you'll just allow me . . ." He made a neat

unobtrusive movement and stood up with the revolver in his large gloved hand.

Breezy gaped at it and then pointed a quivering hand at Lord Pastern.

" That's not my gun," he chattered. " Don't you think it is. It's his. It's his lordship's. He fired it at poor old Carlos and poor old Carlos fell down like he wasn't meant to. That's right, isn't it, chaps? Isn't it, Caesar? God, won't somebody speak up for me and tell the Inspector? His lordship handed me that gun."

" Don't you fret," Fox said comfortably. " We'll have a chat about it presently." He dropped the revolver into his pocket. His sharp glance travelled again over the group of men. " Well, thank you, gentlemen," he said, and opened the door. " We'll need to trouble you a little further, Doctor, but I'll ask the others to wait in here, if you please."

They filed into the main office. Four men already waited there. Fox nodded and three of them joined him in the inner room. They carried black cases and a tripod.

" This is Dr. Curtis, Dr. Allington," said Fox. He unbuttoned his overcoat and laid his bowler on the table. " Will you two gentlemen take a look? We'll get some shots when you're ready, Thompson."

One of the men set up a tripod and camera. The doctors behaved like simultaneous comedians. They hitched up their trousers, knelt on their right knees and rested their forearms on their left thighs.

" I was supping here," said Dr. Allington. " He was dead when I got to him, which must have been about three to five minutes after this "—he jabbed a forefinger at the blotch on Rivera's shirt—" had happened. When I got here they had him where he is now. I made a superficial examination and rang the Yard."

" Nobody tried to withdraw the weapon?" said Dr. Curtis, and added : " Unusual, that."

" It seems that one of them, Lord Pastern it was, said it shouldn't be touched. Some vague idea of an effusion of blood following the withdrawal. They realised almost at once that he was dead. At a guess, would you say there'd been considerable penetration of the right ventricle? I haven't touched a thing, by the way. Can't make out what it is."

"We'll take a look in a minute," said Dr. Curtis. "All right, Fox."

"All right, Thompson," said Fox.

They moved away. Their shadows momentarily blotted the wall as Thompson's lamp flashed. Whistling under his breath he manœuvered his camera, flashed and clicked.

"O.K., Mr. Fox," he said at last.

"Dabs," said Fox. "Do what you can about the weapon, Bailey."

The fingerprint expert, a thin dark man, squatted by the body.

Fox said, "I'd like to get a statement about the actual event. You can help us there, Doctor Allington? What exactly was the set-up? I understand a gun was used against the deceased in the course of the entertainment."

He had folded his overcoat neatly over the back of his chair. He now sat down, his knees apart, his spectacles adjusted, his note-book flattened out on the table. "If I may trouble you, Doctor," he said. "In your own words, as we say."

Dr. Allington fitted his glass in position and looked apologetic. "I'm afraid I'm not going to be a success," he said. "To be quite frank, Inspector, I was more interested in my guest than in the entertainment. And, by the way, I'd like to make my apologies to her as soon as possible. She must be wondering where the devil I've got to."

"If you care to write a note, sir, we'll give it to one of the waiters."

"What? Oh, all right," said Dr. Allington fretfully. A note was taken out by Thompson. Through the opened door they caught a glimpse of a dejected group in the main office. Lord Pastern's voice, caught mid-way in a sentence, said shrilly : ". . . entirely wrong way about it. Making a mess, as usual . . ." and was shut off by the door.

"Yes, Doctor?" said Fox placidly.

"Oh, God, they were doing some kind of idiotic turn. We were talking and I didn't pay much attention except to say it was a pretty poor show, old Pastern making an ass of himself. This chap, here," he looked distastefully at the body, "came out from the far end of the restaurant and made a hell of a noise on his concertina or whatever it is, and there was a terrific bang. I looked up and saw old Pastern with a gun of some sort in his hand. This chap did a fall, the conductor dropped a wreath on him and then he was carried out. About three minutes later they sent for me."

" I'll just get that down, if you please," said Fox. With raised eyebrows and breathing through his mouth, he wrote at a steady pace. "Yes," he said comfortably, "and how far, Doctor, would you say his lordship was from the deceased when he fired?"

" Quite close. I don't know. Between five and seven feet. I don't know."

" Did you notice the deceased's behaviour, sir, immediately after the shot was fired? I mean, did it strike you there was anything wrong?"

Dr. Allington looked impatiently at the door. "Strike me!" he repeated. "I wasn't struck by anything in particular. I looked up when the gun went off. I think it occurred to me that he did a very clever fall. He was a pretty ghastly looking job of work, all hair-oil and teeth."

"Would you say . . ." Fox began and was interrupted.

" I really wouldn't say anything, Inspector. I've given you my opinion from the time I examined the poor devil. To go any further would be unprofessional and stupid. I simply wasn't watching and therefore don't remember. You'd better find somebody who did watch and does remember."

Fox had raised his head and now looked beyond Dr. Allington to the door. His hand had poised motionless over his note-book. His jaw had dropped. Dr. Allington slewed round and was confronted with a very tall dark man in evening dress.

" I was watching," said this person, "and I think I remember. Shall I try, Inspector?"

4

" Good lor'!" Fox said heavily and rose. "Well, thank you, Doctor Allington," he said. "I'll have a typed statement sent round to you to-morrow. Would you be good enough to read it through and sign it if it's in order? We'll want you for the inquest, if you please."

" All right. Thanks," said Dr. Allington, making for the door which the newcomer opened. " Thanks," he repeated. " Hope you make a better fist of it than I did, what?"

" Most unlikely, I'm afraid," the other rejoined pleasantly, and closed the door after him. " You're in for a party, Fox," he said, and walked over to the body. Bailey, the fingerprint expert, said : " Good-evening, sir," and moved away, grinning.

" *If* I may ask, sir," said Fox, " how do you come to be in on it?"

" May I not take mine ease in mine restaurant with mine wife? Shall there be no more cakes and ale? None for you, at all events, you poor chap," he said, bending over Rivera. " You haven't got the thing out yet, I see, Fox."

" It's been dabbed and photographed. It can come out."

Fox knelt down. His hand wrapped in his handkerchief closed round the object that protruded from Rivera's chest. It turned with difficulty. " Tight," he said.

" Let me look, may I?"

Fox drew back. The other knelt beside him. " But what is it?" he said. " Not an orthodox dart. There's a thread at the top. It's been unscrewed from something. Black. Silver mounted. Ebony, I fancy. Or a dark bronze. What the devil is it? Try again, Fox."

Fox tried again. He twisted. Under the wet silk the wound opened slightly. He pulled steadily. With a jerk and a slight but horrible sound, the weapon was released. Fox laid it on the floor and opened out the handkerchief. Bailey clicked his tongue.

Fox said : " Will you look at that. Good lord, what a set-up! It's a bit of an umbrella shaft, turned into a dart or bolt."

" A black and white parasol," said his companion. Fox looked up quickly but said nothing. " Yes. There's the spring clip, you see. That's why it wouldn't come out readily. An elaborate affair, almost a museum piece. The clip's got tiny jewels in it. And look, Fox."

He pointed a long finger. Protruding from one end was a steel, about two inches long, wide at the base and tapering sharply to a point. " It looks like some sort of awl or stiletto. Probably it was originally sunk in a short handle. It's been driven into one end of this bit of parasol shaft and sealed up somehow. Plastic wood, I fancy. The end of the piece of shaft you see was hollow. Probably the longer section of the parasol screwed into it and a knob or handle of some kind, in turn, was screwed on the opposite end." He took out his note-book and made a rapid sketch which he showed to Fox. " Like this," he said. " It'll be a freak of a parasol. French, I should think. I remember seeing them in the enclosure at Longchamps when I was a boy. The shaft's so thin that they have to put a separate section in to take the clip and groove. This is the section. But why in the name of high fantasy use a bit of parasol shaft as a sort of dagger?"

" We'll have another shot of this, Thompson." Fox rose stiffly and after a long pause said : " Where were you sitting, Mr. Alleyn?"

" Next door to the Pastern party. A few yards off the dais."

" What a bit of luck," said Fox simply.

" Don't be too sure," rejoined Chief-Inspector Alleyn. He sat on the table and lit a cigarette. " This is no doubt a delicate situation, Br'er Fox. I mustn't butt in on your job, you know."

Fox made a short derisive noise. " You'll take over, sir, of course."

" I can at least make my report. I'd better warn you at the outset, I was watching that extraordinary chap Pastern most of the time. What a queer cup of tea it is, to be sure."

" I suppose," said Fox stolidly, " you'll be telling me, sir, that you were his fag at Eton."

Alleyn grinned at this jibe. " If I had been I should probably have spent the rest of my life in a lunatic asylum. No, I was going to say that I watched him to the exclusion of the others. I noticed, for instance, that he really pointed his gun—a revolver of some sort—at this man and that he stood not more than seven feet off him when he did it."

" This is more like it," Fox said and reopened his book. " You don't mind, Mr. Alleyn?" he added primly.

Alleyn said, " You're gloating over this, aren't you? Very well. They did a damn' silly turn, revolving umbrellas and parasols like a bunch of superannuated chorus girls and I noticed that one parasol, a very pansy Frenchified affair of black and white lace, seemed to giving trouble. The chap had to shove his hand up to hold it."

"Is that so?" Fox looked at Thompson. "You might get hold of the umbrella." Thompson went out. Bailey moved forward with an insufflator and bent over the weapon.

"I'd better describe the final turn, I suppose," said Alleyn, and did so. His voice moved on quietly and slowly. Thompson returned with the black and white parasol. "This is it, sure enough, sir," he said. "A section of the shaft's gone. Look here! No clip anywhere to keep it shut." He laid it beside the dart.

"Good enough," Fox said. "Get your shots, will you."

Thompson, having taken three further photographs of the weapon, folded it in the handkerchief and put it in Fox's case. "I'll fix it up with proper protection when we're finished, Mr. Fox," he said. On a nod from Fox, he and Bailey went out with their gear.

". . . when the shot was fired," Alleyn was saying, "he had swung round, facing Lord Pastern, with his back half-turned to the audience and fully turned to the conductor. He was inclined backwards at a grotesque angle, with the instrument raised. He was directly under the point of the metronome which was motionless. After the report he swung round still further and straightened up a bit. The piano accordion, if that's what it is, ran down the scale and let out an infernal bleat. His knees doubled and he went down on them, sat on his heels and then rolled over, fetching up on his back with his instrument between himself and the audience. At the same time one of the bandsmen aped being hit. I couldn't see Rivera clearly because the spotlight had switched to old Pastern who, after a moment's hesitation, loosed off the other rounds. Three more of the band chaps did comic staggers as if he'd hit them. Something seemed a bit out of joint here. They all looked as if they weren't sure what came next. However, Pastern gave his gun to Bellairs, who pointed it at him and pulled the trigger. The last round had been used, so there was only a click. Bellairs registered disgust, broke the revolver, pocketed it and gestured as much as to say: 'I've had it. Carry on,' and Lord

Pastern then went to market in a big way and generally raised hell. He looked extraordinary. Glazed eyes, sweating, half-smiling and jerking about over his drums. An unnerving exhibition from a middle-aged peer but of course he's as mad as a March hare. Troy and I were snobbishly horrified. It was then that the metronome went into action in a blaze of winking lights. It'd been pointing straight down at Rivera before. A waiter chucked a wreath to the conductor who knelt down by this chap Rivera and dumped it on his chest. He felt his heart and then looked closely at Rivera and bent over his body, groping inside the wreath. He turned in a startled sort of way to old Pastern. He said something to the blokes with the stretcher. The wreath hid the face and the accordion was half across the stomach. Bellairs spoke to the pianist and then to Lord Pastern who went out with him when they finished their infernal din. I smelt trouble, saw a waiter speak to Allington and stop a chap in Lady Pastern's party. I had a long argument with myself, lost it and came out here. That's all. Have you looked at the revolver?"

"I've taken it off Bellairs. It's in my pocket." Fox put his glove on, produced the revolver and laid it on the table. "No known make," he said.

"Probably been used for target-shooting," Alleyn muttered. He laid the dart beside it. "It'd fit, Fox. Look. Had you noticed?"

"We haven't got very far."

"Of course not."

"I don't know quite what line to take about all the folk in there." Fox jerked his head in the direction of the restaurant.

"Better get names and addresses. The waiters can do it. They'll know a lot of them already. They can say it's a new police procedure on extension nights. It's our good fortune, Br'er Fox, that the public will believe any foolishness if they are told we are the authors of it. The Pastern party had better be held."

"I'll fix it," Fox said. He went out, revealing for a moment the assembly in the outer office. " . . . hang about kickin' my heels all night . . ." Lord Pastern's voice protested and was shut off abruptly.

Alleyn knelt by the body and began to search it. The coat

was turned and the breast pocket had been pulled out. Four letters and a gold cigarette case had slipped down between the body and the coat. The case was half-filled and bore an inscription : "From Félicité." He searched the other pockets. A jade holder. Two handkerchiefs. A wallet with three pound notes. He laid these objects out in a row and turned to the piano accordion. It was a large, heavily ornamental affair. He remembered how it had glittered as Rivera swung it across his chest in the last cacophony before he fell. As Alleyn lifted it, it raised a metallic wail. He put it down hastily on the table and returned to his contemplation of the body. Fox came back. "That's all fixed up," he said.

"Good."

Alleyn stood up. "He was a startling fellow to look at," he said. "One felt one had seen him in innumerable Hollywood band-features, ogling the camera man against an exotic background. We might cover him up, don't you think? The management can produce a clean tablecloth."

"The mortuary van will be outside now, Mr. Alleyn," said Fox. He glanced down at the little collection on the floor. "Much obliged, sir," he said. "Anything useful?"

"The letters are written in Spanish. Postmark. He'll have to be dusted, of course."

"I rang the Yard, Mr. Alleyn. The A.S.M.'s compliments and he'll be glad if you'll take over."

"That's a thumping great lie," said Alleyn mildly. "He's in Godalming."

"He's come back, sir, and happened to be in the office. Quite a coincidence."

"You go to hell, Fox. Damn it, I'm out with my wife."

"I sent a message in to Mrs. Alleyn. The waiter brought back a note."

Alleyn opened the folded paper and disclosed a lively drawing of a lady asleep in bed. Above her, encircled by a balloon, Alleyn and Fox crawled on all fours inspecting, through a huge lens, a nest from which protruded the head of a foal, broadly winking. "A very stupid woman, I'm afraid, poor thing," Alleyn muttered, grinning, and showed it to Fox. "Come on," he said. "We'll take another look at the revolver and then get down to statements."

CHAPTER SIX

DOPE

I

ABOVE THE door leading from the foyer of the Metronome to
the office was a clock with chromium hands and figures. As
the night wore on, the attention of those persons who were
congregated there became increasingly drawn to this clock, so
that when at one in the morning the long hand jumped to
the hour, everyone observed it. A faint sigh, and a dreary
restlessness stirred them momentarily.

The members of the band, who were assembled at the end
of the foyer, sat in dejected attitudes on gilded chairs that
had been brought in from the restaurant. Syd Skelton's hands
dangled between his knees, tapping each other flaccidly.
Happy Hart was stretched back with his legs extended. The
light found out patches on his trousers, worn shiny by the
pressure of his thighs against the under-surface of his piano.
The four saxophonists sat with their heads together, but they
had not spoken for some time and inertia, not interest, held
them in these postures of intimacy. The double-bass, a thin
man, rested his elbows on his knees and his head on his hands.
Breezy Bellairs, in the centre of his Boys, fidgeted, yawned,
wiped his hands over his face, and bit feverishly at his nails.
Near the band stood four waiters and the spotlight operator,
whose interrogation had just ended, quite fruitlessly.

At the opposite end of the foyer, in a muster of easier
chairs, sat Lady Pastern and her guests. Alone of the whole
assembly, she held an upright posture. The muscles of her
face sagged a little; its lines were clogged with powder and
there were greyish marks under her eyes, but her wrists and
ankles were crossed composedly, her hair was rigidly in order.
On her right and left the two girls drooped in their chairs.
Félicité, chain-smoking, gave her attention fitfully to the
matter in hand and often took a glass from her bag and looked

resentfully at herself, repainting her lips with irritable gestures.

Carlisle, absorbed as usual with detail, watched the mannerisms of her companions through an increasing haze of sleepiness and was only half-aware of what they said. Ned Manx listened sharply as if he tried to memorize all that he heard. Lord Pastern was never still. He would throw himself into a chair with an air of abandon and in a moment spring from it and walk aimlessly about the room. He looked with distaste at the speaker of the moment. He grimaced and interjected. At one side, removed from the two main groups, stood Caesar Bonn and the secretary, David Hahn. These two were watchful and pallid. Out of sight, in the main office, Dr. Curtis, having seen to the removal of Rivera's body, jotted down notes for his report.

In the centre of the foyer, Inspector Fox sat at a small table with his note-book open before him and his spectacles on his nose. His feet rested side by side on the carpet and his large knees were pressed together. He contemplated his notes with raised eyebrows.

Behind Fox stood Chief Detective-Inspector Alleyn, and to him the attention of the company, in some cases fitfully, in others constantly, was drawn. He had been speaking for about a minute. Carlisle, though she tried to listen to the sense of his words, caught herself thinking how deep his voice was and how free from mannerisms his habit of speech. " A pleasant chap," she thought, and knew by the small affirmative noise Ned Manx made when Alleyn paused that he agreed with her.

" . . . so you see," Alleyn was saying now, " that a certain amount of ground must be covered here and that we must ask you to stay until it *has* been covered. That can't be helped."

" Damned if I see . . ." Lord Pastern began and fetched up short. " What's your name?" he said. Alleyn told him. " I thought so," said Lord Pastern with an air of having found him out in something. " Point is : are you suggestin' I dug a dart in the chap or aren't you? Come on."

" It doesn't, at the moment, seem to be a question, as far as you are concerned, sir, of digging."

" Well, shootin' then. Don't split straws."

"One may as well," Alleyn said mildly, "be accurate."

He turned aside to Fox's case which lay on a table. From it he took an open box containing the weapon that had killed Rivera. He held the box up, tilting it towards them.

"Will you look at this?" They looked at it. "Do any of you recognise it? Lady Pastern?"

She had made an inarticulate sound, but now she said indifferently: "It looks like part of a parasol handle."

"A black and white parasol?" Alleyn suggested, and one of the saxophonists looked up quickly.

"Possibly," said Lady Pastern. "I don't know."

"Don't be an ass, C.," said her husband. "Obviously it's off that French thing of yours. We borrowed it."

"You had no right whatever, George . . ."

Alleyn interrupted. "We've found that one of the parasols used in the 'Umbrella Man" number is minus a few inches of its shaft." He glanced at the second saxophonist. "I think you had some difficulty in managing it?"

"That's right," the second saxophonist said. "You couldn't shut it properly, I noticed. There wasn't a clip or anything."

"This is it: five inches of the shaft containing the clip. Notice that spring catch. It is jewelled. Originally, of course, it kept the parasol closed. The actual handle or knob on its own piece of shaft has been engaged with the main shaft of the parasol. Can you describe it?" He looked at Lady Pastern, who said nothing. Lord Pastern said: "Of course you can, C. A damn-fool thing like a bird with emeralds for eyes. French."

"You're sure of that, sir?"

"Of course, I'm sure. Damn it, I took the thing to bits when I was in the ballroom."

Fox raised his head and stared at Lord Pastern with a sort of incredulous satisfaction. Edward Manx swore under his breath, the women were rigidly horrified.

"I see," Alleyn said. "When was this?"

"After dinner. Breezy was with me. Weren't you, Breezy?" Breezy shied violently and then nodded.

"Where did you leave the bits, sir?"

"On the piano. Last I saw of 'em."

"Why," Alleyn asked, "did you dismemember the parasol?"

"For fun."

"*Mon Dieu, mon Dieu,*" Lady Pastern moaned.

"I knew it'd unscrew and I unscrewed it."

"Thank you," Alleyn said. "For the benefit of those of you who haven't examined the parasol closely, I'd better describe it a little more fully. Both ends of this piece of shaft are threaded, one on the outer surface to engage with the top section, the other on the inner surface to receive the main shaft of the parasol. It has been removed and the outer sections screwed together. Now look again at this weapon made from the section that has been removed. You will see that a steel tool has been introduced into this end and sunk in plastic wood. Do any of you recognise this tool? I'll hold it a little closer. It's encrusted with blood and a little difficult to see."

He saw Carlisle's fingers move on the arms of her chair. He saw Breezy rub the back of his hand across his mouth and Lord Pastern blow out his cheeks. "Rather unusual," he said, "isn't it? Wide at the base and tapering. Keen pointed. It might be an embroidery stiletto. I don't know. Do you recognise it, Lady Pastern?"

"No."

"Anybody?" Lord Pastern opened his mouth and shut it again. "Well," Alleyn murmured after a pause. He replaced the box containing the weapon and took up Lord Pastern's revolver. He turned it over in his hands.

"If that's the way you chaps go to work," said Lord Pastern, "I don't think much of it. That thing may be smothered with fingerprints, for all you know, and you go pawin' it about."

"It's been printed," Alleyn said without emphasis. He produced a pocket-lens and squinted through it down the barrel. "You seem to have given it some rough usage," he said.

"No, I haven't," Lord Pastern countered instantly. "Perfect condition. Always has been."

"When did you last look down the barrel, sir?"

"Before we came here. In my study, and again in the ballroom. Why?"

"George," said Lady Pastern, "I suggest for the last time that you send for your solicitor and refuse to answer any questions until he is here."

"Yes, Cousin George," Edward murmured. "I honestly think . . ."

"My solicitor," Lord Pastern rejoined, "is a snufflin' old ass. I'm perfectly well able to look after myself, C. What's all this about my gun?"

"The barrel," Alleyn said, "is, of course, fouled. That's from the blank rounds. But under the stain left by the discharges there are some curious marks. Irregular scratches, they seem to be. We'll have it photographed but I wonder if in the meantime you can offer an explanation?"

"Here," Lord Pastern ejaculated. "Let me see."

Alleyn gave him the revolver and lens. Grimacing hideously he pointed the barrel to the light and squinted down it. He made angry noises and little puffing sounds through his lips. He examined the butt through the lens and muttered indistinguishable anathemas. Most unexpectedly, he giggled. Finally he dumped it on the table and blew loudly. "Hankypanky," he said briefly and returned to his chair.

"I beg your pardon?"

"When I examined the gun in my study," Lord Pastern said forcibly, "it was as clean as a whistle. As clean, I repeat, as a whistle. I fired one blank from it in my own house and looked down the barrel afterwards. It was a bit fouled and that was all. All right. There y'are!"

Carlisle, Félicité, Manx and Lady Pastern stirred uneasily. "Uncle George," Carlisle said. "Please."

Lord Pastern glared at her. "Therefore," he said, "I repeat, hanky-panky. The barrel was unmarked when I brought the thing here. I ought to know. It was unmarked when I took it into the restaurant."

Lady Pastern looked steadily at her husband. "You *fool*, George," she said.

"George."

"Cousin George."

"Uncle George . . ."

The shocked voices overlapped and faded out.

Alleyn began again. "Obviously you realise the significance of all this. When I tell you that the weapon—it is, in effect, a dart, or bolt, isn't it?—is half an inch shorter than the barrel of the revolver and somewhat less in diameter . . ."

"All right, all right," Lord Pastern interjected.

"I think," said Alleyn, "I should point out . . ."

"You needn't point anything out. And you," Lord Pastern added, turning on his relatives "can all shut up. I know what you're gettin' at. The barrel was unscratched. By God, I ought to know. And what's more, I noticed when Breezy and I were in the ballroom, that this bit of shaft would fit in the barrel. I pointed it out to him."

"Here, here, here!" Breezy expostulated. "I don't like the way this is going. Look here——"

"Did anyone else examine the revolver?" Alleyn interposed adroitly.

Lord Pastern pointed at Skelton. "He did," he said. "Ask him."

Skelton moved forward, wetting his lips.

"Did you look down the barrel?" Alleyn asked.

"Glanced," said Skelton reluctantly.

"Did you notice anything unusual?"

"No."

"Was the barrel quite unscarred?"

There was a long silence. "Yes," said Skelton at last.

"There y' are," said Lord Pastern.

"It would be," Skelton added brutally, "seeing his lordship hadn't put his funny weapon in it yet."

Lord Pastern uttered a short, rude and incredulous word.

"Thanks," said Skelton and turned to Alleyn.

Edward Manx said: "May I butt in, Alleyn?"

"Of course."

"It's obvious that you think this thing was fired from the revolver. It's obvious, in my opinion, that you are right. How else could he have been killed? But isn't it equally obvious that the person who used the revolver could have known nothing about it? If he had wanted to shoot Rivera he could have used a bullet. If, for some extraordinary reason, he preferred a sort of rifle grenade or dart or what-not, he would surely have used something less fantastic than the affair you have just shown us. The only object in using the piece of parasol shaft, if it has in fact been so used, would have been this: the spring catch, which is jewelled, by the way, would keep the weapon fixed in the barrel and it wouldn't fall out if

the revolver was pointed downwards and the person who fired
the revolver would therefore be unaware of the weapon in
the barrel. You wouldn't," Edward said with great energy,
" fix up an elaborate sort of thing like this unless there was a
reason for it and there would be no reason if you yourself
had full control of the revolver and could load it at the last
moment. Only an abnormally eccentric . . ." He stopped short,
floundered for a moment, and then said : " That's the point
I wanted to make."

" It's well taken," Alleyn said. " Thank you."

" Hi!" said Lord Pastern.

Alleyn turned to him.

" Look here," he said. " You think these scratches were
made by the jewels on that spring thing. Skelton says they
weren't there when he looked at the gun. If anyone was fool
enough to try and shoot a feller with a thing like this, he'd fire
it off first of all to see how it worked. In private. Follow
me?"

" I think so, sir."

" All right, then," said Lord Pastern with a shrill cackle,
" why waste time jabberin' about scratches?"

He flung himself into his chair.

" Did any of you who were there," Alleyn said, " take
particular notice when Mr. Skelton examined the revolver?"

Nobody spoke. Skelton's face was very white. " Breezy
watched," he said, and added quickly : " I was close to Lord
Pastern. I couldn't have . . . I mean . . ."

Alleyn said : " Why did you examine it, Mr. Skelton?"

Skelton wetted his lips. His eyes shifted their gaze from
Lord Pastern to Breezy Bellairs. " I—was sort of interested.
Lord Pastern had fixed up the blanks himself and I thought
I'd like to take a look. I'd gone in to wish him luck. I
mean . . ."

" *Why don't you tell him!*"

Breezy was on his feet. He had been yawning and fidgeting
in his chair. His face was stained with tears. He had seemed
to pay little attention to what was said but rather to be in the
grip of some intolerable restlessness. His interruption shocked
them all by its unexpectedness. He came forward with a
shambling movement and grinned at Alleyn.

"I'll tell you," he said rapidly. "Syd did it because I asked him to. He's a pal. I told him. I told him I didn't trust his lordship. I'm a nervous man where firearms are concerned. I'm a nervous man altogether if you can understand." His fingers plucked at his smiling lips. "Don't look at me like that," he said, and his voice broke into a shrill falsetto. "Everybody's staring as if I'd done something. Eyes. Eyes. Eyes. Oh, God, give me a smoke!"

Alleyn held out his cigarette case. Breezy struck it out of his hand and began to sob. "Bloody sadist," he said.

"I know what's wrong with you, you silly chap," Lord Pastern said accusingly.

Breezy shook a finger at him. "You *know*!" he said. "You started it. You're as good as a murderer. You *are* a murderer, by God!"

"Say that again, my good Bellairs," Lord Pastern rejoined with relish, "and I'll have you in the libel court. Action for slander, b'George."

Breezy looked wildly round the assembly. His light eyes with their enormous pupils fixed their gaze on Félicité. He pointed a trembling hand at her. "Look at that girl," he said, "doing her face and sitting up like Jackie with the man she was supposed to love lying stiff and bloody in the morgue. It's disgusting."

Caesar Bonn came forward, wringing his hands. "I can keep silent no longer," he said. "If I am ruined, I am ruined. If I do not speak, there are others who will." He looked at Lord Pastern, at Edward Manx and at Hahn.

Edward said: "It's got to come out, certainly. In common fairness."

"Certainly. Certainly."

"What," Alleyn asked, "has got to come out?"

"Please, Mr. Manx. You will speak."

"All right, Caesar. I think," Edward said slowly, turning to Alleyn, "that you should know what happened before any of you arrived. I myself had only just walked into the room. The body was where you saw it." He paused for a moment. Breezy, watched him, but Manx did not look at Breezy. "There was a sort of struggle going on," he said. "Bellairs was on the floor by Rivera and the others were pulling him off."

"Damned indecent thing," said Lord Pastern virtuously, "trying to go through the poor devil's pockets."

Breezy whimpered.

"I'd like a closer account of this, if you can give it to me. When exactly did this happen?" Alleyn asked.

Caesar and Hahn began talking at once. Alleyn stopped them. "Suppose," he said, "we trace events through from the point where Mr. Rivera was carried out of the restaurant!" He began to question the four waiters who had carred Rivera. The waiters hadn't noticed anything wrong with him. They were a bit flustered anyway because of the confusion about which routine was to be followed. There had been so many contradictory orders that in the end they just watched to see who fell down and then picked up the stretcher and carried him out. The wreath covered his chest. As they lifted him on to the stretcher, Breezy had said quickly: "He's hurt. Get him out." They had carried him straight to the office. As they put the stretcher down they heard him make a noise, a harsh rattling noise, it had been. When they looked closer they found he was dead. They fetched Caesar Bonn and Hahn and then carried the body into the inner room. Then Caesar ordered them back to the restaurant and told one of them to fetch Dr. Allington.

Lord Pastern, taking up the tale, said that while they were still on the dais, after the removal of Rivera, Breezy had gone to him and muttered urgently: "For God's sake come out. Something's happened to Carlos." The pianist, Happy Hart, said that Breezy had stopped at the piano on his way out and had told him in an aside to keep going.

Caesar took up the story. Breezy and Lord Pastern came to the inner office. Breezy was in a fearful state, saying he'd seen blood on Rivera when he put the wreath on his chest. They were still gathered round Rivera's body, laying him out tidily on the floor. Breezy kept gibbering about the blood and then he caught sight of the body and turned away to the wall, retching and scrabbling in his overcoat pockets for one of his tablets and complaining because he had none. Nobody did anything for him and he went into the lavatory off the inner office and was heard vomiting in there. When he came back he looked terrible and stood gabbling about how he felt.

At this point Breezy interrupted Caesar. "I told them," he said shrilly. "I told them. It was a terrible shock to me when he fell. It was a shock to all of us, wasn't it, Boys?"

The Boys stirred themselves and muttered in unison that it had been a great shock.

"When he fell?" Alleyn said quickly. "Then, definitely, he wasn't supposed to fall?"

They all began to explain at once with great eagerness. Two routines had been rehearsed. There had been a lot of argument about which should be followed. Right up to the last neither Lord Pastern nor Rivera could make up his mind which he preferred. In the one routine Lord Pastern was to have fired the revolver four times at Rivera, who should have smiled and gone on playing. At each of the shots a member of the band was to have played a note in a descending scale and aped having been hit. Then Rivera was to have made his exit and the whole turn continued as they had seen it done, except that it would have ended with Lord Pastern doing a comic fall. Breezy would have then placed the wreath on him and he would have been carried out. In the alternative routine, Rivera was to do the fall. Carlos, the Boys explained, hadn't liked the idea of falling with his instrument so the original plan had been adopted at the last moment.

"When I saw him drop," Breezy chattered, "I was rocked all to hell. I thought he'd done it to put one across us. He was like that, poor old Carlos. He was a bit that way. He didn't fancy the idea of falling, yet he didn't fancy his lordship getting the big exit. He was funny that way. It was a shock to all of us."

"So the end was an improvisation?"

"Not exactly," Lord Pastern said. "I kept my head, of course, and followed the correct routine. It was a bit of a facer but there you were, what? The waiters saw Carlos fall and luckily had the sense to bring the stretcher. It would've been awkward if they hadn't as things turned out. Damn' awkward. I emptied the magazine as we'd arranged and these other fellers did their staggers. Then I handed the gun to Breezy and he snapped it and then broke it open. I always thought my first idea of Carlos getting shot was best. Though of course I did rather see that it ought to be me who was carried out."

"And I thought," Breezy said, "I'd better drop that ruddy wreath on Carlos, like we first said. So I did." His voice jumped into falsetto. "When I saw the blood I thought at first he'd coughed it up. I thought he'd had one of those things —you know—a hæmorrhage. At first. And then the wreath stuck on something. You'd scarcely credit it, would you, but I thought: for chrisake I'm hanging it on a peg. And then I saw. I told you that, all of you. You can't say I didn't."

"Certainly you told us," Caesar agreed, eyeing him nervously. "In the office." Breezy made a petulant sound and crouched back in his chair. Caesar went on quickly to relate that just before they heard Dr. Allington's voice in the main office, Breezy had darted over to the body and had crouched down beside it, throwing back the coat and thrusting his hand into the breast pocket. He had said: "I've got to get it. He's got in on him," or something like that. They had been greatly shocked by this behaviour. He and Caesar and Hahn had pulled Breezy off and he had collapsed. It was during this scene that Edward Manx had arrived.

"Do you agree that this is a fair account of what happened, Mr. Bellairs?" Alleyn asked after a pause.

For a moment or two it seemed as if he would get some kind of answer. Breezy looked at him with extraordinary concentration. Then he turned his head as if his neck was stiff. After a moment he nodded.

"What did you hope to find in the deceased's pockets?" Alleyn said.

Breezy's mouth stretched in its mannikin-grin. His eyes were blank. He raised his hands and the fingers trembled.

"Come," Alleyn said, "what did you hope to find?"

"Oh, God!" said Lord Pastern fretfully. "Now he's goin' to blub again."

This was an understatement. Hysteria took possession of Breezy. He screamed out some unintelligible protest or appeal, broke into a storm of sobbing laughter and stumbled to the entrance. A uniformed policeman came through the door and held him. "Now, now," said the policeman. "Easy does it, sir, easy does it."

Dr. Curtis came out of the office and stood looking at Breezy thoughtfully. Alleyn nodded to him and he went to Breezy.

Breezy sobbed: "Doctor! Doctor! Listen!" He put his heavy arm about Dr. Curtis's shoulders and with an air of mystery whimpered in his ear. "I think, Alleyn . . .?" said Dr. Curtis. "Yes," Alleyn said, "in the office, will you?"

When the door had shut behind them, Alleyn looked at Breezy's Boys.

"Can any of you tell me," he said, "how long he's been taking drugs?"

2

Lord Pastern, bunching his cheeks, said to nobody in particular. "Six months."

"You knew about it, my lord, did you?" Fox demanded and Lord Pastern grinned savagely at him. "Not bein' a detective-inspector," he said, "I don't have to wait until a dope-fiend throws fits and passes out before I know what's wrong with him."

He balanced complacently, toe and heel, and stroked the back of his head. "I've been lookin' into the dope racket," he volunteered. "Disgraceful show. Runnin' sore in the body politic and nobody with the guts to tackle it." He glared upon Breezy's Boys. "You chaps!" he said, jabbing a finger at them, "what did you do about it? Damn all."

Breezy's Boys were embarrassed and shocked. They fidgeted, cleared their throats, and eyed one another.

"Surely," Alleyn said, "you must have guessed. He's in a bad way, you know."

They hadn't been sure, it appeared. Happy Hart said they knew Breezy took some kind of stuff for his nerves. It was some special kind of dope. Breezy used to get people to buy it for him in Paris. He said it was some kind of bromide, Hart added vaguely. The double-bass said Breezy was a very nervous type. The first saxophone muttered something about hitting the high spots and corpse-revivers. Lord Pastern loudly pronounced a succinct but unprintable comment and they eyed him resentfully. "I told him what it'd come to," he announced. "I threatened the chap. Only way. 'If you don't take a pull, by God,' I said, 'I'll give the whole story to the papers. *Harmony* f'r instance.' I told him so, to-night."

Edward Manx uttered a sharp ejaculation and looked as if he wished he'd held his tongue.

"Who searched him for his bloody tablet?" Skelton demanded, glaring at Lord Pastern.

"The show," Lord Pastern countered virtuously, "had to go on, didn't it? Don't split straws, my good ass."

Alleyn intervened. The incident of the lost tablet was related. Lord Pastern described how he went through Breezy's pockets and boasted of his efficiency. "You fellers call it fannin' a chap," he explained kindly, to Alleyn.

"This was immediately after Mr. Skelton had inspected the revolver and handed it back to Lord Pastern?" Alleyn asked.

"That's right," said one or two of the Boys.

"Lord Pastern, did you at any time after he'd done this lose sight of the revolver or put it down?"

"Certainly not. I kept it in my hip pocket from the time Skelton gave it to me until I went on the stage."

"Did you look down the barrel after Mr. Skelton returned it to you?"

"No."

"I won't have this," said Skelton loudly.

Alleyn glanced thoughtfully at him and returned to Lord Pastern. "Did you, by the way," he said, "find anything in Mr. Bellairs' pockets?"

"A wallet, a cigarette-case and his handkerchief," Lord Pastern rejoined importantly. "The pill was in the handkerchief."

Alleyn asked for a closer description of this scene and Lord Pastern related with gusto how Breezy had stood with his hands up, holding his baton as if he were about to give his first down-beat and how he himself had explored every pocket with the utmost despatch and thoroughness. "If," he added, "you're thinkin' that he might have had the dart on him, you're wrong. He hadn't. And he couldn't have got at the gun if he had, what's more. And he didn't pick anything up afterwards. I'll swear to that."

Ned Manx said with some violence, "For God's sake, Cousin George, think what you're saying."

"It is useless, Edward," said Lady Pastern. "He will destroy himself out of sheer complacency." She addressed herself to Alleyn. "I must inform you that in my opinion and that of many of his acquaintances, my husband's eccentricity is of a degree that renders his statements completely unreliable."

"That be damned!" shouted Lord Pastern. "I'm the most truthful man I know. C., you're an ass."

"So be it," said Lady Pastern in her deepest voice, and folded her hands.

"When you came out on the dais," Alleyn went on, disregarding this interlude, "you brought the revolver with you and put it on the floor under a hat. It was near your right foot, I think, and behind the drums. Quite near the edge of the dais."

Félicité had opened her bag and for the fourth time had taken out her lipstick and mirror. She made an involuntary movement of her hands, jerking the lipstick away as if she threw it. The mirror fell at her feet. She half rose. Her open bag dropped to the floor, and the glass splintered under her heel. The carpet was littered with the contents of her bag and blotted with powder. Alleyn moved forward quickly. He picked up the lipstick and a folded paper with typewriting on it. Félicité snatched the paper from his hand. "Thank you. Don't bother. What a fool I am," she said breathlessly.

She crushed the paper in her hand and held it while, with the other hand, she gathered up the contents of her bag. One of the waiters came forward, like an automaton, to help her.

"Quite near the edge of the dais," Alleyn repeated. "So that, for the sake of argument, you, Miss de Suze, or Miss Wayne, or Mr. Manx, could have reached out to the sombrero. In fact, while some of your party were dancing, anyone who was left at the table could also have done this. Do you all agree?"

Carlisle was acutely aware of the muscles of her face. She was conscious of Alleyn's gaze, impersonal and deliberate, resting on her eyes and her mouth and her hands. She remembered noticing him, how many hours ago? when he sat at the next table. "I mustn't look at Fée or at Ned," she thought.

She heard Edward move stealthily in his chair. The paper in Félicité's hand rustled. There was a sharp click and Carlisle jumped galvanically. Lady Pastern had flicked open her lorgnette and was now staring through it at Alleyn.

Manx said: "You were next to our table, I think, weren't you, Alleyn?"

"By an odd coincidence," Alleyn rejoined pleasantly.

"I think it better for us to postpone our answers."

"Do you?" Alleyn said lightly. "Why?"

"Obviously, the question about whether we could have touched this hat, or whatever it was . . ."

"You know perfectly well what it was, Ned," Lord Pastern interjected. "It was my sombrero, and the gun was under it. We've had all that."

". . . this sombrero," Edward amended, "is a question that has dangerous implications for all of us. I'd like to say that quite apart from the possibility, which we have not admitted, of any of us touching it, there is surely no possibility at all that any of us could have taken a revolver from underneath it, shoved a bit of a parasol up the barrel and replaced the gun, without anything being noticed. If you don't mind my saying so, the suggestion of any such manœuvre is obviously ridiculous."

"Oh, I don't know," said Lord Pastern with an air of judicial impartiality. "All that switchin' about of the light and the metronome waggin' and everybody naturally watchin' me, you know. I should say, in point of fact, it was quite possible. I wouldn't have noticed, I promise you."

"George," Félicité whispered fiercely, "do you *want* to do us in?"

"I want the truth," her stepfather shouted crossly. "I was a Theosophist, once," he added.

"You are and have been and always will be an imbecile," said his wife, shutting her lorgnettes.

"Well," Alleyn said, and the attention of the band, the employees of the restaurant, and its guests, having been diverted to this domestic interchange, swung back to him, "ridiculous or not, I shall put the question. You are, of course, under no compulsion to answer it. Did any of you handle Lord Pastern's sombrero?"

They were silent. The waiter, who had gathered up the pieces of broken mirror, faced Alleyn with an anxious smile. "Excuse me, sir," he said.

"Yes?"

"The young lady," said the waiter, bowing towards Félicité, "did put her hand under the hat. I was the waiter for that table, sir, and I happened to notice. I hope you will excuse me, Miss, but I did happen to notice."

Fox's pencil whispered over the paper.

"Thank you," said Alleyn.

Félicité cried out: "This is the absolute *end*. Suppose I said it's not true."

"I shouldn't," Alleyn said. "As Mr. Manx has pointed out, I was sitting next to your table."

"Then why ask?"

"To see if you would frankly admit that you did, in fact, put your hand under the sombrero."

"People," said Carlisle suddenly, "think twice about making frank statements all over the place when a capital crime is involved."

She looked up at Alleyn and found him smiling at her. "How right you are," he said. "That's what makes homicide cases so tiresome."

"Are we to hang about all night," Lord Pastern demanded, "while you sit gossipin'? Never saw such a damned amateur set-up in all m' life. Makes you sick."

"Let us get on by all means, sir. We haven't very much more ground to cover here. It will be necessary, I'm afraid, for us to search you before we can let you off."

"All of us?" Félicité said quickly.

They looked, with something like awe, at Lady Pastern.

"There is a wardress in the ladies' cloakroom," Alleyn said, "and a detective-sergeant in the men's. We shall also need your fingerprints, if you please. Sergeant Bailey will attend to that. Shall we set about it? Perhaps you, Lady Pastern, will go in first?"

Lady Pastern rose. Her figure, tightly encased, seemed to enlarge itself. Everybody stole uneasy glances at it. She faced her husband. "Of the many indignities you have forced upon me," she said, "this is the most intolerable. For this I shall never forgive you."

"Good lord, C.," he rejoined, "what's the matter with being searched. Trouble with you is you've got a dirty mind. If you'd listened to my talks on the Body Beautiful that time in Kent . . ."

"*Silence!*" she said (in French) and swept into the ladies' cloakroom. Félicité giggled nervously.

"Anybody may search *me*," Lord Pastern said, generously, "come on."

He led the way to the men's cloakroom.

Alleyn said: "Perhaps, Miss de Suze, you would like to go with your mother. It's perfectly in order, if you think she'd prefer it."

Félicité was sitting in her chair with her left hand clutching her bag and her right hand out of sight. "I expect she'd rather have a private martyrdom, Mr. Alleyn," she said.

"Suppose you go and ask her? You can get your part of the programme over when she is free."

He stood close to Félicité, smiling down at her. She said: "Oh, all right. If you like." Without enthusiasm, and with a backward glance at Manx, she followed her mother. Alleyn immediately took her chair and addressed himself to Manx and Carlisle.

"I wonder," he said, "if you can help me with one or two routine jobs that will have to be tidied up. I believe you were both at the dinner party at Lord Pastern's house—it's in Duke's Gate, isn't it?—before this show to-night."

"Yes," Edward said. "We were there."

"And the rest of the party? Bellairs and Rivera and of course Lord and Lady Pastern. Anyone else?"

"No," Carlisle said, and immediately corrected herself. "I'd forgotten. Miss Henderson."

"Miss Henderson?"

"She used to be Félicité's governess and stayed on as a sort of general prop and stay to everybody."

"What is her full name?"

"I—I really don't know. Ned, have you ever heard Hendy's Christian name?"

"No," Edward said. "Never. She's simply Hendy. I should think it might be Edith. Wait a moment, though," he added after a moment, "I do know. Fée told me years ago. She saw it on an electoral roll or something. It's Petronella Xantippe."

"I don't believe you."

"People so seldom have the names you expect," Alleyn murmured vaguely. "Can you give me a detailed description of your evening at Duke's Gate? You see, as Rivera was there, the dinner party assumes a kind of importance."

Carlisle thought: "We're waiting too long. One of us ought to have replied at once."

"I want," Alleyn said at last, "if you can give it to me, an account of the whole thing. When everybody arrived. What you talked about. Whether you were all together most of the time or whether you split up, for instance, after dinner and were in different rooms. That kind of thing."

They began to speak together and stopped short. They laughed uncomfortably, apologised and invited each other to proceed.

At last Carlisle embarked alone on a colourless narrative. She had arrived at Duke's Gate at about five and had seen her aunt and uncle and Félicité. Naturally there had been a good deal of talk about the evening performance. Her uncle had been in very good spirits.

"And Lady Pastern and Miss de Suze?" Alleyn said. Carlisle replied carefully that they were in much their usual form. "And how is that?" he asked. "Cheerful? Happy family atmosphere, would you say?"

Manx said lightly: "My dear Alleyn, like most families they rub along together without—without——"

"Were you going to say 'without actually bursting up'?"

"Well—well——"

"Ned," Carlisle interjected, "it's no good pretending Uncle George and Aunt Cecile represent the dead norm of British family life. Presumably Mr. Alleyn reads the papers. If I say they were much as usual it means they were much as usual on their own lines." She turned to Alleyn. "On their own lines, Mr. Alleyn, they were perfectly normal."

"If you'll allow me to say so, Miss Wayne," Alleyn rejoined

warmly, "you are evidently an extremely sensible person. May I implore you to keep it up."

"Not to the extent of letting you think a routine argument to them is matter for suspicion to you."

"They argue," Manx added, "perpetually and vehemently. It means nothing. Well, you've heard them."

"And did they, for example, argue about Lord Pastern's performance in the band?"

"Oh, yes," they said together.

"And about Bellairs or Rivera?"

"A bit," said Carlisle, after a pause.

"Boogie-woogie merchants," Manx said, "are not, in the nature of things, my cousin Cecile's cups-of-tea. She is, as you may have noticed, a little in the *grande dame* line of business."

Alleyn leant forward in his chair and rubbed his nose. He looked, Carlisle thought, like a bookish man considering some point that had been raised in an interminable argument.

"Yes," he said at last. "That's all right, of course. One can see the obvious and rather eccentric *mise en scène*. Everything you've told me is no doubt quite true. But the devil of it is, you know, that you're going to use the palpable eccentricities as a sort of smoke-screen for the more profound disturbances."

They were astonished and disconcerted. Carlisle said tentatively that she didn't understand. "Don't you?" Alleyn murmured. "Oh, well! Shall we get on with it? Bellairs has suggested an engagement between Rivera and Miss de Suze. Was there an engagement, if you please?"

"No, I don't think so. Was there, Lisle?"

Carlisle said that she didn't think so, either. Nothing had been announced.

"An understanding?"

"He wanted her to marry him, I think. I mean," Carlisle amended with heightened colour, "I know he did. I don't think she was going to. I'm sure she wasn't."

"How did Lord Pastern feel about it?"

"Who can tell?" Edward muttered.

"I don't think it bothered him much one way or the other," Carlisle said. "He was too busy planning his début."

But into her memory came the figure of Lord Pastern, bent over his task of drawing bullets from cartridges, and she heard again his grunted, "much better leave things to me."

Alleyn began to lead them step by step through the evening at Duke's Gate. What had they talked about before dinner? How had the party been divided, and into which rooms? What had they themselves done and said? Carlisle found herself landed with an account of her arrival. It was easy to say that her aunt and uncle had argued about whether there should be extra guests for dinner. It was not so easy when he led her back to the likelihood of an engagement between Rivera and Félicité, asking if it had been discussed and by whom, and whether Félicité had confided in her. "These seem impertinent questions," Alleyn said, and anticipated her attempt to suggest as much. "But, believe me, they are entirely impersonal. Irrelevant matters will be most thankfully rejected and forgotten. We want to tidy up the field of inquiry; that's all." And then it seemed to Carlisle that evasions would be silly and wrong and she said that Félicité had been worried and unhappy about Rivera.

She sensed Edward's uneasiness and added that there had been nothing in the Félicité-Rivera situation, nothing at all. "Félicité makes emotional mountains out of sentimental·molehills," she said. "I think she enjoys it." But she knew while she said this that Félicité's outburst had been more serious than she suggested and she heard her voice lose its integrity and guessed that Alleyn heard this too. She began to be oppressed by his quiet insistence and yet her taste for detail made her a little pleased with her own accuracy, and she felt something like an artist's reluctance to slur or distort. It was easy again to recall her solitary time before dinner in the ballroom. As soon as she began to speak of it the sensation of nostalgia flashed up in her memory and she found herself telling Alleyn that her coming-out ball had been there, that the room had a host of associations for her and that she had stood there, recollecting them.

"Did you notice if the umbrellas and parasols were there?"

"Yes," she said quickly. "I did. They were there on the piano. I remembered the French parasol. It was Aunt 'Cile's. I remembered Félicité playing with it as a child. It takes to

pieces." She caught her breath. " But you know it does that,"
she said.

" And it was intact then, when you saw it? No bits gone
out of the shaft?"

" No, no."

" Sure?"

" Yes. I picked it up and opened it. That's supposed to be
unlucky, isn't it? It was all right then."

" Good. And after this you went into the drawing-room.
I know this sounds aimlessly exacting but what happened
next, do you remember?"

Before she knew where she was she had told him about
the magazine, *Harmony*, and there seemed no harm in repeating her notion that Félicité had written one of the letters on
G.P.F.'s page. Alleyn gave no sign that this was of interest.
It was Edward who, unaccountably, made a stifled ejaculation.
Carlisle thought : " Have I blundered?" and hurried on to an
account of her visit to her uncle's study when he drew the
bullets from the cartridges. Alleyn asked casually how he had
set about this and seemed to be diverted from the matter in
hand, amused at Lord Pastern's neatness and dexterity.

Carlisle was accustomed to being questioned about Lord
Pastern's eccentricities. She considered him fair game and
normally enjoyed trying to make sharp, not unkindly, little
word-sketches of him for her friends. His notoriety was so
gross that she had always felt it would be ridiculous to hesitate.
She slipped into this habit now.

Then the picture of the drawer, pulled out and laid on the
desk at his elbow, suddenly presented itself. She felt a kind
of shrinking in her midriff and stopped short.

But Alleyn had turned to Ned Manx and Ned, dryly and
slowly, answered questions about his own arrival in the
drawing-room. What impression did he get of Bellairs and
Rivera? He hadn't spoken to them very much. Lady Pastern
had taken him apart to show him her embroidery.

" *Gros-point?*" Alleyn asked.

" And *petit-point*. Like most Frenchwomen of her period,
she's pretty good. I really didn't notice the others, much."

The dinner party itself came next. The conversation, Ned

was saying, had been fragmentary, about all sorts of things. He couldn't remember in detail.

"Miss Wayne has an observer's eye and ear," Alleyn said, turning to her. "Perhaps you can remember, can you? What did you talk about? You sat, where?"

"On Uncle George's right."

"And on your other hand?"

"Mr. Rivera."

"Can you remember what he spoke about, Miss Wayne?" Alleyn offered his cigarette case to her. As he lit her cigarette Carlisle looked past him at Ned who shook his head very slightly.

"I thought him rather awful, I'm afraid," she said. "He really was a bit too thick. All flowery compliments and too Spanish-grandee for anyone to swallow."

"Do you agree, Mr. Manx?"

"Oh, yes. He was quite unreal and rather ridiculous, I thought."

"Offensively so, would you say?"

They did not look at each other. Edward said: "He just bounded sky-high, if you call that offensive."

"Did they speak of the performance to-night?"

"Oh, yes," Edward said. "And I must say I'm not surprised that the waiters were muddled about who they were to carry out. It struck me that both Uncle George and Rivera wanted all the fat and that neither of them could make up his mind to letting the other have the stretcher. Bellairs was clearly at the end of his professional tether about it."

Alleyn asked how long the men had stayed behind in the dining-room. Reluctantly—too reluctantly Carlisle thought, with a rising sense of danger—Ned told them that Lord Pastern had taken Breezy away to show him the blank cartridges. "So you and Rivera were left with the port?" Alleyn said.

"Yes. Not for long."

"Can you recall the conversation?"

"There was nothing that would be any help to you."

"You never know."

"I didn't encourage conversation. He asked all sorts of

questions about our various relationships to each other and I
snubbed him."

"How did he take that?"

"Nobody enjoys being snubbed, I suppose, but I fancy he
had a tolerably thick hide on him."

"Was there actually a quarrel?"

Edward stood up. "Look here, Alleyn," he said, "if I was
in the slightest degree implicated in this business I should
have followed my own advice and refused to answer any of
your questions. I am not implicated. I did not monkey with
the revolver. I did not bring about Rivera's death."

"And now," Carlisle thought in despair, "Ned's going to
give him a sample of the family temper. Oh, God!" she
thought, "please don't let him."

"Good," Alleyn said, and waited.

"Very well, then," Edward said grandly and sat down.
"So there was a quarrel."

"I merely," Edward shouted, "showed the man I thought
he was impertinent and he walked out of the room."

"Did you speak to him again after this incident?"

Carlisle remembered a scene in the hall. The two men
facing each other, Rivera with his hand clapped to his ear.
What was it Ned had said to him? Something ridiculous, like
a perky schoolboy. "Put that in your hurdy-gurdy and squeeze
it," he had shouted with evident relish.

"I merely ask these questions," Alleyn said, "because the
bloke had a thick ear, and I wondered who gave it to him.
The skin's broken and I noticed you wear a signet ring."

3

In the main office, Dr. Curtis contemplated Breezy Bellairs
with the air of wary satisfaction. "He'll do," he said, and
stepping neatly behind Breezy's chair, he winked at Alleyn.
"He must have got hold of something over and above the
shot I gave him. But he'll do."

Breezy looked up at Alleyn and gave him the celebrated
smile. He was pallid and sweating slightly. His expression

was one of relief, of well-being. Dr. Curtis washed his syringe
in a tumbler of water on the desk and then returned it to his
case.

Alleyn opened the door into the foyer and nodded to Fox,
who rose and joined him. Together they returned to the contemplation of Breezy.

Fox cleared his throat: "Alors," he said cautiously, and
stopped. "Evidement," he said, "il y a un advancement, n'est
ce pas?"

He paused, slightly flushed, and looked out of the corners
of his eyes at Alleyn.

"Pas grand'chose," Alleyn muttered. "But as Curtis says,
he'll do for our purpose. You go, by the way, Br'er Fox, from
strength to strength. The accent improves."

"I still don't get the practice though," Fox complained.
Breezy, who was looking with complete tranquillity at the
opposite wall, laughed comfortably. "I feel lovely, now," he
volunteered.

"He's had a pretty solid shot," Dr. Curtis said. "I don't
know what he'd been up to before but it seems to have packed
him up a bit. But he's all right. He can answer questions,
can't you, Bellairs?"

"I'm fine," Breezy rejoined dreamily. "Box of birds."

"Well . . ." Alleyn said dubiously. Fox added in a sepulchral undertone: "Faut de mieux." "Exactly," Alleyn said
and, drawing up a chair, placed himself in front of Breezy.

"I'd like you to tell me something," he said. Breezy lazily
withdrew his gaze from the opposite wall and Alleyn found
himself staring into eyes that, because of the enormous size
of their pupils, seemed mere structures and devoid of intelli-
gence.

"Do you remember," he said, "what you did at Lord
Pastern's house?"

He had to wait a long time for an answer. At last Breezy's
voice, detached and remote, said: "Don't let's talk. It's nicer
not talking."

"Talking's nice too, though."

Dr. Curtis walked away from Breezy and murmured to no
one in particular, "Get him started and he may go on."

" It must have been fun at the dinner party," Alleyn suggested. "Did Carlos enjoy himself?"

Breezy's arm lay curved along the desk. With a luxurious sigh, he slumped further into the chair and rested his cheek on his sleeve. In a moment or two his voice began again, independently, it seemed, with no conscious volition on his part. It trailed through his scarcely moving lips in a monotone.

" I told him it was silly but that made no difference at all. ' Look,' I said, ' you're crazy.' Well, of course I was sore on account of he held back on me, not bringing me my cigarettes."

" What cigarettes?"

" He never did anything I asked him. I was so good to him. I was as good as gold. I told him. I said, ' Look,' I said, ' she won't take it from you, Boy. She's as sore as hell,' I said, ' and so's he, and the other girl isn't falling so what's the point?' I knew there'd be trouble. ' And the old bastard doesn't like it,' I said. ' He pretends it doesn't mean a thing to him, but that's all hooey because he just naturally wouldn't like it.' No good. No notice taken."

" When was this?" Alleyn asked.

" Off and on. Most of the time you might say. And when we were in the taxi and he said how the guy had hit him, I said: ' There you are, what was I telling you?' "

" Who hit him?"

There was a longer pause. Breezy turned his head languidly.

" Who hit Carlos, Breezy?"

" I heard you the first time. What a gang, though! The Honourable Edward Manx in serious mood while lunching at the Tarmac with Miss Félicité de Suze who is, of course, connected with him on the distaff side. Her stepfather is Lord Pastern and Bagott, but if you ask me it's a punctured romance. Cherchez la femme."

Fox glanced up from his notes with an air of bland interest.

" The woman in this case," Alleyn said, " being . . .?"

" Funny name for a girl."

" Carlisle?"

" Sounds dopey to me, but what of that? But that's the sort

of thing they do. Imagine having two names. Pastern and Bagott. And I can look after both of them, don't you worry. Trying to swing one across me. What a chance! Bawling me out. Saying he'll write to this bloody paper. Him and his hot gunning and where is he now."

"Swing one across you?" Alleyn repeated quietly. He had pitched his voice on Breezy's level. Their voices ran into and away from each other. They seemed to the two onlookers to speak as persons in a dream, with tranquillity and secret understanding.

"He might have known," Breezy was saying, "that I wouldn't come at it but you've got to admit it was awkward. A permanent engagement. Thanks a lot. How does the chorus go?"

He laughed faintly, yawned, whispered: "Pardon me," and closed his eyes.

"He's going," Dr. Curtis said.

"Breezy," Alleyn said loudly. "*Breezy.*"

"What?"

"Did Lord Pastern want you to keep him on permanently?"

"I told you. Him and his blankety blankety blank cartridges."

"Did he want you to sack Skelton?"

"It was all Carlos's fault," Breezy said quite loudly and on a plaintive note. "He thought it up. God, was he angry!"

"Was who angry?"

With a suggestion of cunning the voice murmured: "That's telling."

"Was it Lord Pastern?"

"Him? Don't make me laugh!"

"Syd Skelton?"

"When I told him," Breezy whispered faintly, "he looked like murder. Honest, I *was* nervy."

He rolled his face over on his arm and fell into a profound sleep. "He won't come out of that for eight hours," said Dr. Curtis.

4

At two o'clock the cleaners came in; five middle-aged women who were admitted by the police and who walked through the foyer into the restaurant with the tools of their trade. Caesar Bonn was greatly distressed by their arrival and complained that the pressmen, who had been sent away with a meagre statement that Rivera had collapsed and died, would lie in wait for these women and question them. He sent the secretary, David Hahn, after the cleaners. " They are to be silenced at all costs. At all costs, you understand." Presently the drone of vacuum cleaners arose in the restaurant. Two of Alleyn's men had been there for some time. They now returned to the foyer and, joining the policemen on duty there, glanced impassively at its inhabitants.

Most of the Boys were asleep. They were sprawled in ungainly postures on their small chairs. Trails of ash lay on their clothes. They had crushed out their cigarette butts on empty packets, on the soles of their shoes, on match boxes or had pitched them at the floor containers. The smell of dead butts seemed to hang over the entire room.

Lady Pastern appeared to sleep. She was inclined backwards in her arm-chair and her eyes were closed. Purplish shadows had appeared on her face and deep grooves ran from her nostrils to the corners of her mouth. Her cheeks sagged. She scarcely stirred when her husband, who had been silent for a considerable time, said : " Hi, Ned !"

" Yes, Cousin George?" Manx responded guardedly.

" I've got to the bottom of this."

" Indeed?"

" I know who did it."

" Really? Who?"

" I disagree entirely and emphatically with capital punishment," Lord Pastern said, puffing out his cheeks at the group of police officials. " I shall therefore keep my knowledge to myself. Let 'em muddle on. Murder's a matter for the psychiatrist, not the hangman. As for judges they're a pack of conceited old sadists. Let 'em get on with it. They'll have no help from me. For God's sake, Fée, stop fidgetin'."

Félicité was curled up in the chair she had used earlier in the evening. From time to time she thrust her hands out of sight, exploring, it seemed, the space between the upholstered arms and seat. She did this furtively with sidelong glances at the others.

Carlisle said : " What *is* it, Fée? What have you lost?"

" My hanky."

" Here, take mine, for pity's sake," said Lord Pastern, and threw it at her.

The searching had gone forward steadily. Carlisle, who liked her privacy, had found the experience galling and unpleasant. The wardress was a straw-coloured woman with large artificial teeth and firm pale hands. She had been extremely polite and uncompromising.

Now the last man to be searched, Syd Skelton, returned from the men's cloakroom and at the same time Alleyn and Fox came out of the office. The Boys woke up. Lady Pastern opened her eyes.

Alleyn said : " As the result of these preliminary inquiries . . ." (" Preliminary!" Lord Pastern snorted.) " . . . I think we have got together enough information and may allow you to go home. I'm extremely sorry to have kept you here so long."

They were all on their feet. Alleyn raised a hand. " There's one restriction, I'm afraid. I think you'll all understand, and I hope, respect it. Those of you who were in immediate communication with Rivera or who had access to the revolver used by Lord Pastern, or who seem to us, for sufficient reasons, to be in any way concerned in the circumstances leading to Rivera's death, will be seen home by police officers. We shall provide ourselves with search warrants. If such action seems necessary, we shall use them."

" Of all the footlin', pettifoggin' . . ." Lord Pastern began, and was interrupted.

" Those of you who come under this heading," Alleyn said, " are Lord Pastern and the members of his party, Mr. Bellairs and Mr. Skelton. That's all, I think. Thank you, ladies and gentlemen."

" I'm damned if I'll put up with this. Look here, Alleyn . . ."

" I'm sorry, sir. I must insist, I'm afraid."

"George," said Lady Pastern, "you have tried conclusions with the law on more than one occasion and as often as you have done so you have made a fool of yourself. Come home."

Lord Pastern studied his wife with an air of detachment. "Your hair-net's loose," he pointed out, "and you're bulgin' above your waist. Comes of wearin' stays. I've always said . . ."

"I, at least," Lady Pastern said directly to Alleyn, "am prepared to accept your conditions. So, I am sure, are my daughter and my niece. Félicité! Carlisle!"

"Fox!" said Alleyn.

She walked with perfect composure to the door and waited there. Fox spoke to one of the plain-clothes men who detached himself from the group near the entrance. Félicité held out a hand towards Edward Manx. "Ned, you'll come, won't you? You'll stay with us?"

After a moment's hesitation he took her hand. "Dearest Edward," said Lady Pastern from the door. "We should be so grateful."

"Certainly, Cousin Cecile. Of course."

Félicité still held his hand. He looked at Carlisle. "Coming?" he asked.

"Yes, of course. Good-night, Mr. Alleyn," said Carlisle.

"Good-night, Miss Wayne."

They went out, followed by the plain-clothes man.

"I should like to have a word with you, Mr. Skelton," Alleyn said. "The rest of you," he turned to the Boys, the waiters, and the spotlight man, "may go. You will be given notice of the inquest. Sorry to have kept you up so late. Good-night."

The waiters and the electrician went at once. The band moved forward in a group. Happy Hart said: "What about Breezy?"

"He's sound asleep and will need a bit of rousing. I shall see he's taken home."

Hart shuffled his feet and looked at his hands. "I don't know what you're thinking," he said, "but he's all right. Breezy's O.K., really. I mean, he's just been making the pace a bit too hot for himself as you might say. He's a very nervy type, Breezy. He suffers from insomnia. He took the stuff for his nerves. But he's all right."

"He and Rivera got on well, did they?"

Several of the Boys said quickly: "That's right. Sure. They were all right." Hart added that Breezy was very good to Carlos and gave him his big chance in London.

All the boys agreed fervently with this statement except Skelton. He stood apart from his associates. They avoided looking at him. He was a tall darkish fellow with narrow eyes and a sharp nose. His mouth was small and thin-lipped. He stooped slightly.

"Well, if that's all," Happy Hart said uneasily, "we'll say good-night."

"We've got their addresses, haven't we, Fox? Good. Thank you. Good-night."

They filed out, carrying their instruments. In the old days when places like the Metronome and Quags and the Hungaria kept going up to two in the morning the Boys had worked through, sometimes going on to parties in private houses. They were Londoners who turned homewards with pale faces and blue jaws at the time when fans of water from giant hose-pipes strike across Piccadilly and Whitehall. They had been among the tag-ends of the night in those times, going soberly to their beds as the first milk carts jangled. In summer-time they had undressed in the dawn to the thin stir of sparrows. They shared with taxi-drivers, cloakroom attendants, waiters and commissionaires, a specialised disillusionment.

Alleyn watched them go and then nodded to Fox. Fox approached Caesar Bonn and David Hahn, who lounged gloomily near the office door. "Perhaps you gentlemen wouldn't mind coming into the office," he suggested. They followed him in. Alleyn turned to Skelton. "Now, Mr. Skelton."

"What's the idea," Skelton said, "keeping me back? I've got a home, same as everybody else. Though how the hell I'm going to get there's nobody's business."

"I'm sorry. It's a nuisance for you, I know, but it can't be helped."

"I don't see why."

The office door was opened from inside. Two constables came out with Breezy Bellairs hanging between them like a cumbersome puppet. His face was lividly pale, his eyes half open. He breathed stertorously and made a complaining noise

like a wretched child. Dr. Curtis followed. Bonn and Hahn
watched from inside the office.

"All right?" Alleyn said.

"He'll do. We'll just get him into his coat."

They held Breezy up while Curtis, with difficulty, crammed
him into his tight-fitting overcoat. During this struggle
Breezy's baton fell to the floor. Hahn came forward and
picked it up. "You wouldn't think," Hahn said, contemplating it sadly, "how good he was. Not to look at him now."

Dr. Curtis yawned. "These chaps'll see him into his bed,"
he said. "I'll be off, if you don't want me, Rory."

"Right." The dragging procession disappeared. Fox returned to the office and shut the door.

"That's a nice way," Skelton said angrily, "for a first-
class band leader to be seen going home. Between a couple of
flatties."

"They'll be very tactful," Alleyn rejoined. "Shall we sit
down?"

Skelton said he'd sat down for so long that his bottom was
numb. "Let's get cracking, for God's sake. I've had it.
What's the idea?"

Alleyn took out his note-book.

"The idea," he said, "is further information. I think you
can give it to us. By all means let's get cracking."

"Why pick on me? I know no more than the others."

"Don't you?" Alleyn said vaguely. He glanced up. "What's
your opinion of Lord Pastern as a tympanist?"

"Dire. What of it?"

"Did the others hold this opinion?"

"They knew. Naturally. It was a cheap stunt. Playing up
the snob-value." He thrust his hands down in his pockets and
began to walk to and fro, impelled, it seemed, by resentment.
Alleyn waited.

"It's when something like this turns up," Skelton announced
loudly, "that you see how rotten the whole set-up really is.
I'm not ashamed of my work. Why the hell should I be? It
interests me. It's not easy. It takes doing and anybody that
tells you there's nothing to the best type of our kind of music
talks through his hat. It's got something. It's clever and there's
a lot of hard thinking behind it."

"I don't know about music," Alleyn said, "but I can imagine that from the technical point of view your sort can be almost purely intellectual. Or is that nonsense?"

Skelton glowered at him. "You're not far out. A lot of the stuff we have to play is wet and corny, of course. They," he jerked his head at the empty restaurant, "like it that way. But there's other stuff that's different. If I could pick my work I'd be in an outfit that went for the real mackay. In a country where things were run decently I'd be able to do that. I'd be able to say: 'This is what I can do and it's the best I can do,' and I'd be directed into the right channels. I'm a Communist," he said loudly.

Alleyn was suddenly and vividly reminded of Lord Pastern. He said nothing and after a pause Skelton went on.

"I realise I'm working for the rottenest section of a crazy society but what can I do? It's my job and I have to take it. But this affair! Walking out and letting a dopey old deadbeat of a lord make a fool of himself with my instruments, and a lot of deadbeat effects added to them! Looking as if I like it! Where's my self-respect?"

"How," Alleyn asked, "did it come about?"

"Breezy worked it because . . ."

He stopped short and advanced on Alleyn. "Here!" he demanded. "What's all this in aid of? What do you want?"

"Like Lord Pastern," Alleyn said lightly, "I want the truth. Bellairs, you were saying, worked it because—of what?"

"I've told you. Snob-value."

"And the others agreed?"

"They haven't any principles. Oh, yes. They took it."

"Rivera, for instance, didn't oppose the idea?"

Skelton flushed deeply. "No," he said.

Alleyn saw his pockets bulge as the hidden hands clenched. "Why not?" he asked.

"Rivera was hanging his hat up to the girl. Pastern's step-daughter. He was all out to make himself a hero with the old man."

"That made you very angry, didn't it?"

"Who says it made me angry?"

"Bellairs said so."

"Him! Another product of our so-called civilisation. Look at him."

Alleyn asked him if he knew anything about Breezy's use of drugs. Skelton, caught, as it seemed, between the desire of a zealot to speak his mind and an undefined wariness, said that Breezy was the child of his age and circumstances. He was a by-product, Skelton said, of a cynical and disillusioned social set-up. The phrases fell from his lips with the precision of slogans. Alleyn listened and watched and felt his interest stirring. "We all knew," Skelton said, "that he was taking some kind of dope to keep him going. Even *he* knew—old Pastern. He'd nosed it out all right and I reckon he knew where it came from. You could tell. Breezy's changed a hell of a lot. He used to be a nice sort of joker in a way. Bit of a wag. Always having us on. He got off-side with the dago for that."

"Rivera?"

"That's right. Breezy used to be crazy on practical jokes. He'd fix a silly squeaker in one of the saxes or sneak a wee bell inside the piano. Childish. He got hold of Rivera's p.a. and fixed it with little bits of paper between the keys so's it wouldn't go. Only for rehearsal, of course. Rivera came out all glamour and hair oil and swung his p.a. Nothing happened. There was Breezy grinning like he'd split his face and the Boys all sniggering. You had to laugh. Rivera tore the place up: he went mad and howled out he'd quit. Breezy had a hell of a job fixing him. It was quite a party."

"Practical jokes," Alleyn said. "A curious obsession, I always think."

Skelton looked sharply at him. "Here!" he said, "you don't want to get ideas. Breezy's all right. Breezy wouldn't come at anything like this." He laughed shortly, and added with an air of disgust: "Breezy fix Rivera! Not likely."

"About this drug habit——" Alleyn began. Skelton said impatiently: "Well, there you are! It's just one of those things. I told you: we all knew. He used to go to parties on Sundays with some gang."

"Any idea who they were?"

"No, I never asked. I'm not interested. I tried to tell him

he was heading for a crash. Once. He didn't like it. He's my boss and I shut up. I'd have turned it up and gone over to another band but I'm used to working with these boys and they do better stuff than most."

" You never heard where he got his drug, whatever it is?" Skelton muttered, " I never *heard*. Naturally."

" But you formed an opinion, perhaps?"

" Perhaps."

" Going to tell me about it?"

" I want to know what you're getting at. I've got to protect myself, haven't I? I like to get things straight. You've got some notion that because I looked at Pastern's gun I might have shoved this silly umbrella what-have-you up the muzzle. Why don't you come to the point?"

" I shall do so," Alleyn said. " I've kept you behind because of this circumstance and because you were alone with Lord Pastern for a short time after you left the platform and before he made his entrance. So far as I can see at the moment there is no connection between your possible complicity and the fact that Bellairs takes drugs. As a police officer I'm concerned with drug addicts and their source of supply. If you can help me with any information, I'll be grateful. Do you know, then, where Bellairs got whatever he took?"

Skelton deliberated, his brows drawn together, his lower lip thrust out. Alleyn found himself speculating about his background. What accumulation of circumstances, ill-adjustments or misfortunes had resulted in this particular case? What would Skelton have been if his history had been otherwise? Were his views, his truculence, his suspicions, rooted in honesty or in some indefinable sense of victimisation? To what lengths would they impel him? And finally Alleyn asked himself the inevitable question : could this be a killer?

Skelton wetted his lips. " The drug-racket," he said, " is like any other racket in a capitalistic government. The real criminals are the bosses, the barons, the high-ups. They don't get pulled in. It's the little blokes that get caught. You have to think it out. Silly sentiment and big talk won't work. I've got no tickets on the police department in this country. A fairly efficient machine working for the wrong ideas. But drug-taking's no good from any point of view. All right. I'll co-operate this far. I'll tell you where Breezy got his dope."

"And where," said Alleyn patiently, "did Breezy get his dope?"

"From Rivera," said Skelton. "Now! From Rivera."

CHAPTER SEVEN

DAWN

I

SKELTON had gone home, and Caesar Bonn and David Hahn. The cleaners had retired into some remote part of the building. Only the police remained: Alleyn and Fox, Bailey, Thompson, the three men who had searched the restaurant and band room and the uniformed constable who would remain on duty until he was relieved after daybreak. The time was now twenty minutes to three.

"Well, Foxkin," said Alleyn, "where are we? You've been very mousey and discreet. Let's have your theory. Come on."

Fox cleared his throat and placed the palms of his hands on his knees. "A very peculiar case," he said disapprovingly. "Freakish, you might say. Silly. Except for the corpse. Corpses," Mr. Fox observed with severity, "are never silly."

Detective-sergeants Bailey and Thompson exchanged winks.

"In the first place, Mr. Alleyn," Fox continued, "I ask myself: why do it that way? Why fire a bit of an umbrella handle from a revolver when you might fire a bullet? This applies in particular to his lordship. And yet it seems it must have been done. You can't get away from it. Nobody had a chance of stabbing the chap while he was performing, did they now?"

"Nobody."

"All right, then. Now, if anybody pushed this silly weapon up the gun after Skelton examined it, they had the thing concealed about their person. Not much bigger than a fountain-

pen but sharp as hell. Which brings us to Bellairs, for one. If
you consider Bellairs, you have to remember that his lordship
seems to have searched him very thoroughly before he went
out to perform.''

" Moreover his lordship in the full tide of his own alleged
innocence declares that the wretched Breezy didn't get a
chance to pocket anything after he had been searched—or to
get at the gun.''

" Does he really?'' said Fox. " Fancy!''

" In fact his lordship, who, I submit, is no fool, has been at
peculiar pains to clear everybody but himself.''

" No fool, perhaps,'' Fox grunted, " but would you say a
bit off the plumb, mentally?''

" Everybody else says so, at all events. In any case, Fox,
I'll give sworn evidence that nobody stabbed Rivera before or
at the time he was shot at. He was a good six feet away from
everybody except Lord Pastern, who was busy with his blasted
gun.''

" There you are! And it wasn't planted among the music
stands because they were used by the other band. And anyway none of the musicians went near his lordship's funny hat
where the gun was, and being like that, I ask myself, isn't his
lordship the most likely to use a silly fanciful method if he'd
made up his mind to do a man in? It all points to his lordship. You can't get away from it. And yet he seems so pleased
with himself and kind of unruffled. Of course you do find that
attitude in homicidal mania.''

" You do. What about motive?''

" Do we know what he thought about his stepdaughter
keeping company with the deceased? The other young lady
suggested that he didn't seem to care one way or the other but
you never know. Something else may turn up. Personally, as
things stand at the moment, I favour his lordship. What
about you, Mr. Alleyn?''

Alleyn shook his head. " I'm stumped,'' he said. " Perhaps
Skelton could have got the thing into the revolver when he
examined it but Lord Pastern, who undoubtedly is as sharp as
a needle, swears he didn't. They were alone together for a
minute while Breezy made his announcement, but Skelton
says he didn't go near Lord Pastern, who had the gun in his

hip pocket. It's not likely to be a lie because Pastern could deny it. You didn't hear Skelton. He's an odd chap. A truculent Communist. Australian, I should say. A hard, determined thinker. Nobody's fool and completely sincere. One-track minded. There's no doubt he detested Rivera, both on general principles and because Rivera backed up Lord Pastern's appearance to-night. Skelton bitterly resented this and says so. He felt he was prostituting what he is pleased to regard as his art and conniving at something entirely against his social principles. I believe him to be fanatically sincere in this. He looked on Rivera and Lord Pastern as parasites. Rivera, by the way, supplied Breezy Bellairs with his dope, whatever it is. Curtis says cocaine, and it looks as if he found himself something to go on with when he searched the body. We'll have to follow that one up, Fox."

"Dope," said Fox profoundly. "There you are! When we do get a windfall it's a dead man. Still, there may be something in his rooms to give us a lead. South America, now. That may link up with the Snowy Santos gang. They operate through South America. It'd be nice," said Mr. Fox, whose talents for some time had been concerned with the sale of illicit drugs, " it'd be lovely, in fact, to get the tabs on Snowy Santos."

"Lovely, wouldn't it?" Alleyn agreed absently. "Get on with your argument, Fox."

"Well, now, sir. Seeing Rivera wasn't meant to fall down and *did*, you can say he was struck at that moment. I know that sounds like a glimpse of the obvious, but it cuts out any idea that there was some kind of jiggery-pokery *after* he fell because nobody knew he was going to fall. And unless you feel like saying somebody threw the weapon like a dart at the same time as his lordship fired the first shot—well," said Fox disgustedly, " that would be a fat-headed sort of notion, wouldn't it? So we come back to the idea it was fired from the revolver. Which is supported by the scratches in the barrel. Mind, we'll have to get the experts going there."

"We shall, indeed."

"But saying, for the moment, that the little jewelled clip, acting as a sort of stop, did mark the barrel, we come to Skelton's statement that the scratches were not there when he examined it. And that looks like his lordship again. Look at it how you will, you get back to his lordship, you know."

"Miss de Suze," Alleyn said, rubbing his nose in vexation, "did grope under that damned sombrero. I saw her and so did Manx and so did the waiter. Manx seemed to remonstrate and she laughed and withdrew her hand. She couldn't have got the weapon in then but it shows that it was possible for anyone sitting on her chair to get at the gun. Lady Pastern was left alone at their table while the others danced."

Fox raised his eyebrows and looked puffy. "Very icy," he said. "A haughty sort of lady and with a will and temper of her own. Look how she's stood up to his lordship in the past. Very masterful."

Alleyn glanced at his old colleague and smiled. He turned to the group of waiting men. "Well, Bailey," he said, "we've about got to you. Have you found anything new?"

Bailey said morosely: "Nothing to write home about, Mr. Alleyn. No prints on this dart affair. I've packed it up with protection and can have another go at it."

"The revolver?"

"Very plain sailing there, Mr. Alleyn. Not a chance for latents."

"That's why I risked letting him handle it."

"Yes, sir. Well now," said Bailey with a certain professional relish, "the revolver. Lord Pastern's prints on the revolver. And this band leader's Breezy Bellairs or whatever he calls himself."

"Yes. Lord Pastern handed the gun to Breezy."

"That's right, sir. So I undersand."

"Thompson," said Alleyn suddenly, "did you get a good look at Mr. Manx's left hand when you dabbed him?"

"Yes, sir. Knuckles a bit grazed. Very slight. Wears a signet ring."

"How about the band platform, Bailey?"

Bailey looked at his boots and said he'd been over the floor-space round the tympani and percussion stand. There were traces of four fingertips identifiable as Miss de Suze's. No others.

"And Rivera? On the body?"

"Not much there," Bailey said, "but they would probably

bring up latent prints where Bellairs and the doctor had handled him. That was all, so far."

"Thank you. What about you other chaps in the restaurant and band room? Find anything? Gibson?"

One of the plain-clothes men came forward. "Not much, sir. Nothing out of the ordinary. Cigarette butts and so on. We picked up the wads and shells and Bellairs' handkerchief, marked, on the platform."

"He mopped his unpleasant eyes with it when he did his stuff with the wreath," Alleyn muttered. "Anything else?"

"There was a cork," said Detective-Sergeant Gibson apologetically, "on the band platform. Might have been dropped by a waiter, sir."

"Not up there. Let's see it."

Gibson produced an envelope from which he shook out a smallish cork on to the table. Alleyn looked at it without touching it. "When was the band platform cleaned?"

"Polished in the early morning, Mr. Alleyn, and mopped over before the evening clients came in."

"Where exactly did you find this thing?"

"Half-way back and six feet to left of centre. I've marked the place."

"Good. Not that it'll help much." Alleyn used his lens. "It's got a black mark on it." He stopped and sniffed. "Boot polish, I think. It was probably kicked about the place by bandsmen. But there's another smell. Not wine or spirit and anyway it's not that sort of cork. It's smaller and made with a narrow end and a wide top. No trade-mark. What *is* this smell? Try, Fox."

Fox's sniff was stentorian. He rose, meditated and said: "Now, what am I reminded of?" They waited. "Citronella," Fox pronounced gravely. "Or something like it."

"How about gun-oil?" said Alleyn.

Fox turned and contemplated his superior with something like indignation. "Gun-oil? You're not going to tell me, Mr. Alleyn, that in addition to stuffing jewelled parasol handles up a revolver somebody stopped it with a cork like a ruddy pop-gun?"

Alleyn grinned. "The case is taking liberties with your credulity, Br'er Fox." He used his lens again. "The bottom surface has been broken, I fancy. It's a forlorn hope, Bailey, but we might try for dabs."

Bailey put the cork away. Alleyn turned to the others. " I think you can pack up," he said. " I'm afraid I'll have to keep you, Thompson, and you, Bailey, with us. It's a non-stop show. Gibson, you'll pick up a search warrant and go on to Rivera's rooms. Take someone with you. I want a complete search there. Stott and Watson are attending to Bellairs' rooms and Sallis has gone with Skelton. You'll all report back to me at the Yard at ten. Get people to relieve you when you've finished. Bellairs and Skelton will both have to be kept under observation, damn it, though I fancy that for the next eight hours Breezy won't give anybody a headache except himself. Inspector Fox and I will get extra men to attend to Duke's Gate. All right. We'll move."

In the office a telephone bell rang. Fox went in to answer it and was heard uttering words of reproach. He came out looking scandalised.

" It's that new chap we sent back with his lordship's party, Marks. And what do you suppose he's done?" Fox glared round upon his audience and slapped the palm of his hand on the table. " Silly young chump! When they get in they say they're all going to the drawing-room. 'Oh,' said Marks, ' then it's my duty, if you please, to accompany you.' The gentlemen say they want to retire first, and they go off to the downstairs cloakroom. The ladies have the same idea and they go upstairs and Sergeant Expeditious Marks tries to tear himself in halves which is nothing to what I'll do for him. And while he's exhausting himself running up and down keeping observation, what happens? One of the young ladies slips down the servants' stairs and lets herself out by the back door."

" Which one?" Alleyn asked quickly.

" Don't," said Mr. Fox with bitter scorn, " ask too much of Detective-Sergeant Marks, sir. Don't make it too rough. He wouldn't know which one. Oh, no. He comes bleating to the phone while I daresay the rest of 'em are lighting off wherever the fancy takes 'em. Sergeant ruddy Police-College Marks! What is it?"

A uniformed constable had come in from the front entrance. "I thought I'd better report, sir," he said. "I'm on duty outside. There's an incident."

"All right," said Alleyn. "What incident?"

"A taxi's pulled up some distance away, sir, and a lady got out."

"A lady!" Fox demanded so peremptorily that the constable glanced nervously at him.

"Yes, Mr. Fox. A young lady. She spoke to the driver. He's waiting. She looked round and hesitated. I was in the entrance, sir, well in the shadow, and I don't think she saw me."

"Recognise her?" Alleyn asked.

"I wouldn't be sure, sir. The clothes are different but I reckon it's one of the ladies in Lord Pastern's party."

"Have you locked the doors behind you?"

"Yes, sir."

"Unlock them and make yourself scarce. Clear out, all of you. Scatter. Step lively."

The foyer was emptied in five seconds. The doors into the office and the band room closed noiselessly. Alleyn darted to the light switches. A single lamp was left to glow pinkly against the wall. The foyer was filled with shadow. He slipped to his knees behind a chair in the corner farthest from the light.

The clock ticked discreetly. Somewhere in a distant basement a pail clanked and a door slammed. Innumerable tiny sounds closer at hand became evident : the tap of a blind cord somewhere in the restaurant, a stealthy movement and scuffle behind the walls, an indefinable humming from the main switchboard. Alleyn smelt carpet, upholstery, disinfectant, and stale tobacco. Entrance into the foyer from outside must be effected through two sets of doors; those giving on the street and those inside made of plate-glass and normally open but now swung-to. Through these he could see only a vague greyness crossed by reflections in the glass itself. The image of the one pink lamp floated midway up the right-hand pane. He fixed his gaze on this. Now, beyond the glass doors, there came a paleness. The street door had been opened.

The face appeared quite suddenly against the plate glass,

obscuring the reflected lamp and distorted by pressure. One door squeaked faintly as it opened.

She stood for a moment, holding her head-scarf half across her face. Then she moved forward swiftly and was down on her knees before an arm-chair. Her fingernails scrabbled on its tapestry. So intent was she upon her search that she did not hear him cross the thick carpet behind her, but when he drew the envelope from his pocket it made a slight crackle. Still kneeling, she swung round, saw him and cried out sharply.

"Is this what you are hunting for, Miss Wayne?" Alleyn asked.

2

He crossed over to the wall and switched up the lights. Without moving, Carlisle watched him. When he returned he still held the envelope. She put her hand to her burning face and said unsteadily: "You think I'm up to no good, I suppose. I suppose you want an explanation."

"I should be glad of an answer to my question. Is this what you want?"

He held the envelope up, but did not give it to her. She looked at it doubtfully. "I don't know—I don't think——"

"The envelope is mine. I'll tell you what it contains. A letter that had been thrust down between the seat and the arm of the chair you have been exploring."

"Yes," Carlisle said. "Yes. That's it. May I have it, please?"

"Do sit down," Alleyn rejoined. "We'd better clear this up, don't you think?"

He waited while she rose. After a moment's hesitation, she sat in the chair.

"You won't believe me, of course," she said, "but that letter —I suppose you have read it, haven't you—has nothing whatever to do with this awful business to-night. Nothing in the wide world. It's entirely personal and rather important."

"Have you even read it?" he asked. "Can you repeat the contents? I should like you to do that, if you will."

"But—not absolutely correctly—I mean——"

" Approximately."

" It—it's got an important message. It concerns someone
—I can't tell you in so many words——"

" And yet it's so important that you return here at three
o'clock in the morning to try and find it." He paused, but
Carlisle said nothing. " Why," he said, " didn't Miss de Suze
come and collect her own correspondence?"

" Oh, dear!" she said. " This is difficult."

" Well, for pity's sake keep up your reputation and be honest
about it."

" I am being honest, damn you!" said Carlisle with spirit.
" The letter's a private affair and—and—extremely confiden-
tial. Félicité doesn't want anyone to see it. I don't know
exactly what's in it."

" She funked coming back herself?"

" She's a bit shattered. Everyone is."

" I'd like you to see what the letter's about," said Alleyn
after a pause. She began to protest. Very patiently he repeated his usual argument. When someone had been killed
the nicer points of behaviour had to be disregarded. He had
to prove to his own satisfaction that the letter was immaterial,
and then he would forget it. " You remember," he said, " this
letter dropped out of her bag. Did you notice how she snatched
it away from me? I see you did. Did you notice what she
did after I said you would all be searched? She shoved her
hand down between the seat and arm of that chair. Then she
went off to be searched and I sat in the chair. When she came
back she spent a miserable half-hour fishing for the letter and
trying to look as if she wasn't. All right."

He drew the letter from the envelope and spread it out
before her. " It's been fingerprinted," he said, " but without
any marked success. Too much rubbing against good solid
chair-cover. Will you read it or——"

" Oh, all right," Carlisle said angrily.

The letter was typed on a sheet of plain notepaper. There
was no address and no date.

" MY DEAR :" Carlisle read, " Your loveliness is my undoing.
Because of it I break my deepest promise to myself and to
others. We are closer than you have ever dreamed. I wear a

white flower in my coat to-night. It is yours. But as you value our future happiness, make not the slightest sign—even to me. Destroy this note, my love, but keep my love.
                                                                "G.P.F."

Carlisle raised her head, met Alleyn's gaze and avoided it quickly. "A white flower," she whispered. "G.P.F.? *G.P.F.?* I don't believe it."

"Mr. Edward Manx had a white carnation in his coat, I think."

"I won't discuss this letter with you," she said strongly. "I should never have read it. I won't discuss it. Let me take it back to her. It's nothing to do with this other thing. Nothing. Give it to me."

Alleyn said, "You must know I can't do that. Think for a moment. There was some attachment, a strong attachment of one kind or another, between Rivera and your cousin—your step-cousin. After Rivera is murdered, she is at elaborate pains to conceal this letter, loses it, and is so anxious to retrieve it that she persuades you to return here in an attempt to recover it. How can I disregard such a sequence of events?"

"But you don't know Fée! She's always in and out of tight corners over her young men. It's nothing. You don't understand."

"Well," he said, looking good-humouredly at her, "help me to understand. I'll drive you home. You can tell me on the way. Fox."

Fox came out of the office. Carlisle listened to Alleyn giving his instructions. The other men appeared from the cloakroom, held a brief indistinguishable conversation with Fox and went out through the main entrance. Alleyn and Fox collected their belongings and put on their coats. Carlisle stood up. Alleyn returned the letter to its envelope and put it in his pocket. She felt tears stinging under her eyelids. She tried to speak and produced only an indeterminate sound.

"What is it?" he said, glancing at her.

"It can't be true," she stammered. "I won't believe it. I won't."

"What? That Edward Manx wrote this letter?"

"He couldn't. He couldn't write like that to her."

"No?" Alleyn said casually. "You think not? But she's quite good-looking, isn't she? Quite attractive, don't you think?"

"It's not that. It's not that at all. It's the letter itself. He couldn't write like that. It's so bogus."

"Have you ever noticed love-letters that are read out in court and published in the papers? Don't they sound pretty bogus? Yet some of them have been written by extremely intelligent people. Shall we go?"

It was cold out in the street. A motionless pallor stood behind the rigid silhouette of roofs. "Dawn's left hand," Alleyn said to nobody in particular and shivered. Carlisle's taxi had gone but a large police car waited. A second man sat beside the driver. Fox opened the door and Carlisle got in. The two men followed. "We'll call at the Yard," Alleyn said.

She felt boxed-up in the corner of the seat and was conscious of the impersonal pressure of Alleyn's arm and shoulder. Mr. Fox, on the farther side, was a bulky man. She turned and saw Alleyn's head silhouetted against the bluish window. An odd notion came into her head. "If Fée happens to calm down and take a good look at him," she thought, "it'll be all up with G.P.F. and the memory of Carlos and everybody." And with that her heart gave a leaden thump or two. "Oh, Ned," she thought, "how you *could*!" She tried to face the full implication of the letter but almost at once shied away from it. "I'm miserable," she thought, "I'm unhappier than I've been for years and years."

"What," Alleyn's voice said close beside her, "I wonder, is the precise interpretation of the initials: 'G.P.F.'? They seem to ring some bell in my atrocious memory but I haven't got there yet. Why do you imagine 'G.P.F.'?" She didn't answer and after a moment he went on. "Wait a bit, though. Didn't you say something about a magazine you were reading before you visited Lord Pastern in his study? *Harmony*? Was that it?" He turned his head to look at her and she nodded. "And the editor of the tell-it-all-to-auntie page calls himself Guide, Philosopher and Friend? How does he sign his recipes for radiant living?"

Carlisle mumbled: "Like that."

" And you had wondered if Miss de Suze had written to him," Alleyn said tranquilly. " Yes. Now, does this get us anywhere, do you imagine?"

She made a non-committal sound. Unhappy recollections forced themselves upon her. Recollections of Félicité's story about a correspondence with someone she had never met who had written her a " marvellous " letter. Of Rivera reading her answer to this letter and making a scene about it. Of Ned Manx's article in *Harmony*. Of Félicité's behaviour after they all met to go to the Metronome. Of her taking the flower from Ned's coat. And of his stooping his head to listen to her as they danced together.

" Was Mr. Manx," Alleyn's voice asked, close beside her, " wearing his white carnation when he arrived for dinner?"

" No," she said, too loudly. " No. Not till afterwards. There were white carnations on the table at dinner."

" Perhaps it was one of them."

" Then," she said quickly, " it doesn't fit. The letter must have been written before he ever saw the carnation. It doesn't fit. She said the letter came by district messenger. Ned wouldn't have known."

" By district messenger, did she? We'll have to check that. Perhaps we'll find the envelope. Would you say," Alleyn continued, " that he seemed to be very much attached to her?"

(Edward had said : " About Fée. Something very odd has occurred. I can't explain but I'd like to think you understand.")

" Strongly attracted, would you think?" Alleyn said.

" I don't know. I don't know what to think."

" Do they see much of each other?"

" I don't know. He—he stayed at Duke's Gate while he was flat hunting."

" Perhaps an attachment developed then. What do you think?"

She shook her head. Alleyn waited. Carlisle now found his unstressed persistence intolerable. She felt her moorings go and was adrift in the darkness. A wretchedness of spirit that she was unable to control or understand took possession of her. " I won't talk about it," she stammered. " It's none of my business. I can't go on like this. Let me go, please. Please let me go."

"Of course," Alleyn said. "I'll take you home."

3

When they arrived at Duke's Gate, dawn was so far established that the houses with their blind windows and locked doors were clearly distinguishable in a wan half-light.

The familiar street, emerging from night, had an air of emaciation and secrecy, Carlisle thought, and she was vaguely relieved when milk bottles jingled up a side alley, breaking across the blank emptiness. "Have you got a key?" Alleyn said. He and Fox and the man from the front seat waited, while she groped in her bag. As she opened the door a second car drew up and four men got out. The men from the front seat joined them. She thought : "This makes us all seem very important. This is an important case. A case of murder."

In the old days she had come back from parties once or twice with Ned Manx at this hour. The indefinable house-smell made itself felt as they entered. She turned on a lamp and it was light in the silent hall. She saw herself reflected in the inner glass doors, her face stained with tears. Alleyn came in first. Standing there, in evening dress, with his hat in his hand, he might have been seeing her home, about to wish her good-bye. The other men followed quickly. "What happens now?" she wondered. "Will he let me go now? What are they going to do?"

Alleyn had drawn a paper from his pocket. "This is a search warrant," he said. "I don't want to hunt Lord Pastern out of his bed. It will do, I think, if——"

He broke off, moved quickly to the shadowed staircase and up half a dozen steps. Fox and the other men stood quiet inside the doors. A little French clock in the stairwell ticked flurriedly. Upstairs on the first floor a door was flung open. A faint reflected light shone on Alleyn's face. A voice, unmistakably Lord Pastern's, said loudly : "I don't give a damn how upset you are. You can have kittens if you like but you don't go to bed till I've got my time-table worked out. Sit down."

With a faint grin Alleyn moved upstairs and Carlisle, after a moment's hesitation, followed him.

They were all in the drawing-room. Lady Pastern, still in evening dress and now very grey about the eyes and mouth, sat in a chair near the door. Félicité, who had changed into a housecoat and reduced her make-up, looked frail and lovely. Edward had evidently been sitting near her and had risen on Alleyn's entrance. Lord Pastern, with his coat off and his sleeves turned up, sat at a table in the middle of the room. Sheets of paper lay before him and he had a pencil between his teeth. A little removed from this group, her hands folded in the lap of her woollen dressing-gown and her grey hair neatly braided down her back, sat Miss Henderson. A plain-clothes officer stood inside the door. Carlisle knew all about him. He was the man who had escorted them home : hours ago, it seemed, in another age. She had given him the slip when she returned to the Metronome and now wondered, for the first time, how dim a view the police would take of this manœuvre. The man looked awkwardly at Alleyn, who seemed about to speak to him as Carlisle entered, but stood aside to let her pass. Edward came quickly towards her. "Where have you been?" he said angrily. "What's the matter? I——" He looked into her face. "Lisle," he said. "What is it?"

Lord Pastern glanced up. "Hallo," he said. "Where the devil did you get to, Lisle? I want you. Sit down."

"It's like a scene from a play," she thought. "All of them sitting about exhausted, in a grand drawing-room. The third act of a thriller." She caught the eye of the plain-clothes officer who was looking at her with distaste.

"I'm sorry," she said. "I'm afraid I just walked out by the back door."

"I realise that, Miss," he said.

"We can't be in two places at once, can we?" Carlisle added brightly. She was trying to avoid Félicité. Félicité was look-ing at her anxiously, obviously, with inquiring eyebrows.

Lord Pastern said briskly : "Glad you've come, Alleyn, though I must say you've taken your time about it. I've been doin' your job for you. Sit down."

Lady Pastern's voice, sepulchral with fatigue, said : "May I suggest, George, that as in all probability this gentleman is about to arrest you, your choice of phrase is inappropriate."

"That's a damn' tiresome sort of thing to say, C.," her husband rejoined. "Gets you nowhere. What you want," he continued, darting his pencil at Alleyn, "is a time-table. You want to know what we were all doin' with ourselves before we went to the Metronome. System. All right. I've worked it out for you." He slapped the paper before him. "It's incomplete without Breezy's evidence, of course, but we can get that to-morrow. . Lisle, there are one or two things I want from you. Come here."

Carlisle stood behind him and looked at Alleyn. His face was politely attentive, his eyes were on Lord Pastern's notes. In her turn and in response to an impatient tattoo of the pencil, she too looked at them.

She saw a sort of table, drawn up with ruled lines. Across the top, one each at the head of nine columns, she read their names : her own, Lady Pastern's, Félicité's, Edward's, Lord Pastern's, Bellairs', Rivera's, Miss Henderson's, and Spence's. Down the left hand side, Lord Pastern had written a series of times, beginning at 8.45 and ending at 10.30. These were ruled off horizontally and in the spaces thus formed, under each name, were notes as to the owner's whereabouts. Thus, at "9.15 approx." it appeared that she and Lady Pastern had been in the drawing-room, Miss Henderson on her way upstairs, Félicité in the study, Rivera in the hall, Lord Pastern and Breezy Bellairs in the ballroom, and Spence in the servants' quarters.

"The times," Lord Pastern explained importantly, "are mostly only approximate. We know some of them for certain but not all. Thing is : it shows you the groupin'. Who was with who and who was alone. Method. Here y'are, Lisle. Go over it carefully and check up your entries."

He flung himself back in his chair and ruffled his hair. He reeked of complacency. Carlisle took up the pencil and found that her hand trembled. Exhaustion had suddenly overwhelmed her. She was nauseated and fuddled with fatigue. Lord Pastern's time-table swam before her. She heard her voice saying, "I think you've got it right," and felt a hand under her arm. It was Alleyn's. "Sit down," he said from an enormous distance. She was sitting down and Ned, close beside her, was making some sort of angry protest. She leant forward, propping her head on her hands. Presently it cleared and she listened, with an extraordinary sense of detachment, to what Alleyn was now saying.

" . . . very helpful, thank you. And now, I'm sure, you'll all be glad to get to bed. We shall be here during what's left of the night : hardly anything, I'm afraid, but we shan't disturb you."

They were on their feet. Carlisle, feeling very sick, wondered what would happen if she got to hers. She looked at the others through her fingers and thought that there was something a little wrong, a little misshapen, about all of them. Her aunt, for instance. Why had she not seen before that Lady Pastern's body was too long and her head too big? It was so. And surely Félicité was fantastically narrow. Her skeleton must be all wrong : a tiny pelvis with the hip-bones jutting out from it like rocks. Carlisle's eyes behind their sheltering fingers turned to Lord Pastern, and she thought how monstrous it was that his forehead should overhang the rest of his face : a blind over a shop-window; that his monkey's cheeks should bunch themselves up when he was angry. Even Hendy : Hendy's throat was like some bird's and now that her hair was braided one saw that it was thin on top. Her scalp showed. They were caricatures, really, all of them. Subtly off-pitch : instruments very slightly out of tune. And Ned? He was behind her, but if she turned to look at him, what, in the perceptiveness born of nervous exhaustion, would she see? Were not his eyes black and small? Didn't his mouth, when it smiled, twist and show canine teeth a little too long? But she would not look at Ned.

And now, thought the bemused Carlisle, here was Uncle George at it again. "I've no intention of goin' to bed. People sleep too much. No need for it : look at the mystics. Workin' from this time-table I can show you . . ."

"That's extremely kind of you, sir." Alleyn's voice was clear and pleasant. "But I think not. We have to get through our routine jobs. They're dreary beyond words and we're best left to ourselves while we do them."

"Routine," shouted Lord Pastern. "Official synonym for inefficiency. Things are straightened out for you by someone who takes the trouble to use his head and what do you do? Tell him to go to bed while you gallop about his house makin' lists like a bum-bailiff. Be damned if I'll go to bed. Now!"

"Oh, God!" Carlisle thought desperately. "How's he going to cope with this." She felt the pressure of a hand on her shoulder and heard Ned's voice.

"May I suggest that whatever Cousin George decides to do there's no reason why the rest of us should keep a watch of supererogation."

"None at all," Alleyn said.

"Carlisle, my dear," Lady Pastern murmured as if she was giving the signal to rise from a dinner party, "shall we?" Carlisle stood up. Edward was close by and it seemed to her to her that he still looked angry. "Are you all right?" he asked.

"Perfectly," she said. "I don't know what possessed me. I got a bit run down in Greece and I suppose——" Her voice died. She was thinking of the long flight of stairs up to her room.

"My dearest child," her aunt said, "I shall never forgive myself that you have been subjected to this ordeal."

"But she's wondering," Carlisle thought, "what I've been up to. They're all wondering."

"Perhaps some wine," her aunt continued, "or whisky. It is useless to suggest, George, that you . . ."

"I'll get it," Edward said quickly.

But Miss Henderson had already gone and now returned with a glass in her hand. As she took it from her, Carlisle smelt Hendy's particular smell of soap and talcum powder. "Like a baby," she thought, and drank. The almost neat whisky made her shudder convulsively. "Hendy!" she gasped. "You do pack a punch. I'm all right. Really. It's you, Aunt Cecile, who should be given corpse revivers."

Lady Pastern closed her eyes momentarily upon this vulgarism. Félicité, who had been perfectly silent ever since Alleyn and Carlisle came in, said: "I'd like a drink, Ned. Let's have a pub crawl in the dining-room, shall we?"

"The decanter's here if you want it, dear." Miss Henderson also spoke for the first time.

" In that case," Edward said, " if it's all right by you, Alleyn, I'll take myself off."

" We've got your address, haven't we? Right."

" Good-bye, Cousin 'Cile. If there's anything I can do . . ." Ned stood in the doorway. Carlisle did not look at him. " Good-bye, Lisle," he said. " Good-bye, Fée."

Félicité moved swiftly to him and with an abrupt compulsive movement put her arm round his neck and kissed him. He stood for a moment with his head stooped and his hand on her arm. Then he was gone.

Beneath the heavy mask of exhaustion that her aunt wore, Carlisle saw a faint glimmer of gratification. " Come, my children," Lady Pastern said, almost briskly. " Bed." She swept them past Alleyn, who opened the door for them. As Carlisle turned, with the others, to mount the stairs, she heard Lord Pastern.

" Here I am," he shouted, " and here I stick. You don't turf me off to bed or anywhere else, short of arresting me."

" I'm not, at the moment, proposing to do that," Alleyn said distinctly, " though I think, sir, I should warn you . . ."

The door shut off the remainder of his sentence.

4

Alleyn shut the door on the retiring ladies and looked thoughtfully at Lord Pastern. " I think," he repeated, " I should warn you that if you do decide, against my advice, to stay with us, what you do and say will be noted and the notes may be used . . ."

" Oh, fiddle-faddle!" Lord Pastern interrupted shrilly. " All this rigmarole. I didn't do it and you can't prove I did. Get on with your precious routine and don't twaddle so."

Alleyn looked at him with a sort of astonishment. " You bloody little old fellow," he thought. Lord Pastern blinked and smirked and bunched up his cheeks.

" All right, sir," Alleyn said. " But you're going to be given the customary warning, twaddle or not, and what's more I'll have a witness to it."

He crossed the landing, opened the ballroom door, said, "Fox, can you give me a moment?" and returned to the drawing-room, where he waited in silence until Inspector Fox came in. He then said: "Fox, I've asked Lord Pastern to go to bed and he refuses. I want you to witness this. I warn him that from now onwards his words and behaviour will be noted and that the notes may later on be used in evidence. It's a nuisance, of course, but short of taking a much more drastic step, I don't see what else can be done about it. Have the extra men turned up?"

Fox, looking with marked disapproval at Lord Pastern, said that they had.

"Tell them to keep observation, will you? Thank you, Fox, I'll carry on here."

"Thank you, Mr. Alleyn," said Fox. "I'll get on with it in the study, then."

He turned to the door. Lord Pastern said: "Hi! Where're you goin'? What're you up to?"

"If you'll excuse me for passing the remark, my lord," said Fox severely, "you're acting very foolishly. Very ill-advised and foolish, what you're doing, if I may say so." He went out.

"Great ham-fisted ass of a chap," Lord Pastern remarked.

"On the contrary, sir," Alleyn rejoined with perfect politeness, "an extremely efficient officer and should have had his promotion long ago."

He left Lord Pastern, walked to the centre of the long drawing-room and surveyed it for some minutes with his hands in his pockets. A clock on the landing struck five. Alleyn began a closer inspection of the room. He traversed it slowly, moving across and across it and examining any object that lay in his path. Lord Pastern watched him and sighed and groaned audibly. Presently Alleyn came to a chair beside which stood an occasional table. On the table was an embroidery frame and a work-box of elaborate and elegant design. He opened the lid delicately and stooped to examine the contents. Here, neatly disposed, were innumerable skeins of embroidery silks. The box was fitted with every kind of tool, each in its appointed slot: needle-cases, scissors, bodkins, a thimble, an ivory measure, a tape in a cloisonné case, stilettos held in their places by silken sheaths. One slot was untenanted. Alleyn sat down and began, with scrupulous care, to explore the box.

" Pity you didn't bring your sewin'," said Lord Pastern, " isn't it?"

Alleyn took out his note-book, glanced at his watch and wrote briefly.

" I'd thank you," Lord Pastern added, " to keep your hands out of m'wife's property." He attempted to repress a yawn, shed a tear over the effort and barked suddenly : " Where's your search warrant, b'God?"

Alleyn completed another note, rose and exhibited his warrant. " Tscha!" said Lord Pastern.

Alleyn had turned to examine Lady Pastern's embroidery. It was stretched over a frame and was almost completed. A riot of cupids in postures of extreme insouciance circled about a fabulous nosegay. The work was exquisite. He gave a slight appreciative chuckle which Lord Pastern instantly parodied. Alleyn resumed his search. He moved steadily on at a snail's pace. Half-an-hour crawled by. Presently an odd little noise disturbed him. He glanced up. Lord Pastern, still on his feet, was swaying dangerously. His eyes were glazed and horrible and his mouth was open. He had snored.

Alleyn tiptoed to the door at the far end of the room, opened it and slipped into the study. He heard a sort of roaring noise behind him, shut the door and, finding a key in the lock, turned it.

Inspector Fox, in his shirt sleeves, was examining the contents of an open drawer on the top of the desk. Laid out in front of him were a tube of plastic wood, an empty bottle marked " gun-oil," with no cork in it, and a white ivory handle into which some tool had once fitted.

5

Fox laid a broad finger on the desk beside these exhibits, not so much for an index, as to establish their presence and significance. Alleyn nodded and crossed quickly to the door that gave on the landing. He locked it and waited near it with his head cocked. " Here he comes," he said.

There was a patter of feet outside. The handle of the door was turned and then rattled angrily. A distant voice said: " I'm sorry, my lord, but I'm afraid that room's under inspection just now."

" Who the hell d'you think you are?"

" Sergeant Marks, my lord."

" Then let me tell you . . ."

The voices faded out.

" He won't get into the ballroom either," said Fox, " unless he tries a knock-up with Sergeant Whitelaw."

" How about the dining-room?"

" They've finished there, Mr. Alleyn."

" Anything?"

" Wine had been spilt on the carpet. Port, I'd say. And there's a bit of a mark on the table near the centre flower-bowl as if a drop or two of water had lain there. White carnations in the bowl. Nothing else. The table had been cleared, of course."

Alleyn looked at the collection on the desk. " Where did you beat this lot up, Foxkin?"

" In this drawer which was pulled out and left on top of the desk like it is now. Half a junk shop in it, isn't there, sir? These articles were lying on the surface of the other mess."

" Bailey had a go at it?"

" Yes. No prints on any of 'em," said Fox " Which is funny."

" How about the typewriter?"

" We've printed it. Only his lordship's dabs, and they're very fresh."

" No cap on the plastic wood tube."

" It was on the floor."

Alleyn examined the tub. " It's set hard, of course, at the open end, but not very deep. Tube's three-quarter full."

" There are crumbs of plastic wood in the drawer and on the desk and the carpet."

Alleyn said absently: " Are there, by gum!" and turned his attention to the small white handle. " Exhibit B," he said. " Know what it is, Fox?"

" I can make a healthy guess, I fancy, Mr. Alleyn."

" It's the fellow of a number of gadgets in a very elegant French work-box in the drawing-room. Crochet hooks, scissors and so on. They're fixed inside the lid, in slots. One slot's empty."

" This is just a handle, you'll notice, sir."

" Yes. Do you think it ought to have an embroidery stiletto fitted in the hollow end?"

" It's what I reckoned."

" I think you're right."

Fox opened his bag and took out a narrow cardboard box. In this, secured and protected by strings, was the dart. The jewels in the spring clip, tiny emeralds and brilliants, glittered cheerfully. Only a narrow platinum band near the top and the stiletto itself were dulled with Rivera's blood.

" Bailey'll have to go for latent prints," Fox said.

" Yes, of course. We can't disturb it. Later on it can be dismembered, but on looks, Fox, we've got something."

Alleyn held the ivory handle beside the stiletto. " I'll swear they belong," he said, and put it down. " Here's exhibit C. An empty gun-oil bottle. Where's that cork?"

Fox produced it. " It fits," he said. " I've tried. It fits and it has the same stink. Though why the hell it should turn up on the bandstand . . ."

" Ah, me," Alleyn said. " Why the hell indeed? Well, look what turns up in your particular fancy's very own drawer in his very own study! Could anything be more helpful?"

Fox shifted bulkily in his chair and contemplated his superior officer for some moments. " I know it seems funny," he said at last. " Leaving evidence all over the place : making no attempt to clear himself : piling up a case against himself, you might say. But then he *is* funny. Would you say he was not responsible within the meaning of the act?"

" I'm never sure what is the precise meaning of the infernal act. Responsible. Not responsible. Who's to mark a crucial division in the stream of human behaviour running down from something we are pleased to call sanity into raving lunacy? Where's the point at which a human being ceases to be a responsible being? Oh, I know the definitions, and I know we do our best with them, but it seems to me it's here, over this business of the pathology of behaviour, that any system of corrective and coercive law shows at its dimmest. Is this decidedly rum peer so far south in the latitude of behaviour that he would publicly murder a man by a ridiculously elaborate method that points directly to himself, and then, in effect, do everything in his power to get himself arrested? There have been cases of the sort, but is this going to be one of them?"

"Well, sir," said Fox stolidly, "I must say I think it is. It's early days yet, but as far as we've got I think it looks like it. This gentleman's previous record and his general run of behaviour points to a mental set-up that, without going beyond the ordinary view, is eccentric. Everyone knows he's funny."

"Yes. Everyone. Everyone knows," Alleyn agreed. "Everyone would say: 'It's in character. It's just like him!'"

With as near an approach to exasperation as Alleyn had ever heard from him, Fox said: "All right, Mr. Alleyn, then. I know what you're getting at. But who could have planted it on him? Tell me that. Do you believe any of the party at the table could have got at the revolver when it was under the sombrero and shoved this silly dart or bolt or what-have-you up it? Do you think Bellairs could have planted the bolt and picked it up after his lordship searched him? Where could he have planted it? In a bare band room with nothing in it but musical instruments and other men? And how could he have got it into the revolver when his lordship had the revolver on his person and swears to it that it never left him? Skelton? Skelton handled the gun while a roomful of people watched him do it. Could Skelton have palmed this thing up the barrel? The idea's laughable. Well, then."

"All right, old thing," Alleyn said. "Let's get on with it. The servants will be about soon. How far have you got in here?"

"Not much further than what you've seen, sir. The drawer was a daisy. The bullets he extracted when he made his dummies are in the waste-paper basket there."

"Carlisle Wayne watched him at that. How about the ballroom?"

"Bailey and Thompson are in there."

"Oh, well. Let's have another look at Lord Pastern's revolver, Fox."

Fox lifted it from his bag and laid it on the desk. Alleyn sat down and produced his lens.

"There's a very nice lens here, in his lordship's drawer," Fox remarked. Alleyn grunted. He was looking into the mouth of the barrel.

"We'll get a photomicrograph of this," he muttered. "Two longish scratches and some scrabbles." He gave the revolver to Fox, who was sitting in the chair which, nine hours earlier, Carlisle had occupied. Like Carlisle, Fox used Lord Pastern's lens.

"Did you notice," Alleyn said, "that when I gave the thing to that old freak to look at, it was the underside of the butt near the trigger guard that seemed to interest him? I can't find anything there. The maker's plate's on the heel. What was he up to, do you suppose?"

"God knows," Fox grunted crossly. He was sniffing at the muzzle. "You look like an old maid with smelling salts," Alleyn observed.

"So I may, sir, but I don't smell anything except gun-oil."

"I know. That's another thing. Listen."

In some distant part of the house there was movement. A door slammed, shutters were thrown back and a window opened.

"The servants are stirring," Alleyn said. "We'll seal this room, leave a man to watch it and come back to it later on. Let's collect everything we've picked up, find out what the others have got and catch three hours' sleep. Yard at ten o'clock, don't forget. Come on."

But he himself did not move. Fox looked dubiously at him and began to pack away the revolver, the plastic wood, the empty bottle and the ivory handle.

"No, blast it," Alleyn said, "I'll work through. Take those things, Fox, and dispatch them off to the experts. Fix up adequate relief for surveillance here, and away you go. I'll see you at ten. What's the matter?"

"I'd as soon stay, Mr. Alleyn."

"I know all about that. Zealous young officer. Away you go."

Fox passed his hand over his short grizzled hair and said:

" I keep very fit, really. Make a point of never thinking about the retiring age. Well, thank you very much, Mr. Alleyn."

" I might have another dig at the witnesses."

" The party upstairs won't wake before ten."

" I'll stir 'em up if I need 'em. Why should they have all the fun? I want to ring up my wife. Good-morning to you, Mr. Fox."

Fox unlocked the door on to the landing and turned the handle. The door flew inwards, striking his shoulder. He stepped back with an oath and Lord Pastern's body fell across his feet.

6

It remained there for perhaps three seconds. Its eyes were open and glared furiously. Fox bent over it and the mouth also opened.

" What the hell d'you think you're doin'?" Lord Pastern demanded.

He rolled over neatly and got to his feet. His jaw and cheeks glistened with a sort of hoar-frost, his eyes were bloodshot and his evening-dress disordered. A window on the landing shed the cruel light of early morning upon him and he looked ghastly in it. His manner, however, had lost little of its native aggressiveness. " What are you starin' at?" he added.

" We might fairly ask you," Alleyn rejoined, " what you were up to, sitting, it appears, on the landing with your back to the door."

" I dozed off. Pretty state of affairs when a man's kept out of his own rooms at five o'clock in the morning."

" All right, Fox," Alleyn said wearily, " you get along."

" Very well, sir," said Fox. " Good-morning, my lord." He side-stepped Lord Pastern and went out leaving the door ajar. Alleyn heard him admonishing Sergeant Marks on the landing : " What sort of surveillance do you call this?"

" I was only told to keep observation, Mr. Fox. His lordship fell asleep as soon as he touched the floor. I thought he might as well be there as anywhere."

Fox growled majestically and passed out of hearing.

Alleyn shut the study door and went to the window. "We haven't finished in this room," he said, "but I think I may disturb it so far."

He drew back the curtains and opened the window. It was now quite light outside. A fresh breeze came in through the window, emphasising, before it dismissed them, the dense enclosed odours of carpet, leather and stale smoke. The study looked inhospitable and unkempt. The desk lamp still shed a raffish yellowness on the litter that surrounded it. Alleyn turned from the window to face Lord Pastern and found him rummaging with quick inquisitive fingers in the open drawer on the desk.

"I wonder if I can show you what you're hunting for," Alleyn said. He opened Fox's bag and then took out his note-book. "Don't touch anything please, but will you look in that case?"

He did look, but impatiently, and, as far as Alleyn could see, without any particular surprise.

"Where'd you find that?" Lord Pastern demanded, pointing a not very steady finger at the ivory handle.

"In the drawer. Can you identify it?"

"I might be able to," he muttered.

Alleyn pointed to the weapon. "The stiletto that's been sunk in the end with plastic wood might have belonged to this ivory handle. We shall try it. If it fits, it came originally from Lady Pastern's work-box in the drawing-room."

"So you say," said Lord Pastern insultingly. Alleyn made a note.

"Can you tell me if this stiletto was in your drawer, here, sir? Before last night?"

Lord Pastern was eyeing the revolver. He thrust out his under lip, shot a glance at Alleyn, and darted his hand towards it.

"All right," Alleyn said, "you may touch it, but please answer my questions about the stiletto."

"How should I know?" he said indifferently. "I don't know." Without removing it from the case, he tipped the revolver over and, snatching up his lens, peered at the under side of the butt. He gave a shrill cackle of laughter.

"What did you expect to see?" Alleyn asked, casually.

"Hoity-toity," Lord Pastern rejoined. "*Wouldn't* you like to know!"

He stared at Alleyn. His bloodshot eyes twinkled insolently. "It's devilish amusin'," he said. "Look at it whatever way you like, it's damn' funny."

He dropped into an arm-chair, and with an air of gloating relish rubbed his hands together.

Alleyn shut down the lid of Fox's case and succeeded in snatching back his temper. He stood in front of Lord Pastern and deliberately looked into his eyes. Lord Pastern immediately shut them very tight and bunched up his cheeks.

"I'm sleepy," he said.

"Listen to me," Alleyn said. "Have you any idea at all of the personal danger you are in? Do you know the consequences of withholding or refusing crucial information when a capital crime has been committed? It's my duty to tell you that you are under grave suspicion. You've had the formal warning. Confronted with the body of a man whom, one assumes, you were supposed to hold in some sort of regard, you've conducted yourself appallingly. I must tell you, sir, that if you continue in this silly affectation of frivolity, I shall ask you to come to Scotland Yard, where you will be questioned and, if necessary, detained."

He waited. Lord Pastern's face had gradually relaxed during this speech. His mouth now pouted and expelled a puff of air that blew his moustache out. He was, apparently, asleep again.

Alleyn contemplated him for some moments. He then seated himself at the desk in a position that enabled him to keep Lord Pastern in sight. After a moment's cogitation, he pulled the typewriter towards him, took Félicité's letter from his pocket, found a sheet of paper and began to make a copy.

At the first rattle of the keys Lord Pastern's eyes opened, met Alleyn's gaze and shut again. He mumbled something indistinguishable and snored with greater emphasis. Alleyn completed his copy and laid it beside the original. They had been typed on the same machine.

On the floor, beside the chair Carlisle had used on the previous night, lay the magazine, *Harmony*. He took it up and ruffled the pages. A dozen or more flopped over and then the binding opened a little. He was confronted with G.P.F.'s page and noticed, as Carlisle had noticed, the cigarette ash in the groove. He read the letter signed Toots, turned a few more pages and came upon the anti-drug racket article and a dramatic review signed by Edward Manx. He once more confronted that preposterous figure in the arm-chair.

"Lord Pastern," he said loudly, "wake up. Wake up."

Lord Pastern jerked galvanically, made a tasting noise with his tongue and lips, and uttered a nightmarish sound.

"A-a-ah?"

"Come now, you're awake. Answer me this," said Alleyn, and thrust the copy of *Harmony* under his nose. "How long have you known that Edward Manx was G.P.F.?"

CHAPTER EIGHT

MORNING

I

LORD PASTERN blinked owlishly at the paper, swung round in his chair and eyed the desk. The letter and the copy lay conspicuously beside the typewriter.

"Yes," Alleyn said, "that's how I know. Will you give me an explanation of all this?"

Lord Pastern leant forward and, resting his forearm on his knees, seemed to stare at his clasped hands. When he spoke his voice was subdued and muffled.

"No," he said, "I'll be damned if I do. I'll answer no questions. Find out for yourself. I'm for bed."

He pulled himself out of the chair and squared his shoulders. The air of truculence was still there but Alleyn thought it overlaid a kind of indecision. With the nearest approach to civility that he had yet exhibited, he added: "I'm within my rights, aren't I?"

"Certainly," Alleyn said at once. "Your refusal will be noted. That's all. If you change your mind about sending for your solicitor, we shall be glad to call him in. In the meantime, I'm afraid, sir, I shall have to place you under very close observation."

"D'you mean some damn' bobby's goin' to follow me about like a hulkin' great poodle?"

"If you care to put it that way. It's no use, I imagine, for me to repeat any warnings about your own most equivocal position?"

"None whatever." He went to the door and stood with his back to Alleyn, holding the knob and leaning heavily on it. "Get them to give you breakfast," he said without looking round, and went slowly out and up the stairs. Alleyn called his thanks after him and nodded to Marks who was on the landing. Marks followed Lord Pastern upstairs.

Alleyn returned to the study, shut the window, had a last look round, packed Fox's bag, removed it to the landing and finally locked and sealed the door. Marks had been replaced on the landing by another plain-clothes man. "Hallo, Jimson," Alleyn said. "Just come on?"

"Yes, sir. Relieving."

"Have you seen any of the staff?"

"A maid came upstairs just now, Mr. Alleyn. Mr. Fox left instructions they were to be kept off this floor so I sent her down again. She seemed very much put about."

"She would," Alleyn said. "All right. Tactful as you can, you know, but don't miss anything."

"Very good, sir."

He crossed the landing and entered the ballroom where he found Thompson and Bailey packing up. Alleyn looked at the group of chairs round the grand piano and at a sheet of notepaper Bailey had collected. On it was pencilled the band programme for the previous night. Bailey pointed out the light coating of dust on the piano top and showed Alleyn where they had found clear traces of the revolver and the parasol and umbrellas. It was odd, Bailey and Thompson thought, but it appeared that quantities of dust had fallen after these objects had rested in this place. Not so very odd, Alleyn suggested, as Lord Pastern had, on his own statement, fired off a blank round in the ballroom and that would probably have brought down quite a lot of dust from the charming but ornately moulded ceiling. "Happy hunting ground," he muttered. "Whose are the prints round these traces of the parasol section and knob? Don't tell me," he added wearily. "His lordship's?"

"That's right," Thompson and Bailey said together. "His lordship's and Breezy's." Alleyn saw them go and then came out and sealed the ballroom doors.

He returned to the drawing-room, collected Lady Pastern's work-box, debated with himself about locking this room up too and decided against it. He then left all his gear under the eye of the officer on the landing and went down to the ground floor. It was now six o'clock.

The dining-room was already prepared for breakfast. The bowl of white carnations, he noticed, had been removed to a side-table. As he halted before a portrait of some former Settinjer who bore a mild resemblance to Lord Pastern, he heard a distant mingling of voices beyond the service door. The servants, he thought, having their first snack. He pushed open the door, found himself in a servery with a further door which led, it appeared, into the servants' hall. The best of all early morning smells, that of freshly brewed coffee, was clearly discernable. He was about to go forward when a voice, loud, dogged and perceptibly anxious, said very slowly:

"Parlez, monsieur, je vous en prie, plus lentment, et peut tre je vouês er er—comprendrai—No, blast it, as you were, je vous pouverai——"

Alleyn pushed open the door and discovered Mr. Fox seated cosily before a steaming cup of coffee, flanked by Spence and a bevy of attentive ladies and vis-à-vis with a dark imposing personage in full chef's regalia.

There was only a fractional pause while Alleyn surveyed this tableau. Fox then rose.

"Perhaps you'd like a cup of coffee, Mr. Alleyn," he suggested, and addressing the chef, added carefully: "C'est Monsieur—er—le chef—Inspecteur Alleyn, monsieur. Mr. Alleyn, this is Miss Parker, the housekeeper, and Mademoiselle Hortense. And these girls are Mary and Myrtle. This is Mr. Spence and this is Monsieur Dupont and the young chap over there is William. Well!" concluded Fox, beaming upon the company, "this is what I call cosy."

Alleyn took the chair placed for him by William and stared

fixedly at his subordinate. Fox responded with a bland smile. "I was just leaving, sir," he said, "when I happened to run into Mr. Spence. I knew you'd want to inform these good people of our little contretemps so here, in point of fact, I am."

"Fancy," said Alleyn.

Fox's technique on the working side of the green baize doors was legendary at the Yard. This was the first time Alleyn had witnessed it in action. But even now, he realised, the fine bloom of the exotic was rubbed off and it was his own entrance which had destroyed it. The atmosphere of conviviality had stiffened. Spence had risen, the maids hovered uneasily on the edges of their chairs. He did his best and it was a good best, but evidently Fox, who was an innocent snob, had been bragging about him and they all called him "sir."

"Well," he said cheerfully, "if Mr. Fox has been on this job there'll be no need for me to bother any of you. This is the best coffee I've drunk for years."

"I am gratified," said M. Dupont in fluent English. "At present, of course, one cannot obtain the fresh beans as readily as one desires."

Mademoiselle Hortense said: "Naturally," and the others made small affirmative noises.

"I suppose," Fox said genially, "his lordship's very particular about his coffee. Particular about everything, I dare say?" he added, invitingly.

William, the footman, laughed sardonically and was checked by a glance from Spence. Fox prattled on. It would be her ladyship, of course, who was particular about coffee. Being of Mlle. Hortense's and M. Dupont's delightful nationality. He attempted this compliment in French, got bogged down, and told Alleyn that M. Dupont had been giving him a lesson. Mr. Alleyn, he informed the company, spoke French like a native. Looking up, Alleyn found Spence gazing at him with an expression of anxiety.

"I'm afraid this is a great nuisance for all of you," Alleyn said.

"It's not that, sir," Spence rejoined slowly. "It does put us all about very much, I can't deny. Not being able to get things done in the usual way——"

"I'm sure," Miss Parker intervened, "I don't know what her ladyship's going to say about the first floor. Leaving everything. It's very awkward."

"Exactly. But the worrying thing," Spence went on, "is not knowing what it's all about. Having the police in, sir, and everything. Just because the party from this house happens to be present when this Mr. Rivera passes away in a restaurant."

"Quite so," said Miss Parker.

"The circumstances," Alleyn said carefully, "are extraordinary. I don't know if Inspector Fox has told you——"

Fox said that he had been anxious not to distress the ladies. Alleyn thought that the ladies looked as if they were half-dead with curiosity, agreed that Fox had shown great delicacy but added that it would have to come out sometime.

"Mr. Rivera," he said, "was killed."

They stirred attentively. Myrtle, the younger of the maids, ejaculated "Murdered?" clapped her hand over her mouth and suppressed a nervous giggle. Alleyn said it looked very much like it and added that he hoped they would all co-operate as far as they were able in helping to clear the ground. He had known, before he met it, what their response would be. People were all very much alike when it came to homicide cases. They wanted to be removed to a comfortable distance where curiosity could be assuaged, prestige maintained, and personal responsibility dissolved. With working people this wish was deepened by a heritage of insecurity and the necessity to maintain caste. They were filled with a kind of generic anxiety: at once disturbed by an indefinite threat and stimulated by a crude and potent assault on their imagination.

"It's a matter," he said, "of clearing innocent people, of tidying them up. I'm sure you would be glad to help us in this, if you can."

He produced Lord Pastern's time-table, spread it out before Spence, and told them who had compiled it.

"If you can help us check these times, any of you, we shall be very grateful," he said.

Spence put on his spectacles and with an air of slight embarrassment began to read the time-table. The others, at

Alleyn's suggestion, collected round him, not altogether unwillingly.

"It's a bit elaborate, isn't it?" Alleyn said. "Let's see if it
can be simplified at all. You see that between half-past eight
and nine the ladies left the dining-room and went to the
drawing-room. So we get the two groups in the two rooms.
Can any of you add to or confirm that?"

Spence could. It was a quarter to nine when the ladies went
to the drawing-room. When he came away from serving their
coffee he passed Lord Pastern and Mr. Bellairs on the landing.
They went into his lordship's study. Spence continued on
through the dining-room, paused there to see that William
had served coffee to the gentlemen and noticed that Mr. Manx
and Mr. Rivera were still sitting over their wine. He then
went into the servants' hall, where a few minutes later he
heard the nine o'clock news on the wireless.

"So now," Alleyn said, "we have three groups. The ladies
in the drawing-room, his lordship and Mr. Bellairs in the study,
and Mr. Manx and Mr. Rivera in the dining-room. Can anyone tell us when the next move came and who made it?"

Spence remembered coming back into the dining-room and
finding Mr. Manx there alone. His reticence at this point became more marked, but Alleyn got from him the news that
Edward Manx had helped himself to a stiff whisky. He asked
casually if there was anything about his manner which was
at all remarkable, and got the surprising answer that Mr.
Edward seemed to be very pleased and said he'd had a wonderful surprise.

"And now," Alleyn said, "Mr. Rivera has broken away
from the other groups. Where has he gone? Mr. Manx is in
the dining-room, his lordship and Mr. Bellairs in the study, the
ladies in the drawing-room, and where is Mr. Rivera?"

He looked round the group of faces with their guarded un-
willing expressions until he saw William, and in William's eye
he caught a zealous glint. William, he thought, with any luck
read detective magazines and spent his day-dreams sleuthing.
"Got an idea?" he asked.

"Well, sir," William said, glancing at Spence, "if you'll
excuse me, I think his lordship and Mr. Bellairs have parted

company where you've got to. I was tidying the hall, sir, and I heard the other gentleman, Mr. Bellairs, come out of the study. I glanced up at the landing, like. And I heard his lordship call out he'd join him in a minute and I saw the gentleman go into the ballroom. I went and got the coffee-tray from the drawing-room, sir. The ladies were all there. I put it down on the landing and was going to set the study to rights, when I heard the typewriter in there. His lordship doesn't like being disturbed when he's typing, sir, so I took the tray by the staff-stairs to the kitchen and after a few minutes came back. And his lordship must have gone into the ballroom while I was downstairs because I could hear him talking very loudly to Mr. Bellairs, sir."

"What about, do you remember?"

William glanced again at Spence and said: "Well, sir, it was something about his lordship telling somebody something if Mr. Bellairs didn't want to. And then there was a terrible loud noise. Drums. And a report like a gun. They all heard it down here in the hall, sir."

Alleyn looked at the listening staff. Miss Parker said coldly that his lordship was no doubt practising, as if Lord Pastern was in the habit of loosing off firearms indoors and there was nothing at all remarkable in the circumstance. Alleyn felt that both she and Spence were on the edge of giving William a piece of their minds and he hurried on.

"What did you do next?" he asked William.

He had been, it appeared, somewhat shattered by the report, but had remembered his duties. "I crossed the landing, sir, thinking I'd get on with the study, but Miss de Suze came out of the drawing-room. And then—well, the murdered gentleman, he came from the dining-room and they met and she said she wanted to speak to him alone and they went into the study."

"Sure of that?"

Yes, it appeared that William was perfectly certain. He had lingered evidently at the end of the landing. He even remembered that Miss de Suze had something in her hand. He wasn't sure what it was. Something bright, it might have been, he said doubtfully. After she and the gentleman had gone into

the study and shut the door, Miss Henderson had come out of
the drawing-room and gone upstairs.

Alleyn said : "Now, that's a great help. You see it corres-
ponds exactly so far with his lordship's time-table. I'll just
check it over, Fox, if you . . ."

Fox took the tip neatly and, while Alleyn affected to study
Lord Pastern's notes, continued what he liked to call the
painless extraction method with William. It must, he said,
have been awkward for William. You couldn't go barking in
on a tête-à-tête, could you, and yet a chap liked to get his job
done. Life, said Fox, was funny when you came to think of it.
Here was this poor young lady happily engaged in conversation with, well, he supposed he wasn't giving any secrets away
if he said with her fiancé, and little did she think that in a
couple of hours or so he would be lying dead. Miss Parker
and the maids were visibly moved by this. William turned
extremely red in the face and shuffled his feet. "She'll treasure
every word of that last talk, I'll be bound," said Fox. "Every
word of it." He looked inquiringly at William, who, after a
longish pause, blurted out very loud : "I wouldn't go so far
as to say that, Mr. Fox."

"That'll do, Will," said Spence quietly, but Fox's voice
over-rode him.

"Is that so?" Fox inquired blandly. "You wouldn't? Why
not?"

"Because," William announced boldly, "they was at it
hammer-and-tongs."

"*Will!*"

William turned to his superior. "I ought to tell the truth,
didn't I, Mr. Spence? To the police?"

"You ought to mind your own business," said Miss Parker
with some emphasis, and Spence murmured his agreement.

"All right, then," William said, huffily. "I'm sure I don't
want to push myself in where I'm not welcome."

Fox was extremely genial and complimented William on
his natural powers of observation and Miss Parker and Spence
upon their loyalty and discretion. He suggested, without
exactly stating as much and keeping well on the safe side of
police procedure, that any statements anybody offered would,

by some mysterious alchemy, free all concerned of any breath
of suspicion. In a minute or two he had discovered that sharp-
eared William, still hovering on the landing, had seen Rivera
go into the ballroom and had overheard most of his quarrel
with Breezy Bellairs. To this account Spence and Miss Parker
raised no objections and it was tolerably obvious that they had
already heard it. It became clear that Mlle. Hortense was stifl-
ing with repressed information. But she had her eye on Alleyn
and it was to him that she addressed herself. She had that
particular knack, that peculiar talent commanded by so many
of her countrywomen, of making evident, without the slightest
emphasis, her awareness of her own attractions and those of
the man to whom she was speaking. Alleyn, she seemed to
assume, would understand perfectly that she was the confidante
of Mademoiselle. M. Dupont, who had remained aloof, now
assumed an air of gloomy acquiescence. It was understood,
he said, that the relationship between a personal maid and her
mistress was one of delicacy and confidence.

"About *l'affaire Rivera* . . .?" suggested Fox, doggedly
Gallic.

Hortense lifted her shoulders and rocked her head slightly.
She addressed herself to Alleyn. Undoubtedly this M. Rivera
had been passionately attached. That was evident. And Mademoiselle had responded, being extremely impressionable. But
an engagement? Not precisely. He had urged it. There had
been scenes. Reconciliations. Further scenes. But last night!
She suddenly executed a complicated and vivid gesture with
her right hand as if she wrote something off on the air. And
against the unuttered but almost tangible disapproval of the
English servants, Hortense, with a darting incisiveness, said:
"Last night everything was ended. But irrevocably *ended*."

2

It appeared that at twenty to ten Hortense was summoned
to Lady Pastern's bedroom, where she prepared her for the
road, putting her into a cloak, and adding, Alleyn supposed,
some kind of super-gloss to that already immaculate surface.
Hortense kept an eye on the time as the car was ordered for

10.30 and Lady Pastern liked to have leisure. About ten
minutes later Miss Henderson had come in with the news that
Félicité was extremely excited and wished to make an elaborate change in her *toilette*. She herself was sent to Félicité's
room.

" And conceive the scene, Monsieur ! " said Hortense, breaking into her native tongue. " The room is complete disarray
and Mademoiselle in *déshabille*. There must be a completely
new *toilette,* you understand. Everything, from the founda-
tion, is it not? And while I dress her she relates the whole
story. With M. Rivera it is as if it had never been. There has
been a formidable quarrel. She had dismissed him forever and
in the meantime a letter has arrived in romantic circumstances.
It is a letter from a journalistic gentleman she has never seen
but with whom she has corresponded frequently. He is about
to reveal himself. He declares his passionate attachment. Yet
secrecy must be observed. And for myself," Hortense added
with conscious rectitude, " I would never, never have allowed
myself to repeat one syllable of this matter if it had not become my duty to assure Monsieur that as far as Mademoiselle
is concerned, she had no further interest in M. Rivera and
was happily released from him and that this is not therefore
a *crime passionelle.*"

" I see," Alleyn said. " Yes, perfectly. It is understood."
Hortense gave him a soubrettish glance and a hard smile.

" And do you know," he said, " who this person was? The
letter writer?"

Félicité, it appeared, had shown her the letter. And as the
party was leaving for the Metronome, Hortense had run downstairs with Lady Pastern's vinaigrette and had seen (with
what emotion!) M. Edward Manx wearing a white flower in
his coat. All was revealed! And how great, Hortense had
reflected as Spence closed the front door on their departure,
how overwhelming would be the joy of her ladyship, who had
always desired this union! Hortense had been quite unable to
conceal her own gratification and had sung for pure joy as she
rejoined her colleagues in the servants' hall. Her colleagues,
with the exception of M. Dupont, now cast black glances at
her and refrained from comment.

Alleyn checked over the events related by Hortense and

found that they corresponded as nearly as made no difference
with the group movements suggested by Lord Pastern's notes.
From the nucleus of persons, further individuals had broken
away. Manx had been alone in the drawing-room. Lady Pastern had been alone in her room until Hortense arrived. Hortense herself, and William, had cruised about the house and
so had Spence. Alleyn was about to lay down his pencil when
he remembered Miss Henderson. She had gone to her room
earlyish in the evening and had presumably stayed there until
she was visited by Félicité and herself reported this incident to
Lady Pastern. It was odd, he thought, that he should have forgotten Miss Henderson.

But there were still a good many threads to be caught up
and introduced into the texture. He referred again to Lord
Pastern's notes. At 9.26, the notes declared specifically, Lord
Pastern, then in the ballroom, had suddenly recollected the
sombrero which he desired to wear in his own number. He
had glanced at his watch, perhaps, and taken alarm. The note
merely said : " 9.26. Self. Ballroom. Sombrero. Search for.
All over house. William. Spence. Etc."

Questioned on this matter the servants willingly recalled
the characteristic hullaballo that had been raised in this search.
It set in immediately after the last event related by William.
Félicité and Rivera were in the study, Miss Henderson was on
her way upstairs and William himself was hovering on the
landing, when Lord Pastern shot out of the ballroom, shout-
ing : "Where's my sombrero?" In no time the hunt was in
full cry. Spence, William and Lord Pastern scattered in various
directions. The sombrero was finally discovered by Miss Henderson (she was no doubt the " etc." of the notes) in a cupboard on the top landing. Lord Pastern appeared with the
thing on his head and re-entered the ballroom in triumph.
During this uproar Spence, questing in the hall, had found a
letter on the table addressed to Miss de Suze.

Here the narrative was interrupted by a dignified passage-
of-arms between Spence, William and the parlourmaid, Mary.
Mr. Spence, William said resentfully, had torn a strip off him
for not taking the letter in to Miss Félicité as soon as it
came. William had denied knowledge of the letter and had
not opened the door to any district messenger. Nor had Mary.

Nor had anyone else. Spence obviously considered that some-one was lying. Alleyn asked if any of them had seen the envelope. Hortense, needlessly dramatic, cried out that she had tidied an envelope up from the floor of Mademoiselle's bedroom. Fox held a smothered colloquy about rubbish bins with William, who made an excited exit and returned, flushed with modest triumph, to lay a crushed and stained envelope on the table before Alleyn. Alleyn recognised the eccentricities of Lord Pastern's typewriter and pocketed the envelope.

" It's my belief, Mr. Spence," William announced boldly, " that there never was a district messenger."

Leaving them no time to digest this theory, Alleyn con-tinued with the business of checking Lord Pastern's time-table. Spence, still very anxious, said that having discovered the letter on the hall table, he had come upstairs and taken it into the drawing-room, where he found only his mistress, Miss Wayne, and Mr. Manx, who, he thought, had not long arrived there from the dining-room. On returning to the landing Spence encountered Miss de Suze, coming out of the study, and gave her the letter. Sounds of the sombrero-hunt reached him from upstairs. He was about to join it when a cry of triumph from Lord Pastern reassured him, and he returned to the servants' quarters. He had noticed the time: 9.45.

" And at that time," Alleyn said, " Lady Pastern and Miss Wayne are about to leave Mr. Manx alone in the drawing-room and go upstairs. Miss de Suze and Miss Henderson are already in their rooms and Lord Pastern is about to descend, wearing his sombrero. Mr. Bellairs and Mr. Rivera are in the ballroom. We have 45 minutes to go before the party leaves for the Metronome. What happens next?"

But he had struck a blank. Apart from Hortense's previous account of her visits to the ladies upstairs there was little to be learned from the servants. They had kept to their own quar-ters until a few minutes before the departure to the Metro-nome, Spence and William had gone into the hall, assisted the gentlemen into their overcoats, given them their hats and gloves, and seen them into their cars.

" Who," Alleyn asked, " helped Mr. Rivera into his coat?" William had done this.

"Did you notice anything about him? Anything at all out of the ordinary, however slight?"

William said sharply: "The gentleman had a—well, a funny ear, sir. Red and bleeding a bit. A cauliflower ear, as you might say."

"Had you noticed this earlier in the evening? When you leant over his chair, serving him, at dinner, for instance?"

"No, sir. It was all right then, sir."

"Sure?"

"Swear to it," said William crisply.

"You think carefully, Will, before you make statements," Spence said uneasily.

"I know I'm right, Mr. Spence."

"How do you imagine he came by this injury?" Alleyn asked.

William grinned, pure Cockney. "Well, sir, if you'll excuse the expression, I'd say somebody handed the gentleman a fourpenny-one."

"Who, at a guess?"

William rejoined promptly: "Seeing he was holding his right hand, tender-like, in his left and seeing the way the murdered gentleman looked at him so fierce, I'd say it was Mr. Edward Manx, sir."

Hortense broke into a spate of excited and gratified comment. M. Dupont made a wide, conclusive gesture and exclaimed: "Perfectly! It explains itself!" Mary and Myrtle ejaculated incoherently while Spence and Miss Parker, in a single impulse, rose and shouted awfully: "That WILL DO, William."

Alleyn and Fox left them, still greatly excited, and retraced their steps to the downstairs hall.

"What have we got out of that little party," Alleyn grunted, "beyond confirmation of old Pastern's time-table up to half an hour before they all left the house?"

"Damn all, sir. And what does that teach us?" Fox grumbled. "Only that every man-jack of them was alone at some time or another and might have got hold of the parasol handle, taken it to the study, fixed this silly little stiletto affair in the end with plastic wood and then done Gawd-knows-what. Every man-jack of 'em."

" And every woman-jill?"

" I suppose so. Wait a bit, though."

Alleyn gave him the time-table and his own notes. They had moved into the entrance lobby, closing the inner glass-doors behind them. " Mull it over in the car," Alleyn said. " I think there's a bit more to be got out of it, Fox. Come on."

But as Alleyn was about to open the front door Fox gave a sort of grunt and he turned back to see Félicité de Suze on the stairs. She was dressed for the day and in the dim light of the hall looked pale and exhausted. For a moment they stared at each other through the glass panel and then tentatively, uncertainly, she made an incomplete gesture with one hand. Alleyn swore under his breath and re-entered the hall.

" Do you want to speak to me?" he said. " You're up very early."

" I couldn't sleep."

" I'm sorry," he said formally.

" I think I do want to speak to you."

Alleyn nodded to Fox, who re-entered the hall.

" Alone," said Félicité.

" Inspector Fox is acting with me in this case."

She glanced discontentedly at Fox. " All the same," she said, and then as Alleyn made no answer : " Oh, well !"

She was on the third step from the foot of the stairs, standing there boldly, aware of the picture she made. " Lisle told me," she said, " about you and the letter. Getting it from her, I mean. I suppose you take rather a dim view of my sending Lisle to do my dirty work, don't you?"

" It doesn't arise."

" I was all bouleversée. I know it was rather awful letting her go, but I think in a way she quite enjoyed it." He noticed that her upper lip was fuller than the under one and that when she smiled it curved richly. " Darling Lisle," she said, " doesn't have much fun and she's so madly interested always in other people's little flutters." She watched Alleyn out of the corners of her eyes and added : " We're all devoted to her."

" What do you want to ask me, Miss de Suze?"

" Please may I have the letter back? Please !"

" In due course," he said. " Certainly."

" Not now?"

"I'm afraid, not now."

"That's rather a bore," said Félicité. "I suppose I'd better come clean in a big way."

"If it's relevant to the matter in hand," Alleyn agreed. "I am only concerned with the death of Mr. Carlos Rivera."

She leant back against the banister, stretching her arms along it and looking downwards, arranging herself for him to look at. "I'd suggest we went somewhere where we could sit down," she said, "but here seems to be the only place where there's no lurking minor detective."

"Let it be here, then."

"You are not," Félicité said, "making this very easy."

"I'm sorry. I shall be glad to hear what you have to say, but to tell the truth, there's a heavy day's work in front of us."

They stood there, disliking each other. Alleyn thought: "She's going to be one of the tricky ones. She may have nothing to say; I know the signs but I can't be sure of them." And Félicité thought: "I didn't really notice him last night. If he'd known what Carlos was like he'd have despised me. He's taller than Ned. I'd like him to be on my side thinking how courageous and young and attractive I am. Younger than Lisle, for instance, with two men in love with me. I wonder what sort of women he likes. I suppose I'm frightened."

She slid down into a sitting position on the stairs and clasped her hands about her knees; young and a bit boyish, a touch of the *gamine*.

"It's about this wretched letter. Well, not wretched at all, really, because it's from a chap I'm very fond of. You've read it, of course."

"I'm afraid so."

"My dear, I don't *mind*. Only, as you've seen, it's by way of being number one secrecy and I'll feel a bit low if it all comes popping out, particularly as it's got utterly *no* connection with your little game. It just couldn't be less relevant."

"Good."

"But I suppose I've got to prove that, haven't I?"

"It would be an excellent move if you can."

"Here we go, then," said Félicité.

Alleyn listened wearily, pinning his attention down to the
recital, shutting out the thought of time sliding away, and of
his wife who would soon wake and look to see if he was there.
Félicité told him that she had corresponded with G.P.F. of
Harmony and that his advice had been too marvellously understanding and that she had felt an urge like the kick of a mule
to meet him but that although his replies had grown more
and more come-to-ish he had insisted that his identity must
remain hidden. " All Cupid-and-Psycheish only definitely less
rewarding," she said. And then the letter had arrived and
Edward Manx had appeared with a white flower in his coat
and, suddenly, after never having gone much for old Ned,
she had felt astronomically uplifted. Because, after all, it was
rather bracing, wasn't it, to think that all the time Ned was
G.P.F. and writing these really gorgeous things and falling for
one like a dray-load of bricks? Here Félicité paused and then
added rather hurriedly and with an air of hauteur : " You'll
understand that by this time poor Carlos had, from my point
of view, become comparatively a dim figure. I mean, to be as
bald as an egg about it, he just faded out. I mean it couldn't
have mattered less about Carlos because clearly I wasn't his
cup-of-tea and we'd both gone tepid on it and I knew he
wouldn't mind. You do see what I mean about that, don't
you?"

" Are you trying to tell me that you and Rivera had parted
as friends?"

Félicité shook her head vaguely and raised her eyebrows.
" Even that makes it sound too important," she said. " It all
just came peacefully unstuck."

" And there was no quarrel, for instance, when you and he
were in the study between a quarter and half-past nine? Or
later, between Mr. Manx and Mr. Rivera?"

There was a long pause. Félicité bent forward and jerked at
the strap of her shoe. " What in the world," she said indistinctly, " put these quaint little notions into your head?"

" Are they completely false?"

" I know," she said loudly and cheerfully. She looked up
into his face. " You've been gossiping with the servants." She
appealed to Fox. " Hasn't he?" she demanded playfully.

" I'm sure I couldn't say, Miss de Suze," said Fox blandly.

"How could you!" she accused Alleyn. "Which of them was it? Was it Hortense? My poor Mr. Alleyn, you don't know Hortense. She's the world's most accomplished liar! She just can't help herself, poor thing. It's pathological."

"So there was no quarrel?" Alleyn said. "Between any of you?"

"My dear, haven't I told you?"

"Then why," he asked, "did Mr. Manx punch Mr. Rivera over the ear?"

Félicité's eyes and mouth opened. Then she hunched her shoulders and caught the tip of her tongue between her teeth. He could have sworn she was astonished and in a moment it was evident that she was gratified.

"No!" she said. "Honestly? Ned did? Well, I must say I call that a handsome tribute. When did it happen? Before we went down to the Met.? After dinner? When?"

Alleyn looked steadily at her. "I thought," he said, "that perhaps you could tell me that."

"I? But I promise you . . ."

"Had he got a trickle of blood on his ear when you talked to him in the study? On the occasion, you know, when you say there was no quarrel?"

"Let me think," said Félicité, and rested her head on her crossed arms. But the movement was not swift enough. He had seen the blank look of panic in her eyes. "No." Her voice muffled by her arms, said slowly, "No, I'm sure . . ."

There was some change of light above, where the stairs ran up to the first landing. He looked up. Carlisle Wayne stood there in the shadow. Her figure and posture still retained the effect of movement, as if while she came downstairs, she had suddenly been held in suspension as the action of a motion picture may be suspended to give emphasis to a specific moment. Over Félicité's bent head, Alleyn with a slight movement of his hand arrested Carlisle's descent. Félicité had begun to speak again.

"After all," she was saying, "one is a bit uplifted. It's not every day in the week that people give other people cauliflower ears for love of one's bright eyes." She raised her face and looked at him. "How naughty of Ned, but how sweet of him. Darling Ned!"

"No, really!" said Carlisle strongly, "this is too much!"
Félicité, with a stifled cry, was on her feet.

Alleyn said : "Hallo, Miss Wayne. Good-morning to you.
Have you any theory about why Mr. Manx gave Rivera a clip
over the ear? He did give him a clip, you know. Why?"

"If you must know," Carlisle said in a high voice, "it was
because Rivera kissed me when we met on the landing."

"Good lord!" Alleyn ejaculated, "why didn't you say so
before? Kissed *you*, did he? Did you like it?"

"Don't be a *bloody* fool!" Carlisle shouted and bolted upstairs.

"I must say," Félicité said, "I call that rather poor of
darling Lisle."

"If you'll excuse us," Alleyn said. He and Fox left her
staring thoughtfully at her fingernails.

3

"A shave," Alleyn said in the car, "a bath and with luck
two hours' sleep. I'll take it out at home. We'll send the stuff
on to the experts. What about you, Fox? Troy will be delighted to fix you up."

"Thank you very much, sir, but I wouldn't think of troubl-
ing Mrs. Alleyn. There's a little place——"

"Be damned to your little place. I've had enough insubor-
dination from you, my lad. To hell with you. You're coming
to us."

Fox accepted this singular invitation in the spirit in which it
was made. He took out his spectacles, Alleyn's note-book and
Lord Pastern's time-table. Alleyn dragged his palm across his
jaw, shuddered, yawned and closed his eyes. "A hideous
curse on this case," he murmured, and appeared to sleep. Fox
began to whisper to himself. The car slipped down Cliveden
Place, into Grosvenor Place, into Hyde Park Corner. "T, t, t,"
Fox whispered over the time-table.

"You sound," Alleyn said without opening his eyes, "like
Dr. Johnson on his way to Streatham. Can you crack your
joints, Foxkin?"

"I see what you mean about this ruddy time-table."

"What *did* I mean? Split me and sink me if I know what I meant."

"Well, sir, our customer, whoever he or she may be, and you know my views on the point, had to be in the ballroom to pick up the bit of umbrella shaft, in the drawing-room to collect the stiletto and alone in the study to fix the stiletto in the bit of umbrella shaft with plastic wood."

"You'll be coming round the mountain when you come."

"It *is* a bit of a mountain and that's a fact. According to what the young lady, Miss Wayne, I mean, told you, sir, this perishing parasol was all right before dinner when she was in the ballroom and handled it, and according to her, his lordship was in the study drawing the bullets out of the cartridges. If that's correct he didn't get a chance to play the fool with the parasol before dinner. What's more it fits in with his lordship's own statement, which Bellairs can speak to, if he ever wakes up, that he took the parasol to bits on the piano *after* dinner. For fun."

"Quite."

"All right. Now where does this get us? If the time-table's correct, his lordship was never alone in the study after that."

"And the only time he was alone at all, moreover, he was up and down the house, bellowing like a bull for his sombrero."

"Doesn't that look like establishing an alibi?" Fox demanded.

"It looks a bit like the original alibi itself, Br'er Fox."

"He might have carried the tube of plastic wood round in his pocket."

"So he might. Together with the bit of parasol and the stiletto, pausing in mid-bellow to fix the job."

"Gah! How about him just taking the stuff in his pocket to the Metronome and fixing everything there?"

"Oh, lord! When? How?"

"Lavatory?" Fox suggested hopefully.

"And when did he put the weapon in the gun? Skelton looked down the barrel just before they started playing, don't forget."

The car had stopped at traffic lights in Piccadilly. Fox contemplated the Green Park with disapproval. Alleyn still kept his eyes shut. Big Ben struck seven.

"By gum!" Fox said, bringing his palm down on his knee, "by gum, how about this? How about his lordship in his damn-your-eyes fashion fitting the weapon into the gun while he sat there behind his drums? In front of everybody, while one of the other turns was on? It's amazing what you can do when you brazen it out. What's that yarn they're always quoting, sir? I've got it. *The Purloined Letter*! Proving that if you make a thing obvious enough nobody notices it?"

Alleyn opened one eye. "*The Purloined Letter*," he said. He opened the other eye. "Fox, my cabbage, my rare edition, *my objet d'art*, my own especial bit of *bijouterie*, be damned if I don't think you've caught an idea. Come on. Let's further think of this."

They talked intensively until the car pulled up, in a cul-de-sac off Coventry Street, before Alleyn's flat.

Early sunlight streamed into the little entrance hall. Beneath a Benozzo Gozzoli, a company of dahlias, paper-white in a blue bowl, cast translucent shadows on a white parchment wall. Alleyn looked about him contentedly.

"Troy's under orders not to get up till eight," he said. "You take first whack at the bath, Fox, while I have a word with her. Use my razor. Wait a bit." He disappeared and returned with towels. "There'll be something to eat at half-past nine," he said. "The visitor's room's all yours, Fox. Sleep well."

"Very kind, I'm sure," said Fox. "May I send my compliments to Mrs. Alleyn, sir?"

"She'll be delighted to receive them. See you later."

Troy was awake in her white room, sitting up with her head aureoled in short locks of hair. "Like a faun," Alleyn said, "or a bronze dahlia. Are you well this morning?"

"Bouncing, thanks. And you?"

"As you see. Unhousled, unannealed and un-everything that's civilised."

"A poor state of affairs," said Troy. "You look like the gentleman in that twenty-foot canvas in the Luxembourg. Boiled shirt in dents and gazing out over Paris through lush curtains. I think it's called 'The Hopeless Dawn'! His floozy is still asleep in an elephantine bed, you remember."

"I don't remember. Talking of floozies, oughtn't you to be asleep yourself?"

"God bless my soul!" Troy complained, "I haven't been bitten by the tsetse-fly. It's getting on for nine hours since I went to bed, damn it."

"O.K. O.K."

"What's happened, Rory?"

"One of the kind we don't fancy."

"Oh, *no*."

"You'll hear about it anyway, so I may as well tell you. It's that florid number we saw playing the piano accordion, the one with the teeth and hair."

"You don't mean——"

"Somebody pinked him with a sort of dagger made out of a bit of a parasol and a needlework stiletto."

"Gatcha!"

He explained at some length.

"Well but . . ." Troy stared at her husband. "When have you got to be at the Yard?"

"Ten."

"All right. You've got two hours and time for breakfast. Good-morning, darling."

"Fox is in the bathroom. I know I'm not fit for a lady's bed-chamber."

"Who said?"

"If you didn't, nobody." He put his arm across her and stooped his head. "Troy," he said, "may I ask Fox this morning?"

"If you want to, my dearest."

"I think I might. How much, at a rough guess, would you say I loved you?"

"*Words* fail me," said Troy, imitating the late Harry Tate.

"And me."

"There's Mr. Fox coming out of the bathroom. Away with you."

"I suppose so. Good-morning, Mrs. Quiverful."

On his way to the bathroom Alleyn looked in upon Fox. He found him lying on the visitor's room bed, without his jacket but incredibly neat; his hair damp, his jaw gleaming, his shirt stretched tight over his thick pectoral muscles. His eyes were closed but he opened them as Alleyn looked in.

"I'll call you at half-past nine," Alleyn said. "Did you know you were going to be a godfather, Br'er Fox?" And as Fox's eyes widened he shut the door and went whistling to the bathroom.

CHAPTER NINE

THE YARD

I

At TEN-THIRTY in the Chief-Inspector's room at New Scotland Yard, routine procedure following a case of homicide was efficiently established.

Alleyn sat at his desk taking reports from Detective-Sergeants Gibson, Watson, Scott and Sallis. Mr. Fox, with that air of good humour crossed with severity, which was his habitual reaction to reports following observation, listened critically to his juniors, each of whom held his official note-book. Six men going soberly about their day's work. Earlier that morning, in other parts of London, Captain Entwhistle, an expert on ballistics, had fitted a dart made from a piece of parasol into a revolver and had fired it into a bag of sand; Mr. Carrick, a Government analyst, had submitted a small cork to various tests for certain oils; and Sir Grantly Morton, the famous pathologist, assisted by Curtis, had opened Carlos Rivera's thorax, and, with the greatest delicacy, removed his heart.

"All right," Alleyn said. "Get yourselves chairs and smoke if you want to. This is liable to be a session."

When they were settled, he pointed the stem of his pipe at a heavy-jawed, straw-coloured detective-sergeant with a habitually startled expression. "You searched the deceased's rooms, didn't you, Gibson? Let's take you first."

Gibson thumbed his note-book open, contemplated it in

apparent astonishment and embarked on a high-pitched recital.

"*The deceased man, Carlos Rivera,*" he said, "*lived at 102 Bedford Mansions, Austerley Square, S.W.1. Service Flat. Rental £500 a year.*"

"Why don't we all play piano accordions?" Fox asked of nobody in particular.

"*At 3 a.m. on the morning of June 1st,*" Gibson continued in a shrillish voice, "*having obtained a search warrant, I effected entrance to above premises by means of a key on a ring removed from the body of the deceased. The flat consists of an entrance lobby, six-by-eight feet, a sitting-room twelve-by-fourteen, and a bedroom nine-by-eleven feet. Furnishings:—Sitting-room: Carpet, purple, thick. Curtains, full length, purple satin.*"

"Stay me with flagons!" Alleyn muttered. "Purple."

"You might call it morve, Mr. Alleyn."

"Well, go on."

"*Couch, upholstered green velvet, three arm-chairs ditto, dining-table, six dining-chairs, open fireplace. Walls painted fawn. Cushions: Seven. Green and purple satin.*" He glanced at Alleyn. "I beg pardon, Mr. Alleyn? Anything wrong?"

"Nothing. Nothing. Go on."

"*Bookcase. Fourteen books. Foreign. Recognised four as on police lists. Pictures: four.*"

"What were *they* like?" Fox asked.

"Never you mind, you dirty old man," said Alleyn.

"Two were nood studies, Mr. Fox, what you might call heavy pin-ups. The others were a bit more so. *Cigarette boxes: four. Cigarettes, commercial product. Have taken one from each box. Wall safe. Combination lock but found note of number in deceased's pocket book. Contents:——*"

"Half a minute," Alleyn said. "Have all the flats got these safes?"

"I ascertained from inquiries, sir, that deceased had his installed."

"Right. Go on."

"*Contents. I removed a number of papers, two ledgers or account books and a locked cash box containing three hundred pounds in notes of low denomination, and thirteen shillings in silver."* Here Gibson paused of his own accord.

"There now!" said Fox. "Now we *may* be on to something."

"*I left a note of the contents of the safe in the safe and I locked the safe,*" said Gibson, on a note of uncertainty, induced perhaps by misgivings about his prose style. "Shall I produce the contents now, sir, or go on to the bedroom?"

"I doubt if I can take the bedroom," Alleyn said. "But go on."

"It was done up in black, sir. Black satin."

"Do you put all this in your notes?" Fox demanded suddenly. "All this about colours and satin?"

"They tell us to be thorough, Mr. Fox."

"There's a medium to all things," Fox pronounced sombrely. "I beg pardon, Mr. Alleyn."

"Not at all, Br'er Fox. The bedroom, Gibson."

But there wasn't anything much to the purpose in Gibson's meticulous account of Rivera's bedroom unless the revelation that he wore black satin pyjamas with embroidered initials could be called, as Alleyn suggested, damning and conclusive evidence as to character. Gibson produced the spoil of the wall-safe and they examined it. Alleyn took the ledgers and Fox the bundle of correspondence. For some time there was silence, broken only by the whisper of papers.

Presently, however, Fox brought his palm down on his knees and Alleyn, without looking up, said: "Hallo?"

"Peculiar," Fox grunted. "Listen to this, sir."

"Go ahead."

"'How tender,'" Mr. Fox began, "is the first burgeoning of love! How delicate the tiny bud, how easily cut with frost! Touch it with gentle fingers, dear lad, lest its fragrance be lost to you forever.'"

"Cor'!" whispered Detective-Sergeant Scott.

"'You say,'" Mr. Fox continued, "'that she is changeable. So is a day in spring. Be patient. Wait for the wee petals to unfold. If you would care for a very special, etc.'" Fox removed his spectacles and contemplated his superior.

"What do you mean by your 'etc.,' Fox? Why don't you go on?"

" That's what it says. Etc. Then it stops. Look."

He flattened a piece of creased blue letter paper out on the desk before Alleyn. It was covered with typing, closely spaced. The Duke's Gate address was stamped on the top.

Alleyn said : " What's that you're holding back?"

Fox laid his second exhibit before him. It was a press-cutting and printed on paper of the kind used in the more exotic magazines. Alleyn read aloud : " ' Dear G.P.F., I am engaged to a young lady who at times is very affectionate and then again goes cold on me. It's not halitosis because I asked her and she said it wasn't and wished I wouldn't harp on about it. I am twenty-two, five-foot eleven in my socks and well built. I drag down £550 per annum. I am an A grade motor mechanic and I have prospects of a rise. She reckons she loves me and yet she acts like this. What should be my attitude? Spark-plug.' "

" I should advise a damn' good hiding," Alleyn said. " Poor old Spark-plug."

" Go on, sir. Read the answer."

Alleyn continued : " ' Dear Spark-plug. Yours is not as unusual a problem as perhaps you, in your distress of mind, incline to believe. How tender is the first burgeoning——!' Yes, here we go again. Yes. All right, Fox. You've found, apparently, a bit of the rough draft and the finished article. The draft, typed on Duke's Gate letter-paper, looks as if it had been crumpled up in somebody's pocket, doesn't it? Half a minute."

He opened his own file and in a moment the letter Félicité had dropped from her bag at the Metronome had been placed beside the other. Alleyn bent over them. " It's a pot-shot, of course," he said, " but I'm ready to bet it's the same machine. The ' s ' out of alignment. All the usual indications."

" Where does this lead us?" Fox asked. Gibson, looking gratified, cleared his throat. Alleyn said : " It leads us into a bit of a tangle. The letter to Miss de Suze was typed on the machine in Lord Pastern's study on the paper he uses for that purpose. The machine carried his dabs only. I took a chance and asked him, point-blank, how long he'd known that Edward Manx was G.P.F. He wouldn't answer but I'll swear I rocked him. I'll undertake he typed the letter after he saw Manx put a white carnation in his coat, marked the envelope, ' By District Messenger' and put it on the hall table where it was discovered by the butler. All right. Now, not so long ago, Manx stayed at Duke's Gate for three weeks and I suppose it's reasonable to assume that he may have used the typewriter and the blue letter-paper in the study when he was jotting down notes for his nauseating little G.P.F. numbers in *Harmony*. So this draft may have been typed by Manx. But, as far as we know, Manx met Rivera for the first time last night and incidentally dotted him what William pleasingly called a fourpenny one, because Rivera kissed, *not* Miss de Suze but Miss Wayne. Now, if we're right so far, how and when the hell did Rivera get hold of Manx's rough draft of this sickening G.P.F. stuff? Not last night, because we've got it from Rivera's safe, and he didn't go back to his rooms. Answer me that, Fox."

" Gawd knows."

" We don't, at all events. And if we find out, is it going to tie up with Rivera's murder? Well, press on, chaps, press on."

He returned to the ledger and Fox to the bundle of papers. Presently Alleyn said : " Isn't it extraordinary how business-like they are?"

" Who's that, Mr. Alleyn?"

" Why, blackmailers to be sure. Mr. Rivera was a man of parts, Fox. Piano accordions, drug-running, blackmail. Almost a pity we've got to nab his murderer. He was ripe for bumping off, was Mr. Rivera. This is a neatly kept record of monies and goods received and disbursed. On the 3rd of February, for instance, we have an entry. ' Cash, £150, 3rd instalment, S.F.F.' A week later, a cryptic note on the debit side : ' 6 doz. per S.S., £360,' followed by a series of credits : ' J.C.M., £10.' ' B.B. £100,' and so on. These entries are in a group by themselves. He's totted them up and balanced the whole thing, showing a profit of £200 on the original outlay of £360."

" That'll be his dope racket, by gum. ' S.S., did you say, Mr. Alleyn? By gum, I wonder if he *is* in with the Snowy Santos bunch."

" And ' B.B.' on the paying side. ' B.B.' is quite a profitable number on the paying side."

"Breezy Bellairs?"

"I shouldn't wonder. It looks to me, Fox, as if Rivera was a medium high-up in the drug racket. He was one of the boys we don't catch easily. It's long odds he never passed the stuff out direct to the small consumer. With the exception, no doubt, of the wretched Bellairs. No, I fancy Rivera's business was confined to his purple satin parlour. At the smallest sign of our getting anywhere near him, he'd have burnt his books and, if necessary, returned to his native hacienda or what have you."

"Or got in first by laying information against the small man. That's the line they take as often as not."

"Yes, indeed. As often as not. What else have you got in your lucky dip, Br'er Fox?"

"Letters," said Fox. "A sealed package. And the cash."

"Anything that chimes in with his book-keeping, I wonder."

"Wait a bit, sir. I wouldn't be surprised. Wait a bit."

They hadn't long to wait. The too-familiar raw material of the blackmailer's trade was soon laid out on Alleyn's desk: the dingy, colourless letters, paid for again and again, yet never redeemed, the discoloured clippings from dead newspapers, one or two desperate appeals for mercy, the inexorable entries on the credit side. Alleyn's fingers seemed to tarnish as he handled them but Fox rubbed his hands.

"This is something like," Fox said, and after a minute or two: "Look at this, Mr. Alleyn."

It was a letter signed "Félicité" and was some four months old. Alleyn read it through and handed it back to Fox, who said: "It establishes the relationship."

"Apparently."

"Funny," said Fox. "You'd have thought from the look of him, even when he was dead, that any girl in her senses would have picked him for what he was. There are two other letters. Much the same kind of thing."

"Yes."

"Yes. Well now," said Fox slowly. "Leaving the young lady aside for the moment, where, if anywhere, does this get us with his lordship?"

"Not very far, I fancy. Unless you find something reveal-

ing a hitherto unsuspected irregularity in his lordship's past
and he doesn't strike me as one to hide his riotings."

"All the same, sir, there may be something. What about
his lordship encouraging this affair with his stepdaughter?
Doesn't that look as if Rivera had a hold on him?"

"It might," Alleyn agreed, "if his lordship was anybody
but his lordship. But it might. So last night, having decided
to liquidate Rivera, he types this letter purporting to come from
G.P.F. with the idea of throwing the all-too-impressionable
Miss de Suze into Edward Manx's arms!"

"There you are!"

"How does Lord Pastern know Manx as G.P.F.? And if
Rivera used this G.P.F. copy to blackmail Manx it wasn't a
very hot instrument for his purpose, being typed. Anybody at
Duke's Gate might have typed it. He would have to find it on
Manx and try a bluff. And he hadn't met Manx. All right.
For purposes of your argument we needn't pursue that one at
the moment. All right. It fits. In a way. Only . . . only . . ."
He rubbed his nose. "I'm sorry, Fox, but I can't reconcile the
flavour of Pastern and Manx with all this. A most untenable
argument, I know. I won't try to justify it. What's in that
box?"

Fox had already opened it and shoved it across the desk.
"It'll be the stuff itself," he said. "A nice little haul, Gibson."

The box contained neat small packages, securely sealed and,
in a separate carton, a number of cigarettes.

"That'll be it," Alleyn agreed. "He wasn't the direct receiver, evidently. This will have come in by the usual damned
labyrinth." He glanced up at Detective-Sergeant Scott, a young
officer. "You haven't worked on any of these cases, I think,
Scott. This is probably cocaine or heroin, and has no doubt
travelled long distances in bogus false teeth, fat men's navels,
dummy aids to hearing, phoney bayonet fitments for electric
light bulbs and God knows what else. As Mr. Fox says,
Gibson, it's a nice little haul. We'll leave Rivera for the
moment, I think." He turned to Scott and Watson. "Let's
hear how you got on with Breezy Bellairs."

Breezy, it appeared, lived in a furnished flat in Pikestaff
Row, off Ebury Street. To this address Scott and Watson had
conveyed him, and with some difficulty put him to bed. Once

there, he had slept stertorously through the rest of the night. They had combed out the flat which, unlike Rivera's, was slovenly and disordered. It looked, they said, as if Breezy had had a frantic search for something. The pockets of his suits had been pulled out, the drawers of his furniture disembowelled and the contents left where they lay. The only thing in the flat that was at all orderly was Breezy's pile of band-parts. Scott and Watson had sorted out a bundle of correspondence consisting of bills, dunning reminders, and his fan-mail, which turned out to be largish. At the back of a small bedside cupboard they had found a hypodermic syringe which they produced, and a number of torn and empty packages which were of the same sort as those found in Rivera's safe.

"Almost too easy," said Mr. Fox with the liveliest satisfaction. "We knew it already, of course, through Skelton, but here's positive proof Rivera supplied Bellairs with his dope. By gum," he added deeply, "I'd like to get this line on the dope-racket followed in to one of the high-ups. Now, I wonder. Breezy'll be looking for his stuff and won't know where to find it. He'll be very upset. I ask myself if Breezy won't be in the mood to talk."

"You'd better remind yourself of your police code, old boy."

"It'll be the same story," Fox muttered. "Breezy won't know how Rivera got it. He won't know."

"He hasn't been long on the injection method," Alleyn said. "Curtis had a look for needle-marks and didn't find so very many."

"He'll be fretting for it, though," said Fox, and after a moment's pondering: "Oh, well. It's a homicide we're after."

Nothing more of interest had been found in Breezy's flat and Alleyn turned to the last of the men. "How did you get on with Skelton, Sallis?"

"Well, sir," said Sallis, in a loud public-school voice, "he didn't like me much to begin with. I picked up a search warrant on the way and he took a very poor view of that. However, we talked sociology for the rest of the journey and I offered to lend him *The Yogi and The Commissar*, which bent the barriers a little. He's Australian by birth, and I've been out there, so that helped to establish a more matey attitude."

"Get on with your report now," Fox said austerely. "Don't

meander. Mr. Alleyn isn't concerned to know how much Syd
Skelton loves you."

"I'm sorry, sir."

"Use your notes and get on with it," Fox counselled.

Sallis opened his note-book and got on with it. Beyond a
quantity of communistic literature there was little out of the
ordinary to be found in Skelton's rooms, which were in the
Pimlico Road. Alleyn gathered that Sallis had conducted his
search during a lively exchange of ideas and could imagine
Skelton's guarded response to Sallis's pinkish, facile and con-
sciously ironical observations. Finally, Skelton, in spite of
himself, had gone to sleep in his chair and Sallis then turned
his attention stealthily to a table which was used as a desk.

"I'd noticed that he seemed rather uneasy about this table,
sir. He stood by it when we first came in and shuffled the
papers about. I had the feeling there was something there that
he wanted to destroy. When he was safely off, I went through
the stuff on the table and I found this. I don't know if it's
much cop, really, sir, but here it is."

He gave a sheet of paper to Alleyn, who opened it up. It
was an unfinished letter to Rivera, threatening him with exposure if he continued to supply Breezy Bellairs with drugs.

2

The other men had gone and Alleyn invited Fox to embark
upon what he was in the habit of calling "a hag." This involved the ruthless taking to pieces of the case and a fresh
attempt to put the bits together in their true pattern. They
had been engaged upon this business for about half an hour
when the telephone rang. Fox answered it and announced
with a tolerant smile that Mr. Nigel Bathgate would like to speak
to Mr. Alleyn.

"I was expecting this," Alleyn said. "Tell him that for
once in a blue moon I want to see him. Where is he?"

"Down below."

"Hail him up."

Fox said sedately : "The Chief would like to see you, Mr.

Bathgate," and in a few moments Nigel Bathgate of the *Evening Chronicle* appeared, looking mildly astonished.

" I must say," he said, shaking hands, " that this is uncommonly civil of you, Alleyn. Have you run out of invectives or do you at last realise where the brains lie?"

" If you think I asked you up with the idea of feeding you with banner headlines you're woefully mistaken. Sit down."

" Willingly. How are you, Mr. Fox?"

" Nicely, thank you, sir. And you?"

Alleyn said : "Now, you attend to me. Can you tell me anything about a monthly called *Harmony*?"

" What sort of things? Have you been confiding in G.P.F., Alleyn?"

" I want to know who he is."

" Has this got anything to do with the Rivera case?"

" Yes, it has."

" I'll make a bargain with you. I want a nice meaty bit of stuff straight from the Yard's mouth. All about old Pastern and how you happened to be there and the shattered romance . . ."

" Who've you been talking to?"

" Charwomen, night porters, chaps in the band. And I ran into Ned Manx a quarter of an hour ago."

" What had he got to say for himself?"

" He hung out on me, blast him. Wouldn't utter. And he's not on a daily, either. Unco-operative twerp."

" You might remember he's the chief suspect's cousin."

" Then there's no doubt about it being old Pastern?"

" I didn't say so and you won't suggest it."

" Well, hell, give me a story."

" About this paper. *Do* you know G.P.F.? Come on."

Nigel lit a cigarette and settled down. " I don't know him," he said. " And I don't know anyone who does. He's a chap called G. P. Friend, I'm told, and he's supposed to own the show. If he does, he's on to a damn' useful thing. It's a mystery, that paper. It breaks all the rules and rings the bell. It first came out about two years ago with a great fanfare of trumpets. They bought out the old *Triple Mirror*, you know, and took over the plant and the paper and in less than no time trebled the sales. God knows why. The thing's a freak. It mixes sound criticism with girly-girly chat and runs top-

price serials alongside shorts that would bring a blush to the
cheeks of *Peg's Weekly*. They tell me it's G.P.F.'s page that
does the trick. And look at it! That particular racket blew
out before the war and yet he gets by with it. I'm told the
personal letters at five bob a time are a gold mine in themselves. He's said to have an uncanny knack of hitting on the
things all these women want him to say. The types that write
in are amazing. All the smarties. Nobody ever sees him. He
doesn't get about with the boys and the chaps who free-lance
for the rag never get past a sub who's always very bland and
entirely uncommunicative. There you are. That's all I can tell
you about G.P.F."

"Ever heard what he looks like?"

"No. There's a legend he wears old clothes and dark
glasses. They say he's got a lock on his office door and never
sees anybody on account he doesn't want to be recognised. It's
all part of an act. Publicity. They play it up in the paper itself
—'Nobody knows who G.P.F. is.'"

"What would you think if I told you he was Edward
Manx?"

"Manx! You're not serious."

"Is it so incredible?"

Nigel raised his eyebrows. "On the face of it, yes. Manx
is a reputable and very able specialist. He's done some pretty
solid stuff. Leftish and fairly authoritative. He's a coming
man. He'd turn sick in his stomach at the sight of G.P.F., I'd
have thought."

"He does their dramatic reviews."

"Yes, I know, but that's where they're freakish. Manx has
got a sort of damn-your-eyes view about theatre. It's one of
his things. He wants state-ownership and he'll scoop up any
chance to plug it. And I imagine their anti-vice parties
wouldn't be unpleasing to Manx. He wouldn't go much for
the style, which is tough and coloured, but he'd like the policy.
They give battle in a big way, you know. Names all over the
place and a general invitation to come on and sue us for libel
and see how you like it. Quite his cup of tea. Yes, I imagine
Harmony runs Manx to give the paper *cachet* and Manx
writes for *Harmony* to get at their public. They pay. Top
prices." Nigel paused and then said sharply: "But Manx as

G.P.F.! That's different. Have you actually good reason to suspect it? Are you on to something?"

" The case is fluffy with doubts at the moment."

" The Rivera case? It ties up with that?"

" Off the record, it does."

" By God," said Nigel profoundly, " if Ned Manx spews up that page it explains the secrecy! By God, it does."

" We'll have to ask him," Alleyn said. " But I'd have liked to have a little more to go on. Still, we can muscle in. Where's the *Harmony* office?"

" 5 Materfamilias Lane. The old *Triple Mirror* place."

" When does this blasted rag make its appearance? It's a monthly, isn't it?"

" Let's see. It's the 27th to-day. It comes out in the first week of the month. They'll be going to press any time now."

" So G.P.F.'s likely to be on tap at the office?"

" You'd think so. Are you going to burst in on Manx with a brace of manacles?"

" Never you mind."

" Come on," Nigel said. " What do I get for all this?"

Alleyn gave him a brief account of Rivera's death and a lively description of Lord Pastern's performance in the band.

" As far as it goes, it's good," Nigel said, " but I could get as much from the waiters."

" Not if Caesar Bonn knows anything about it."

" Are you going to pull old Pastern in?"

" Not just yet. You write your stuff and send it along to me."

" It's pretty!" Nigel said. " It's as pretty as paint. Pastern's good at any time but like this he's marvellous. May I use your typewriter?"

" For ten minutes."

Nigel retired with the machine to a table at the far end of the room. " I can say you were there, of course," he said hurriedly.

" I'll be damned if you can."

" Come, come, Alleyn, be big about this thing."

" I know you. If we don't ring the bell you'll print some revolting photograph of me looking like a half-wit. Caption:

'Chief Inspector who watched crime but doesn't know who-dunit!'"

Nigel grinned. "And would that be a story, and won't that be the day! Still, as it stands, it's pretty hot. Here we go, chaps." He began to rattle the keys.

Alleyn said, "There's one thing, Fox, that's sticking out of this mess like a road-sign and I can't read it. Why did that perishing old mountebank look at the gun and then laugh himself sick? Here! Wait a moment. Who was in the study with him when he concocted his dummies and loaded his gun? It's a thin chance but it might yield something." He pulled the telephone towards him. "We'll talk once more to Miss Carlisle Wayne."

3

Carlisle was in her room when the call came through and she took it there, sitting on her bed and staring aimlessly at a flower print on the wall. A hammer knocked at her ribs and her throat constricted. In some remote part of her mind she thought: "As if I was in love, instead of frightened sick."

The unusually deep and clear voice said: "Is that you, Miss Wayne? I'm sorry to bother you again so soon but I'd like to have another word with you."

"Yes," said Carlisle. "Would you? Yes."

"I can come to Duke's Gate or, if you would rather, can see you here at the Yard." Carlisle didn't answer at once and he said: "Which would suit you best?"

"I—I think—I'll come to your office."

"It might be easier. Thank you so much. Can you come at once?"

"Yes. Yes, I can, of course."

"Splendid." He gave her explicit instructions about which entrance to use and where to ask for him. "Is that clear? I shall see you in about twenty minutes, then."

"In about twenty minutes," she repeated, and her voice cracked into an absurd cheerful note as if she was gaily making a date with him. "Right-ho," she said and thought with horror: "But I never say 'right-ho.' He'll think I'm demented."

"Mr. Alleyn," she said loudly.

"Yes? Hallo?"

"I'm sorry I made such an ass of myself this morning. I don't know what happened. I seemed to have gone extremely peculiar."

"Never mind," said the deep voice easily.

"Well—all right. Thank you. I'll come straight away."

He gave a small polite not unfriendly sound and she hung up the receiver.

"Booking a date with the attractive inspector, darling?" said Félicité from the door.

At the first sound of her voice Carlisle's body had jerked and she had cried out sharply.

"You *are* jumpy," Félicité said, coming nearer.

"I didn't know you were there."

"Obviously."

Carlisle opened her wardrobe. "He wants to see me. Lord knows why."

"So you're popping off to the Yard. Exciting for you."

"Marvellous, isn't it?" Carlisle said, trying to make her voice ironical. Félicité watched her change into a suit. "Your face wants a little attention," she said.

"I know." She went to the dressing-table. "Not that it matters."

When she looked in the glass she saw Félicité's face behind her shoulder. "Stupidly unfriendly," she thought, dabbing at her nose.

"You know, darling," Félicité said, "I'm drawn to the conclusion you're a dark horse."

"Oh, Fée!" she said impatiently.

"Well, you appear to have done quite a little act with my late best young man, last night, and here you are having a sly assignation with the dynamic inspector."

"He probably wants to know what kind of tooth-paste we all use."

"Personally," said Félicité, "I always considered you were potty about Ned."

Carlisle's hand shook as she pressed powder into the tear-stains under her eyes.

"You *are* in a state, aren't you?" said Félicité.

Carlisle turned on her. "Fée, for pity's sake come off it. As if things weren't bad enough without your starting these monstrous hares. You *must* have seen that I couldn't endure your poor wretched incredibly phoney young man. You *must* see that Mr. Alleyn's summons to Scotland Yard has merely frightened seven bells out of me. How you *can*!"

"What about Ned?"

Carlisle picked up her bag and gloves. "If Ned writes the monstrous bilge you've fallen for in *Harmony* I never want to speak to him again," she said violently. "For the love of Mike pipe down and let me go and be grilled."

But she was not to leave without further incident. On the first-floor landing she encountered Miss Henderson. After her early-morning scene with Alleyn on the stairs, Carlisle had returned to her room and remained there, fighting down the storm of illogical weeping that had so suddenly overtaken her. So she had not met Miss Henderson until now.

"Hendy!" she cried out, "what's the matter?"

"Good-morning, Carlisle. The matter, dear?"

"I thought you looked—I'm sorry. I expect we all look a bit odd. Are you hunting for something?"

"I've dropped my little silver pencil somewhere. It can't be here," she said, as Carlisle began vaguely to look. "Are you going out?"

"Mr. Alleyn wants me to call and see him."

"Why?" Miss Henderson asked sharply.

"I don't know. Hendy, isn't this awful, this business? And to make matters worse I've had a sort of row with Fée."

The light on the first landing was always rather strange, Carlisle told herself, a cold reflected light coming from a distant window making people look greenish. It must be that, because Miss Henderson answered her quite tranquilly and with her usual lack of emphasis. "Why, of all mornings, did you two want to have a row?"

"I suppose we're both scratchy. I told her I thought the unfortunate Rivera was ghastly and she thinks I'm shaking my curls at Mr. Alleyn. It was too stupid for words."

" I should think so, indeed."

" I'd better go."

Carlisle touched her lightly on the arm and crossed to the stairs. She hesitated there, without turning to face Miss Henderson, who had not moved. " What is it?" Miss Henderson said. " Have you forgotten something?"

" No. Hendy, you know, don't you, about the fantastic thing they say killed him? The piece of parasol with an embroidery stiletto in the end?"

" Yes."

" Do you remember—I know this is ridiculous—but do you remember, last night when there was that devastating bang from the ballroom? Do you remember you and Aunt 'Cile and Fée and I were in the drawing-room and you were sorting Aunt 'Cile's work-box?"

" Was I?"

" Yes. And you jumped at the bang and dropped something."

" Did I?"

" And Fée picked it up."

" Did she?"

" Hendy, was it an embroidery stiletto?"

" I remember nothing about it. Nothing at all."

" I didn't notice where she put it. I wondered if you had noticed."

" If it was something from the work-box, I expect she put it back. Won't you be late, Carlisle?"

" Yes," Carlisle said without turning. " Yes, I'll go."

She heard Miss Henderson walk away into the drawing-room. The door closed gently and Carlisle went downstairs. There was a man in a dark suit in the hall. He got up when he saw her and said: " Excuse me, Miss, but are you Miss Wayne?"

" Yes, I am."

" Thank you, Miss Wayne."

He opened the glass doors for her and then the front door. Carlisle went quickly past him and out into the sunshine. She was quite unaware of the man who stepped out from the corner a little way down Duke's Gate and who, glancing impatiently at his watch, waited at the bus stop and journeyed with her to

Scotland Yard. " Keep observation on the whole damn' boiling," Alleyn had said irritably at six o'clock that morning. " We don't know *what* we want."

She followed a constable who looked oddly domesticated without his helmet down a linoleumed corridor to the Chief Inspector's room. She thought : " They invite people to come and make statements. It means something. Suppose they suspect me. Suppose they've found out some little thing that makes them think I've done it." Her imagination galloped wildly. Suppose, when she went into the room, Alleyn said : " I'm afraid this is serious. Carlisle Loveday Wayne, I arrest you for the murder of Carlos Rivera and I warn you . . ." They would telephone for any clothes she wanted. Hendy, perhaps, would pack a suitcase. Perhaps, secretly, they would all be a little lightened, almost pleasurably worried, because they would no longer be in fear for themselves. Perhaps Ned would come to see her.

" In here, if you please, Miss," the constable was saying with his hand on the doorknob.

Alleyn rose quickly from his desk and came towards her. " Punctilious," she thought. " He's got nice manners. Are his manners like this when he's going to arrest people?"

" I'm so sorry," he was saying. " This must be a nuisance for you."

The solid grizzled detective was behind him. Fox. That was Inspector Fox. He had pulled up a chair for her and she sat in it, facing Alleyn. " With the light on my face," she thought. " That's what they do."

Fox moved away and sat behind a second desk. She could see his head and shoulders but his hands were hidden from her.

" You'll think my object in asking you to come very aimless, I expect," Alleyn said, " and my first question will no doubt strike you as being completely potty. However, here it is. You told us last night that you were with Lord Pastern when he made the dummies and loaded the revolver."

" Yes."

" Well, now, did anything happen, particularly in respect of the revolver, that struck you both as being at all comic?"

Carlisle gaped at him. "'Comic.'"

"I told you it was a potty question," he said.

"If you mean did we take one look at the revolver and then shake with uncontrollable laughter, we didn't."

"No," he said. "I was afraid not."

"The mood was sentimental if anything. The revolver was one of a pair given to Uncle George by my father and he told me so."

"You were familiar with it, then?"

"Not in the least. My father died ten years ago, and when he lived was not in the habit of showing me his armoury. He and Uncle George were both crack shots, I believe. Uncle George told me my father had the revolvers made for target shooting."

"You looked at the gun last night? Closely?"

"Yes—because——" Beset by nervous and unreasoned caution she hesitated.

"Because?"

"My father's initials are scratched on it. Uncle George told me to look for them."

There was a long pause. "Yes, I see," Alleyn said.

She found she had twisted her gloves tightly together and doubled them over. She felt a kind of impatience with herself and abruptly smoothed them out.

"It was one of a pair," Alleyn said. "Did you look at both of them?"

"No. The other was in a case in the drawer on his desk. I just saw it there. I noticed it because the drawer was under my nose, almost, and Uncle George kept putting the extra dummies, if that's what you call them, into it."

"Ah, yes. I saw them there."

"He made a lot more than he wanted, in case," her voice faltered, "in case he was asked to do his turn again sometime."

"I see."

"Is that all?" she said.

"As you've been kind enough to come," Alleyn said with a smile, "perhaps we should think up something more."

"You needn't bother, thank you."

He smiled more broadly. "Fée was doing her stuff for him on the stairs this morning," Carlisle thought. "Was she actually showing the go-ahead signal or was she merely trying to stall him off?"

" It's about the steel end in this eccentric weapon. The bolt or dart," Alleyn said, and her attention snapped taut again. " We are almost certain that it's the business end of an embroidery stiletto from the work-box in the drawing-room. We found the discarded handle. I wonder if by any chance you remember when you last noticed the stiletto. If, of course, you happen to have noticed it?"

" So this is it," she thought. " The revolver was nothing, it was a red herring. He's really got me here to talk about the stiletto."

She said : " I don't think the work-box was open when I was in the drawing-room before dinner. At any rate I didn't notice it."

" I remember you told me that Lady Pastern showed you and Manx her *petit-point*. That *was* when you were all in the drawing-room before dinner, wasn't it? We found the *petit-point*, by the way, beside the work-box."

" Therefore," she thought, " Aunt 'Cile or Ned or I might have taken the stiletto." She repeated : " I'm sure the box wasn't open."

She had tried not to think beyond that one time, that one safe time about which she could quickly speak the truth.

" And after dinner?" Alleyn said casually.

She saw again the small gleaming tool drop from Miss Henderson's fingers when the report sounded in the ballroom. She saw Félicité automatically stoop and pick it up and a second later burst into tears and run furiously from the room. She heard her loud voice on the landing : " I've got to speak to you," and Rivera's : " But certainly, if you wish it."

" After dinner?" she repeated flatly.

" You were in the drawing-room then. Before the men came in. Perhaps Lady Pastern took up her work. Did you, at any time, see the box open or notice the stiletto?"

How quick was thought? As quick as people said? Was her hesitation fatally long? Here she moved, on the brink of speech. She could hear the irrevocable denial, and yet she had not made it. And suppose he had already spoken to Félicité about the stiletto? "What am I looking like?" she thought in a panic. "I'm looking like a liar already."

"Can you remember?" he asked. So she had waited too long.

"I—don't think I can." Now, she had said it. Somehow it wasn't quite as shaming to lie about remembering as about the fact itself. If things went wrong she could say afterwards : "Yes, I remember, now, but I had forgotten. It had no significance for me at the time."

"You don't *think* you can." She had nothing to say but he went on almost at once : "Miss Wayne, will you please try to look squarely at this business. Will you try to pretend that it's an affair that you have read about and in which you have no personal concern. Not easy. But try. Suppose, then, a group of complete strangers was concerned in Rivera's death and suppose one of them, not knowing much about it, unable to see the factual wood for the emotional trees, was asked a question to which she knew the answer. Perhaps the answer seems to implicate her. Perhaps it seems to implicate someone she is fond of. She doesn't in the least know, it may be, what the implications are but she refuses to take the responsibility of telling the truth about one detail that may fit in with the whole truth. She won't, in fact, speak the truth if by doing so she's remotely responsible for bringing an extraordinarily callous murderer to book. So she lies. At once she finds that it doesn't end there. She must get other people to tell corroborative lies. She finds herself, in effect, whizzing down a dangerous slope with her car out of control, steering round some obstacles, crashing into others, doing irreparable damage and landing herself and possibly other innocent people in disaster. You think I'm overstating her case, perhaps. Believe me, I've seen it happen very often."

"Why do you say all this to me?"

"I'll tell you why. You said just now that you didn't remember noticing the stiletto at any time after dinner. Before you made this statement you hesitated. Your hands closed on your gloves and suddenly twisted them. Your hands behaved with violence and yet they trembled. After you had spoken they continued to have a sort of independent life of their own. Your left hand kneaded the gloves and your right hand moved rather aimlessly across your neck and over your face. You blushed deeply and stared very fixedly at the top of my head. You presented me, in fact, with Example A from any handbook on behaviour of the lying witness. You were a glowing demonstration of the bad liar. And now, if all this is nonsense, you can tell counsel for the defence how I bullied you and he will treat me to as nasty a time as his talents suggest when I'm called to give evidence. Now I come to think of it, he'll be very unpleasant indeed. So, however, will prosecuting counsel if you stick to your lapse of memory."

Carlisle said angrily: "My hands feel like feet. I'm going to sit on them. You don't play fair."

"My God!" Alleyn said, "this isn't a game! It's murder."

"He was atrocious. He was much nastier than anyone else in the house."

"He may have been the nastiest job of work in Christendom. He was murdered and you're dealing with the police. This is not a threat but it's a warning: we've only just started: a great deal more evidence may come our way. You were not alone in the drawing-room after dinner."

She thought: "But Hendy won't tell and nor will Aunt 'Cile. But William came in some time, about then. Suppose he saw Fée on the landing? Suppose he noticed the stiletto in her hand? And then she remembered the next time she had seen Félicité. Félicité had been on top of the world, in ecstasy, because of the letter from G.P.F. She had changed into her most gala dress and her eyes were shining. She had already discarded Rivera as easily as she had discarded all her previous young men. It was fantastic to tell lies for Félicité. There was something futile about this scene with Alleyn. She had made a fool of herself for nothing.

He had taken an envelope from a drawer of his desk and now opened it and shook its contents out before her. She saw a small shining object with a sharp end.

"Do you recognise it?" he asked.

"The stiletto."

"You say that because we've been talking about the stiletto. It's not a bit like it really. Look again."

She leant over it. "Why," she said, "it's a—a pencil."

"Do you know whose pencil?"

She hesitated. " I think it's Hendy's. She wears it on a chain like an old-fashioned charm. She always wears it. She was hunting for it on the landing this morning."

" This is it. Here are her initials. P.X.H. Very tiny. You almost need a magnifying glass. Like the initials you saw on the revolver. The ring at the end was probably softish silver and the gap in it may have opened with the weight of the pencil. I found the pencil in the work-box. Does Miss Henderson ever use Lady Pastern's work-box?"

This at least was plain sailing. " Yes. She tidies it very often for Aunt 'Cile." And immediately Carlisle thought : " I'm no good at this. Here it comes again."

" Was she tidying the box last night? After dinner?"

" Yes," Carlisle said flatly. " Oh, yes. Yes."

" Did you notice, particularly? When exactly was it?"

" Before the men came in. Well, only Ned came in actually. Uncle George and the other two were in the ballroom."

" Lord Pastern and Bellairs were at this time in the ballroom, and Rivera and Manx in the dining-room. According to the time-table." He opened a file on his desk.

" I only know that Fée had gone when Ned came in."

" She had joined Rivera in the study by then. But to return to this incident in the drawing-room. Can you describe the scene with the work-box? What were you talking about?"

Félicité had been defending Rivera. She had been on edge, in one of her moods. Carlisle had thought : " She's *had* Rivera but she won't own up." And Hendy, listening, had moved her fingers about inside the work-box. There was the stiletto in Hendy's fingers and, dangling from her neck, the pencil on its chain.

" They were talking about Rivera. Félicité considered he'd been snubbed a bit and was cross about it."

" At about this time Lord Pastern must have fired off his gun in the ballroom," Alleyn muttered. He had spread the time-table out on his desk. He glanced up at her. His glance, she noticed, was never vague or indirect, as other people's might be. It had the effect of immediately collecting your attention. " Do you remember that?" he said.

" Oh, yes."

" It must have startled you, surely?"

What were her hands doing now? She was holding the side of her neck again.

"How did you all react to what must have been an infernal racket? What for instance did Miss Henderson do? Do you remember?"

Her lips parted dryly. She closed them again, pressing them together.

"I think you do remember," he said. "What did she do?"

Carlisle said loudly: "She let the lid of the box drop. Perhaps the pencil was caught and pulled off the chain."

"Was anything in her hands?"

"The stiletto," she said, feeling the words grind out.

"Good. And then?"

"She dropped it."

Perhaps that would satisfy him. It fell to the carpet. Anyone might have picked it up. Anyone, she thought desperately. Perhaps he will think a servant might have picked it up. Or even Breezy Bellairs, much later.

"Did Miss Henderson pick it up?"

"No."

"Did anyone?"

She said nothing.

"You? Lady Pastern? No. Miss de Suze?"

She said nothing.

"And a little while afterwards, a very little while, she went out of the room. Because it was immediately after the report that William saw her go into the study with Rivera. He noticed that she had something shiny in her hand."

"She didn't even know she had it. She picked it up automatically. I expect she just put it down in the study and forgot all about it."

"We found the ivory handle there," Alleyn said, and Fox made a slight gratified sound in his throat.

"But you mustn't think there was any significance in all this."

"We're glad to know how and when the stiletto got into the study, at least."

"Yes," she said. "I suppose so. Yes."

Someone tapped on the door. The bareheaded constable came in with a package and an envelope. He laid them on the desk. " From Captain Entwhistle, sir. You asked to have them as soon as they came in."

He went out without looking at Carlisle.

" Oh, yes," Alleyn said. " The report on the revolver, Fox. Good. Miss Wayne, before you go, I'll ask you to have a look at the revolver. It'll be one more identification check."

She waited while Inspector Fox came out from behind his desk and unwrapped the parcel. It contained two separate packages. She knew the smaller one must be the dart and wondered if Rivera's blood was still encrusted on the stiletto. Fox opened the larger package and came to her with the revolver.

" Will you look at it?" Alleyn said. " You may handle it. I would like your formal identification."

Carlisle turned the heavy revolver in her hands. There was a strong light in the room. She bent her head and they waited. She looked up, bewildered. Alleyn gave her his pocket lens. There was a long silence.

" Well, Miss Wayne?"

" But . . . But it's extraordinary. I can't identify it. There are no initials. This isn't the same revolver."

CHAPTER TEN

THE REVOLVER, THE STILETTO AND
HIS LORDSHIP

I

" AND WHAT," Alleyn asked when Carlisle had left them, " is the betting on the favourite now, Br'er Fox?"

" By gum," Fox said, " you always tell us that when a homicide case is full of fancy touches, it's not going to give much trouble. Do you stick to that, sir?"

" I'll be surprised if this turns out to be the exception, but I must say it looks like it at the moment. However, the latest development does at least cast another ray of light on your playmate. Do you remember how the old devil turned the gun over when we first let him see it at the Metronome? D'you remember how he squinted through the lens at the butt? And I told you how he took another look at it in the study and then had an attack of the dry grins and when I asked him what he expected to see, had the infernal nerve to come back at me with : ' Hoity-toity '—yes ' hoity-toity—wouldn't you like to know ! ' "

" Ugh ! "

" He'd realised all along, of course, that this wasn't the weapon he loaded in the study and took down to the Metronome. Yes," Alleyn added as Fox opened his mouth, " and don't forget he showed Skelton the gun a few minutes before it was fired. Miss Wayne says he pointed out the initials to Skelton."

" *That* looks suspicious in itself," Fox said instantly. " Why go to the trouble of pointing out initials to two people? He was getting something fixed up for himself. So he could turn round and say : ' That's not the gun I fired.' "

" Then why didn't he say so at once?"

" Gawd knows."

" If you ask me he was sitting pretty, watching us make fools of ourselves."

Fox jabbed his finger at the revolver. " If this isn't the original weapon," he demanded, " what the hell is it? It's the one this projectile-dart-bolt or what-have-you was fired from because it's got the scratches in the barrel. That means someone had this second gun all ready loaded with the dart and ammunition and substituted it for the original weapon. Here! What's the report say, Mr. Alleyn?"

Alleyn was reading the report. " Entwhistle," he said, " has had a ballistic orgy over the thing. The scratches could have been made by the brilliants in the parasol clip. In his opinion they were so made. He's sending photo-micrographs to prove it. He's fired the bolt—let's stick to calling this hybrid a bolt, shall we?—from another gun with an identical bore and it is ' somewhat similarly scratched,' which is a vile phrase. He pointed out that wavering, irregular scars were made when the bolt was shoved up the barrel. The spring-clip was pressed back with the thumb while it was being inserted and then sprang out once it was inside the barrel, thus preventing the bolt from falling out if the weapon was pointed downwards. The bolt was turned slightly as it was shoved home. The second scar was made by the ejection of the bolt, the clip retaining its pressure while being expelled. He says that the scars in the revolver we submitted don't extend quite as deep up the barrel as those made by the bolt which he fired from his own gun, but he considers that they were made by the same kind of procedure and the same bolt. At a distance of four feet, the projectile shoots true. Over long distances there are ' progressive divergences caused by the weight of the clip on one side or by air-resistance. Entwhistle says he's very puzzled by the fouling from the bore, which is quite unlike anything in his experience. He removed it and sent it along for analysis. The analyst finds that the fouling consists of particles of carbon and of various hydro-carbons including members of the paraffin series, apparently condensed from vapour."

" Funny."

" That's all."

" All right," Fox said heavily. " All right. That looks fair enough. The bolt that plugged Rivera *was* shot out of this weapon. This weapon is not the one his lordship showed Miss Wayne and Syd Skelton. But unless you entertain the idea of somebody shooting off another gun at the same instant, this is the one that killed Rivera. You accept that, sir?"

" I'll take it as a working premise. With reservations and remembering our conversation in the car."

" All right. Well, after Skelton examined the gun with the initials, did his lordship get a chance to substitute this one and fire it off? Could he have had this one on him all the time?"

" Hobnobbing, cheek by jowl with a dozen or so people at close quarters? I should say definitely not. And, he didn't know Skelton would ask to see the gun. And what did he do with the first gun afterwards? We searched him, remember."

" Planted it? Anyway, where is it?"

" Somewhere at the Metronome if we're on the right tack and we've searched the Metronome. But go on."

" Well, sir, if his lordship didn't change the gun who did?"

" His stepdaughter could have done it. Or any other member of his party. They were close to the sombrero, remember. They got up to dance and moved round between the table and the edge of the dais. Lady Pastern was alone at the table for some time. I didn't see her move but I wasn't watching her, of course. All the ladies had largish evening bags. The catch in that theory, Br'er Fox, is that they wouldn't have known they were going to be within reach of the sombrero and it's odds on they didn't know he was going to put his perishing gun under his sombrero, anyway.''

Fox bit at his short grizzled moustache, planted the palms of his hands on his knees and appeared to go into a short trance. He interrupted it to mutter : '' Skelton, now. Syd Skelton. Could Syd Skelton have worked the substitution? You're going to remind me they were all watching him, but were they watching all that closely? Syd Skelton.''

'' Go on, Fox.''

'' Syd Skelton's on his own, in a manner of speaking. He left the band platform before his lordship came on for his turn. Syd walked out. Suppose he had substituted this gun for the other with the initials? Suppose he walked right out and dropped the other one down the first grating he came to? Syd knew he was going to get the chance, didn't he?''

'' How, when and where did he convert the bit of parasol shaft and stiletto into the bolt and put it up the barrel of the second revolver? Where did he get his ammunition? And when did he get the gun? *He* wasn't at Duke's Gate.''

'' Yes,'' Fox said heavily, '' that's awkward. I wonder if you could get round that one. Well, leave it for the time being. Who else have we got? Breezy. From the substitution angle, can we do anything about Breezy?''

'' He didn't get alongside Pastern, on either of their statements, from the time Skelton looked at the gun until after Rivera was killed. They were alone together in the bandroom before Breezy made his entrance but Pastern, with his usual passionate industry in clearing other people, says Breezy didn't go near him. And Pastern had his gun in his hip pocket, remember.''

Fox returned to his trance.

'' I think,'' Alleyn said, '' it's going to be one of those affairs where the whittling away of impossibilities leaves one face-to-face with a mere improbability which, as you would say, ' faut de mieux,' one is forced to accept. And I think, so far, Fox, we haven't found my improbable notion an impossibility. At least it has the virtue of putting the fancy touches in a more credible light."

" We'll never make a case of it, I reckon, if it does turn out to be the answer."

" And we'll never make a case of it if we pull in his lord-ship and base the charge on the assumption that he substituted this gun for the one he loaded and says he fired. Skelton's put up by the defence and swears he examined the thing at his own request and saw the initials and that this is not the same weapon. Counsel points out that three minutes later Lord Pastern goes on for his turn."

Fox snarled quietly to himself and presently broke out. " We call this blasted thing a bolt. Be damned if I don't think we'll get round to calling it a dart. Be damned if I'm not be-ginning to wonder if it was used like one. Thrown at the chap from close by. After all it's not impossible."

" Who by? Breezy?"

" No," Fox said slowly. " No. Not Breezy. His lordship cleared Breezy in advance by searching him. Would you swear Breezy didn't pick anything up from anywhere after he came out to conduct?"

" I believe I would. He walked rapidly through the open door and down an alley-way between the musicians. He stood in a spotlight a good six feet or more away from anything, conducting like a great jerking jellyfish. They all say he couldn't have picked anything up after Pastern searched him, and in any case I would certainly swear he didn't put his hands near his pockets and that up to the time Rivera fell he was conducting with both hands and that none of his extraordinary antics in the least resembled dart-throwing. I was watching him. They rather fascinated me, those antics. And if you want any more, Br'er Fox, Rivera had his back turned to Breezy when he fell."

" All right. His lordship, then. His lordship was facing Rivera. Close to him. *Blast.* Unless he's ambidextrous, how'd he fire off a gun and throw a dart all in a split second? This is getting me nowhere. Who else, then?"

" Do you fancy Lady Pastern as a dart queen?"

Fox chuckled. " That *would* be the day, sir, wouldn't it?

But how about Mr. Manx? We've got a motive for Manx. Rivera had proof that Manx wrote these sissy articles in *Harmony*. Manx doesn't want that known. Blackmail," said Fox without much conviction.

" Foxkin," Alleyn said, " let there be a truce to these barren speculations. May I remind you that up to the time he fell Rivera was raising hell with a piano accordion?"

Fox said, after another long pause : " You know I like this case. It's got something. Yes. And may I remind *you*, sir, that he wasn't meant to fall. None of them expected him to fall. Therefore he fell because somebody planted a bloody little steel embroidery gadget on a parasol handle in his heart before he fell. So where, if you don't object to the inquiry, Mr. Alleyn, do we go from here?"

" I think," Alleyn said, " that you institute a search for the missing gun and I pay a call on Miss Petronella Xantippe Henderson." He got up and fetched his hat. " And I think, moreover," he added, " that we've been making a couple of perishing fools of ourselves."

" About the dart?" Fox demanded. " Or the gun?"

" About *Harmony*. Think this one over while I call on Miss Henderson and then tell me what you make of it."

Five minutes later he went out, leaving Fox in a concentrated trance.

2

Miss Henderson received him in her room. It had the curiously separate, not quite congenial air that seems to be the characteristic of sitting-rooms that are permanently occupied by solitary women in other people's houses. There were photographs : of Félicité, as a child, as a schoolgirl and in her presentation dress; one intimidating portrait of Lady Pastern and one, enlarged, it would seem, from a snapshot, of Lord Pastern in knickerbockers and shooting boots, with a gun under his arm, a spaniel at his heels, a large house at his back and an expression of impertinence on his face. Above the desk hung a group of women-undergraduates clad in the tube-like brevity of the nineteen-twenties. A portion of Lady Margaret Hall loomed in the background.

Miss Henderson was dressed with scrupulous neatness, in a dark suit that faintly resembled a uniform or habit. She received Alleyn with perfect composure. He looked at her hair, greyish, quietly fashionable in its controlled grooming, at her eyes, which were pale, and at her mouth, which was unexpectedly full.

"Well, Miss Henderson," he said, "I wonder if you will be able to throw any light on this very obscure business."

"I'm afraid it's most unlikely," she said tranquilly.

"You never know. There's one point, at least, where I hope you will help us. You were present at last night's party in this house, both before and after dinner, and you were in the drawing-room when Lord Pastern, with the help of all the people concerned, worked out and wrote down the time-table which he afterwards gave to me."

"Yes," she agreed, after he had waited for a second or two.

"Would you say that as far as your personal observations and recollections cover them, the movements set down in the time-table are accurate?"

"Oh, yes," she said at once, "I think so. But of course, they don't go very far—my recollections. I was the last to arrive in the drawing-room, you know, before dinner, and the first to leave after dinner."

"Not quite the first, according to the time-table, surely?"

She drew her brows together as if perturbed at the suggestion of inaccuracy. "Not?" she said.

"The time-table puts Miss de Suze's exit from the drawing-room a second or two before yours."

"How stupid of me. Félicité did go out first but I followed almost at once. I forgot for the moment."

"You were all agreed on this point, last night, when Lord Pastern compiled his time-table?"

"Yes. Perfectly."

"Do you remember that just before this there was a great rumpus in the ballroom? It startled you and you dropped a little stiletto on the carpet. You were tidying Lady Pastern's work-box at the time. Do you remember?"

He had thought at first that she used no more make-up

than a little powder but he saw now that the faint warmth of her cheeks was artificial. The colour became isolated as the skin beneath and about it bleached. Her voice was quite even and clear.

" It was certainly rather an alarming noise," she said.

" Do you remember, too, that Miss de Suze picked up the stiletto? I expect she meant to return it to you or to the box but she was rather put out just then. She was annoyed, wasn't she, by the, as she considered, uncordial reception given to her fiancé?"

" He was not her fiancé. They were not engaged."

" Not officially, I know."

" Not unofficially. There was no engagement."

" I see. In any case, do you remember that instead of replacing the stiletto, she still had it in her hand when, a moment later, she left the room?"

" I'm afraid I didn't notice."

" What did you do?"

" Do?"

" At that moment? You had been tidying the box. It was exquisitely neat when we found it this morning. Was it on your knees? The table was a little too far from your chair for you to have used it, I think."

" Then," she said, with her first hint of impatience, " the box was on my knees."

" So that was how the miniature silver pencil you wear on a chain came to be in the box?"

Her hands went to the bosom of her dress, fingering it. " Yes, I suppose so. Yes. I didn't realise . . . was that where it was?"

" Perhaps you dropped the lid and caught the pencil, dragging it off the chain."

" Yes," she repeated. " Yes. I suppose so. Yes, I remember I did do that."

" Then why did you hunt for it this morning on the landing?"

" I had forgotten about catching it in the box," she said rapidly.

" Not," Alleyn murmured apologetically, " a frightfully good memory."

" These are trivial things that you ask me to remember. In this house we are none of us at the moment concerned with trivial things."

" Are you not? Then, I suggest that you searched the landing, not for your trinket, which you say was a trivial thing, but for something that you knew could not be in the work-box because you had seen Miss de Suze take it out with her when she left the drawing-room in a rage. The needlework stiletto."

" But Inspector Alleyn, I told you I didn't notice anything of the sort."

" Then what were you looking for?"

" You have apparently been told. My pencil."

" A trivial thing but your own. Here it is."

He opened his hand, showed her the pencil. She made no movement and he dropped it in her lap. " You don't seem to me," he remarked casually, " to be an unobservant woman."

" If that's a compliment," she said, " thank you."

" Did you see Miss de Suze again, after she left the drawing-room with the stiletto in her hand and after she had quarrelled with Rivera when they were alone together in the study?"

" Why do you say they quarrelled?"

" I have it on pretty good authority."

" Carlisle?" she said sharply.

" No. But if you cross-examine a policeman about this sort of job, you know, he's not likely to be very communicative."

" One of the servants, I suppose," she said, dismissing it and him without emphasis. He asked her again if she had seen Félicité later that evening and after watching him for a moment she said that she had. Félicité had come to this room and had been in the happiest possible mood. " Excited?" he suggested, and she replied that Félicité had been pleasurably excited. She was glad to be going out with her cousin, Edward Manx, to whom she was attached, and was looking forward to the performance at the Metronome.

" After this encounter you went to Lady Pastern's room, didn't you? Lady Pastern's maid was with her. She was dismissed, but not before she had heard you say that Miss de Suze was very much excited and that you wanted to have a word with her mother about this."

" Again, the servants."

"Anybody," Alleyn said, "who is prepared to speak the truth. A man has been murdered."

"I have spoken nothing but the truth." Her lips trembled and she pressed them together.

"Good. Let's get on with it then, shall we?"

"There's nothing at all that I can tell you. Nothing at all."

"But at least you can tell me about the family. You understand, don't you, that my job, at the moment, is not so much finding the guilty person as clearing persons who may have been associated with Rivera but are innocent of his murder. That may, indeed it does, take in certain members of this household. It takes in the inter-communications of the household, the detailed as well as the general set-up. Now, in your position . . ."

"My position!" she muttered, with a sort of repressed contempt. Almost inaudibly she added: "What do you know of my position?"

Alleyn said pleasantly: "I've heard you're called the Controller of the Household." She didn't answer and he went on: "In any case it has been a long association and I suppose, in many ways, an intimate one. With Miss de Suze, for instance. You have brought her up, really, haven't you?"

"Why do you keep speaking about Félicité? This has nothing to do with Félicité." She got up, and stood with her back towards him, changing the position of an ornament on the mantelpiece. He could see her carefully kept and very white hand steady itself on the edge of the shelf. "I'm afraid I'm not behaving very well, am I?" she murmured. "But I find your insistence rather trying."

"Is that because, at the moment, it's directed at Miss de Suze and the stiletto?"

"Naturally, I'm uneasy. It's disturbing to feel that she will be in the smallest degree involved." She leant her head against her hand. From where he stood, behind her, she looked like a woman who had come to rest for a moment and fallen into an idle speculation. Her voice came to him remotely from beyond her stooped shoulders as if her mouth was against her hand. "I suppose she simply left it in the study. She didn't even realise she had it in her hand. It was not in her hand when she came upstairs. It had no importance for her at all."

She turned and faced him. "I shall tell you something," she said. "I don't want to. I'd made up my mind I'd have no hand in this. It's distasteful to me. But I see now that I must tell you."

"Right."

"It's this. Before dinner last night, and during dinner, I had opportunity to watch those—those two men."

"Rivera and Bellairs?"

"Yes. They were extraordinary creatures and I suppose in a sort of way I was interested."

"Naturally. In Rivera at all events."

"I don't know what servants' gossip you have been listening to, Inspector Alleyn."

"Miss Henderson, I've heard enough from Miss de Suze herself to tell me that there was an understanding between them."

"I watched those two men," she said exactly as if he hadn't spoken. "And I saw at once there was bad blood between them. They looked at each other—I can't describe it—with enmity. They were both, of course, incredibly common and blatant. They scarcely spoke to each other but during dinner, over and over again, I saw the other one, the conductor, eyeing him. He talked a great deal to Félicité and to Lord Pastern but he listened to . . ."

"To Rivera?" Alleyn prompted. She seemed to be incapable of pronouncing his name.

"Yes. He listened to him as if he resented every word he spoke. That would have been natural enough from any of us."

"Was Rivera so offensive?"

An expression of eagerness appeared on her face. Here was something, at last, about which she was ready to speak.

"Offensive?" she said. "He was beyond everything. He sat next to Carlisle and even she was nonplussed. Evidently she attracted him. It was perfectly revolting."

Alleyn thought distastefully : "Now what's behind all this? Resentment? At Carlisle rather than Félicité attracting the atrocious Rivera? Or righteous indignation? Or what?"

She had raised her head. Her arm still rested on the mantel-piece and she had stretched out her hand to a framed photograph of Félicité in presentation dress. He moved slightly and saw that her eyes were fixed on the photograph. Félicité's eyes, under her triple plumage, stared back with the glazed distaste (so suggestive of the unwitting influence of Mr. John Gielgud) that characterises the modish photograph. Miss Henderson began to speak again and it was as if she addressed herself to the photograph. " Of course, Félicité didn't mind in the least. It was nothing to her. A relief, no doubt. Anything rather than suffer his odious attentions. But it was clear to me that the other creature and he had quarrelled. It was quite obvious."

" But if they hardly spoke to each other how could . . ."

" I've told you. It was the way the other person, Bellairs, looked at him. He watched him perpetually."

Alleyn now stood before her. They made a formal conversation piece with the length of the mantelpiece between them. He said : " Miss Henderson, who was beside you at the dinner-table?"

" I sat next to Lord Pastern. On his left."

" And on your left?"

She made a fastidious movement with her shoulders. " Mr. Bellairs."

" Do you remember what he talked to you about?"

Her mouth twisted. " I don't remember that he spoke to me at all," she said. " He had evidently realised that I was a person of no importance. He devoted himself to Félicité who was on his other side. He gave me his shoulder."

Her voice faded out almost before she had uttered the last word as if, too late, she had tried to stop herself.

" If he gave you his shoulder," Alleyn said, " how did it come about that you could see this inimical stare of his?"

The photograph of Félicité crashed on the hearth. Miss Henderson cried out and knelt. " How clumsy of me," she whispered.

" Let me do it. You may cut your fingers."

" No," she said sharply, " don't touch it."

She began to pick up the slivers of glass from the frame and drop them in the grate. " There's a looking-glass on the wall of the dining-room," she said. " I could see him in that." And in a flat voice that had lost all its urgency she repeated : " He watched him perpetually."

"Yes," Alleyn said, "I remember the looking-glass. I accept that."

"Thank you," she said ironically.

"One more question. Did you go into the ballroom at any time after dinner?"

She looked up at him warily and after a moment said: "I believe I did. Yes. I did."

"When?"

"Félicité had lost her cigarette-case. It was when they were changing and she called out from her room. She had been in the ballroom during the afternoon and thought she might have left it there."

"Had she done so?"

"Yes. It was on the piano. Under some music."

"What else was on the piano?"

"A bundle of parasols."

"Anything else?"

"No," she said. "Nothing."

"Or on the chairs or floor?"

"Nothing."

"Are you sure?"

"Perfectly sure," she said, and dropped a piece of glass with a little tinkle in the grate.

"Well," Alleyn said, "if I can't help you, perhaps I'd better take myself off."

She seemed to examine the photograph. She peered at it as if to make certain there were no flaws or scratches on Félicité's image. "Very well," she said, and stood up, holding the face of the photograph against her flattish chest. "I'm sorry if I haven't told you the kind of things you want to be told. The truth is so seldom what one really wants to hear, is it? But perhaps you don't think I have told you the truth."

"I think I am nearer to it than I was before I visited you."

He left her, with the broken photograph still pressed against the bosom of her dark suit. On the landing he encountered Hortense. Her ladyship, Hortense said, smiling knowledgeably at him, would be glad to see him before he left. She was in her boudoir.

3

It was a small, delicately appointed room on the same floor. Lady Pastern rose from her desk, a pretty Empire affair, as he came in. She was firmly encased in her morning-dress. Her hair was rigid, her hands ringed. A thin film of make-up had been carefully spread over the folds and shadows of her face. She looked ghastly but completely in order.

"It is so good of you to spare me a moment," she said, and held out her hand. This was unexpected. Evidently she considered that her change of manner required an explanation, and without wasting time, she let him have it.

"I did not realise last night," she said concisely, "that you must be the younger son of an old friend of my father's. You are Sir George Alleyn's son, are you not?"

Alleyn bowed. This, he thought, is going to be tiresome.

"Your father," she said, "was a frequent visitor at my parents' house in the Faubourg St. Germaine. He was, in those days, an attaché, I think, at your Embassy in Paris." Her voice faded and an extraordinary look came over her face. He was unable to interpret it.

"What is it, Lady Pastern?" he asked.

"Nothing. I was reminded, for a moment, of a former conversation. We were speaking of your father. I remember that he and your mother called upon one occasion, bringing their two boys with them. Perhaps you do not recollect the visit."

"It is extremely kind of you to do so."

"I had understood that you were to be entered in the British Diplomatic Service."

"I was entirely unsuited for it, I'm afraid."

"Of course," she said, with a sort of creaking graciousness, "young men after the first war began to find their vocation in unconventional fields. One understands and accepts these changes, doesn't one?"

"Since I am here as a policeman," Alleyn said politely, "I hope so."

Lady Pastern examined him with that complete lack of reticence which is often the characteristic of royal personages.

It occurred to him that she herself would also have shaped up well, in an intimidating way, as a policewoman.

"It is a relief to me," she announced, after a pause, "that we are in your hands. You will appreciate my difficulties. It will make an enormous difference."

Alleyn was familiar enough with this point of view, and detested it. He thought it advisable, however, to say nothing. Lady Pastern, erecting her bust and settling her shoulders, continued :

"I need not remind you of my husband's eccentricities. They are public property. You have seen for yourself to what lengths of imbecility he will go. I can only assure you that though he may be, and indeed is, criminally stupid, he is perfectly incapable of crime as the word is understood in the profession you have elected to follow. He is not, in a word, a potential murderer. Or," she added, apparently as an afterthought, "an actual one. Of that you may be assured." She looked affably at Alleyn. Evidently, he thought, she had been a dark woman. There was a tinge of sable in her hair. Her skin was sallow and he thought she probably used something to deal with a darkness of the upper lip. It was odd that she should have such pale eyes. "I cannot blame you," she said, as he was still silent, "if you suspect my husband. He has done everything to invite suspicion. In this instance, however, I am perfectly satisfied that he is guiltless."

"We shall be glad to find proof of his innocence," Alleyn said.

Lady Pastern closed one hand over the other. "Usually," she said, "I comprehend entirely his motives. But entirely. On this occasion, however, I find myself somewhat at a loss. It is obvious to me that he develops some scheme. But what? Yes : I confess myself at a loss. I merely warn you, Mr. Alleyn, that to suspect my husband of this crime is to court acute embarrassment. You will gratify his unquenchable passion for self-dramatisation. He prepares a denouement."

Alleyn took a quick decision. "It's possible," he said, "that we've anticipated him there."

"Indeed?" she said quickly. "I'm glad to hear it."

"It appears that the revolver produced last night was not

the one Lord Pastern loaded and took to the platform. I think
he knows this. Apparently it amuses him to say nothing."

" Ah!" She breathed out a sound of immense satisfaction.
" As I thought. It amuses him. Perfectly! And his innocence
is established, no doubt?"

Alleyn said carefully : " If the revolver produced is the one
he fired, and the scars in the barrel suggest that it is, then a
very good case could be made out on the lines of substitution."

" I'm afraid I do not understand. A good case?"

" To the effect that Lord Pastern's revolver was replaced by
this other one which was loaded with the bolt that killed
Rivera. That Lord Pastern fired it in ignorance of the substitution."

She had a habit of immobility but her stillness now declared
itself as if until this moment she had been restless. The creased
lids came down like hoods over her eyes. She seemed to look
at her hands. " Naturally," she said, " I make no attempt to
understand these assuredly very difficult complexities. It is
enough, little as he deserves to escape, that my husband clears
himself."

" Nevertheless," Alleyn said, " it remains necessary to dis-
cover the guilty person." And he thought : " Damn it, I'm
beginning to talk like a French phrase book myself!"

" No doubt," she said.

" And the guilty person, it seems obvious, was one of the
party who dined here last night."

Lady Pastern now closed her eyes completely. " A most distressing possibility," she murmured.

" Hands," Alleyn thought, " Carlisle Wayne's hands fingering her neck. Miss Henderson's hand jerking the photograph
off the mantelpiece. Lady Pastern's hands closing upon each
other like vices. Hands."

" Furthermore," he said, " if the substitution theory is right,
the time-field is narrowed considerably. Lord Pastern put his
revolver under his sombrero on the edge of the band dais, you
remember."

" I made a point of disregarding him," his wife said instantly. " The whole affair was entirely distasteful to me. I
did not notice and therefore I do *not* remember."

"That's what he did, however. The possibilities as far as substitution goes are therefore limited to the people who were within easy reach of his sombrero."

"No doubt you will question the waiters. The man was of the type which makes itself insufferable to servants."

"By gum!" Alleyn thought, "you're almost one up on me there, old girl." But he said: "We must remember that the substituted weapon was charged with a bolt and blank cartridges. The bolt was made out of a section of your parasol handle and its point of a stiletto from your work-box." He paused. Her fingers were more closely interlocked, but she didn't move or speak. "And the blanks," he added, "were, it is almost certain, made by Lord Pastern and left in his study. The waiters are ruled out, I think."

Her lips parted and closed again. She said: "Am I, perhaps, being stupid? It seems to me that this theory of substitution may embrace a wider field. Why could the change of weapons not have been effected before my husband appeared? He was later than the others in appearing. So, for example, was Mr. Bellairs. I believe that is the conductor's name."

"Lord Pastern insists that neither Bellairs nor anyone else had an opportunity to get at his revolver, which he says he carried in his hip pocket, until he put it under the sombrero. I am persuaded that the change-over was effected after Lord Pastern made his entrance on the band dais and it's obvious that the substituted revolver must have been prepared by someone who had access to your parasol . . ."

"In the restaurant," she interrupted quickly. "Before the performance. The parasols must have been within reach of all of them."

". . . and also access to the study in this house."

"Why?"

"To get the stiletto which was carried there."

She drew in her breath sharply. "It may have been an entirely different stiletto, I imagine."

"Then why has this particular one disappeared from the study? Your daughter took it away from the drawing-room when she left for her interview in the study with Rivera. Do you remember that?"

He could have sworn that she did if only because she made

no sign whatsoever. She couldn't achieve the start of astonishment or dismay which this statement should have produced if she hadn't been prepared for it.

" I remember nothing of the sort," she said.

" That is what happened, however," Alleyn said, " and it appears that the steel was removed in the study since we found the ivory handle there."

After a moment she lifted her chin and looked directly at him. " It is with the greatest reluctance that I remind you of the presence of Mr. Bellairs in this house last night. I believe he was in the study with my husband after dinner. He had ample opportunity to return there."

" According to Lord Pastern's time-table to which you have all subscribed he had from about a quarter-to-ten until half-past when, with the exception of Rivera and Mr. Edward Manx, the rest of the party was upstairs. Mr. Manx, I remember, said he was in the drawing-room during this period. He had, by the way, punched Rivera on the ear shortly beforehand."

" Ah!" Lady Pastern breathed out her small ejaculation. She took a moment or two over digesting this information and Alleyn thought she was very well pleased with it. She said : " Dear Edward is immensely impulsive."

" He was annoyed, I gather, because Rivera had taken it upon himself to kiss Miss Wayne."

Alleyn would have given a lot to have Lady Pastern's thoughts floating above her head in clear letters, encased by a balloon as in one of Troy's little drawings, or to have heard them through spectral earphones. Were there four elements? Desire that Manx should be concerned only with Félicité? Gratification that Manx should have gone for Rivera? Resentment that Carlisle and not Félicité had been the cause? And fear : fear that Manx should be more gravely involved? Or some deeper fear?

" Unfortunately," she said, " he was a totally impossible person. It is, I feel certain, an affair of no significance. Dear Edward."

Alleyn said abruptly : " Do you ever see a magazine called *Harmony*?" and was startled by her response. Her eyes widened. She looked at him as if he had uttered some startling impropriety.

"Never!" she said loudly. "Certainly not. Never."

"There is a copy in the house. I thought perhaps . . ."

"The servants may take it. I believe it is the kind of thing they read."

"The copy I saw was in the study. It has a correspondence page, conducted by someone who calls himself G.P.F."

"I have not seen it. I do not concern myself with this journal."

"Then," Alleyn said, "there's not much point in my asking if you suspected that Edward Manx was G.P.F."

It was not possible for Lady Pastern to leap to her feet: her corsets alone prevented such an exercise. But, with formidable energy and comparative speed, she achieved a standing position. He saw with astonishment that her bosom heaved and that her neck and face were suffused with a brickish red.

"*Impossible!*" she panted. "Never! I shall never believe it. An insufferable suggestion."

"I don't quite see . . ." Alleyn began, but she shouted him down.

"Outrageous! He is utterly incapable." She shot a fusillade of adjectives at him. "I cannot discuss such a fantasy. Incredible! Monstrous! Libellous! Libel of the grossest kind! Never!"

"But why do you say that? On account of the literary style?"

Lady Pastern's mouth opened and shut. She stared at him with an air of furious indecision. "You may say so," she said at last. "You may put it in that way. Certainly. On account of style."

"And yet you have never read the magazine?"

"Obviously it is a vulgar publication. I have seen the cover."

"Let me tell you," Alleyn suggested, "how the theory has arisen. I really should like you to understand that it's not based on guesswork. May we sit down?"

She sat down abruptly. He saw, and was bewildered to see, that she was trembling. He told her about the letter Félicité had received and showed her the copy he had made. He reminded her of the white flower in Manx's coat and of Félicité's change of manner after she had seen it. He said that Félicité believed Manx to be G.P.F. and had admitted as much. He said they had discovered original drafts of articles that had subsequently appeared on G.P.F.'s page and that these drafts had been typed on the machine in the study. He reminded her that Manx had stayed at Duke's Gate for three weeks. Throughout this recital she sat bolt upright, pressing her lips together and staring, inexplicably, at the top right-hand drawer of her desk. In some incomprehensible fashion he was dealing her blow after shrewd blow, but he kept on and finished the whole story. " So you see, don't you," he ended, " that, at least, it's a probability?"

" Have you asked him?" she said pallidly. " What does he say?"

" I have not asked him yet. I shall do so. Of course, the whole question of his identity with G.P.F. may be irrelevant as far as this case is concerned."

" Irrelevant!" she ejaculated, as if the suggestion was wildly insane. She was looking again at her desk. Every muscle of her face was controlled but tears now began to form in her eyes and trickle over her cheeks.

" I'm sorry," Alleyn said, " that you find this distressing."

" It distresses me," she said, " because I find it is true. I am in some confusion of mind. If there is nothing more . . ."

He got up at once. " There's nothing more," he said. " Good-bye, Lady Pastern."

She recalled him before he reached the door. " One moment."

" Yes?"

" Let me assure you, Mr. Alleyn," she said, pressing her handkerchief against her cheek, " that my foolishness is entirely unimportant. It is a personal matter. What you have told me is quite irrelevant to this affair. It is of no consequence whatever, in fact." She drew in her breath with a sound that quivered between a sigh and a sob. " As for the identity of the person who has perpetrated this outrage, I mean the murder, not the journalism, I am persuaded it was one of his own kind. Yes, certainly," she said more vigorously, " one of his own kind. You may rest assured of that." And finding himself dismissed, he left her.

4

As Alleyn approached the first landing on his way down he was surprised to hear the ballroom piano. It was being played somewhat unhandily and the strains were those of hotly syncopated music taken at a funereal pace. Detective-Sergeant Jimson was on duty on the landing, Alleyn jerked his head at the ballroom doors, which were ajar. "Who's that playing?" he asked. "Is it Lord Pastern? Who the devil opened that room?"

Jimson, looking embarrassed and scandalised, replied that he thought it must be Lord Pastern. His manner was so odd that Alleyn walked past him and pushed open the double doors.

Inspector Fox was discovered seated at the piano with his spectacles on his nose. He was inclined forward tensely, and followed with concentration a sheet of music in manuscript. Facing him, across the piano, was Lord Pastern who, as Alleyn entered, beat angrily, but rhythmically, upon the lid and shouted : "No, no, my good ass, not a bit like it. N'yah—yo. Bo bo bo. Again." He looked up and saw Alleyn. "Here!" he said, "can you play?"

Fox rose without embarrassment, and removed his spectacles.

"Where have you come from?" Alleyn demanded.

"I had a little matter to report, sir, and as you were engaged for the moment I've been waiting in here. His lordship was looking for someone to try over a piece he's composing but I'm afraid . . ."

"I'll have to get one of these women," Lord Pastern cut in impatiently. "Where's Fée? This chap's no good."

"I haven't sat down to the piano since I was a lad," said Fox mildly.

Lord Pastern made for the door but Alleyn intercepted him. "One moment, sir," he said.

"It's no good worryin' me with any more questions," Lord Pastern snapped at him. "I'm busy."

"Unless you'd prefer to come to the Yard, you'll answer this one, if you please. When did you first realise that the revolver we produced after Rivera was killed was not the one you loaded in the study and carried on to the band platform?"

Lord Pastern smirked at him. "Nosed that out for yourselves, have you?" he remarked. "Fascinatin', the way our police work."

"I still want to know when you made this discovery."

"About eight hours before you did."

"As soon as you were shown the substitute and noticed there were no initials?"

"Who told you about initials? Here!" Lord Pastern said with some excitement, "have you found my other gun?"

"Where do you suggest we look for it?"

"If I knew where it was, my good fathead, I'd have got it for meself. I value that gun, by God!"

"You handed over the weapon you fired at Rivera to Breezy Bellairs," Fox said suddenly. "Was it that one, my lord? The one with the initials? The one you loaded in this house? The one that's missing?"

Lord Pastern swore loudly. "What d'you think I am?" he shouted. "A bloody juggler. Of course it was."

"And Bellairs walked straight into the office with you and I took it off him a few minutes later and it *wasn't* the same gun. That won't wash, my lord," said Fox, "if you'll excuse my saying so. It won't wash."

"In that case," Lord Pastern said rudely, "you can put up with it dirty." Alleyn made a slight, irritated sound and Lord Pastern instantly turned on him. "What are *you* snufflin' about?" he demanded, and before Alleyn could answer he renewed his attack on Fox. "Why don't you ask Breezy about it?" he said. "I should have thought even *you'd* have got at Breezy."

"Are you suggesting, my lord, that Bellairs might have worked the substitution after the murder was committed?"

"I'm not suggestin' anything."

"In which case," Fox continued imperturbably, "perhaps you'll tell me how Rivera was killed?"

Lord Pastern gave a short bark of laughter. "No, really!" he said, "it's beyond belief how bone-headed you are."

Fox said: "May I press this point a little further, Mr. Alleyn?"

From behind Lord Pastern, Alleyn returned Fox's inquiring glance with a dubious one. "Certainly, Fox," he said.

"I'd like to ask his lordship if he'd be prepared to swear on oath that the weapon he handed Bellairs after the fatality was the one that is missing."

"Well, Lord Pastern," Alleyn said, "will you answer Mr. Fox?"

"How many times am I to tell you I won't answer any of your tom-fool questions. I gave you a time-table, and that's all the help you get from me."

For a moment the three men were silent; Fox by the piano, Alleyn near the door and Lord Pastern midway between them like a truculent Pekinese, an animal, it occurred to Alleyn, he closely resembled.

"Don't forget, my lord," Fox said, "that last night you stated yourself that anybody could have got at the revolver while it was under the sombrero. Anybody, you remarked, for all you'd have noticed."

"What of it?" he said, bunching his cheeks.

"There's this about it, my lord. It's a tenable theory that one of the party at your own table could have substituted the second gun, loaded with the bolt, and that you could have fired it at Rivera, without knowing anything about the substitution."

"That cat won't jump," Lord Pastern said, "and you know it. I didn't tell anybody I was going to put the gun under my sombrero. Not a soul."

"Well, my lord," Fox said, "we can make inquiries about that."

"You can inquire till you're blue in the face and much good may it do you."

"Look here, my lord," Fox burst out, "do you *want* us to arrest you?"

"Not sure I don't. It'd be enough to make a cat laugh." He thrust his hands in his trousers pockets, walked round Fox, eyeing him, and fetched up in front of Alleyn. "Skelton," he said, "saw the gun. He handled it just before he went on and when he came out while I waited for my entrance he handled it again. While Breezy did the speech about me, it was."

"Why did he handle it this second time?" Alleyn asked.

"I was a bit excited. Nervy work, hangin' about for your entrance. I was takin' a last look at it and I dropped it and he picked it up and squinted down the barrel in a damn-your-eyes supercilious sort of way. Professional jealousy."

"Why didn't you mention this before, my lord?" Fox demanded, and was ignored. Lord Pastern grinned savagely at Alleyn. "Well," he said with gloating relish, "what about this arrest? I'll come quietly."

Alleyn said: "You know, I do wish that for once in a blue moon you'd behave yourself."

For the first time, he thought, Lord Pastern was giving him his full attention. He was suddenly quiet and wary. He eyed Alleyn with something of the air of a small boy who is not sure if he can bluff his way out of a misdemeanour.

"You really are making the most infernal nuisance of yourself, sir," Alleyn went on, "and, if you will allow me, the most appalling ass of yourself into the bargain."

"See here, Alleyn," Lord Pasten said with a not entirely convincing return to his former truculence, "I'm damned if I'll take this. I know what I'm up to."

"Then have the grace to suppose we know what we're up to, too. After all, sir, you're not the only one to remember that Rivera played the piano accordion."

For a moment Lord Pastern stood quite still with his jaw dropped and his eyebrows half-way up his forehead. He then said rapidly: "I'm late. Goin' to m'club," and incontinently bolted from the room.

CHAPTER ELEVEN

EPISODES IN TWO FLATS AND AN OFFICE

I

"Well, Mr. Alleyn," said Fox, "that settles it, in my mind. It's going to turn out the way you said. Cut loose the trimmings and you come to the—well the *corpus delicti* as you might say.

They were sitting in a police car outside the house in Duke's Gate. Both of them looked past the driver, and through the windscreen, at a jaunty and briskly moving figure, its hat a little to one side and swinging its walking stick.

"There he goes," Fox said, "as cocksure and perky as you please, and there goes our chap after him. Say what you like, Mr. Alleyn, the art of trailing your man isn't what it was in the service. These young fellows think they signed on for the sole purpose of tearing about the place with the Flying Squad." And having delivered himself of his customary grumble, Fox, still contemplating the diminishing figure of Lord Pastern, added : "Where do we go from here, sir?"

"Before we go anywhere you'll be good enough to explain why your duties led you back to Duke's Gate and, more particularly, to playing that old antic's boogy-woogie on the piano."

Fox smiled in a stately manner. "Well, sir," he said, "as to what brought me, it was a bit of stale information, and another bit that's not so stale. Skelton rang up after you left, to say he had inspected his lordship's revolver the second time and was sorry he hadn't mentioned it last night. He said that he and our Mr. Eton-and-Oxford Detective-Sergeant Sallis got into a discussion about the *petit bourgeoisie* or something and it went out of his head. I thought it better not to ring you at Duke's Gate. Extension wires all over the shop in that house. So, as it seemed to settle the question about which gun his lordship took on the platform with him, I thought I'd pop along and tell you."

"And Pastern saved you the trouble?"

"Quite so. And as to the piano, there was his lordship saying he'd been inspired, so to speak, with a new composition and wanted someone to try it over. He was making a great to-do over the ballroom being sealed. Our chaps have finished in there so there seemed no harm in obliging him. I thought it might establish friendly relations," Fox added sadly, "but I can't say it did in the end. Shall we tell this chap where we're going, sir?"

Alleyn said : "We'll call at the Metronome, then we'll have a look at Breezy and see how the poor swine's shaping up this morning. Then we'll have a very brief snack, Br'er Fox, and when that's over it'll be time to visit G.P.F. in his den. If he's there, blast him."

"Ah, by the way," Fox said, as they moved off, "that's the other bit of information. Mr. Bathgate rang the Yard and said he'd got hold of someone who writes regularly for this paper *Harmony* and it seems that Mr. Friend is generally supposed to be in the office on the afternoon and evening of the last Sunday in the month, on account of the paper going to press the following week. This gentleman told Mr. Bathgate that nobody on the regular staff except the editor ever sees Mr. Friend. The story is he deals direct with the proprietors of the paper but popular opinion in Fleet Street reckons he owns the show himself. They reckon the secrecy business is nothing but a build-up."

"Silly enough to be incredible," Alleyn muttered. "But we're knee-deep in imbecility. I suppose we can take it. All the same, I fancy we'll turn up a better reason for Mr. Friend's elaborate incognito before this interminable Sunday is out."

Fox said, with an air of quiet satisfaction : "I fancy we shall, sir. Mr. Bathgate's done quite a nice little job for us. It seems he pressed this friend of his a bit further and got him on to the subject of Mr. Manx's special articles for the paper and it came out that Mr. Manx is often in their office."

"Discussing his special articles. Picking up his galley-sheets or whatever they do."

"Better than that, Mr. Alleyn. This gentleman told Mr. Bathgate that Mr. Manx has been noticed coming out of G.P.F.'s room on several occasions, one of them being a Sunday afternoon."

"Oh."

"Fits, doesn't it?"

"Like a glove. Good for Bathgate. We'll ask him to meet us at the *Harmony* offices. This being the last Sunday in the month, Br'er Fox, we'll see what we can see. But first—the Metronome."

2

When Carlisle left the Yard, it was with a feeling of astonishment and aimless boredom. So it wasn't Uncle George's
revolver after all. So there had been an intricate muddle that
someone would have to unravel. Alleyn would unravel it and
someone else would be arrested and she ought to be
alarmed and agitated because of this. Perhaps, in the hinter-
land of her emotions, alarm and agitation were already established and waited to pounce, but in the meantime she was
only drearily miserable and tired. She was pestered by all sorts
of minor considerations. The thought of returning to Duke's
Gate and trying to cope with the situation there was intolerable. It wasn't so much the idea that Uncle George or Aunt
'Cile or Fée might have murdered Carlos Rivera that Carlisle
found appalling : it was the prospect of their several personalities forcing themselves upon her own; their demands upon
her attention and courtesy. She had a private misery, a galling
unhappiness, and she wanted to be alone with it.

While she walked irresolutely towards the nearest bus stop,
she remembered that not far from here, in a cul-de-sac called
Costers Row, was Edward Manx's flat. If she walked to Duke's
Gate she would pass the entry into this blind street. She was
persuaded that she did not want to see Edward, that an encounter would, indeed, be unbearable; yet, aimlessly, she began to
walk on. Church-going people returning home with an air of
circumspection made a pattering sound in the empty streets.
Groups of sparrows flustered and pecked. The day was mildly
sunny. The Yard man, detailed to keep observation on Carlisle, threaded his way through a trickle of pedestrians and
recalled the Sunday dinners of his boyhood. Beef, he thought,
Yorkshire pudding, gravy, and afterwards a heavy hour or so in
the front room. Carlisle gave him no trouble at all but he was
hungry.

He saw her hesitate at the corner of Costers Row and himself halted to light a cigarette. She glanced along the file of
housefronts and then, at a more rapid pace, crossed the end of
the row and continued on her way. At the same time a dark
young man came out of a house six doors down Costers Row

and descended the steps in time to catch a glimpse of her. He shouted: "Lisle!" and waved his arm. She hurried on, and once past the corner, out of his sight, broke into a run. "Hi Lisle!" he shouted. "Lisle!" and loped after her. The Yard man watched him go by, turn the corner, and overtake her. She spun round at the touch of his hand on her arm and they stood face to face.

A third man who had come out of some doorway farther up the cul-de-sac walked briskly down the path on the same side as the Yard man. They greeted each other like old friends and shook hands. The Yard man offered cigarettes and lit a match. "How's it going, Bob?" he said softly. "That your bird?"

"That's him. Who's the lady?"

"Mine," said the first, whose back was turned to Carlisle.

"Not bad," his colleague muttered, glancing at her.

"I'd just as soon it was my dinner, though."

"Argument?"

"Looks like it."

"Keeping their voices down."

Their movements were slight and casual: acquaintances pausing for a rather aimless chat.

"What's the betting?" said the first.

"They'll separate. I never have the luck."

"You're wrong, though."

"Going back to his place?"

"Looks like it."

"I'll toss you for it."

"O.K." The other pulled his clenched hand out of his pocket. "Your squeak," he said.

"Heads."

"It's tails."

"I never get the luck."

"I'll ring in then and get something to eat. Relieve you in half an hour, Bob."

They shook hands again heartily as Carlisle and Edward Manx, walking glumly towards them, turned into Costers Row.

Carlisle had seen Edward Manx out of the corner of her eye as she crossed the end of the cul-de-sac. Unreasoned panic took hold of her. She lengthened her stride, made a show of looking at her watch, and when he called her name, broke into a run. Her heart pounded and her mouth was dry. She had the sensation of a fugitive in a dream. She was the pursued and, since even in her sudden alarm she was confusedly aware of something in herself that frightened her, she was also the pursuer. This nightmarish conviction was intensified by the sound of his feet clattering after her and of his voice, completely familiar but angry, calling her to stop.

Her feet were leaden, he was overtaking her quite easily. Her anticipation of his seizing her from behind was so vivid that when his hand actually closed on her arm it was something of a relief. He jerked her round to face him and she was glad to feel angry.

"What the hell do you think you're doing?" he said breathlessly.

"That's my business," she panted, and added defiantly: "I'm late. I'll be late for lunch. Aunt 'Cile will be furious."

"Don't be an ass, Lisle. You ran when you saw me. You heard me call out and you kept on running. What the devil d'you mean by it?"

His heavy eyebrows were drawn together and his lower lip jutted out.

"Please let me go, Ned," she said. "I really am late."

"That's utterly childish and you know it. I'm getting to the bottom of this. Come back to the flat. I want to talk to you."

"Aunt 'Cile . . ."

"Oh, for God's sake! I'll ring Duke's Gate and say you're lunching here."

"No."

For a moment he looked furious. He still held her arm and his fingers bit into it, hurting her. Then he said more gently: "You can't expect me to let a thing like this pass: it's a monstrous state of affairs. I must know what's gone wrong. Last night, after we got back from the Metronome, I could tell there was something. Please, Lisle. Don't let's stand here snarling at each other. Come back to the flat."

"I'd rather not. Honestly. I know I'm behaving queerly."

He had slipped the palm of his hand inside her arm, pressing it against him. His hand was gentler now but she couldn't escape it. He began to speak persuasively and she remembered

how, even when they were children, she had never been able to
resist his persuasiveness. " You will, Lisle, won't you? Don't
be queer, I can't bear all this peculiarity. Come along."

She looked helplessly at the two men on the opposite corner,
thinking vaguely that she had seen one of them before. " I
wish I knew him," she thought, " I wish I could stop and speak
to him."

They turned into Costers Row. " There's some food in the
flat. It's quite a nice flat. I want you to see it. We'll have
lunch together, shan't we? I'm sorry I was churlish, Lisle."

His key clicked in the lock of the blue door. They were in a
small lobby. " It's a basement flat," he said, " but not at all
bad. There's even a garden. Down those stairs."

" You go first," she said. She actually wondered if that
would give her a chance to bolt and if she would have the
nerve to do it. He looked fixedly at her.

" I don't believe I trust you," he said lightly. " On you go."

He followed close on her heels down the steep stairs and
took her arm again as he reached past her and unlocked the
second door.

" Here we are," he said, pushing it open. He gave her a
little shove forward.

It was a large, low-ceilinged room, white-washed and oak-
beamed. French windows opened on a little yard with potted
flowers and plane-trees in tubs. The furniture was modern :
steel chairs with rubber-foam upholstery, a carefully planned
desk, a divan bed with a scarlet cover. A rigorous still-life
hung above the fireplace, the only picture in the room. The
bookshelves looked as if they had been stocked completely
from a Left Book Shop. It was a scrupulously tidy room.

" The oaken beams are strict stockbroker's Tudor," he was
saying. " Completely functionless, of course, and pretty revolting. Otherwise not so bad, do you think? Sit down while I
find a drink."

Sat sat on the divan and only half-listened to him. His be-
lated pretence that, after all, this was a pleasant and casual
encounter did nothing to reassure her. He was still angry. She
took the drink he brought and found her hand was shaking so
much she couldn't carry the glass to her lips. The drink spilled.
She bent her head down and took a quick gulp at it, hoping

this would steady her. She rubbed furtively with her handkerchief at the splashes on the cover and knew, without looking,
that he watched her.

" Shall we go in, boots and all, or wait till after lunch?" he
said.

" There's nothing to talk about. I'm sorry to be such an ass,
but after all it was a bit of a night. I suppose murder doesn't
suit me."

" Oh, no," he said, " that won't do. You don't bolt like a
rabbit at the sight of me because somebody killed a piano
accordionist." And after a long pause he added smoothly,
" Unless, by any chance, you think I killed him. Do you?"

" Don't be a dolt," she said, and by some fortuitous mis-
chance, an accident quite beyond her control and unrelated to
any recognisable impulse, her answer sounded unconvincing
and too violent. It was the last question she had expected from
him.

" Well, at least I'm glad of that," he said. He sat on the
table near to her. She did not look up at him but straight
before her at his left hand, lying easily across his knee.
" Come on," he said, " what have I done? There *is* something
I've done. What is it?"

She thought : " I'll have to tell him something : part of it.
Not the real thing itself but the other bit that doesn't matter so
much." She began to search for an approach, a line to take,
some kind of credible presentation, but she was deadly tired
and she astonished herself by saying abruptly and loudly :
" I've found out about G.P.F."

His hand moved swiftly out of her range of sight. She
looked up expecting to be confronted by his anger or astonishment but he had turned aside, skewing round to put his glass
down on the table behind him.

" Have you?" he said. " That's awkward, isn't it?" He
moved quickly away from her and across the room to a wall
cupboard which he opened. With his back turned to her he
said : " Who told you? Did Cousin George?"

" No," she said, wearily surprised. " No, I saw the letter."

" Which letter?" he asked, groping in the cupboard.

" The one to Félicité."

" Oh," said Manx slowly. " That one." He turned round.

He had a packet of cigarettes in his hand and came towards her holding it out. She shook her head and he lit one himself with steady hands. "How did you come to see it?" he said.

"It was lost. It—I—oh, what *does* it matter? The whole thing was perfectly clear. Need we go on?"

"I still don't see why this discovery should inspire you to sprint like an athlete at the sight of me."

"I don't think I know myself."

"What were you doing last night?" he demanded suddenly. "Where did you go after we got back to Duke's Gate? Why did you turn up again with Alleyn? What were you up to?"

It was impossible to tell him that Félicité had lost the letter. That would lead at once to his discovering that Alleyn had read it : worse than that, it would lead inevitably to the admittance, perhaps the discussion, of his new attitude towards Félicité. "He might," she thought, "tell me, point-blank, that he is in love with Fée and I'm in no shape to jump that hurdle."

So she said : "It doesn't matter what I was up to. I can't tell you. In a way it would be a breach of confidence."

"Was it something to do with this G.P.F. business?" Manx said sharply, and after a pause : "You haven't told anybody about this discovery, have you?"

She hadn't told Alleyn. He had found out for himself. Miserably she shook her head.

He stooped over her. "You mustn't tell anybody, Lisle. That's important. You realise how important, don't you?"

Isolated sentences, of an indescribable archness, flashed up in her memory of that abominable page. "You don't need to tell me that," she said, looking away from his intent and frowning eyes, and then suddenly burst out : "It's such ghastly stuff, Ned. That magazine. It's like one of our novelettes gone hay-wire. How you could!"

"My articles are all right," he said, and after a pause : "So that's it, is it? You *are* a purist, aren't you?"

She clasped her hands together and fixed her gaze on them. "I must tell you," she said, "that if, in some hellish muddled way, entirely beyond my comprehension, this G.P.F. business has anything to do with Rivera's death——"

"Well?"

"I mean, if it's going to—I mean——"

"You mean that if Alleyn asks you point-blank about it, you'll tell him?"

"Yes," she said.

"I see."

Carlisle's head ached. She had been unable to face her breakfast and the drink he had given her had taken effect. Their confused antagonism, the sense of being trapped in this alien room, her personal misery : all these circumstances were joined in a haze of uncertainty. The whole scene had become unreal and unendurable. When he put his hands on her shoulders and said loudly : "There's more to it than this. Come on, what is it?" she seemed to hear him from a great distance. His hands were bearing down hard. "I *will* know," he was saying.

At the far end of the room a telephone bell began to ring. She watched him go to it and take the receiver off. His voice changed its quality and became the easy friendly voice she had known for so long.

"Hallo? Hallo, Fée darling. I'm terribly sorry, I should have rung up. They kept Lisle for hours grilling her at the Yard. Yes : I ran into her and she asked me to telephone and say she was so late she'd try for a meal somewhere at hand, so I asked her to have one with me. Please tell Cousin Cecile it's entirely my fault and not hers : I promised to ring for her." He looked at Carlisle over the telephone. "She's perfectly all right," he said. "I'm looking after her."

3

If any painter, a surrealist for choice, attempted to set the figure of a working detective officer against an appropriate and composite background, he would turn his attention to rooms overlaid with films of dust, to objects suspended in unaccustomed dinginess, to ash-trays and tablecloths, unemptied waste-bins, tables littered with powder, dirty glasses, disordered chairs, stale food, and garments that retained an unfresh smell of disuse.

When Alleyn and Fox entered the Metronome at 12.30 on

this Sunday morning, it smelt of Saturday night. The restaurant, serveries and kitchens had been cleaned, but the vestibule and offices were untouched and upon them the aftermath of festivity lay like a thin pall of dust. Three men in shirt sleeves greeted Alleyn with that tinge of gloomy satisfaction which marks an unsuccessful search.

" No luck?" Alleyn said.

" No luck yet, sir."

" There's the passage that runs through from the foyer and behind the offices to the back premises," said Fox. " That's the way the deceased must have gone to make his entrance from the far end of the restaurant."

" We've been along there, Mr. Fox."

" Plumbing?"

" Not yet, Mr. Alleyn."

" I'd try that next." Alleyn pointed through the two open doors of Caesar Bonn's office into the inner room. " Begin there," he said.

He went alone into the restaurant. The table he and Troy had sat at was the second on the right. The chairs were turned up on its surface. He replaced one of them and seated himself. " For twenty years," he thought, " I have trained my memory and trained it rigorously. This is the first time I have been my own witness in a case of this sort. Am I any good or am I rotten?"

Sitting alone there, he recreated his scene, beginning with small things : the white cloth, the objects on the table, Troy's long hand close to his own and just within his orbit of vision. He waited until these details were firm in his memory and then reached out a little farther. At the next table, her back towards him, sat Félicité de Suze in a red dress. She turned a white carnation in her fingers and looked sidelong at the man beside her. He was between Alleyn and the lamp on their table. His profile was rimmed with light. His head was turned towards the band dais. On his right, more clearly visible, more brilliantly lit, was Carlisle Wayne. In order to watch the performance she had swung round with her back half-turned to the table. Her hair curved back from her temples. There was a look of compassion and bewilderment in her face. Beyond Carlisle, with her back to the wall, a heavy shape almost obscured by the others, sat Lady Pastern. As they moved he could see in turn her stony coiffure, her important shoulders, the rigid silhouette of her bust; but never her face.

Raised above them, close to them, a figure gestured wildly among the tympani. This was a vivid picture because it was contained by a pool of light. Lord Pastern's baldish head darted and bobbed. Metallic highlights flashed among his instruments. The spotlight shifted and there, in the centre of the stage, was Rivera, bent backwards, hugging his piano accordion to his chest. Eyes, teeth, and steel and mother-of-pearl ornament glittered. The arm of the metronome pointed fixedly at his chest. Behind, half-shadowed, a plump hand jerked up and down, beating the air with its miniature baton. A wide smile glistened in a moon face. Now Lord Pastern faced Rivera on the perimeter of the light pool. His revolver pointed at the contorted figure, flashed, and Rivera fell. Then the further shots and comic falls and then . . . In the deserted restaurant Alleyn brought his hands down sharply on the table. It had been then, and not until then, that the lights began their infernal blinking. They popped in and out down the length of the metronome and about its frame, in and out, red, green, blue, green, red. Then, and not until then had the arm swung away from the prostrate figure and, with the rest of that winking stuttering bedazzlement, gone into action.

Alleyn got up and mounted the bandstand. He stood on the spot where Rivera had fallen. The skeleton tower of the metronome framed him. The reverse side of this structure revealed its electrical equipment. He looked up at the pointer of the giant arm which was suspended directly above his head. It was a hollow steel or plastic casting studded with miniature lights, and for a moment reminded him fantastically of the jewelled dart. To the right of the bandroom door and hidden from the audience by the piano, a small switchboard was sunk in the wall. Happy Hart, they had told Alleyn, was in charge of the lights. From where he sat at the piano and from where he fell to the floor he could reach out to the switches. Alleyn did so, now, pulling down the one marked " Motor." A hidden whirring sound prefaced the first loud " clack." The giant downward-pointing arm swept semi-circularly across, back, across and back to its own ratchet-like accompaniment. He switched on the lights and stood for a moment, an incongruous figure, motionless at the core of his kaleidoscopic setting. The point of the arm, flashing its lights, swept within four inches of his head and away and back and away again. " If you watched the damn' thing for long enough, I believe it'd mesmerise you," he thought, and turned off the switches.

Back in the offices he found Mr. Fox in severe control of two plumbers who were removing their jackets in the lavatory.

" If we can't find anything fishing with wires, Mr. Alleyn," Fox said, " it'll be a case of taking down the whole job."

" I don't hold out ecstatic hopes," Alleyn said, " but get on with it."

One of the plumbers pulled the chain and contemplated the ensuing phenomena.

" Well?" said Fox.

" I wouldn't say she was a sweetly running job," the plumber diagnosed, " and yet again she *works* if you can understand me." He raised a finger, and glanced at his mate.

" Trap-trouble?" ventured his mate.

" Ar."

" We'll leave you to it," Alleyn said, and withdrew Fox into the office. " Fox," he said, " let's remind ourselves of the key pieces in this jig-saw atrocity. What are they?"

Fox said promptly : " The set-up at Duke's Gate. The drug racket. *Harmony.* The substitution. The piano accordion. The nature of the weapon."

" Add one more. The metronome was motionless when Rivera played. It started its blasted tick-tack stuff after he fell and after the other rounds had been fired."

" I get you, sir. Yes," said Fox, placidly, " there's that too. Add the metronome."

" Now, let's mug over the rest of the material and see where we are."

Sitting in Caesar Bonn's stale office, they sorted, discarded, correlated and dissociated the fragments of the case. Their voices droned on to the intermittent accompaniment of plumbers' aquatics. After twenty minutes Fox shut his notebook, removed his spectacles and looked steadily at his superior officer.

" It amounts to this," he said. " Setting aside a handful of insignificant details, we're short of only one piece." He poised his hand, palm down, over the table. " If we can lay hold of that and if, when we've got it, it fits; well, our little picture's complete."

"If," Alleyn said, "and when."

The door of the inner office opened and the senior plumber entered. With an air of false modesty he extended a naked arm and bleached hand. On the palm of the hand dripped a revolver. " Would this," he asked glumly, " be what you was wanting?"

4

Dr. Curtis waited for them outside the main entrance to Breezy's flat.

" Sorry to drag you out, Curtis," Alleyn said, " but we may need your opinion about his fitness to make a statement. This is Fox's party. He's the drug baron."

" How do you expect he'll be, Doctor?" Fox asked.

Dr. Curtis stared at his shoes and said guardedly : " Heavy hangover. Shaky. Depressed. May be resentful. May be placatory. Can't tell."

" Suppose he decides to talk, is it likely to be truthful?"

" Not very. They usually lie."

Fox said : " What's the line to take. Tough or coaxing?"

" Use your own judgment."

" You might tip us the wink, though, Doctor."

" Well," said Curtis, " let's take a look at him."

The flats were of the more dubious modern kind and brandished chromium steel almost in the Breezy Bellairs Manner —showily and without significance. Alleyn, Fox and Curtis approached the flat by way of a rococo lift and a tunnel-like passage. Fox pressed a bell and a plain-clothes officer answered the door. When he saw them he snibbed back the lock and closed the door behind him.

" How is he?" Alleyn asked.

" Awake, sir. Quiet enough, but restless."

" Said anything?" Fox asked. " To make sense, I mean."

" Nothing much, Mr. Fox. Very worried about the deceased,

he seems to be. Says he doesn't know what he's going to do without him."

"*That* makes sense at all events," Fox grunted. "Shall we go in, sir?"

It was an expensive and rather characterless flat, only remarkable for its high content of framed and signed photographs and its considerable disorder. Breezy, wearing a dressing-gown of unbelievable sumptuousness, sat in a deep chair into which he seemed to shrink a little further as they came in. His face was the colour of an uncooked fowl and as flabby. As soon as he saw Dr. Curtis he raised a lamentable wail.

"Doc," he whined, "I'm all shot to heaps. Doc, for petesake take a look at me and tell them."

Curtis picked up his wrist.

"Listen," Breezy implored him, "you know a sick man when you see one—listen——"

"Don't talk."

Breezy pulled at his lower lip, blinked at Alleyn and, with the inconsequence of a ventriloquist's doll, flashed his celebrated smile.

"Excuse us," he said.

Curtis tested his reflexes, turned up his eyelid and looked at his tongue.

"You're a bit of a mess," he said, "but there's no reason why you shouldn't answer any questions these gentlemen like to put to you." He glanced at Fox. "He's quite able to take in the usual warning," he said.

Fox administered it and drew up a chair, facing Breezy, who shot out a quavering finger at Alleyn.

"What's the idea," he said, "shooing this chap on to me? What's wrong with talking to me yourself?"

"Inspector Fox," Alleyn said, "is concerned with investigations about the illicit drug trade. He wants some information from you."

He turned away and Fox went into action.

"Well, now, Mr. Bellairs," Fox said, "I think it's only fair to tell you what we've ascertained so far. Save quite a bit of time, won't it?"

"I can't tell you a thing. I don't know a thing."

" We're aware that you're in the unfortunate position," Fox said, " of having formed the taste for one of these drugs. Gets a real hold on you, doesn't it, that sort of thing?"

Breezy said : " It's only because I'm overworked. Give me a break and I'll cut it out. I swear I will. But gradually. You have to make it gradual. That's right, isn't it, Doc?"

" I believe," Fox said comfortably, " that's the case. That's what I understand. Now, about the supply. We've learnt on good authority that the deceased, in this instance, was the source of supply. Would you care to add anything to that statement, Mr. Bellairs?"

" Was it the old bee told you?" Breezy demanded. " I bet it was the old bee. Or Syd. Syd knew. Syd's had it in for me. Dirty bolshevik! Was it Syd Skelton?"

Fox said that the information had come from more than one source and asked how Lord Pastern knew Rivera had provided the drugs. Breezy replied that Lord Pastern nosed out all sorts of things. He refused to be drawn further.

" I understand," Fox went on, " that his lordship tackled you in the matter last evening."

Breezy at once became hysterical. " He'd ruin me! That's what he'd do. Look! Whatever happens don't let him do it. He's crazy enough to do it. Honest. Honest he is."

" Do what?"

" Like what he said. Write to that bloody paper about me."

" *Harmony*?" Fox asked, at a venture. " Would that be the paper?"

" That's right. He said he knew someone—God, he's got a thing about it. You know—the stuff. Damn and blast him," Breezy screamed out, " he'll kill me. He killed Carlos and now what'll *I* do, where'll I get it? Everybody watching and spying and I don't *know*. Carlos never told me. I don't *know*."

" Never told you?" Fox said peacefully. " Fancy that now! Never let on how he got it! And I bet he made it pretty hot when it came to paying up. Um?"

" God, you're telling me!"

" And no reduction made, for instance, if you helped him out?"

Breezy shrank back in his chair. " I don't know anything about that. I don't get you at all."

"Well, I mean to say," Fox explained, "there'd be opportunities, wouldn't there? Ladies, or it might be their partners, asking the band leader for a special number. A note changes hands and it might be a tip or it might be payment in advance, and the goods delivered next time. We've come across instances. I wondered if he got you to oblige him. You don't have to say anything if you don't want to, mind. We've the names and addresses of all the guests last night and we've got our records. People that are known to like it, you know. So I won't press it. Don't let it worry you. But I thought that he might have had some arrangement with you. Out of gratitude as you might put it——"

"Gratitude!" Breezy laughed shrilly. "You think you know too much," he said profoundly, and drew in his breath. He was short of breath and had broken into a sallow, profuse sweat. "I don't know what I'll do without Carlos," he whispered. "Someone'll have to help me. It's all the old bee's fault. Him and the girl. If I could just have a smoke——" He appealed to Dr. Curtis. "Not a prick. I know you won't give me a prick. Just one little smoke. I don't usually in the mornings but this is exceptional, Doc. Doc, couldn't you——"

"You'll have to hang on a bit longer," Dr. Curtis said, not unkindly. "Wait a bit. We won't let it go longer than you can manage. Hang on."

Suddenly and inanely Breezy yawned, a face-splitting yawn that bared his gums and showed his coated tongue. He rubbed his arms and neck. "I keep feeling as if there's something under my skin. Worms or something," he said, fretfully.

"About the weapon," Fox began.

Breezy leant forward, his hands on his knees, aping Fox. "About the weapon?" he mimicked savagely. "You mind your business about the weapon. Coming here tormentin' a chap. Whose gun was it? Whose bloody sunshade was it? Whose bloody stepdaughter was it? Whose bloody business is it? Get out!" He threw himself back in his chair, panting. "Get out. I'm within my rights. Get out."

"Why not?" Fox agreed. "We'll leave you to yourself. Unless Mr. Alleyn . . .?"

"No," Alleyn said.

Dr. Curtis turned at the door. "Who's your doctor, Breezy?" he asked.

"I haven't got a doctor," Breezy whispered. "Nothing ever used to be wrong with me. Not a thing."

"We'll find someone to look after you."

"Can't *you*? Can't you look after me, Doc?"

"Well," Dr. Curtis said, "I might."

"Come on," said Alleyn, and they went out.

5

One end of Materfamilias Lane had suffered a bomb and virtually disappeared, but the other stood intact, a narrow City street with ancient buildings, a watery smell, dark entries and impenitent charm.

The *Harmony* offices were in a tall building at a corner where Materfamilias Lane dived downhill and a cul-de-sac called Journeyman's Steps led off to the right. Both were deserted on this Sunday afternoon. Alleyn's and Fox's feet rang loudly on the pavement as they walked down Materfamilias Lane. Before they reached the corner they came upon Nigel Bathgate standing in the arched entry to a brewer's yard.

"In me," Nigel said, "you see the detective's ready-reckoner and pocket-guide to the City."

"I hope you're right. What have you got for us?"

"His room's on the ground floor with the window in this street. The nearest entrance is round the corner. If he's there the door to his office'll be latched on the inside with an 'Engaged' notice displayed. He locks himself in."

"He's there," Alleyn said.

"How do you know?"

"He's been tailed. Our man rang through from a call-box and he should be back on the job by now."

"Up the side street if he's got the gumption," Fox muttered. "Look out, sir!"

"Softly does it," Alleyn murmured.

Nigel found himself neatly removed to the far end of the archway, engulfed in Fox's embrace and withdrawn into a recess. Alleyn seemed to arrive there at the same time.

"You cry mum and I'll cry budget!" Alleyn whispered. Someone was walking briskly down Materfamilias Lane. The approaching footsteps echoed in the archway as Edward Manx went by in the sunlight.

They leant motionless against the dark stone and clearly heard the bang of a door.

"Your sleuth-hound," Nigel pointed out with some relish, "would appear to be at fault. Whom do you suppose he's been shadowing? Obviously, not Manx."

"Obviously," Alleyn said, and Fox mumbled obscurely.

"Why are we waiting?" Nigel asked fretfully.

"Give him five minutes," Alleyn said. "Let him settle down."

"Am I coming in with you?"

"Do you want to?"

"Certainly. One merely," Nigel said, "rather wishes that one hadn't met him before."

"May be a bit of trouble, you know," Fox speculated.

"Extremely probable," Alleyn agreed.

A bevy of sparrows flustered and squabbled out in the sunny street, an eddy of dust rose inconsequently, and somewhere, out of sight, halliards rattled against an untenanted flagpole.

"Dull," Fox said, "doing your beat in the City of a Sunday afternoon. I had six months of it as a young chap. Catch yourself wondering why the blazes you were there and so on."

"Hideous," Alleyn said.

"I used to carry my Police Code and Procedure on me and try to memorise six pages a day. I was," Fox said simply, "an ambitious young chap in those days."

Nigel glanced at his watch and lit a cigarette.

The minutes dragged by. A clock struck three and was followed by an untidy conclave of other clocks, overlapping each other. Alleyn walked to the end of the archway and looked up and down Materfamilias Lane.

"We may as well get under way," he said. He glanced again up the street and made a sign with his hand. Fox and Nigel followed him. A man in a dark suit came down the footpath. Alleyn spoke to him briefly and then led the way to the corner. The man remained in the archway.

They walked quickly by the window, which was uncurtained

and had the legend *Harmony* painted across it and turned into
the cul-de-sac. There was a side door with a brass plate beside
it. Alleyn turned the handle and the door opened. Fox and
Nigel followed him into a dingy passage which evidently led
back into a main corridor. On their right, scarcely discernible
in the sudden twilight, was a door. The word "Engaged,"
painted in white, showed clearly. From beyond it they heard
the rattle of a typewriter.

Alleyn knocked. The rattle stopped short and a chair
scraped on boards. Someone walked towards the door and a
voice, Edward Manx's, said: "Hallo? Who is it?"

"Police," Alleyn said.

In the stillness they looked speculatively at each other.
Alleyn poised his knuckles at the door, waited, and said:
"May we have a word with you, Mr. Manx?"

After a second's silence the voice said: "One moment. I'll
come out."

Alleyn glanced at Fox, who moved in beside him. The word
"Engaged" shot out of sight noisily and was replaced by the
letters "G.P.F." A latch clicked and the door opened inwards.
Manx stood there with one hand on the jamb and the other
on the door. There was a wooden screen behind him.

Fox's boot moved over the threshold.

"I'll come out," Manx repeated.

"On the contrary, we'll come in, if you please," Alleyn said.

Without any particular display of force or even brusqueness,
but with great efficiency, they went past him and round the
screen. He looked for a second at Nigel and seemed not to
recognise him. Then he followed them and Nigel unobtru-
sively followed him.

There was a green-shaded lamp on a desk at which a figure
was seated with its back towards them. As Nigel entered, the
swivel-chair creaked and spun round. Dingily dressed and
wearing a green eyeshade, Lord Pastern faced them with
bunched cheeks.

CHAPTER TWELVE

G.P.F.

I

HE MADE a high-pitched snarling noise as they closed round him and reached out his hand towards an ink-pot on the desk.

Fox said: "Now, my lord, don't you do anything you'll be sorry for," and moved the ink-pot.

Lord Pastern sunk his head with a rapid movement between his shoulders. From behind them Edward Manx said: "I don't know why you've done this, Alleyn. It'll get you no further."

Lord Pastern said: "Shut up, Ned," and glared at Alleyn. "I'll have you kicked out of the force," he said. "Kicked out, by God!" And after a silence: "You don't get a word from me. Not a syllable."

Alleyn pulled up a chair and sat down facing him. "That will suit us very well," he said. "You are going to listen, and I advise you to do so with as good a grace as you can muster. When you've heard what I've got to say you may read the statement I've brought with me. You can sign it, alter it, dictate another or refuse to do any of these things. But in the meantime, Lord Pastern, you are going to listen."

Lord Pastern folded his arms tightly across his chest, rested his chin on his tie and screwed up his eyes. Alleyn took a folded typescript from his breast pocket, opened it and crossed his knees.

"This statement was prepared," he said, "on the assumption that you are the man who calls himself G. P. Friend and writes the articles signed G.P.F. in *Harmony*. It is a statement of what we believe to be fact and doesn't concern itself overmuch with motive. I, however, will deal rather more fully with motive. In launching this paper and in writing these articles, you found it necessary to observe complete anonymity. Your reputation as probably the most quarrelsome man in England, your loudly publicised domestic rows, and your notorious eccentricities would make an appearance in the role of Guide

Philosopher and Friend a fantastically bad joke. We presume, therefore, that through a reliable agent you deposited adequate security in a convenient bank with the specimen signature of G. P. Friend as the negotiating instrument. You then set up the legend of your own anonymity and launched yourself in the role of oracle. With huge success."

Lord Pastern did not stir but a film of complacency overspread his face.

" This success," Alleyn went on, " it must always be remembered, depends entirely upon the preservation of your anonymity. Once let *Harmony's* devotees learn that G.P.F. is none other than the notoriously unharmonious peer whose public quarrels have been the punctual refuge of the penny-press during the silly season—once let that be known and G.P.F. is sunk, and Lord Pastern loses a fortune. All right. Everything goes along swimmingly. You do a lot of your journalism at Duke's Gate, no doubt, but you also make regular visits to this office wearing dark glasses, the rather shabby hat and scarf which are hanging on the wall there, and the old jacket you have on at this moment. You work behind locked doors and Mr. Edward Manx is possibly your only confidant. You enjoy yourself enormously and make a great deal of money. So, perhaps, in his degree, does Mr. Manx."

Manx said : " I've no shares in the paper if that's what you mean. My articles are paid for at the usual rate."

" Shut up, Ned," said his cousin automatically.

" The paper," Alleyn continued, " is run on eccentric but profitable lines. It explodes bombs. It exposes rackets. It mingles soft-soap and cyanide. In particular it features an extremely efficient and daringly personal attack on the drug-racket. It employs experts, it makes accusations, it defies and invites prosecution. Its information is accurate and if it occasionally frustrates its own professed aims by warning criminals before the police are in a position to arrest them, it is far too much inflated with crusaders' zeal and rising sales to worry its head about *that*."

" Look here, Alleyn . . ." Manx began angrily, and simultaneously Lord Pastern shouted : " What the hell do you think you're getting at?"

" One moment," Alleyn said. Manx thrust his hands in his

pockets and began to move about the room. "Better to hear this out, after all," he muttered.

"Much better," Alleyn agreed. "I'll go on. Everything prospered in the *Harmony* set-up until you, Lord Pastern, discovered an urge to exploit your talents as a tympanist and allied yourself with Breezy Bellairs and His Boys. Almost immediately there were difficulties. First: your stepdaughter, for whom I think you have a great affection, became attracted by Carlos Rivera, the piano accordionist in the band. You are an observant man: for a supreme egoist, surprisingly so. At some time of your association with the Boys, I don't know precisely when, you became aware that Breezy Bellairs was taking drugs and, more important, that Carlos Rivera was supplying them. Through your association with *Harmony*, you are well up in the methods of drug-distribution and you are far too sharp not to realise that the usual pattern was being followed. Bellairs was in a position to act as a minor distributing agent. He was introduced to the drug, acquired a habit for it, was forced to hand it out to clients at the Metronome, and as a reward was given as much as Rivera thought was good for him at the usual exorbitant rate."

Alleyn looked curiously at Lord Pastern who, at that moment, met his eye and blinked twice.

"It's an odd situation," Alleyn said, "isn't it? Here we have a man of eclectic, violent and short-lived enthusiasms suddenly confronted with a situation where his two reigning passions and his one enduring attachment are brought into violent opposition."

He turned to Manx, who had stopped still and was looking fixedly at him.

"A situation of great possibilities from your professional point of view, I should imagine," Alleyn said. "The stepdaughter whom Lord Pastern loves falls for Rivera, who is engaged in an infamous trade which Lord Pastern is zealous in fighting. At the same time Rivera's dupe is the conductor of the band in which Lord Pastern burns to perform. As a final twist in an already tricky situation, Rivera has discovered, perhaps amongst Lord Pastern's music during a band rehearsal, some rough drafts for G.P.F.'s page, typed on Duke's Gate letter-paper. He is using them, no doubt, to force on his

engagement to Miss de Suze. 'Either support my suit or . . .'
For Rivera, in addition to running a drug racket, is an accomplished blackmailer. How is Lord Pastern to play the drums,
break the engagement, preserve his anonymity as G.P.F. and
explode the drug racket?"

"You can't possibly," Manx said, "have proof of a quarter
of all this. It's the most brazen guesswork."

"A certain amount is guesswork. But we have enough information and hard fact to carry us some way. I think that
between you, you are going to fill out the rest."

Manx laughed shortly. "What a hope!" he said.

"Well," Alleyn murmured, "let us go on and see. Lord
Pastern's inspiration comes out of a clear sky while he is
working on his copy for G.P.F.'s page in *Harmony*. Among the
letters in his basket, seeking guidance, philosophy and friendship is one from his stepdaughter." He stopped short. "I
wonder," he said, "if at some time or another there is also one
from his wife? Asking perhaps for advice in her marital
problems."

Manx looked quickly at Lord Pastern and away again.

"It might explain," Alleyn said thoughtfully, "why Lady
Pastern is so vehement in her disapproval of *Harmony*. If she
did write to G.P.F., I imagine the answer was one of the five
shilling Private Chat Letters and extremely displeasing to her."

Lord Pastern gave a short bark of laughter and shot a glance
at his cousin.

"However," Alleyn went on, "we are concerned, at this
point, with the fact that Miss de Suze does write for guidance.
Out of this coincidence, an idea is born. He answers the letter.
She replies. The correspondence goes on, becoming, as Miss
de Suze put it to me, more and more come-to-ish. Lord
Pastern is an adept. He stages (again I quote Miss de Suze)
a sort of Cupid-and-Psyche act at one remove. She asks if they
may meet. He replies ardently but refuses. He has all the fun
of watching her throughout in his own character. Meanwhile
he appears to Rivera to be supporting his suit. But the ice gets
thinner and thinner and his figure-skating increasingly hazardous. Moreover, here he is with a golden opportunity for a
major journalistic scoop. He could expose Bellairs, represent
himself as a brilliant investigator who has worked on his own

in the band and now hands the whole story over to *Harmony*. And yet—and yet—there are those captivating drums, those entrancing cymbals, those stimulating wire whisks. There is his own composition. There is his début. He skates on precariously but with exhilaration. He fiddles with the idea of weaning Bellairs from his vice and frightens him into fits by threatening to supplant Syd Skelton. He——"

"Did you," Lord Pastern interrupted, "go to that police school or whatever it is? Hendon?"

"No," Alleyn said. "I didn't."

"Well, get on, get on," he snapped.

"We come to the night of the début and of the great inspiration. Lady Pastern quite obviously desires a marriage between her daughter and Mr. Edward Manx."

Manx made an expostulatory sound. Alleyn waited for a moment. "Look here, Alleyn," Manx said, "you can at least observe some kind of decency. I object most strongly——" He glared at Nigel Bathgate.

"I'm afraid you'll have to lump it," Alleyn said mildly. Nigel said: "I'm sorry, Manx. I'll clear out if you like, but I'll hear it all, in any case."

Manx turned on his heel, walked over to the window and stood there with his back to them.

"Lord Pastern," Alleyn continued, "seems to have shared this hope. And now, having built up a spurious but ardent mystery round G.P.F., he gets his big idea. Perhaps he notices Mr. Manx's instant dislike of Rivera and perhaps he supposes this dislike to arise from an attachment to his stepdaughter. At all events he sees Mr. Manx put a white carnation in his coat, he goes off to his study and he types a romantic note to Miss de Suze in which G.P.F. reveals himself as the wearer of a white carnation. The note swears her to secrecy. Miss de Suze, coming straight from a violent quarrel with Rivera, sees the white flower in Mr. Manx's jacket and reacts according to plan."

Manx said: "Oh, my *God*!" and drummed with his fingers on the window-pane.

"The one thing that seems to have escaped Lord Pastern's notice," Alleyn said, "is the fact that Mr. Manx is enormously attracted, not by Miss de Suze, but by Miss Carlisle Wayne."

"Hell!" said Lord Pastern sharply, and slewed round in his swivel chair. "Hi!" he shouted. "Ned!"

"For pity's sake," Manx said impatiently, "let's forget it. It couldn't matter less." He caught his breath. "In the context," he added.

Lord Pastern contemplated his cousin's back with extreme severity and then directed his attention once more upon Alleyn. "Well?" he said.

"Well," Alleyn repeated, "so much for the great inspiration. But your activity hasn't exhausted itself. There is a scene with Bellairs in the ballroom, overheard by your footman and in part related to me by the wretched Breezy himself. During this scene you suggest yourself as a successor to Syd Skelton, and tick Bellairs off about his drug habit. You go so far, I think, as to talk about writing to *Harmony*. The idea, at this stage, would appear to be a comprehensive one. You will frighten Breezy into giving up cocaine, expose Rivera, and keep on with the band. It was during this interview that you behaved in a rather strange manner. You unscrewed the end section of Lady Pastern's parasol, removed the knob and absentmindedly pushed the bit of shaft a little way up the muzzle of your revolver, holding down the spring clip as you did so. You found that it fitted like a miniature ramrod or bolt. Or, if you like, a rifle grenade."

"*I* told you that meself."

"Exactly. Your policy throughout has been to pile up evidence against yourself. A sane man, and we are presuming you sane, doesn't do that sort of thing unless he believes he has an extra trick or two in hand, some conclusive bits of evidence that must clear him. It was obvious that you thought you could produce some such evidence and you took great glee in exhibiting the devastating frankness of complete innocence. Another form of figure-skating on thin ice. You would let us blunder about making clowns of ourselves, and, when the sport palled or the ice began to crack, you would, if you'll excuse the mixed metaphor, plank down the extra tricks."

A web of thread-like veins started out on Lord Pastern's blanched cheek-bones. He brushed up his moustache and, finding his hand shook, looked quickly at it, and thrust it inside the breast of his coat.

"It seemed best," Alleyn said, "to let you go your own gait and see how far it would take you. You wanted us to believe that Mr. Manx was G.P.F.: there was nothing to be gained, we thought, and there might be something lost in letting you see we recognised the equal possibility of your being G.P.F. yourself. This became a probability when the drafts of copy turned up amongst Rivera's blackmailing material. Because Rivera had never met Manx but was closely associated with you."

Alleyn glanced up at his colleague. "It was Inspector Fox," he said, "who first pointed out that you had every chance, during the performance, while the spotlight was on somebody else, to load the revolver with that fantastic bolt. All right. But there remained your first trump card—the substituted weapon. The apparently irrefutable evidence that the gun we recovered from Breezy was not the one you brought down to the Metronome. But when we found the original weapon in the lavatory beyond the inner office that difficulty, too, fell into place in the general design. We had got as far as abundant motive and damning circumstance. Opportunity began to appear."

Alleyn stood up, and with him Lord Pastern, who pointed a quivering finger at him.

"You bloody fool!" he said, drawing his lips back from his teeth. "You can't arrest me—you——"

"I believe I could arrest you," Alleyn rejoined, "but not for murder. Your second trump card is unfortunately valid. You didn't kill Rivera because Rivera was not killed by the revolver."

He looked at Manx. "And now," he said, "we come to you."

2

Edward Manx turned from the window and walked towards Alleyn with his hands in his pockets. "All right," he said. "You come to me. What have you nosed out about me?"

"This and that," Alleyn rejoined. "On the face of it there's the evidence that you quarrelled with Rivera and clipped him over the ear. Nosing, as you would put it, beneath the surface, there's your association with *Harmony*. You, and perhaps you alone, knew that Lord Pastern was G.P.F. If he told you Rivera was blackmailing him——"

" He didn't tell me."

"——and if, in addition, you knew Rivera was a drug merchant——" Alleyn waited for a moment but Manx said nothing. "——why then, remembering your expressed loathing of this abominable trade, something very like a motive began to appear."

" Oh, nonsense," Manx said lightly. " I don't go about devising quaint deaths for everyone I happen to think a cad or a bad lot."

" One never knows. There have been cases. And you could have changed the revolvers."

" You've just told us that he wasn't killed by the revolver."

" Nevertheless the substitution was made by his murderer."

Manx laughed acidly. " I give up," he said, and threw out his hands. " Get on with it."

" The weapon that killed Rivera couldn't have been fired from the revolver because at the time Lord Pastern pulled the trigger, Rivera had his piano accordion across his chest and the piano accordion is uninjured."

" I could have told you that," said Lord Pastern, rallying.

" It was a patently bogus affair, in any case. How, for instance, could Lord Pastern be sure of shooting Rivera with such a footling tool? A stiletto in the end of a bit of stick? If he missed by a fraction of an inch Rivera might not die instantly and might not die at all. No. You have to be sure of getting the right spot and getting it good and proper, with a bare bodkin."

Manx lit a cigarette with unsteady hands. " Then in that case I can't for the life of me see "—he stopped—" whodunit," he said, " and how."

" Since it's obvious Rivera wasn't hurt when he fell," Alleyn said, " he was stabbed after he fell."

" But he wasn't meant to fall. They'd altered the routine. We've had that till we're sick of the sound of it."

" It will be our contention that Rivera did not know that the routine had been altered."

" Bosh ! " Lord Pastern shouted so unexpectedly that they all jumped. "He wanted it changed. I didn't. It was Carlos wanted it."

"We'll take that point a bit later," Alleyn said. "We're considering how, and when, he was killed. Do you remember the timing of the giant metronome? It was motionless, wasn't it, right up to the moment when Rivera fell; motionless and pointing straight down at him. As he leant backwards its steel tip was poised rather menacingly, straight at his heart."

"Oh, for pity's sake!" Manx said disgustedly. "Are you going to tell us somebody dropped the bolt out of the metronome?"

"No. I'm trying to dismiss the fancy touches, not add to them. Immediately after Rivera fell, the arm of the metronome went into action. Coloured lights winked and popped in and out along its entire surface and that of the surrounding tower-frame. It swung to and fro with a rhythmic clack. The whole effect of course, carefully planned, was dazzling and unexpected. One's attention was drawn away from the prostrate figure and what actually happened during the next ten seconds or so was quite lost on the audience. To distract attention still further from the central figure, a spotlight played on the tympani where Lord Pastern could be seen in terrific action. But what seemed to happen during those ten confusing seconds?"

He waited again and then said : "Of course you remember, both of you. A waiter threw Breezy a comic wreath of flowers. He knelt down and, pretending to weep, using his handkerchief, opened Rivera's coat and felt for his heart. He felt for his heart."

3

Lord Pastern said : "You're wrong, Alleyn, you're wrong. I searched him. I'll swear he had nothing on him then and I'll swear he didn't get a chance to pick anything up. Where the devil was the weapon? You're wrong. I searched him."

"As he intended you to do. Yes. Did you notice his baton while you searched him?"

"I told you, damn it. He held it above his head. Good God!" Lord Pastern added, and again, "Good God!"

" A short black rod. The pointed steel was held in his palm, protected by the cork out of an empty gun-oil bottle in your desk. Fox reminded me this morning of Poe's story *The Purloined Letter*. Show a thing boldly to unsuspecting observers and they will think it's what they expect it to be. Breezy conducted your. programme last night with a piece of parasol handle and a stiletto. You saw the steel mounting glinting as usual at the tip of an ebony rod. The stiletto was concealed in his palm. It really was quite like his baton. Probably that gave him the idea when he handled the dismembered parasol in the ballrom. I think you asked him, didn't you, to put it together."

" Why the hell," Lord Pastern demanded, " didn't you tell us this straight away? Tormentin' people. It's a damn' scandal. I'll take you up on this, Alleyn, by God I will."

" Did you," Alleyn asked mildly, " go out of your way to confide in us? Or did you wilfully and dangerously play a silly lone hand? I think I may be forgiven, sir, for giving you a taste of your own tactics. I wish I could believe it had shaken you a bit : but that, I'm afraid, is too much to hope for." Lord Pastern bunched up his cheeks and swore extensively, but Manx said, with a grin : " You know, Cousin George, I rather think we bought it. We've hindered the police in the execution of their duty."

" Serve 'em damn' well right."

" I'm still sceptical," Manx said. " Where's your motive? Why should he kill the man who supplied him with his dope?"

" One of the servants at Duke's Gate overheard a quarrel between Bellairs and Rivera when they were together in the ballroom. Breezy asked Rivera for cigarettes—drugged cigarettes, of course—and Rivera refused to give him any. He intimated that their association was ended and talked about writing to *Harmony*. Fox will tell you that sort of thing's quite a common gambit when these people fall out."

" Oh, yes," Fox said. " They do it, you know. Rivera would have a cast-iron story ready to protect himself and get in first with the information. We'd pick Breezy up and be no further on. We might suspect Rivera but we wouldn't get on to anything. Not a thing."

" Because," Lord Pastern pointed out, " you're too thickheaded to get your man when he's screamin' for arrest under your great noses. That's why. Where's your initiative? Where's your push and drive? Why can't you "—he gestured wildly—" stir things up? Make a dust?"

"Well, my lord," said Fox placidly, "we can safely leave that kind of thing to papers like *Harmony*, can't we?"

Manx muttered : "But to kill him—no, I can't see it. And to think all that nonsense up in an hour——"

"He's a drug addict," Alleyn said. "He's been drawing near the end of his tether for some time, I fancy, with Rivera looming up bigger and bigger as his evil genius. It's a common characteristic for the addict to develop an intense hatred of the purveyor upon whom he is so slavishly dependent. This person becomes a sort of Mephistopheles-symbol for the addict. When the purveyor is also a blackmailer and for good measure in a position where he can terrify his victim by threats of withdrawal, you get an excruciating twist to the screw. I fancy the picture of you, Lord Pastern, firing point-blank at Rivera had begun to fascinate Bellairs long before he saw you fit the section into the barrel of the gun. I believe he had already played with the idea of frigging round with the ammunition. You added fuel to his fire."

"That be damned——" Lord Pastern began to shout, but Alleyn went on steadily.

"Breezy," he said, "was in an ugly state. He was frantic for cocaine, nervous about his show, terrified of what you would do. Don't forget, sir, you, too, had threatened him with exposure. He planned for a right-and-left coup. You were to hang, you know, for the murder. He has always had a passion for practical jokes."

Manx gave a snort of nervous laughter. Lord Pastern said nothing.

"But," Alleyn went on, "it was all too technicolor to be credible. His red-herrings were more like red whales. The whole set-up has the characteristic unreason and fantastic logic of the addict. A Coleridge creates Kubla Khan but a Breezy Bellairs creates a surrealistic dagger made of a parasol handle and a needlework stiletto. An Edgar Allan Poe writes *The Pit and the Pendulum* but a Breezy Bellairs steals a revolver and makes little scratches in the muzzle with a stiletto; he smokes it with a candle end and puts it in his overcoat pocket.

Stung to an intolerable activity by his unsatisfied lust for cocaine he plans grotesquely but with frantic precision. He may crack at any moment, lose interest or break down, but for a crucial period he goes to work like a demon. Everything falls into place. He tells the band but *not* Rivera, that the other routine will be followed. Rivera had gone to the end of the restaurant to make his entrance. He persuades Skelton to look at Lord Pastern's revolver at the last minute. He causes himself to be searched, holding his dagger over his head, trembling with strangled laughter. He conducts. He kills. He finds Rivera's heart, and with his hands protected by a hand-kerchief and hidden from the audience by a comic wreath, he digs his stiletto in and grinds it round. He shows distress. He goes to the room where the body lies and shows greater distress. He changes carefully the scarred revolver in his over-coat pocket with the one Lord Pastern fired. He goes into the lavatory and makes loud retching noises while he disposes of Lord Pastern's unscarred gun. He returns, and being now at the end of his course, frantically searches the body and pro-bably finds the dope he needs so badly. He collapses. That, as we see it, is the case against Breezy Bellairs."

" Poor dope," Manx said. " If you're right."

" Poor dope. Oh, yes," Alleyn said. " Poor dope."

Nigel Bathgate murmured : " Nobody else could have done it."

Lord Pastern glared at him but said nothing.

" Nobody," Fox said.

" But you'll never get a conviction, Alleyn."

" That," Alleyn said, " may be. It won't ruin our lives if we don't."

" How young," Lord Pastern demanded suddenly, " does a feller have to be to get into detection?"

" If you'll excuse me, Alleyn," Edward Manx said hurriedly, " I think I'll be off."

" Where are you goin', Ned?"

" To see Lisle, Cousin George. We lunched," he explained, " at cross-purposes. I thought she meant she knew it was you. I thought she meant the letter was the one Fée got from *Harmony*. But I see now : she thought it was me."

" What the hell are you talkin' about?"

" It doesn't matter. Good-bye."

" Hi, wait a minute. I'll come with you." They went out into the deserted sunlight, Lord Pastern locking the door behind him.

" I'll be off too, Alleyn," said Nigel as they stood watching the two figures, one lean and loose-jointed, the other stocky and dapper, walk briskly away up Materfamilias Lane. " Unless—what are you going to do?"

" Have you got the warrant, Fox?"

" Yes, Mr. Alleyn."

" Come on, then."

4

" The Judges' Rules," Fox said, " may be enlightened but there are times when they give you the pip. I suppose you don't agree with that, Mr. Alleyn."

" They keep you and me in our place, Br'er Fox, and I fancy that's a good thing."

" If we could confront him," Fox burst out. " If we could break him down."

" Under pressure he might make a hysterical confession. It might not be true. That would appear to be the idea behind the Judges' Rules."

Fox muttered something unprintable.

Nigel Bathgate said : " Where are we heading?"

" We call on him," Alleyn grunted. " And with any luck we find he already has a visitor. Caesar Bonn of the Metronome."

" How d'you know?"

" Information received," said Fox. " He made an arrangement over the telephone."

" And so, what do you do about it?"

" We pull Bellairs in, Mr. Bathgate, for receiving and distributing drugs."

" Fox," said Alleyn, " thinks there's a case against him. Through the customers."

" Once he's inside," Fox speculated dismally, " he *may* talk. In spite of the Usual Caution. Judges' Rules!"

"He's a glutton for limelight," Alleyn said unexpectedly.

"So what?" Nigel demanded.

"Nothing. I don't know. He may break out somewhere. Here we go."

It was rather dark in the tunnel-like passage that led to Breezy's flat. Nobody was about but a plain-clothes man on duty at the far end : a black figure against a mean window.

Walking silently on the heavy carpet, they came up to him. He made a movement of his head, murmured something that ended with the phrase : "hammer and tongs."

"Good," Alleyn said, and nodded. The man stealthily opened the door into Breezy's flat.

They moved into an entrance lobby where they found a second man with a note-book pressed against the wall and a pencil poised over it. The four silent men almost filled the cramped lobby.

In the living-room beyond, Caesar Bonn was quarrelling with Breezy Bellairs.

"Publicity!" Caesar was saying. "But of what a character! No, no! I am sorry. I regret this with all my heart. For me as for you it is a disaster."

"Listen, Caesar, you're all wrong. My public won't let me down. They'd *want* to see me." The voice rose steeply. "They *love* me," Breezy cried out, and after a pause : "You bloody swine, they *love* me."

"I must go."

"All right. You'll see. I'll ring Carmarelli. Carmarelli's been trying to get me for years. Or the Lotus Tree. They'll be fighting for me. And your bloody clientiele'll follow me. They'll eat us. I'll ring Stein. There's not a restaurateur in Town——"

"One moment." Caesar was closer to the door. "To spare you discomfiture, I feel I must warn you. Already I have discussed this matter with these gentlemen. An informal meeting. We are all agreed. It will not be possible for you to appear at any first-class restaurant or club."

They heard a falsetto whining. Caesar's voice intervened. "Believe me," he said, "when I say I mean this kindly. After all, we are old friends. Take my advice. Retire. You can afford to do so, no doubt." He gave a nervous giggle. Breezy

had whispered. Evidently they were close together on the
other side of the door. "No, no!" Caesar said loudly. "I can
do nothing about it. Nothing! Nothing!"

Breezy screamed out abruptly: "I'll ruin you!" and the
pencil skidded across the plain-clothes officer's note-book.

"You have ruined yourself," Caesar gabbled. "You will
keep silence. Understand me: there must be complete silence.
For you there is no more spotlight. You are finished. *Keep
off!*" There was a scuffle and a stifled ejaculation. Something
thudded heavily against the door and slid down its surface.
"There, now!" Caesar panted. He sounded scandalised and
breathlessly triumphant. Unexpectedly, after a brief pause, he
went on in a reflective voice. "No, truly you are too stupid.
This decides me. I am resolved. I inform the police of your
activities. You will make a foolish appearance in court. Everyone will laugh a little and forget you. You will go to gaol or
perhaps to a clinic. If you are of good behaviour you may, in
a year or so, be permitted to conduct a little band."

"*Christ!* Tell them, then! *Tell them!*" Beyond the door
Breezy stumbled to his feet. His voice broke into falsetto.
"But it's me that'll tell the tale; me! If I go to the dock, by
God, I'll wipe the grins off all your bloody faces. You haven't
heard anything yet. Try any funny business with ME! Finished! By God, I've only just started. You're all going to hear
how I slit up a bloody dago's heart for him."

"This is it," Alleyn said, and opened the door.

Fontana Books

Fontana is best known as one of the leading paperback publishers of popular fiction and non-fiction. It also includes an outstanding, and expanding section of books on history, natural history, religion and social sciences.

Most of the fiction authors need no introduction. They include Agatha Christie, Hammond Innes, Alistair MacLean, Catherine Gaskin, Victoria Holt and Lucy Walker. Desmond Bagley and Maureen Peters are among the relative newcomers.

The non-fiction list features a superb collection of animal books by such favourites as Gerald Durrell and Joy Adamson.

All Fontana books are available at your bookshop or newsagent; or can be ordered direct. Just fill in the form below and list the titles you want.

FONTANA BOOKS, Cash Sales Department, P.O. Box 4, Godalming, Surrey. Please send purchase price plus 5p postage per book by cheque, postal or money order. No currency.

NAME (Block letters) _____

ADDRESS _____

_____

_____